WINTERSTRIKE

Also by Liz Williams

The Ghost Sister

Empire of Bones

The Poison Master

Nine Layers of Sky

Banner of Souls

Darkland

Bloodmind

The Snake Agent

The Demon and the City

Precious Dragon

The Shadow Pavilion

The Banquet of the Lords of Night and Other Stories

LIZ WILLIAMS

WINTERSTRIKE

TOR

First published 2008 by Tor
an imprint of Pan Macmillan Ltd
Pan Macmillan, 20 New Wharf Road, London N1 9RR
Basingstoke and Oxford
Associated companies throughout the world
www.panmacmillan.com

ISBN 978-0-230-70931-7

1 3 5 7 9 8 6 4 2

A CIP catalogue record for this book is available from
the British Library.

Typeset by Intype Libra, London
Printed and bound in the UK by
CPI Mackays, Chatham, Kent ME5 8TD

To Veronica, Ken and Trevor

Acknowledgements

With special thanks to
Peter Lavery and Stef Bierwerth at Macmillan,
Shawna McCarthy,
everyone at the Milford workshop.

ONE

Essegui Harn — Winterstrike

The coldest night of the year in Winterstrike is always the night on which the festival of Ombre is held, or Wintervale if you are young and disdain the older dialects. The Matriarchy knows how to predict these things, how to read the subtle signatures in snow-drift and the length of icicles, the messages formed by the freezing of the breath upon the air, the crackling of the icy skin of the great canals.

In the centre of Winterstrike, Mars's first city, in the middle of the meteorite crater that gave the city its name, stands the fortress: a mass of vitrified stone striped as white as a bone and as red as a still-beating heart. It has a shattered turret, from some long-forgotten war, in which verminous birds fight and nest and cry. And on one particular night, at the top of the fortress and on the eve of war, at the summit of another tower so high that from it one could see out across the basalt walls to the dim, shimmering slopes of Olympus, stood a woman. She was surrounded by four glass windows: crimson, white, black, and transparent. She stood before a brazier and beneath a bell. She wore triple gloves: a thin membrane of weedworm silk, then the tanned leather of vulpen skin, then a pair of woollen mittens knitted by a grandmother. In spite of this, and the spitting coals of the brazier, her hands were still cold.

When the night froze below a certain point, and the signs were relayed to her by antiscribe, she turned, nearly overthrowing the brazier in her haste, and rushed to the windows. She threw them open, letting in a great gust of cold air which made the coals crackle, then struck the bell three times. It rang out, fracturing the chill. The woman ran down the stairs to the warm depths of the tower before the echo had even died. One by one, the coals hissed into silence as the bell note faded.

This all took place shortly before dawn, in the blue light before the sun rose. The woman was myself, Essegui Harn. The day was that of Ombre. And all Winterstrike could hear the bell, except for one woman, and except for one woman, all Winterstrike answered. I knew that across the city, women were throwing aside their counterpanes, rushing to the basins to wash, and then, still dressed in their nightclothes, running upstairs to the attics of mansions, or to the cellars of community shacks, to retrieve costumes forgotten over the course of the previous year, all six hundred and eighty-seven days of it. From chests and boxes, they would pull masks depicting the creatures of the Age of Children and the Lost Epoch, the long muzzles of cenulae, or the narrow, inhuman faces of demotheas and gaezelles. They would try them on, laughing at one another, then fall silent as they stood, masked, their concealed faces suddenly foolish above the thick nightdresses.

By Second Hour the robes, too, would have been retrieved: confections of lace and metal, leather and stiffened velvet, scarlet and ochre and amethyst, sea-green and indigo and pearl. Above these, the masks would no longer appear silly or sinister, but natural and full of grace. Then the women of Winterstrike would set them aside and, frantic throughout the short day, make sweet dumplings and fire-cakes for the night ahead, impatient for the fall of twilight.

*

2

After my stint in the bell tower I was in equal haste, rushing back to the mansion of Calmaretto, which lay not far from the fortress. I hurried through the streets, pounding snow into ice under my boots and churning it into powder against the swing of the hem of my heavy coat. I was thinking of the festival, of my new friend Vanity, whom I was planning to seduce tonight (or be seduced by, even more hopefully), of my cousin Hestia, vanished from the city a week ago and rumoured to have gone to Caud.

I didn't like to think about that. Caud was gearing up for war, over yet another territorial matter of a disputed sacred site, and given Hestia's occupation – a matter of some subtle conjecture – that city wasn't a safe place for her to be.

But thinking about Hestia was still easier than thinking about my sister. It was difficult *not* to think of her, especially when the walls of Calmaretto rose up before me: black weedwood, glittering with silver and frost. The tall arched windows were covered by heavy drapes, ostensibly to keep out the cold but in reality to conceal the house from the eyes of the peasantry, which, to my mothers Alleghetta and Thea, meant most people.

When I reached the main entrance I did not hesitate but put my eye to the haunt-lock. The scanner glowed with blacklight, an eldritch sparkle, as the lock read my soul-engrams through the hollow of my eye. The door opened. I stepped through into a maelstrom of activity.

Both my mothers were shouting at one another, at the servants, and then, without even a pause for breath, at me.

'. . . there is not enough sugar and only a little haemomon? Why didn't you order more?'

'. . . Canteley's best dress has a stain, she refuses to wear it even under her robes . . .'

'And Jhule cannot find the tracing-spoon anywhere!'

Thea started to wheeze and put a plump hand to her heart. Alleghetta's proud face became even frostier with contempt. She'd had her hair done for Ombre and it laced her head in a series of

3

small, tight curls as if she was wearing a helmet; Thea, on the other hand, had chosen a loose, piled-up style which did not do a great deal for a round countenance. Her hair was starting to descend.

'*Do* stop *fussing*, Thea!' Alleghetta snapped.

Thea's mouth turned down, heralding tears.

It was *always* the same. My head started to pound. I said, 'What about Shorn?'

Immediate, tense silence. My mothers stared at me, then at one another.

'What about her?'

'You know very well,' I said. I was speaking too loud, too fast, despite my best efforts, but I couldn't help it. 'You have to let her out. Tonight.'

Upstairs, in the windowless heart of Calmaretto, my sister Shorn Harn sat alone. Her birth name was Leretui, but she had been told that this was no longer her name: she had been shorn of it, and this verb was the only name she could take from now on. She would not know that it was the day of Ombre, because the sound of the bell rung by her sister, myself, had not penetrated the walls of Calmaretto. Nor would she be able to witness the haste and bustle outside in the street, the skaters skimming up and down Canal-the-Less, because she was not allowed to set foot in a room which had windows. She was permitted books, but not writing materials or an antiscribe, in case she found a way to send a message.

At this thought, my mouth gave a derisive twist. There would be little point in composing a message, since the one for whom it would be intended could not read, could not be taught to read, and was unlikely ever to communicate with someone literate. But my mothers would not countenance even the slightest possibility that a message might be sent, and thus Shorn was no longer allowed to see our little sister Canteley, as Canteley was young enough to view the scenario as romantic, no matter how many times our mothers had impressed upon her that Shorn was both transgressor and pervert. Shorn was occasionally permitted to see me, since I pretended to be of a similar mind to our mothers.

I usually only put my head around the door once a week, though Shorn found it difficult to estimate the days. Even so, I think she was surprised when the door hissed open and I strode through, snow falling in flakes from my outdoor coat.

'Essegui?' Shorn turned her head away and did not rise. She looked older than she was: not a surprise, given what had befallen her. She could have been my own age, a full five years older. Her long dark hair, a clone-mark of Alleghetta and Calmaretto, streamed down her back and I could tell that she hadn't bothered to brush it for several days; it had knotted into locks. For a moment, I longed to sit behind her and comb it through, as we'd done when we were children. Her face, so like my own and those of Alleghetta, Hestia and Canteley, stretched white over its bones like snow on broken ground. Blue shadows had pooled in the hollows of her eyes.

'What is it?' Shorn said, dully.

'Ombre falls today. I've told our mothers that you are to be allowed out, when the gongs ring for dusk.'

Shorn's mouth fell open to reveal her silver-latticed teeth, an affectation Alleghetta had insisted she adopt when our mothers were still trying to marry her off. She stared at me.

'*Outside*? And they agreed?'

'They hate it. But it is your last remaining legal right, ancient custom, and they have no choice.'

Shorn said, slowly and disbelieving, 'I am to be allowed out? In the mask-and-gown? *Tonight*? This is mockery.'

I leaned forward, hands on either arm of the chair, and spoke clearly. 'Mockery maybe. Understand this. If you use the mask-and-gown as a cover to flee the city, our mothers will go to the Matriarchy and ask for a squadron of scissor-women to hunt you down. The city will, of course, be closed from dusk onward, and they will know if anyone tries to leave. Or if any*thing* tries to get in.'

'I will not try to leave,' Shorn whispered. 'Where would I go?'

'To that which brought you to this plight?'

Shorn gave a small, hard laugh like a bark. 'I repeat, where indeed?'

'True enough. To the mountains, in winter? You would die of cold before you got halfway across the Demnotian Plain. And the mountains themselves, what then? Men-remnants would tear you to pieces and devour you before you had a chance to find it.' I grimaced. 'Perhaps *it* would even be one of them. I've heard that all women look alike to them. And that's without taking into account factions from Caud. We could go to war very soon, you know. Everyone thinks so.'

'War with Caud?' Shorn looked disdainful. 'What is it this time?'

'Some dispute over Mardian Hill. They were holding talks, but it just escalated. If war does break out, you'd be best off here in Winterstrike, in spite of—' *In spite of everything.*

Shorn lowered her gaze. There was a moment's silence. 'I should reassure you, then, that I will not try to escape.'

'There is a mask waiting for you,' I told her, then turned on my heel and went through the door, leaving it open behind me.

I did not expect her to leave the chamber immediately. She must have been dreaming about this day ever since the evening of her imprisonment, six hundred and eighty-seven days ago. Ombre then was like every other festival for her, a chance for fun and celebration. She did not expect to meet what stepped from under the bridge of the Curve.

The mask was one that I remembered from our childhood: the round, bland face of a crater cat. It was a child's mask: for the last few years, Canteley had been wearing it. Now, however, it was the only one left in the box. I watched as Shorn pulled the gown – a muted grey-and-black brocade – over her head and then, slowly, put the mask on. The cat beamed at her from the mirror; she looked like an overgrown child, no longer the woman they called the Malcontent. She twitched aside the fold of a sash, but the box was empty. There was no sign of the other mask: the long, narrow head, the colour of polished bone, mosaiced with cracks and fractures. She searched through the draperies.

'You won't find it,' I told her. She did not reply.

As we turned to go downstairs, a gaezelle danced in through the door.

'Tui, is that you? Is it?' The gaezelle flung her arms around Shorn and held on tight.

'It's me. But don't call me Tui.' It sounded as though she was spitting. 'That's not my name any more.'

Canteley had grown over the last months: she was almost as tall as me now, though her voice was still as shrill as a waterwhistle. I felt as though an icy mass had lodged deep in my throat.

'Are you coming? Essegui said our mothers are letting you out for the Wintervale. Is it true? You should run away, Tui. You should try to find him.' This last in a whisper.

'I won't be going away, Canteley,' Shorn said, but as she said this she looked to me as though the walls were falling in on her.

'Is it true what they say, that the vulpen steal your soul? That they put you in a trance so that you can't think of anything else?'

'No, that isn't true,' Shorn said. She took our little sister's hand and led her through the door.

I won't be going away. But better the devouring mountains than the windowless room, I thought. Better the quick, clean cold. I should never have let our mothers shut her away, but Shorn herself had been too dazed, with grief and bewilderment and incomprehension, to protest. Now, she'd had time to think, to become as clear as ice, and I needed to know what she was planning.

'Canteley, I'll talk to you later.' She gave our sister a swift hug. 'Go downstairs. I'll join you in a minute.'

I lingered behind the door, watching through a crack. Once Canteley had gone, Shorn took a pair of skates from the wall and stood looking down at the long, curved blades. Then, holding the skates by their laces, she followed our sister down the stairs, and I followed her.

They were all standing in the doorway, staring upward: Canteley and our mothers. Of the two, Thea was by far the shorter, and so it must have been Alleghetta behind the demothea's mask, its white, pointed face wearing a simpering smile. Shorn looked from one to the other before descending. No one spoke. As Shorn reached the last step, our mothers turned and pushed open the double doors that led out onto the steps to the street. Blacklight crackled, a weir-ward shrieked, and winter filled the hallway. The gongs rang out in the twilight, filling the street and the house with sound. It must have seemed very loud to Shorn, used as she had become to the cushioned silence of the windowless room.

The mothers grasped Canteley firmly by each hand and pulled her through the doors, so decisively that I was the only one who had time to turn and see a flickering twitch of Thea's head in the direction of Shorn. As for myself, I was wearing a cenulae's mask: a fragile countenance, painted in green. When I stepped out, I saw the bland cat face smiling back at me. Then Shorn ran, stumbling on unaccustomed feet across the black-and-white mosaic of the hall floor, through the scents of snow and fire-cake and polish, out through the doors and into the street to stand uncertainly in the snow.

Canal-the-Less, on which Calmaretto stood, was frozen solid and filled with skaters bearing snow-lamps. They wove in and out of one another with insect skill. Shorn, breath coming in short gasps in the cold, was evidently tempted to take the round cat's face from her own and fling it into the drifts, but she did not, though I saw her hands trembling around her face. She tied on the skates with quivering fingers and lowered herself over the bank of the canal onto the ice. Then she was off, winging down Canal-the-Less towards the culvert that leads to the Great Canal. I followed.

The Canal itself was thronged with skaters, milling about before the start of the procession. Shorn twisted this way and that, keeping to the side of the Canal at first, then moving out to where the light was less certain. The great houses that lined the Canal were blazing with snow-lamps and torches, mirrored in the ice so that Shorn and I glided across a glassy, shimmering expanse. She was heading for the Curve and the labyrinth of canals that led to the island of Midis and then the Great North Gate.

Behind us, the crowds of skaters fell away. Ahead, I could see a mass of red gowns, the start of the procession, led by the Matri-archs. Our mothers, not quite so elevated, would be just behind, amongst their peers. A pair of scissor-women sped by, the raw mouths of holographic wounds displayed across the surface of their armour. They were unmasked. Their faces were as sharp as their blades and I flinched behind the mask, until I realized that to them, Shorn was nothing more than a tall child, and not the Malcontent of Calmaretto. But I watched them go all the same, then slunk behind my sister from the Great Canal and into the maze.

It was much quieter here. The houses along the waterways had already emptied and there were only a few stray women lin-gering beneath the lamps or the bridges, waiting no doubt for assignations. Shorn skated on, though the long months of forced inactivity must have taken their toll. Even my own calves were burning. I did not want to think of what would befall Shorn if she made it past the North Gate: the vast expanse of snow-covered plain, the mountains beyond. I hoped only that it would be a swift death and that she made it out of Winterstrike. It would be her revenge on the city and on Calmaretto, to die beyond its walls. I knew that this was not rational, but Shorn and I had left reason by a canal bank, a year before.

In summer, the Curve is lined with cafés and weedwood trees, black-branched, with the yellow flower balls spilling pollen into the water until it lies there as heavy as oil, perfuming the air with a subtle musk. Now, the cafés were cold and closed – all the trade would have moved down the Canal for the night.

My heart pounded with exertion and memory. It was here, a year ago, on this stretch of the Curve beneath the thin-arched bridge, that something – some*one*, I corrected myself, angry at my own use of our mothers' term – had drifted from the darkness to stand as still as snow.

Shorn glided to a halt. I'd been out on the canal that night, but not with Shorn. I had replayed this scene over and over in my mind ever since I'd first learned what had happened: the figure outlined against the black wall and pale ice, the long head swivelling to meet Shorn's gaze, the frame shifting under the layers of robes and the sudden realization that this was not just another reveller, but real: the mild dark eyes set deep in the hollow of the skull, the ivory barbs of its teeth. What she had taken for the curve of skate blades beneath the hem of the robe was its feet. One of the Changed, a vulpen, from the mountains: the genetically altered remnant of ancient man.

They were said to tear women limb from limb in vengeance for old woes: the phasing out of the male by Matriarch geneticists. But this one merely looked at her, she told me, and held out its hand. She should have fled; instead, she took its long fingers in her own. It led her along the Curve, skating alongside with inhuman skill. Nothing else befell her. The vulpen gazed at her as they moved, blinking its mild eyes. It said: *I have been waiting for you.*

And as it spoke, they turned the bend and ran into a squadron of scissor-women. Unlike Shorn, the warriors took only a moment to realize what was before them. They skated forward, scissors snicking. One of them seized Shorn, who cried 'No!' and struggled in the warrior's grasp. The other three surrounded the vulpen, who suddenly was springing upward to land on the bank on all fours, blade-feet skidding, casting the disguising robes away to reveal a pale, narrow form, the vertebral tail whipping around. Its erection resembled a bone, and when they saw it the scissor-women shrieked in fury. Then it was gone, into the snowy night.

They took Shorn back to Calmaretto on a chain, and sat with her until her family returned, laughing and exhausted, at dawn.

Remembering this now, I was moved to wonder if any of it was even real. It seemed long ago and far away – and then it was as though I had stepped sideways into Shorn's own memory, for the figure of a vulpen once more skated from beneath the arch. I think I cried out, but whether in hope or dismay, I could not have said. It held out its hands, but did not attempt to touch her. Shorn skated with it, back along the Curve in a haze and a dream, myself following behind, flying through the winter dark, until we were once more out onto the Great Canal, passing the Long Reach that led down to the Winter Palace of the Matriarchy, then the curving wall of the Matriarchy parliament itself.

The procession had passed. Circling, whirling, Shorn and the vulpen danced out to the middle of the Great Canal, and now I was beginning to understand that this was, after all, nothing more than a woman in a mask. Thoughts of Shorn's flight, of dying beyond Winterstrike, skated through my head and were gone.

She let the woman in the vulpen's mask lead her back to Calmaretto. As they stepped through the door, the woman pulled off the mask and I saw that it was not a woman after all, but a girl. It was Canteley.

'I could not let you go,' Canteley said, and Shorn, exhausted, merely nodded. Together, Canteley and I led her up the stairs to the windowless room and closed the door behind her.

In the morning, Winterstrike was quiet. Ribbons littered the ice and the snow was trodden into filth. I woke late, my head ringing with explanations that I would later have to make to Vanity. I went to the heart of the house and opened the door of the windowless room.

Shorn sat where we had left her, upright, the cat's face beaming.

'Shorn?' There was no reply. I went haltingly forward and touched my sister's shoulder, thinking that she slept. But the brocade gown was stiff and unyielding, moulded in the form of a woman's figure. I tugged at the cat's mask, but it would not budge. It remained fixed, staring sightlessly across the windowless room, and slowly I stepped away, and once more closed the door.

TWO

Hestia Mar — Caud

I was in a tea-house in Caud when the ghost warrior walked in. I turned, hoping to see everyone staring at her, tea glasses suspended halfway to gaping mouths, eyes wide. But the only person they were staring at was me, responding to my sudden movement. I couldn't afford to attract attention. I looked back down at my place and the glances slid away. Conversation resumed about normal subjects: the depth of last night's snow, the day's horoscopes, the prospect of war.

Under my lashes, I watched the warrior. I was alone in Caud, knowing no one, trying to be unobtrusive. The tea-house was close to the principal gate of the city and was thus filled with travellers, mostly from the Martian north, but some from the more southerly parts of the Crater Plain, Ardent, perhaps, or Ord. I saw no one who looked as though they might be from Winterstrike. I had taken pains to disguise myself: bleaching my hair to the paleness of a northern woman, lightening my skin a shade or so with pigmentation pills. All my family looked the same, the result of snobbish and conservative selection in the breeding tanks, and all of us were typical of old Winterstrike: sheaves of straight black hair, grey eyes, sallow faces. Even our mothers had found it hard to tell my cousin Essegui and me apart, growing up.

So disguise was essential. And I had been careful to come anonymously to Caud, travelling in a rented vehicle across the Crater Plain at night, hiring a room in a slum tenement and staying away from any haunt-locks and blacklight devices that might scan my soul-engrams and reveal me for what I was: Hestia Mar, a woman of Winterstrike, an enemy, a spy.

But now the warrior was here, sitting down in the empty seat opposite mine, a flayed ghost. And it seemed that no one else could see her except me.

She moved stiffly beneath the confines of her rust-red armour: without the covering of skin, I could see the interplay of muscles. The flesh looked old and dry, as though the warrior had spent a long time out in the cold. The armour she wore was antique, covered with symbols that I did not recognize. I thought that she must be from the very long ago: the Rune Memory Wars, perhaps, or the Age of Children, though she could be more recent – the time when the Memnos Matriarchy had ruled not only the Crater Plain but Earth itself. But that Matriarchy had fallen long ago, and only a few clan warriors now remained in the hills. I did not think she was one of these.

Her eyes were the wan green of winter ice, staring at me from the ruin of her face. Her mouth moved, but no sound emerged. I knew better than to speak to a ghost. I turned away. People were still shooting covert glances at me. This red, raw visitation was the last way I wanted to draw attention to myself. I rose, abruptly, and went through the door without looking back. At the end of the street I risked a glance over my shoulder, fearing that the thing had followed me, but the only folk to be seen were a few hooded figures hurrying home before curfew. Hastening around the corner, I jumped onto a crowded rider that was heading in the direction of my slum. I resolved not to return to the tea-house: it was too much of a risk.

Thus far, I'd been successful in staying out of sight. My days were spent in the ruin of the great library of Caud, hunting through what was left of the archives. I was not the only searcher, sidling through the fire-blackened racks under the shattered shell of the roof, but we left one another well alone and the Matriarchy of Caud had other things to deal with. Their scissor-women did not come to the ruins, though a less distracted government might have regarded us as looters. Even so, I was as careful as possible, heading out in the dead hours of the afternoon and returning well before twilight and the fall of curfew.

My thoughts dwelt on the warrior as the rider trundled along. I did not know who she was, what she might represent, nor why she had chosen to manifest herself to me. I tried to tell myself that it was an unfortunate coincidence, nothing more. Caud must be full of ghosts these days, and I'd always been able to see them: it was, after all, why I'd been picked by the Matriarchy to do what I did. *Soul stealer, weir reader. Sensitive. Spy.*

Halfway along Gaudy Street the rider broke down, spilling passengers out in a discontented mass. We had to wait for the next available service and the schedule was disrupted. I was near the back of the crowd and though I pushed and shoved, I couldn't get on the next vehicle and had to wait for the one after that. I stood shivering in the snow for almost an hour, looking up at the shuttered faces of the weedwood mansions that lined Gaudy Street. Many of them were derelict, or filled with squatters. I saw the gleam of a lamp within one of them: it looked deceptively welcoming. Above Caud, the stars blazed, and I could see the eldritch glitter of the Chain, dotted with the specks of haunt-ships departing for Earth and beyond.

By the time I reached the tenement, varying my route from the rider stop through the filthy alleys in case of pursuit, it was close to the gongs for curfew. I hurried up the grimy stairs and triple-bolted the steel door behind me. I half expected the flayed warrior to be waiting for me – sitting on the pallet bed, perhaps – but there was no one there. The power was off again, so I lit the lamp and sat down at the antiscribe, hoping that the battery had enough juice to sustain a call to Winterstrike.

Gennera's voice crackled into the air and a moment later her face appeared on the little screen, pasty and familiar. Her bone earrings swung as she leaned forward and one snagged on the black lace of her ruffled collar. Her small eyes were even chillier than usual.

'Anything?'

'No, not yet. I'm still looking.' I did not want to tell her about the warrior.

'You have to find it,' Gennera said. 'And quickly. The situation's degenerating, we're on the brink. The Caud Matriarchy is out of control.' Her mouth pursed primly, as if commenting on a particularly inferior dinner party.

'You're telling me. The city's a mess. Public transport's breaking down, there are scissor-women everywhere. They seek distraction, to blame all their economic problems on us rather than on their own incompetence. The news-views whip up the population, night after night. There are posters everywhere saying we've desecrated Mardian Hill, that the shrine belongs to Caud.'

'Nonsense. The shrine was built by the Matriarchy of Winterstrike, it's documented, no matter what fantasies Caud likes to tell.'

'Caud's constructed on fantasies. Dangerous ones.'

'And that's why we must have a deterrent. Even if we don't go to war, they'll find some other excuse in a year or so's time.'

'If a deterrent is to be found, it will be found in the library. What's left of it.'

'They've delivered an ultimatum. Hand over the shrine, or they'll declare war. You saw that?'

'I saw. I have three days.' There was a growing pressure in my head and I massaged my temples as I spoke into the antiscribe. 'Gennera, this isn't realistic. You know that.'

'Find what you can.'

A fool's errand. I'd said so when the news of the mission first came up, and I hadn't changed my mind. I'd have added that it was me risking my life, not Gennera, but that was part of the deal and always had been: I was indentured and I didn't have a choice. It was pointless to think I could argue the toss.

'I have to go. The battery's running down.' It could have been true.

Gennera frowned. 'Then call me when you can.' *And be careful, look after yourself,* I waited for her to say, but it didn't come. The antiscribe sizzled into closure as I reached out and turned the dial.

I put a pan of dried noodles over the lamp to warm up, then drew out the results of the day's research. There was little of use. Schematics for ships that had ceased to fly a hundred years before, maps of mines that had long since caved in, old philosophical rants that could have been either empirical or theoretical, impossible to say which. I could find nothing resembling the fragile rumour that had sent me here: the story of ancient weapons.

'If we had something that could be deployed as an edge over Caud, it would be enough,' Gennera said. 'We'd never need to use it. It would be enough that we had it, to keep our enemies in check.'

If I believed that, I'd believe anything.

'The Matriarchy remember what you did in Tharsis,' Gennera said. 'You have a reputation for accomplishing the impossible.'

'Tharsis was not impossible, by definition. Only hard. And that was nine years ago, Gennera. I'm not as young as I was.' That sounded pathetic. I was in my late twenties, and making out that I was middle-aged. I certainly *felt* middle-aged. But I wasn't surprised when she gave a snort of derision.

'That should benefit you all the more,' Gennera said.

'If I meet a man-remnant on the Plain, maybe not. My fighting skills aren't what they were, either.'

Even over the antiscribe, I could tell that she was smiling her frozen little smile. 'You'd probably end up selling it something, Hestia.'

But I had not come to Caud to sell, and I was running out of time. Not just my time in Caud, either. When I looked at my life, the years seemed to be slipping away, lost in Gennera's bidding. I'd been indentured to her for a decade now, still knew little about her. I'd had reservations at the start, but she offered a way out from under my mother's Matriarchal thumb, a life that promised adventure. Powerful in her own right, she'd protected me against my mother's temper and my aunt's bids for authority.

And all I'd really done had been to exchange one kind of dependence for another.

In the morning, I returned to the library. I had to dodge down a series of alleyways to avoid a squadron of scissor-women, bearing heavy weaponry. These morning excissiere patrols were becoming increasingly frequent and there were few people on the streets. I hid in the shadows, waiting until they had passed by. Occasionally, there was the whirring roar of orthocopters overhead: Caud was so clearly preparing for conflict. My words to Gennera rose up and choked me.

I reached the ruin of the library much later than I'd hoped. The spars of the blasted roof arched up over the twisted remains of the foremost stacks. The ground was littered with books, still in their round casings. It was like walking along the shores of the Small Sea, when the sand-clams crawl out onto the beaches to mate. I could not help wondering whether the information I sought was even now crunching beneath my boot heel, but these books were surely too recent. If there had been anything among them, the Matriarchy of Caud would be making use of it.

No one knew who had attacked the library. The Matriarchy blamed Winterstrike, which was absurd. My government had far too great a respect for information. Paranoid talk among the tenements suggested that it had been men-remnants from the mountains, an equally ridiculous claim. Awts and hyenae fought with bone clubs and rocks, not missiles, though who knew what weaponry the enigmatic vulpen possessed: they were said to have intelligence, whereas awts and hyenae did not. The most probable explanation was that insurgents had been responsible: Caud had been cracking down on political dissent over the last few years, a dissent spawned by its economic woes, and this was the likely result. I suspected that the library had not been the primary target. If you studied a map, the Matriarchy buildings were on the same trajectory and I was of the opinion that the missile had simply fallen short. But I volunteered this view to no one. I spoke to no one, after all.

Even though this was not my city, however, I could not stem a sense of loss whenever I laid eyes on the library. Caud, like Winterstrike, Tharsis and the other cities of the Plain, went back thousands of years, and the library was said to contain data from very early days, from the time when humans had first come from Earth, to settle Mars. There were folk – the Caud Matriarchy among them – who considered that to be heresy; I considered it to be historical fact. There had been a time when all Mars, dominated by the Memnos Matriarchy, had believed ourselves to be the world on which human life had originated; we were more enlightened these days.

Civilized. Or so it was said.

I made my way as carefully as I could through the wreckage into the archives. No one else was there and it struck me that this might be a bad sign, a result of the increased presence of the scissor-women on the streets. I began to sift through fire-hazed data scrolls, running the short antenna of the antiscribe up each one. In the early days, they had written bottom-to-top and left-to-right, but somewhere around the Age of Children this had changed. I was not sure how much difference, if any, this would make to the antiscribe's pattern-recognition capabilities: hopefully, little enough. I tried to keep an ear out for any interference, but gradually I became absorbed in what I was doing and the world around me receded.

The sound penetrated my consciousness like a beetle in the wall: an insect clicking. Instantly, my awareness snapped back. I was crouched behind one of the stacks, a filmy fragment of documentation in my hand, and there were two scissor-women only a few feet away.

It was impossible to tell if they had seen me, or if they were communicating. Among themselves, the excissieres, as they call themselves, do not use speech if they are within sight of one another, but converse by means of the patterns of holographic wounds that play across their flesh and armour, a language that is impossible for any not of their ranks to comprehend. I could see the images flickering up and down their legs through the gaps in the stack – raw scratches and gaping mouths, mimicking injuries too severe not to be fatal, fading into scars and then blankness, in endless permutation. A cold wind blew across my skin and involuntarily I shivered, causing the scattered documents to rustle. The play of wounds became more agitated. Alarmed, I looked up, to see the ghost of the flayed warrior beckoning at me towards the end of the stack. I hesitated for a moment, weighing risks, then rose silently, muscles aching in protest, and crept towards it, setting the antiscribe to closure as I did so in case of scanning devices.

The ghost led me along a further row, into the shadows. There we waited, while the scissor-women presumably conversed and finally left, heading into the eastern wing of the library. I turned to the ghost to thank it, but it had disappeared.

A moment later, however, it was back. It stood over a small tangle of data cases and it was pointing downwards. I smiled. I didn't see how it could possibly know what I was looking for, but I knew a hint when I saw one. I sidled over to it and crouched down, scooping the data cases into my pack. They didn't look anything special and a couple of them were scorched.

'Well?' I whispered, looking up at the warrior. 'Do you

approve?' But the warrior's face did not change. 'I don't think I should even be trusting you,' I added. The warrior's only reply was to fade. Typical.

I debated whether to leave, but the situation was too urgent. Keeping a watch out for the scissor-women, I collected a further assortment of documents, switching on the antiscribe at infrequent intervals to avoid detection. I did not see the ghost again. Eventually, the sky above the ruined shell grew darker and I had to depart, stowing the handfuls of documentation away in my coat as I did so. They rustled like dried leaves. Then I hurried back to the tenement to examine them more closely.

The ghost might have given me a helping hand, but it wasn't much of one. The data cases themselves were damaged beyond repair, unreadable, and if they'd once contained vital information, it had been lost. Among the cases, however, I found something strange: a small round object like a vitrified egg, gleaming black as coal. The same size as my finger joint, it had a hole through the centre. A memento of Caud, I thought, a souvenir. I considered stringing it on the chain around my neck that held my fake identity chips, but in the end I tied it onto a loose thread in an inner pocket instead and forgetting about it, sought sleep.

The knock on the door came in the early hours of the morning. I sat up in bed, heart pounding. No one good ever knocks at that time of night. The window led nowhere, and in any case was bolted shut behind a grille. I switched on the antiscribe and broadcast the emergency code, just as there was a flash of ire-palm from the door lock and the door fell forward, blasted off its hinges. The room filled with acrid smoke as the lock quickly began to melt. I held little hope of fighting my way out, but I swept one of the scissor-women off her feet and tackled the next. The razor-edged scissors were at my throat within a second and I knew she wouldn't hesitate to kill me. Wounds flickered across her face in a ghastly display of silent communication.

'I'll come quietly,' I said. I raised my hands.

They said nothing, but picked up the antiscribe and stashed it in a hold-all, then made a thorough search of the room. The woman who held the scissors at my throat looked into my face all the while, unblinking. At last, she gestured. 'Come.' They bound my wrists and led me, stumbling, down the stairs.

As we left the tenement and stepped out into the icy night, I saw the flayed warrior standing in the shadows. The scissor-woman who held the chain at my wrists shoved me forward.

'What are you looking at?' Her voice was harsh and guttural. I wondered how often she actually spoke aloud.

'Nothing.'

She grunted and pushed me on, but as they took me towards the vehicle I stole a glance back and saw that the ghost was gone. It occurred to me that it might have led the scissor-women to me, but then in the library, it had helped me, or had seemed to. I did not understand why it should do either.

They took me to the Mote, the Matriarchy's own prison, rather than the city catacombs. This suggested they might have identified me, if not as Hestia Mar, then as a citizen of Winterstrike. That they suspected me of something major was evident by the location, and the immediacy and nature of the questioning. Even Caud had abandoned the art of direct torture, but they had other means of persuasion: haunt-tech and drugs. They tried the haunt-tech on me first.

'You'll be placed in this room,' the doctor on duty explained to me. At first, with a shock, I thought I was looking at Gennera. This woman looked more like a majike than a proper doctor: the tell-tale symbols hanging from her pierced ear lobes, the faded mark of a tattoo visible underneath her greying hairline. Black science, for a world in which what had once been superstition was now fact, and much of that illegal. Even Caud had standards, however often they'd violated them. But then again, Winterstrike was supposed to have standards, too.

'The blacklight matrix covers the walls. There is no way out. When you are ready to talk, which will be soon, squeeze this alarm.' She handed me a small soft black cube and the scissor-women pushed me through the door.

The Matriarchies keep a tight hold on the more esoteric uses of haunt-tech, but all will be familiar with the everyday manifestations: the locks and soul-scans, the weir-wards which guard so many public buildings and private mansions. This chamber was like a magnified version of those wards, conjuring spirits from the psycho-geographical strata of the city's consciousness, bringing them out of the walls and up through the floor. I saw dreadful things: a woman with thorns that pierced every inch of her flesh, a procession of bloated drowned children, vulpen and awts from the high hills with glistening eyes and splinter teeth. But the Matriarchy of Caud was accustomed to breaking peasants. Quite apart from my natural abilities and the training I'd had to develop them, I'd grown up in a weir-warded house, filled with things that swam through the air of my chamber at night. I was used to the nauseous burn that accompanied their presence, the sick shiver of the skin. This was worse, but it was only a question of degree. Fighting the urge to vomit, I knelt in a corner, in a meditational control posture, placed the alarm cube in front of me, and looked only at it.

After an hour, my keepers evidently grew tired of waiting. The blacklight matrix sizzled off with a fierce electric odour, like the air after a thunderstorm. From the corner of my eye, I saw things wink out of sight. I was taken from the chamber and placed in a cell. Next, they tried the drugs.

From their point of view, this may have been more successful. I can't say, since I remember little of what I may or may not have said. That aspect of haunt-tech is supposed to terrify the credulous into speaking the truth. The mind-drugs of the Matriarchies are crude and bludgeon one into confession, but those confessions are all too frequently unreliable, built on fantasies conjured from the psyche's depths. When the drug they had given me began to ebb, I found my captors staring at me, their expressions unreadable. Two were clearly Matriarchy personnel, wearing the jade-and-black of Caud. The scissor-women hovered by the door.

'Put her under,' one of the Matriarchs said. She sounded disgusted. I started to protest, more for the form of it than anything else, and they touched a sleep-pen to my throat. The room fell away around me.

When I came to my senses again, everything was quiet and the lights had been dimmed. I rose, stiffly. My wrists were still bound and the chains had chafed the skin into a raw burn. I peered through the little window set into the door of the cell. One of the scissor-women sat outside. Her armour, and the few inches of exposed skin, were silent, but her eyes were open. She was awake, but not speaking. There was no sign of the majike and I was grateful for that: she'd probably have been able to tell what I was up to. I knocked on the window. I needed the guard's undivided attention for a few minutes and the only way I could think of to do that was by making a full confession.

'I'll talk,' I said, when she came across. 'But only to you.'

I could see indecision in her face. It was never really a question of how intelligent the scissor-women were; they operated on agendas that were partially programmed, and partly opaque to the rest of us. Her voice came through the grille.

'I am activating the recording device,' she said. 'Speak.'

'My name is Aletheria Stole. I am from Tharsis. I assumed another identity, which was implanted. I came here looking for my sister, who married a woman from Caud many years ago . . .'

I continued to speak, taking care to modulate the rhythm of my voice so that it became semi-hypnotic. The scissor-women had programming to avoid mind control, but this was something else entirely. As I spoke, I looked into her pale eyes and glimpsed her soul. I drew it out, as I had done so many years before, when

I was a child and playing with my cousins Essegui and Leretui. Leretui had been the harder of the two, I remembered, and I remembered wondering why, since of the sisters she was the weaker-willed. Odd, to think of that now in the depths of the Mote, but I needed something to distract my conscious attention while my preternatural abilities operated, and nostalgia was pre-occupying enough.

The excissiere's soul spun across the air between us, a darkling glitter . . . Leretui on the lawn of Calmaretto, her soul halfway out of her body, and I recalled that it had a peculiar taste, bitter as aloes and stinging inside my head, so that I'd dropped it like a fumbled ball and Leretui had sunk back into the grass, staring at me with an oddly malicious triumph. Essegui had been much easier and I'd got into trouble for that. You're supposed to give stolen souls back; I'd kept hers for a while, watching her walk jerk-ily around the lawn with no one behind her eyes. Eventually a dawning conscience had prompted me to return it, but by then my aunt Alleghetta had noticed something amiss and swooped . . .

Here came the scissor-woman's soul, like something crawling out of a burrow. The door was no barrier. I opened my mouth and sucked the soul in. It lay in my cheek like a lump of intangi-ble ice.

The excissiere's face grew slack and blank, just as Essegui's had done so many years ago, but this time there was no conscience to trouble me.

'Step away from the door,' I said. My voice was thick, but she did as I told her. I bent my head to the haunt-lock and spat her soul into it, or that is what it felt like. It fled into the lock, trac-ing its engrams through the circuit mechanisms, grateful to be free of me. The door swung open; I stepped through and struck the scissor-woman at the base of the skull. She crumpled without a sound. My antiscribe was nowhere to be seen. I had not expected it to be, but there was a small communications array sitting on a shelf, a standard model, activated. I snatched it up.

Discovery was soon made. I heard a cry behind me, feet drumming on the ceiling above. I headed downward, reasoning that in these old buildings the best chance of escape lay in the catacombs below. When I reached what I judged to be the lowest level, I ducked into a chamber. I found the warrior's ghost before me. Her flayed face wore a grim smile. My guardian spirit, I thought.

'Where, then?' I said aloud, not expecting her to respond, but once more the ghost beckoned. I followed the rust-red figure through the labyrinth, through tunnels swimming with unknown forms: women with the heads of coyu and aspiths, creatures that might have been men. I ignored the weir-wards, careful not to touch them. Sometimes the ghost grew faint before me and I was beginning to suspect why this should be. I could hear no signs of pursuit, but that did not mean that none were following. The scissor-women could be deadly in their silence.

At last we came to a door and the warrior halted. In experiment, I closed down the array and she was no longer there. I put it on again, and she reappeared.

'You're no ghost,' I said. She was speaking. There was still no sound, but the words flickered across the screen.

She was not conversing. The words were lists of archived data: skeins of information scrolling down. 'What are you doing?' I asked. 'What *are* you?'

As I watched, I realized that I had not been entirely correct. She was not a ghost of a warrior at all. She was the ghost of the library itself, the cached archives that we had believed to be destroyed, and that the Caud Matriarchy, in their ignorance, had not managed to find. And intuition told me that she hadn't been pointing to the ruined data cases at all, but to the little round sphere amongst them that still sat in my pocket.

I knew what I had to do. I hastened past the warrior and pushed open the door, kicking and shoving until the ancient hinges gave way. I stumbled out into a frosty courtyard, by a frozen fountain. The mansion before me was dark, but something shrieked out of the shadows: a weir-form, activated, of a woman with long teeth and trailing hair. She shot past my shoulder and disappeared. I heard an alarm sounding inside the house. But the array had a broadcasting signal and that was all that mattered. I called through to Winterstrike, where it was already mid-morning, and downloaded everything into the Matriarchy's data store, along with a message. The warrior's face did not change as she slowly vanished. When she was completely gone, I shut down the array, hid it behind a piece of broken stone, and waited.

The scissor-women were not long in finding me. They took me back to the Mote, to a different, smaller cell, and there I remained.

THREE

Essegui Harn – Winterstrike

My mother Alleghetta turned the colour of ice when I told her what I'd found, there in Shorn's chamber on the morning after Ombre.

'Gone? What do you mean, "gone"?'

'Missing. Absent. *Not there.*'

'Tui's missing?' That was Canteley, wide-eyed from the door-way. Alleghetta spun like a serpent coiling, hissed, '*Go away.*'

Canteley did as she was told; I heard her panicky footsteps pattering down the passage. If she'd overheard, then I doubted the news of my sister's disappearance would remain a secret for long among the servants: they had their own way of finding out about things, information channelled through the weir-wards and whispered along corridors. Secrets permeated the air of Calmaretto like incense.

'How?' Alleghetta didn't care about Shorn's well-being, that much was plain. Bad enough my sister's name had been taken away from her, bad enough she had to be confined, but worse yet that she might have vanished somewhere into Winterstrike and then, I could see it in my mother's face, there would be no controlling the situation.

Next moment, Alleghetta confirmed these thoughts. 'I'm to

assume a position in the Matriarchy in less than two weeks! This could jeopardize everything.' Her face was contorted. It had been bad enough when Shorn had first been disgraced: Alleghetta had been expecting a call to the Matriarchy council then, and they'd not unnaturally postponed it. She'd spent the last year worming her way back in, and now this had happened. I could almost sympathize with her. Almost. 'How?' she asked again.

'I don't *know*, Mother. I have no idea.' I sank down onto the tapestry-covered seat that formed the central point of the parlour and looked down at my ungloved hands. Against the folds of my long leather skirt, the rough nubs of bone buttons, my hands looked very smooth and pale, almost unreal. Almost inhuman. I thought of clawed fingers reaching out to take Leretui's hands, snatching her life and her name. I wished Hestia were here: Hestia would know what to do.

Alleghetta evidently thought that I was ashamed, for she said, the words as grudging as if they'd been dragged up out of a well, 'No one is blaming you, Essegui.'

Not yet, anyway. Alleghetta couldn't keep the sharpness out of her tone and I knew where that was heading. But in truth, I was not ashamed, simply furious – with Alleghetta and Thea for the former's continual grasping at crumbs of status and the latter's weakness, with Canteley for wearing the vulpen mask and bringing the past year so painfully back, and most of all with Shorn, for putting us all in this position in the first place, aligning us like pieces on a game board. It reminded me exactly of that, some strange ancient game where the most significant piece is captured, throwing everything else into shadowy relief.

I did not want to tell my mother how angry I was. I kept my head bowed, my gaze tracing out the lines of the folded leather, then the buttons and straps of my boots, then the muted colours of the faded rug. I'd sat here as a child, also scolded.

'No one is blaming you,' Alleghetta repeated, with even less conviction than before. 'However, Shorn must be found, as quickly as possible before the news spreads. Thea has to look after Canteley and I have my civic duties. You must be the one to find her, Essegui.'

As if from a long distance away, I hear myself saying, 'I won't do it.' I looked up at last. Alleghetta was frozen in astonishment, and I couldn't say I blamed her. In fact, I'd surprised myself. I'd often been intransigent in minor matters, and on more major occasions had either acquiesced, or worked around my mothers' wishes so that a satisfactory compromise was effected: to me, at least. But I couldn't remember a time when I'd directly disobeyed an order and it seemed that Alleghetta could not, either. She gaped, and then she said, as if to herself, 'Very well, then.'

It was my turn to stare. Alleghetta turned her back on me and left the room. I thought, 'I have to get out of here.' But before I did so, I forced myself up the stairs and back to Shorn's chamber.

I half expected, even then, to find her still there, as if the last hour had been a bad dream. But the chamber was empty. The cracked glaze of the mask stared up at me in mute mockery, crumpled up in the folds of the robe. I turned my back on it and went over to the walls, examining them for any traces of exit or ingress. Nothing. I stooped, picked up the corner of the rug, and rolled it up to reveal the worn floorboards. I don't know what I was thinking. I had some nebulous idea, perhaps, that Shorn had somehow over the course of her year's confinement managed to tunnel her way out. In the cold light of day, this was a ridiculous proposition – and yet, people had managed to escape from locked rooms before, histories' worth of it, and it was said that Calmaretto was one of the oldest houses in Winterstrike, built after that ancient terraforming called the Alchemy was complete and the first merchants had come to Mars. Perhaps men had once even lived in the place on which Calmaretto now stood: human men, the *antiques*, before the Matriarchies had taken over control of the birthing processes and phased them out into what had now stolen Shorn's heart. A strange idea, to love something that was male, and not human – for like my little sister Canteley, I had no proof and yet I also had no doubt that Shorn *did* love.

Shorn's chamber provided me with no clues as to where she had gone, however. Her original, windowed room had grown up with Shorn, but the aristocracies of Winterstrike are conservative, traditionalist, and they cleave strangely to childhood, perhaps because adult life can be so rigid. Nor did I know why we all seemed to have escaped this process to some degree: Shorn disastrously, myself quietly, my cousin Hestia secretly, and Canteley with a worrying romanticism that might or might not diminish with age. But my mothers had, perhaps in a semblance of pity, allowed Shorn to take some of the fittings of her old bedroom into the windowless room with her. Now, I crouched in front of a bookcase, running my gaze along a young girl's books: *Growing Up in Tharsis, A Cure for Contemplation, Beyond the Crater Plain.* Books about history, carefully doctored to conceal inconvenient truths for the young; books about animals, about flowers and stars. A picture-book of Earth, showing the Nine Wonders: the arthropod festivals of Malay, the cities of Altai and Thibet, their towers rising above the waves of the Himalayan Sea, the bird-rich marshlands of Ropa with ruined spires gleaming dully above the waters.

I'd never been to Earth. I'd never been *anywhere*. I'd like to visit our sister world someday, and maybe I would, I told myself defiantly, once this whole thing was settled. I had dreams that went far beyond Winterstrike. But I had the sense of walls closing in, all the same.

I put the picture-book back in the bookcase and stood. My leather skirt rustled as I walked across the room: I remember thinking how quiet it was. I thought, again, that I needed to get out of Calmaretto, find a tea-house somewhere and sit down. I'd always liked the day after Ombre itself. No one was working, and a pallidly festive atmosphere still remained without the need for preparation. We'd always had the traditional post-Ombre meal of fricasseed carp, but the servants had leftovers and I envied them that – I had no idea why all this was going through my mind as I shut the door of Shorn's chamber behind me and locked it (force of habit), then descended the long staircase to the hall. Maybe I had some inkling of what was to come, intuition starting to jangle like the Ombre bell.

I hoped to avoid both my mothers and creep out of the house. For a moment, this seemed possible. I'd felt guilty about leaving Canteley to face Alleghetta, but as I came down the stairs I heard her light voice calmly reciting the Litanies and realized that she had been put in the schoolroom as usual with her governess and that lessons were in progress: not a normal occurrence for a festival period, but I could see why my mothers might have insisted upon it. I doubted that the governess was pleased, though.

Then, as I stepped onto the black and red tiles of the hallway, Thea came out of the parlour. Her plump face looked tight and strained, which under the circumstances, was hardly surprising.

'Essegui, dear,' she said, and I was immediately on guard. 'Would you step in here for a moment? There's something we need to talk about.'

I sighed. So Alleghetta, having unexpectedly failed, had set Thea on me. I'd always been able to talk my way round Thea, to some extent, but Thea had always been better at making me feel guilty. She did disappointment rather well, also helplessness. 'All right.' I could hardly plead some other engagement.

I followed her into the parlour and the world caved in. My memories of what followed are jumbled and fragmented, but what I do recall is this:

A small woman rising from the overstuffed chair to the right of the doorway. A crimson veil billowed down from her coil of hair, her eyes were like black pebbles in a waxy face. I saw a necklace of bones around her neck, polished until they gleamed in the firelight, bracelets of bone around her wrists. Her ears were pierced and a tattoo the colour of iron spiralled out over her forehead. She raised a metal rattle and shook it in my face. Thea gasped. I saw letters streaming out from the rattle, glowing scarlet against the panelled walls of the parlour, and at once my whole attention was engaged in trying to read what they said. Then my vision went dark and there were only the letters, congealing into what I thought were words, but not in any language that I could understand. There was a dreadful sense of wrongness about it: this was haunt-tech of some kind, I knew that from the burning-juniper smell and the electric tingle up the back of my neck, as though I'd walked into hostile weir-wards, but much worse. Weir-wards are designed to disable, not to suck your soul out through your eyes – and that made me think of Hestia. Not all of my soul, only a fragment, but I saw it go, a thin finger of light blasting past and coiling down like quick smoke into a small metal box.

The box closed with a snap. I caught a glimpse of the parlour, of Thea's horrified face and Alleghetta's triumphant one. Then, hollowed, my sight pinpointing down into a black tunnel, I slid to the floor.

A thousand stars sparkled against a painted ceiling, and by degrees, I realized where I was: lying on the divan in the parlour. My head was pounding like a drum. Thea was sitting on a stool by my side, with a cloth and a bowl of water. There was the faint smell of vomit over the perfumed wood of the fire, but no trace of it when I squinted down at myself; one good thing about wearing leather, I suppose, is that it makes you easy to clean off. The movement, however, sent a spear of pain through my head and I collapsed back, groaning.

'The majike says that it shouldn't last long,' Thea assured me, anxiously. She leaned forward and I could smell alcohol on her breath, the cheap sherry that was supposed to be odourless, but wasn't.

'The majike? You hired someone who does black science?' I couldn't believe they'd gone this far from respectability. I think it was really only then that I realized that Alleghetta was actually mad. '*Why?*' But I already knew. Something was missing, some piece of me. Some piece of my *soul*, snatched out and now trapped in the majike's box.

'It was Alleghetta's idea, not mine.' Thea had always been quick to blame her spouse; it did not make for peace. Or respect. 'She told me that you'd refused to help – surely you understand the seriousness of this? We could lose all manner of positions, it's been bad enough already. Alleghetta is to join the council in a fort-night's time – surely you'd thought about that? She said that if you would not help, you must be made to.'

'So you've done – what? Put me under a geise? A compulsion?'

I didn't need to ask. I could feel it, a nagging insistence, lodged deep inside my head. A geise. An ancient word for a hyper-hypnotic suggestion, exchanged for a fraction of my essential being.

I could find another practitioner, get it removed. But even if I managed to find one, I'd have to pay and I did not have the money. I wondered how much it had cost my mothers to have this done, in all manner of ways.

'It was Alleghetta's idea,' Thea said again. But now that I seemed to be on the mend – with the pain ebbing, I was able to sit up – I thought I detected a trace of smugness in her face. 'Alleghetta's idea,' I said bitterly, 'but your agreement. You pair of canal-side bitches.'

Thea flinched. 'There's no need—' she began. But I was on my feet and bending over her, trying to ignore the smell of sherry.

'When this is over,' I said, 'When I've found *Leretui* – and I promise you this will happen, are you satisfied now? – we won't be coming back. I'll work passage on a soul-ship and take her to Earth. You can take Calmaretto, and the inheritance. Canteley can have my share. But you won't be seeing either of us again.'

Thea's small mouth worked. But from the doorway, I heard the rustling of skirts. Alleghetta stood in the entrance to the parlour, teeth like bone as she said, 'And that will be a very good thing.'

Interlude: Palace of the Centipede Queen, Malay, Earth

'Madam?' Shurr hesitated at the entrance to the chamber, but there was no reply from within. Her head lowered, she shuffled into the chamber, one hand masking her eyes so that she could, at least, pretend to have seen nothing. Segment Three slid back inside her sleeve as she did so, also observant of the niceties. This was ancient protocol rather than modern pragmatism: the Queen had ways of dealing with true traitors and Shurr was a born-retainer, bonded to the Queen's clan from birth. Even though this Queen had been in office for no more than a few years, Shurr had never questioned her own loyalty, although she did remember the old Queen with a trace of nostalgia: the parades and processions about Khul Pak, the seemingly endless masques and masquerades. This Queen was more private, devoted to less public pleasures, but she had treated Shurr with consideration and for this, Shurr was grateful.

Now, looking neither to right nor left, she made her way across the chamber, memory supplementing the lack of what she did not allow herself to see. The chamber was old, separated by columns of stone and intricately carved wooden screens, with draperies hanging between them. Although Shurr had been visiting this chamber since she herself was a child, there were parts of it that she still had not seen: it occupied the entire fourth storey of the Palace of Lights, and that had been built before the Flood had swept over the eastern lands of Earth. As she stepped across the mosaic floor, blue daylight poured over the tesserae, casting pools and spangles of fire. Shurr blinked as she came out onto the terrace and glanced quickly and covertly around her. There was still no sign of the Queen. Shurr put her hands on the wooden railing and peered down into the courtyard below. A fountain plashed, sending a breath of coolness upwards. Segment Three's pincered head slipped out of Shurr's sleeve and the long body slid part-way along the balcony, claws ticking on stone.

'Back, back,' Shurr murmured and the centipede did so. There was a tickle of protest inside her head. For a moment, she saw the garden below through Segment Three's faceted gaze: a multi-layered hunting ground, filled with moths and beetles, frogs and small birds.

'You're supposed to be a machine,' Shurr said, not without affection. But that was the whole point: Segment Three had been grown, after all. And Segment Three did not possess true consciousness, although sometimes it came to her in dreams, and Shurr wondered then. The beasts belonging to the Queen were quite different, of course.

Shurr watched as a party of kappa made their way across the gravel to the kitchens, their squat bodies and hairless heads glistening with moisture in the heat. They carried baskets filled with market produce and were chattering with animation, but Shurr was too far up to hear what they were saying. Beyond the heavily guarded walls of the Palace, Khul Pak stretched out as far as the white line of the harbour, shimmering in afternoon warmth. The smell of galangal, ginger, sewage and salt drifted by, and the distant sound of tuk tuks and river traffic. Above, a military orthocopter skimmed over the city, too low, amphibious wings arching out beneath the rotor blades in preparation for its landing in the harbour. An ordinary afternoon, Shurr thought, placid in her accustomed place, but then a voice behind her spoke.

'Shurr?'

Shurr turned, bowing low. She could see the Queen's feet: bare and stained with ochre spines. This Queen, though obviously vat-grown, must have had Ropan genes somewhere in the mix, given the pallor of her skin: like milk, or the moon.

'Madam?'

'I was sleeping,' the Queen said. 'You may look up now.'

Shurr did so. The Queen wore her customary harness; information-loaded and singing up the haunt-lines of supple leather. The enemies of the Palace of Light claimed that this inherited costume was made of human skin; Shurr dismissed this, but it was not an impossibility. A necklace of shark's teeth circled the Queen's throat. Her dark hair was braided with orchids; her plum-dark eyes were bright with amusement and perhaps stimulants.

'Shurr,' the Queen purred. Within her sleeve, Shurr felt Segment Three stir in recognition; she tapped her arm sharply, to keep it within. But the spirit of the old Queen's segment was also moving: arching up and over the Queen's head in spectral angularity. The Queen reached up and brushed a hand over nothingness.

'Still awake, Shurr,' the Queen said softly. 'You see?'

Shurr remembered it living, had seen it kill. The old Queen had been more ruthless than this one, or seemed so. Sometimes Shurr thought that it was simply that the new Queen could not be bothered. She bowed her head again, before the ghost.

'Tell me,' the Queen said. 'What's happening below?'

Shurr knew that this meant the laboratories. 'I had a status report late yesterday. It was forwarded to you.'

The Queen gave a fluid shrug. 'I haven't looked yet.'

'The new segment is almost ready.'

The Queen's carefully inscribed eyebrows rose. 'Oh, is that so? Then we need to start preparing for our journey.'

'I've already done so,' Shurr said. 'Against the eventuality.'

'Good,' the Queen said. She looked in the direction of the balcony, where the sky was beginning to change to green. 'You can see it very clearly, when night comes. Like a tiny crimson eye, sparkling back at you. I look at it through the telescope sometimes. I wonder what's there.'

Shurr knew that the Queen was not referring simply to the cities and plains of the red world, and an old cold desire rose inside her throat. For a moment, she could not speak, then she said, 'Ancestries.'

'Oh,' the Queen said softly, 'I certainly hope so.'

Later that evening, Shurr made her way back to the Palace through the marketplace. Corrugated iron awnings rattled in the sea wind; the air smelled of heat and sweat. Shurr walked quickly, glancing to either side at mounds of spice and poisons, at medicines and black-market haunt-circuitry that hummed and whistled as she passed. People got out of her way, were careful not to jostle her, and Shurr felt Segment Three's watchfulness, encased within the flimsy hollow of her sleeve. She kept her veil over her face all the same, a mark of pride rather than modesty. Halfway down the market aisle, she felt the slight nip of the centipede's pincers into the flesh of her arm and then the message came: *Return at once.* Bitterness flooded into her mouth, a signal of emergency, and Shurr's steps quickened, slippers tapping on the concrete floor of the market. Soon she was out of the building and hastening along the quay, past the rattling sampans and the bulk of a huge liner coming in, one of the deep-sea vessels on a rare inshore visit for replenishing. Its shadow passed over her as she hurried, blotting out the aquamarine sky and the prickle of the stars, but she remained conscious of the eye of the red planet, as though it watched her from the heavens, promising change.

As she came through the side gate, she saw that the Palace of Light was quite dark, apart from a dim lamp gleaming in the Queen's chambers. She hurried through the door and Khant came out of the shadows. Segment Five was coiled around his throat like a necklace of bone.

'They've found her,' he said, whispering.

Shurr stared at him. 'What? Are they sure?'

'They seem quite certain. I had the call mid-evening. The daughter of a noble house.'

Shurr instinctively bowed her head. 'Of course. She would be.'

'But there are problems.'

Shurr repressed a smile. *Of course. There would be.*

'What kind of problems?'

'The girl in question has gone missing. She was mistreated by her family, imprisoned, has disappeared.'

'Well, then,' Shurr said. 'All the more reason for us to rescue her.'

FOUR

Hestia Mar — Caud

Locked once more behind the cell door in the Mote of Caud, I started to hallucinate. I don't know, now, whether this was a belated result of the haunt-torture or simply fatigue. I say 'hallucinate', but I didn't see anything that I'd never seen before. The visions that came to me were more like flashbacks, images of childhood from an adult's point of view. I didn't seem to have any control over them, only a distant capacity to reflect. It was distracting, at least, but I could have done without it. I wanted to focus on getting out of there, not indulge in warmly fuzzy memories.

They weren't particularly nostalgic ones, however. One moment I was lying on the filthy floor of the cell, and the next I was standing on the sloping lawn that led down to the bank of Canal-the-Less. It was evening, golden with summer, and the blossoms of the weedwood trees periodically exploded in the heat, sending showers of glistening pollen streamers down into the garden, dappling the immaculate grass. At the bottom of the slope, the water of the canal, too, was gilded: it looked solid enough to walk upon, a shining molten glaze. I knew what I'd see if I turned around and sure enough, there it was: the weedwood mansion, the home of my cousins. Calmaretto.

As I stared at this familiar sight, three figures came out onto the veranda. In winter, which was most of the year, the veranda was enclosed behind thick glass panels, etched with seasonal scenes, but now the panels had been thrown open to let some air into the house, so that the steps that led down to the garden were visible behind the lacing of foliage and so were the people who stood upon them. The adult was my aunt, Alleghetta Harn, and the two smaller figures were Essegui and Leretui, my cousins. Esse was the taller of the two, already rangy in her traditional black-and-bone, a ceremonialist's colours. But Tui was a delicate little thing, held in family lore to be of a weak constitution. My own mother, Alleghetta's sister, maintained that this was a myth and that Leretui malingered, in order to get out of her lessons. I have no idea whether this was true. Mother didn't consider you to be ill unless you were actually on the verge of death, and sometimes not even then.

Essegui waved. I waved back and she broke away from Alleghetta's restraining hand – for all that she was being groomed for ceremonial duties, my aunt thought that Esse was unseemly – and ran down the steps to the lawn.

'Hestia! Where have you been? We've been looking for you.' A glance over her shoulder. 'Mother wanted you at tea.'

'I couldn't face it,' I hissed.

Essegui pulled a face. 'Don't blame you. It was just as you'd expect. Lots of stuffy old Matriarchs and Tui and I having to serve cake and not eat any of it. Then the baby started howling. Alleghetta slapped the nursemaid, in front of everyone.' Essegui's grey eyes were sparkling wide; she looked delighted, and a bit guilty.

'Oh dear,' I said.

'Well, *did* you do it? *Did* you take the boat out?'

I longed to say *Yes*; I wanted to impress Essegui, who was a year younger than I. But instead I told her the truth.

'No. I thought someone might see me. Maybe later, when the

weedwood grows to cover the water – it'll only be another week or so before they're in full leaf. I went to the winter garden instead.' I hid. But I didn't have to tell Essegui that.

'Hestia! Where have you been, wicked child?'

'Sorry, Aunty.' Alleghetta was angry – she would have loved to have Sulie Mar's daughter serve tea in her own drawing chamber, and that was largely why I'd hidden from the tea party – but there were limits to how much annoyance she could express: Mother's position in the Matriarchy saw to that. I think, if I had been the child of a lesser person, Alleghetta would not have permitted her daughters to associate with me: not after I'd shown what I could do. Soul-stealing is a majike ability, not appropriate for a Matriarch's child. But my mother was who she was, and so Alleghetta swallowed whatever distaste she might have felt. Now, she contented herself with a sour scowl instead and told us all to go and play.

Essegui and I, drawn by a single thought, wandered down to the canal bank, followed by Leretui a few steps behind. Tui always was a dreamy child, the sort of kid who won't tell you what she's thinking, but just shakes her head instead and looks down at the ground, scuffs her feet. Essegui and I left her alone, for the most part, but she trailed after us anyway, as if compromising between her own company and that of other children. From this now-perspective, I could see the first faint seeds that had led to her becoming shorn of her name, but as a girl, I thought nothing of her relative muteness. We were all different, after all.

Essegui squinted up into the mirror of the afternoon sky. 'We *could* take the boat, you know.' We'd had this conversation before, and would have it again. Together, she and I ducked underneath the fronds of weedwood, staining our hair with bright strands of pollen so that we were tiger-coloured, and stared down the Curve.

This was the richest quarter of Winterstrike and at that time I'd barely known anything else: sheltered children, my cousins and I, carefully nurtured and with the prospect of suitable marriages and ceremonial duties and respectable civil service careers lying ahead of us. That afternoon, I did not have any inkling that either my own life or Essegui's – or, spirits knew, *Leretui's* – would take the same form as Canal-the-Less: a straight shining line and then, suddenly, unexpectedly, the long sweep of the Curve, throwing us all off the track of our lives like a skater hurled too swiftly past a turn.

But then the windows of the mansions caught the sun, reflecting it back across the water, and the canal, too, shone. A small boat, a taxi-gondola, glided up the bend of the Curve and broke the water into a thousand sparkling shards. All the world was lost in light. Behind the towering peaks and gables of the mansions, I could see the mountains, a distant shadow, with Olympus's improbable cone seeming as high as the stars.

Then, as Essegui and I were gazing longingly at the boat belonging to Calmaretto – a long thing with a curling moon-bow prow and sleek lacquered sides – Leretui cried out. I didn't realize at first what it was: I thought a bird had made some sound from the trees. Essegui and I turned just in time to see Leretui fall, crumpling in slow motion to the emerald grass.

'Tui!' Essegui shouted. She scrambled up the slope to her sister's fallen form and I was close behind. Now, in the Mote in Caud, I felt a sense of wonder at the memory: had this really happened, or was I inventing it, some weird response to the haunt-torment? I didn't recall this – but even as the thought came to me, something stirred at the back of my mind and I thought: yes, this was real. But Leretui had fainted before, and afterwards, too – I remembered a dance at which she'd passed out, blaming the heat or too much Tharsis wine, an occasion at a picnic in the Great Park. And, yes, this had been the first of those fainting fits, I remembered it properly now.

We reached Tui and Essegui dropped to her knees beside her sister. 'Tui, wake up!'

Leretui's head lolled and her eyes rolled upward in her head, flashing the whites. She was whispering.

'What's she saying? Is she ill?' Essegui wailed.

'I don't *know*,' I snapped. 'Get me some water.'

Essegui ran up to the garden tap and filled the bowl that was kept beneath it. When she brought it back, we slopped it as carefully as we could over Leretui's white face. The whispering was still going on, a murmured litany that I could not grasp. Then she said, quite clearly, 'We can help you.' I looked down into her face and her eyes went quite dark, bloomed over with a glaze of light. Leretui blinked.

'What—?' she started to say.

'You fainted.' Anxiety made Essegui brusque. 'Are you all right?'

Leretui frowned. 'I could *hear* someone.'

'You're imagining things.'

'Sometimes people who faint hear ghosts,' I said. I've no idea where I'd got this notion from, only that I believed it in that unreflective way that you do when you're young – possibly it was something I'd overheard from my mother's servants.

Essegui stared at me. 'Nonsense,' she said. 'Why should she hear ghosts?'

'They're all around,' I faltered.

'No, they're not. They're in the locks and the machines and the clocks. That's not "all around".'

'It wasn't a ghost,' Tui said. Her eyes were shocked and wide. 'I don't know what it was.'

'You'd better come inside and sit down,' Essegui told her, with a warning glance at me that said, *Don't encourage her.*

We didn't tell Alleghetta, or my aunt Thea – marginally more sympathetic, but only marginally. I think Essegui and I sensed, without discussing it, that we would be blamed for Leretui's collapse. Neither mother was renowned for being fair, so we kept silent, and Tui said nothing, either. Maybe the 'malingering' charge had hit home.

I watched her closely, all the same, and I knew that Essegui did, too. I was to stay at Calmaretto that night, despite my mild disgrace for failing to appear at tea, and we were taken to a performance of a play, one of the first acknowledgements that Essegui and I, at least, were growing up. But Leretui was allowed to come as well and I wondered, now in the Mote, whether this, combined with her uncertain mood that day, had influenced what was to come: conjured the chancy, dangerous future to her, reeling it in like a fish hooked through the lip.

Impossible to say. I watched now, from the distant viewpoint of my prison, as those long-ago events unscrolled across the screen of my mind's eye. I saw us come down the steps of the mansion: it was fully dark now, and the torches flared and sputtered in their holsters all along the front of Calmaretto, sending fractured reflections of fire over the waters of Canal-the-Less. As daughters of the Matriarchy, we were not allowed to make our way on foot through the streets to the theatre like vulgar people, although Essegui and I, at least, would have preferred to do so, perhaps Leretui too. Instead we were ushered into a waiting carriage by Alleghetta. I saw her sweep her skirts around her, revealing her long buttoned boots with their ancestral buckles, swishing into the carriage in a froth of red lace like foam from a bloody sea. Disorientingly, I caught a glimpse of my own face peering out of the carriage window, and then I was back inside its stuffy velvet confines as we came onto the street that paralleled the Curve.

'I trust you'll enjoy the play,' my aunt said to me. It sounded more like a threat than a wish. 'It's supposed to be rather good – by Benaise, you know.'

I had no idea who this was. Alleghetta had always had literary pretensions, which she presented with a belligerent air, as if defying one to disagree with her. I mumbled something. Beside me, Essegui fidgeted as she stared out of the window, and Leretui looked simply unhappy.

'Does your mother attend the theatre very often?' This was embarrassing, for a number of reasons. Mother had no patience with the arts, and in any case Alleghetta, as her own sister, should not have had to ask me.

'No,' I said, and Alleghetta looked faintly triumphant, as if she'd scored a point. 'She's too busy with her official duties,' I said, unable to resist temptation, and Alleghetta's expression soured.

'I suppose she finds it fulfilling,' she said, dubiously. Alleghetta would have loved to have that much power. I did not say what – even at that young age – I thought, which was that my mother's power had come with a very high price, and crippled her within. I did not want to give my aunt the satisfaction. Instead, I muttered, echoing, 'I suppose so.'

'Look,' Essegui said suddenly. I think she was trying to rescue me from her mother's interrogation. 'Who are *they*?' She pointed out of the window. I looked past her shoulder and saw that we were away from the Curve now and passing the sombre bulk of the official buildings that lined the Great Canal. The water doors had their own magnificence, but these façades, technically the back entrances, were opulently pillared and carved, made of obsidian and Plains red marble: the black bones and red blood of the city. Now, through the window of the carriage, I could see that there were people milling about in front of the columns, dressed in flimsy lace that made them look as insubstantial as spirits. They had spidery hands and their heads were an intricate mass of coils and cones, like many tiny fossils. Their long faces narrowed into muzzles and I saw the glint of their slanted, oval eyes.

'Demotheas!' Leretui breathed.

'Don't be ridiculous!' her mother snapped. 'They are in costume, you silly girl.'

'Why?' Essegui asked, casually, as if to defuse the sting of Alleghetta's words. 'It's not Ombre.'

Alleghetta gave an exasperated sigh. 'Of course not. There are festivals other than Ombre; it is simply that you have not been old enough to attend them. This is one of them, although it is not widely observed, I must admit.'

'What's it called?' Essegui asked.

'Phantome. It is supposed to honour the ancient non-human dead.'

Essegui frowned, watching the procession of demotheas form a slow, vague order. 'I thought demotheas were supposed to be a myth, nothing more?'

'There is *some* evidence that they actually existed,' Alleghetta said grudgingly, 'although it isn't certain. Our ancestors created so many things, here in this very city. Some lived and were real – coyu, aspiths – some did not. Gaezelles, for instance, died out long ago, but were revived in the labs after the fall of the Memnos Matriarchy.' Her tone became didactic.

'But the men-remnants are real, aren't they?' Leretui's voice was startlingly shrill. 'The vulpen, the hyaenae, the awts? They exist, don't they?'

For a moment, I thought Alleghetta might slap her. 'Of course they exist, but it is not seemly to speak of such things.'

Essegui nudged her sister in the ribs. 'Shut up, Tui.'

Leretui subsided, gnawing her lip. The carriage moved on, leaving the demotheas behind. We reached the theatre and sat through the play, which was about political matters and was dull: a propaganda piece against Caud, dealing with Mardian Hill. In retrospect, one could see the seeds of war even then. I wanted to be out on the streets, chasing demotheas that were as sinister and elusive as moths, or back at Calmaretto, messing about with the boat. Beside me, Essegui and Leretui appeared equally bored, but Alleghetta sat with her hands gripping the sides of her chair and a fire burned in her face.

That night, in the room that I shared with Essegui, something woke me. I lay for a moment, staring into the shadows, not quite sure where I was until I remembered. On the other side of the room, Essegui lay in a foetal heap. There was no sign of anything amiss, but my senses were jangling. Then it came again, the creak of a floorboard from the passage outside the room.

Very quietly, I got out of bed and went to the door, opening it a crack. Down the hall, which was lit by a single sconce, there was a whisk of movement just before the stairs. I wasn't sure what it was that I had seen: a servant, perhaps, or maybe one of the weir-wards activating itself as a moth or beetle blundered past. The weir-wards at Calmaretto were highly strung: Alleghetta was either paranoid, or thought that a high level of security created an impression of importance. Either way, I had become accustomed to the wards in my mother's house and I slipped out of the bedroom, leaving Essegui still curled around her dreams, and down the hallway. A very old rug, rather grand but now somewhat worn, scuffed under my feet and I nearly fell. The sound of my elbow striking the wall seemed very loud in the night silence of the mansion and I bit down on a curse. Ahead of me, going down the stairs, footsteps speeded up. I knew where the wards watched, and where they originated. I ducked and dodged along the hallway, taking more care this time, and when I reached the top of the stairs I looked back to a peaceful hall. Whoever ran ahead of me on the staircase obviously knew similar tricks, for the stair, too, was silent. I went down it and found myself out in the torchlit main hall. A breath of wind stirred the drapes by the front door and when I followed it into the parlour, I found that one of the long doors that led to the lawn was open.

Back along the veranda, back down the steps, retracing the path through the weedwood trees to the banks of Canal-the-Less. Leretui was standing on the very edge of the canal, with her hands outstretched. In her long summer nightgown, she looked like a spirit herself: conversing with someone who stood, impossibly, at the very centre of the canal.

I started to say her name but it died upon the air. The thing that stood there was a demothea, and now that I was looking at it, I realized just how unlike it the women in costume had been, how human their movements were. The demothea was dancing, its limbs contorting and flowing at wholly unnatural angles. In the torchlight, its eyes flared a bright brief gold and its flimsy garments billowed out behind it across the water, skeins of material swirling as if in a great wind, though the summer night was humid and still. Leretui took a little step forward and tottered on the brink of the canal. The demothea reached out a long, long hand and beckoned her further yet; I saw its pointed, smiling face upraised, an expression incapable of human interpretation. All this came to me later, glimpsed from the far-away perspective of the Mote: as a young girl, I felt only panic and fear. I called out, '*Leretui*!'

The demothea abruptly vanished. I thought Tui was going to fall into the canal; she gave a faint cry and clawed at the air. I don't remember rushing forward to catch her, but suddenly we were both sprawling on the canal bank and the water was rocking up beneath my face. I edged quickly back. There were said to be things living in the canals, coming up to the surface at night. Leretui sat in a huddle on the damp grass, shaking.

'What happened?' I asked her. 'What were you *doing?*' But she shook her head and would not answer. I took her by her fragile shoulders and hauled her to her feet and we both stumbled up the steps and through the open door. I expected the shriek and whirl of the wards, the running feet of servants, but there was nothing and no one. Calmaretto was quiet. I bundled Leretui up the stairs and into bed, telling her that on no account was she to stir until morning. She gave a mute, unhappy nod; she seemed half asleep already.

As I turned to close and lock the door to her bedroom, a hand fell on my shoulder. I must have jumped a foot in the air.

'Aunt—'

'It's me,' Essegui hissed. 'What's going on?'

I felt myself go limp with relief. I pushed past her into our own room, sank down onto the bed and told her everything. She listened, frowning, and when I had finished she said, 'Well, something's the matter with her, that's for sure. I've heard of people being haunted, though not like this.'

'But where will it lead?' I asked. Somehow, I knew that neither Essegui or myself would be repeating this conversation to my aunts.

And Essegui said, with what from the distance of my time in Caud seemed so bitter a hindsight, 'Nowhere good for her, or us.'

FIVE

Essegui Harn — Winterstrike

I could not look away from the contents of the teacup, swirling like a little galaxy. Trivialities seemed to grip me with an unexpected fascination. On the way to the tea-house, in my stumbling trying-to-be-dignified flight out of Calmaretto, I'd become intrigued by a flashing red neon sign on the side of a building, had stood staring at it with my mouth open for some minutes before the suspicious, curious stares of a couple passing by had brought me to my senses. Was this what it was like to have a piece of your soul gone missing? To be a little bit less than human, to become entranced by human things? I remembered how my cousin Hestia had stolen my soul once, years ago on the lawn of Calmaretto. Hestia had done it just to see if she could, and I didn't recall much about the experience itself, only a bright blankness, as if I was walking into the sun. Later, they told me that I'd stumbled around as if drunk, or bewitched, but I just didn't remember that part of it. The Matriarchy had begun to take an interest in Hestia after that, to Alleghetta's fury.

I still couldn't believe that my mothers had done this to me. If I'd thought it would do any good, I'd have tried to reason with Thea, but I knew how far she was under Alleghetta's thumb. She might regret what had happened, but she wouldn't do anything to stop it – just sink further into the sherry, most likely.

I had no doubt that the geise was working. My sister's disappearance, until recently, had been a source of sorrow, bewilderment, anxiety, and it still was, except that now everything had fused into a nagging compulsion, driving me on through Winterstrike. It took a considerable effort of will to force myself to stop, to sit down, to drink tea and warm my numb hands.

And the ironic thing was, I'd have done it anyway. I'd have gone after her without the geise on me, and if anything would hold me back beneath its lash, it would be the lack of my mothers' trust.

When I looked up from the cup, everyone else looked away. I must have been muttering to myself. Or maybe the geise was visible, in the way that you sometimes looked at people staggering through the streets and knew that there was something wrong with them. There was a lot of it about, these days. *Black science. Majikeise. Whatever you wanted to call it.*

I turned and met my own stare in the metal wall of the tea-house. This was an old place, and the metal was spotted and stained: my skin looked mottled, as though I'd fallen ill. But apart from that you'd never have known, for I looked the same: white face, grey eyes, long black hair. All monochrome, with no colour in me except the stain on my soul. And I looked more like Shorn than I'd have liked, too – her ageing self, gaunt and hunched into her woes.

I wanted to stay here in the tea-house, amongst the steam and the murmured conversations, with the old-fashioned spine trees in pots by the door, signs dating from the last century advertising different kinds of tea, and the burnished metal walls reflecting us all. The conversations were all about the war – about some news report that last night, on the sacred night of Ombre, the heretic matriarchy of Caud had launched an attack on Winterstrike and we had responded with an assault of our own, some new weapon developed by our dedicated scientists and unleashed only at the most extreme provocation.

The murmurs were cynical. I didn't believe it either. And I had other things to worry about. I had to go where Leretui had gone, and the only thing I could think of was that, somehow, impossibly, Leretui had gone to the vulpen. That meant the mountains, and as I had told my sister, the mountains in winter were no place for anyone human. At that thought, the geise snapped my head forward so that I gave a small muffled cry and people looked at me out of the corners of their eyes and started talking to one another a little too loudly. Time to get out of the tea-house. I stood, in a flurry of coat-tails, slapped a few coins down onto the table and went through the door into the icy air.

The geise, I was finding, had not only taken a piece of my soul. It had a soul of its own, and also its own voice, with which it was starting to whisper and prompt: a thin, reptilian hiss.

'*Remember*,' the geise said. '*Remember.*'

And all at once, I did remember: riding in the gliding carriage towards the theatre with Leretui and my cousin Hestia, over fifteen years ago now. I couldn't remember what the play was – some mind-numbing piece which Alleghetta had insisted we go to see – but I had a small, sharp, recollection of looking out of the window of the carriage and seeing a group of women dressed as demotheas, or perhaps not dressed up at all, but demotheas themselves. Vulpen were the Changed, and so were the mythical demotheas, and even though the years of the Thousand Cults of the Age of Children were centuries gone, the remnants of those cults remained. And there was one place where the records were to be found. A place I knew very well.

These days, the Temple of the Changed stands on the very edge of the great crater of Winterstrike. Its fall into the crater itself was predicted every year due to erosion and lack of funds, but somehow the Temple survived, like a tottering drunk, staggering but not falling. A bridge led from it to the fortress where I carried out my own ceremonial duties; where I had rung the Ombre bell. In the undamaged turret of the fortress were kept records: ancient texts and inscriptions dating back to the Age of Children, detailing lost races and antique technologies, vanished abilities that were now no more than myths.

I was thinking of a defenceless girl's sudden ability to vanish from a locked room, leaving defiance and mockery behind her. Something had happened to Leretui during the course of that half-free night of Ombre, and I needed to know what it was. The fortress was not open to the public, but I wasn't an ordinary citizen: I had access.

It was mid-afternoon when I made my way back to the fortress, but the light had already begun to fade and the first of the street-torches had been lit along the Grand Avenue, flaring and hissing into the sleet. The tea-houses were doing a roaring trade all the same, and there was a stream of shoppers going in and out of the state stores, using hoarded savings for the holiday discount, carrying off electrical goods and bags of clothes. Normally I avoided this part of the city at the festivals; Alleghetta had always told us that it was common to seek discounts and had stuff ordered, usually at much greater – and pointless – expense. Thinking of this, I had a sudden desire to rush into the nearest state store and buy lots of cut-price unnecessaries, but the geise, perhaps fortunately, was pushing me on.

The Grand Avenue stretched before me, pointing to the towers of the civic buildings and the circular walls of the Matriarchy, arrow-straight. To my right – through what had ceased to be sleet and was now snow, falling in huge, soft flakes – I could see the bell tower above the roofs. It struck me that I should like to be able to turn back the clock, to be standing there once again, tolling the bell for Ombre and a different outcome. I turned towards its shadowy height, ducking under a sodden red awning down a side alley. The further I walked, the older the city became:

massive walls of ancient marble, pitted with bullet holes and fire strikes, dovetail-jointed in the old manner and so finely done that even now you could not have slid the blade of a scalpel between them. The walls reared up, with windows that were no more than slits high above me, set deep in angled sills. Defensive fortifications, now used for public housing, but the Matriarchy had made no effort to make them less fortress-like. Wise, under recent circumstances. I passed along the alley and came out onto the banks of a narrow canal: one of the secret waterways of Winterstrike. A woman was driving a sledge along the silvery ice, invisible beneath a broad-brimmed hat. She did not look up and I, not wishing to be seen for reasons that I did not fully understand, melted back into the wintry shadows and slipped along the canal, hugging the wall.

Over a little arched bridge I came into a district smelling strongly of food. Someone was frying batter-cakes in a pan of hot oil and the odour cut through the numbness of the winter air, comforting and greasy. Apart from the tea, I'd last eaten at breakfast and I was hungry, but I didn't think I'd be able to keep anything down. Instead, I walked quickly on, down further alleys and snickets running between the fortress walls, until an insistent, rhythmic banging caught my attention and I realized that I was close to the Temple: someone was beating a gong. My heart started to beat in time with it and so did the whisper of the geise, though this time I could not understand what it was saying. I felt as though I'd become a seamless whole with the rest of the world and that world had contracted down to this single hammering pulse. A moment later, I came out into the plaza that led to the crater.

It looked like the surface of some distant moon, an expanse of stone that was pitted and holed with meteorite strikes. Cracks ran along its length, spreading outward from the crater. They could have covered it, rendered it anew, but the Matriarchy preferred to remember this single greatest disaster in the city's history.

At the far end of the plaza, I could see the Temple of the Changed towering up through the falling snow, its façade mottled to a fleshy pink by winter. The gong had stopped but it seemed to me that its reverberations continued, striking out the hour across the city and pulling us all in its wake. Beneath my booted feet, the surface of the plaza was icy, the snow that had been melted by last night's torchlit procession, to mark the start of Ombre, had pooled and frozen. I had to keep my head down in order to retain my footing and was at the steps of the Temple almost before I knew it. I looked up. Two pillars marked the entrance, so coiling and curling with entwined figures that it was difficult to distinguish them from one another, but all of them were representations of the Changed themselves, mythical and real, mainly coyu and aspith, but a few demotheas, cenulae, sultrice, also. Stylized representations of DNA spirals wound amongst them, celebrating difference.

They were the last remnants of the Age of Children. They were supposed to be the future of the human race: created by a cult that had originated here in Winterstrike and which held diversification to be the final product of evolution. Earth had its own peoples: the kappa, the moke, the kajari, and many more. It hadn't really worked. Genetically unstable, often physically frail, the majority of the Changed failed to thrive.

Movement between the pillars attracted my attention. Someone was watching, someone who did not want to be seen any more than I did, but who did not have the skill to remain unobserved. I turned, pretending that I was heading past the Temple, and slipped along the steps in the snowy shadow of the left-hand pillar. I came up behind the watcher. She was hunched against the stone, clinging to it as if it could protect her from the cold.

'Hello,' I breathed. She jumped, and stood shaking. I looked down into a long-muzzled face, the eyes human and sad, the skin covered in a faint fawn down. Her hands were unnatural, the fingers oddly jointed. If the aspith had been engineered for some particular purpose, I could not imagine what it might have been: animal genes seemed to have been thrown into the mix at random, or perhaps selection had bred into particular traits. I half expected her to wring her hands. She was dressed in the customary red of the cult, her hair concealed behind a veil. It reminded me of the majike.

'Why are you watching me?' I demanded, but the aspith turned and ran, her veil streaming out behind her like red smoke. She disappeared through a tall open door into an echoing space that was barely warmer than the plaza outside. I followed the sound of her footsteps, the hem of her skirts rustling against the stone floor like wind in the branches. Far ahead, along the rows of columns, I could see daylight once more, as if the other side of the Temple was open to the crater.

I ran after the aspith past rows of columns – there seemed to be far too many more of them than was necessary to support the roof, and each one depicted a different race. Nightmarish faces glared out at me and I was sure one of the columns represented the vulpen. A long, beak-like skull snaked from top to bottom of the column, as if looking down its nose at me. All at once I felt that the carvings had eyes. The back of my neck prickled with chill. A little scatter of what looked like hail eddied over the floor, blown in from the direction of the crater.

The aspith whisked around a corner and I'd been right, for the Temple did lie open at the far end. Past the bulk of the fortress, I could see the opposite walls of the crater, with the dark hollows of the maze of dwellings visible even through the snow. I could see lights, which looked as though they were floating.

The aspith was nowhere to be seen. I stood in an echoing hall, its walls mirrored like the old stained metal of the tea-house, and casting a fragile light across the black stone floor which sent my reflection, also white and black, spinning into infinity. The fanciful thought came to me that if I could step into one of those reflections and disappear, so much the better.

Disappearing. Leretui, I thought. Oh, Shorn.

It was now almost completely dark, the torches flaring through the sleet across the plaza. Snow starred the tall windows that separated the front façade of the hallway from the outside world; it was marginally warmer in here, but I still kept my coat securely buttoned. I had plans to stay the night in the fortress, perhaps in the tower room, where at least I felt safe. But my mothers would know to look for me there: safety was an illusion. Wild beasts would not have dragged me back to Calmaretto and I thought my presence might prove a liability to one of my friends. I had the odd sensation that the whole world was changing around me, some projected but unrealized future in which this really was the condition of the human race, and that if I walked outside now to the cold plaza, I would find a different city.

I'd wasted enough time on the aspith. I left the Temple and went out onto the plaza, feet scuffling in the drifts of snow that were building up against the steps. The bridge to the fortress lay on the opposite side of the plaza, reaching out over the crater pit. It was a route I'd taken dozens of times, ever since my majority and the days when I'd first been assigned my duties in the bell tower. I'd won the role by birth, not through any merit on my own behalf, but I still thought it was the closest that Alleghetta had come to being proud of me. Now, as I approached the gate, I was filled with a queasy unease, thinking of the aspith, that unlikely spy, and whether Calmaretto might have sent someone after me, to bring me home by force. But there was no one waiting for me at the gate and my other fear, that the majike's black work would have altered my soul-engrams to the point where I'd be unreadable by the matrix of the gate, proved similarly unfounded. The mechanism scanned my eye and I felt the familiar tickling deep inside my head. Then the gate swung open. I stepped through onto the bridge.

The fortress always seemed to be a place of extremes. When you were on the bridge itself, the winds tore at you, snatching at hair and hood and whipping coat and skirts around you. I always hurried at this point, afraid of being snatched up by the wind and blown into the dark pit of the crater. But once I reached the other side – traversing the iron railings, each side with its spindly statue of the fortress spirits, my feet beating on iron – the sound was abruptly cut off. I looked back down the shadows of the bridge to the gate, and once again, no one was watching.

No one that I could see, at any rate. Again I put my eye to a mechanism and again it spoke to my soul, opening the main doors to the fortress. I was glad to shut the night and the weather behind me and step into the empty, echoing corridor that led, ultimately, to the bell tower. All metal and stone, a red floor, punctuated with black and white tiles. Above, the ceiling was fashioned in an ancient style, representing feathers like smooth black wings. I don't know how this conceit had originated. Bronze lamps lit the corridor with a subtle glow and ahead, stairs led up to the bell tower. There was no elevator, though they had certainly possessed the technology: interminable academic speculation suggested various explanations, all of them esoteric, most to do with the journey of the soul. For me, it was workplace and sanctuary, nothing more. But I pretended a mystical leaning, if questioned. It was politic.

And of course, on this occasion, my shattered soul's journey would be correspondingly incomplete. I wasn't going right to the top of the bell tower, but to one of the antechambers that lay halfway up the stairs. These were separated chronologically, their books and records divided according to age: since I was interested in the handful of texts dating from the Age of Children, I would not be climbing very high today.

This particular chamber was lined in bronze, like the lamps, which lent it a pleasantly warm cast when I sat down and asked the light to come on. There were no windows and I was glad about this: I didn't want to see beyond the confines of the bell tower. It reminded me too much of what I'd have to do when I got back out there. An ancient antiscribe stood on the central desk, and it whirred into life as I switched it on and input my entry data.

Some years before, my cousin Hestia had suggested to me that it might be helpful if we manufactured a separate identity for ourselves. This, more than any more tangible evidence, indicated to me that the rumours about my cousin's profession – supposedly that of young-lady-about-town – had some truth. But we didn't discuss it. Hestia was as well aware as I of the difficulties of Calmaretto and I'd agreed with her enthusiastically that it might not be a bad plan. I'd even managed to siphon some money into an additional account, under that name: Aletheria Stole, a name that would be redolent of Tharsis to the casual observer, nothing to connect it to the aristocracy of Winterstrike. I suspected that Hestia might use the same name on occasion, as the account fluctuated, though the sums I placed in it remained scrupulously constant under a separate credit heading.

So *Stole* was the name under which I entered myself into the antiscribe, and the account details which churned ponderously up fell beneath that heading also. Once entered, I began to scan the system for relevant records. Anything religious could be ruled out – I'd had to survey these records once before for a visiting academic and they had proved opaque in the extreme. I don't know whether the woman ever made anything of them in the end, though academics can usually generate some kind of theory to cover available data. But there was a handful of texts that referred to battles, and these I brought up on the scanner and studied.

The first text referred to a journey across the Silent Sea: a catalogue of islands, most of them in all probability imaginary. Interesting, but not apparently of relevance.

The second and third were partial and made little sense: one was a list of curses and the other a list of names. But the fourth was of greater note.

Mantis. A name that rang a bell, somewhere. She'd been one of the warrior matriarchs in the Age of Children, had vanished from a fortress under siege. There had been no clue to how she had done it: her warriors, once the fortress had fallen, maintained that she had been taken by the spirits of the Crater Plain and stuck to their stories despite torture. Mantis the Mad, who had held and ruled the lands around the area that was now known as the Noumenon, a remote mountain matriarchy that no one knew very much about. A closed, secret place, high in the ragged crags beyond the western Plains.

That was the only text that had any vague relevance, and I thought this was probably stretching things. I doubted whether Mantis, mad or not, had really disappeared into thin air: more likely she'd bolted down a tunnel or had been done away with by one of her own troops. But one thing did engage my attention, even though I was sure it was still no more than coincidence: the Noumenon was said to be a haunt of vulpen – not, obviously, within the bounds of the Matriarchy itself, but beyond, in the high crags and rifts. Vulpen were said to haunt ruins, and there were a lot of those in this part of the Crater Plain – also dating from the Age of Children. The geise was tugging at me, but I didn't know how much store to set by that: I didn't think it had any extra knowledge that wasn't also possessed by me, and I directed a swift but heartfelt curse in the direction of Calmaretto for saddling me with this additional set of unreliable instincts.

There were no more records. I closed down the antiscribe, turned off the light, and left the bronze chamber with reluctance.

My feet nearly took me up the stairs to the bell tower, but I made myself turn away, back down the bronze corridor. It seemed warmer, almost stifling, and I thought at first that this was because I was so reluctant to leave. Then I reached the doors and realized. The bridge was on fire.

It didn't look like a normal flame. It was white and blazing, so bright that I had to shield my eyes, and that meant ire-palm. I slammed the doors shut. My hands slipped on the metal, sweating, as I fumbled at the lock. There was no way I could face the bridge, not in those conditions: one touch and I'd go up like a torch. I ran back down the corridor, all longings for the bell tower abandoned: I had a vision of the fortress as a tall iron oven, with myself roasting at its heart.

I'd no inclination to be cooked. I'd never been down into the cellars, but I'd studied the plans of the building when I'd first started working there, and I knew roughly what was there. A spiral staircase led downward, twisting until it was lost in the shadows. I followed it down, footsteps pattering on the metal struts, until I felt dizzy. Looking back up, the ceiling seemed impossibly far away. I thought of fire and kept on descending.

I stepped out into a long, dusty room lined with stone blocks. This looked even older than the rest of the fortress: red Martian sandstone, grooved as though water had at one time flowed along it. Double doors at the far end of the room were heavily bolted, but at some point a more modern haunt-lock had been installed. I ran across and tugged at the bolts, which after some minutes gave way in a shower of rust. Then I put my eye to the haunt-lock and heard the familiar whirring of the soul-scan. The doors swung open, to my mingled relief and apprehension. I didn't know what might be waiting on the other side of the exit.

But they opened onto night and nothing. I came out into the expanse of the crater floor and a bitter smell. Glancing up, I saw the ire-palm burning out on the bridge, and a second after that the centre of the bridge gave way. Outlined against the night-glow of the city, a section of the bridge collapsed, to hang for a moment in the void, and then to fall in seeming slow motion into the crater. There were shouts. An excissiere orthocopter, lights blazing, swung low overhead, veered up, came back around. I flattened myself against the wall of the fortress and watched as the burning section of the bridge came to rest in a blinding flare. The reek of ire-palm filled my mouth and nose; I choked. The floor of the crater was an expanse of ice and snow, melting out from the burning bridge. Dodging out of sight of the craft and hoping that any heat-sensitive equipment would be baffled by the ire-palm, I started to make my way to the crater wall.

I looked back once, saw the vitrified wall of the fortress rising straight up out of the crater. Above, a swarm of figures, tiny as insects, were milling around the shattered bridge. The light from the torches along the lip of the crater flickered, sending my shadow skittering along the snow ahead of me in an uneasy dance. I reached the crater wall and breathed again. But there was life in the hollows and crags of the wall. Eyes glittered out at me as I sidled towards the steep steps that led up the side of the crater. The orthocopter came in lower yet and someone dropped down onto the remains of the bridge; I saw the glint of a wire as she landed. I hadn't done anything wrong, but I still hoped not to be noticed: being in the wrong place at the wrong time in Winterstrike never turned out well, in my experience. So I hitched up my skirts and started to climb, my calves twingeing in protest after the long descent from the fortress. I'd get fitter, at least. If I survived.

SIX

Hestia Mar — Caud

Once the childhood visions had faded, I concentrated on trying to get out of the Mote. I knew this would not be easy: I'd already failed once and it seemed I was a valuable prisoner. The next guard who came to the door of the cell was soulless: I could see the slack lack of it in her face. They'd taken her speech as well. I asked her name and she stared at me vacantly, clearly not comprehending. A slave? But as she raised her arm to shove the meagre bowl of food through the interlock, her sleeve fell back and I saw the tracery of old and intricate scarring upon her skin: a former excissiere, then, subject to the most extreme punishment short of death. It was pointless to try anything more. I ate the food she'd given me in silence and returned the bowl to the lock. Then I sat down to consider my options, which were few.

When I looked up again, the Library was back.

'Hello,' I said.

The flayed face of the warrior tightened into a grimace. 'I can't help you,' I said, aloud. 'I can't help myself.'

The warrior's lips moved but no sound came out. After a moment, as if there was a time-lag in a recording, I heard her say, 'Something is coming.'

'Something? What kind of something?'

The warrior did not reply. Instead, she looked up, as if staring at what lay beyond the ceiling of the cell and the Mote above it.

'Can you hear it?' the warrior whispered.

'Hear what?' But she was right, there *was* something – a thin, whistling noise like a child's flute.

'What—?' I started to say, and the moment I spoke the world exploded. There was a soundless, incandescent flash that had me throwing my arms across my face. Reflections cascaded behind my retinas, a kaleidoscope of fractured colour. I felt something sinewy gripping my wrist, but only for a second, as if the Library had become real and reached out and touched me. I still don't know what it really was, only that it was oddly reassuring. I opened my eyes again and saw that although the afterimages were still blasting through my sight, my vision had cleared enough to allow me to see the rest of the cell.

The walls of the Mote were melting. It looked, to my astonished gaze, as if the stone had turned to wax and been held in a flame. The veins in the marble ran like blood, trickling down to the floor, and the stone sloughed away in its wake. It was like ire-palm, but on a much larger and faster scale; it turned the place into a ruin.

'What in the world?' But the warrior was standing right before me, saying urgently, 'You must go, now, before they see.'

She was right. And I wasn't known for succumbing to dazed stupidity. I went through one of the gaps in the wall and out through the blacklight chambers.

The machinery of the haunt-equipment resembled metal lace, ancient and rusty, corroded almost to nothing, even though I'd seen it in action literally hours before. I touched a panel and it disintegrated under my fingers. I couldn't say I was particularly sorry about that. I pushed past it, slammed my hand against a door that collapsed, showering the floor with brittle splinters, and went out into a passage.

I could hear distant shouts: the Mote had become a hive in panic. I couldn't blame it: looking around, the whole thing seemed to be coming apart. There were huge holes in the ceiling and floor: I had to skirt around them in order to avoid falling through.

But from my own condition, which was unchanged as far as I could tell, and the scurry of voices from somewhere up above, the weapon – if weapon it had been – did not appear to have affected the humans in the Mote. I didn't know of anything that could do that: it was no technology possessed by Winterstrike or, I was fairly sure, by Caud. But I'd heard of much older devices that were able to destroy rock, even mountains: the Fused Cities of the Demnotian Plain gave some truth to those myths, although scientists now thought that this had been caused by some natural phenomena. And the gaping hole where the tower of the old Memnos Matriarchy had once stood was yet another reminder.

But what if they were wrong? And – since this was a strike at the heart of Caud – what if this had been a weapon from data that I'd just delivered to the Matriarchy in Winterstrike?

Hell, I thought. It was certainly impressive, whatever it was.

I flattened myself behind a dripping pillar – the last remnant of one of the walls – as two exicissieres ran by. They were conversing rapidly, the wounds flickering across their skin, and their scissor-weapons were out and at the ready. I did not fancy engaging them in conversation. I waited until they had passed and then I ran back the way they had come, reasoning that they'd emerged from somewhere higher up in the Mote.

This turned out to be correct. As I turned a corner I saw the warrior once more; she had vanished for a time, but now was back, looking ghastlier than ever. The dimming lights made her flayed countenance appear drowned.

'This way?' I asked her. She gestured assent. I ran around the corner and found myself in what might, an hour ago, have been the main hall of the Mote: a massive chamber lined with green marble pillars, now melted into stalagmites. The place swarmed with excissieres and I ducked quickly back behind one of the decaying pillars, but they didn't seem to see me. Some kind of command and control was going on: an armoured woman stood on a platform, rips and tears flickering over the surface of her gear as though she was being invisibly attacked. Excissieres were dispatched in all directions and just as the last group was leaving the chamber, the ceiling caved in.

I was thrown to the floor underneath a shower of plaster. When I raised my head, the stars blazed through the shattered roof. I suppose I should have felt proud, or at least relieved, at the notion that the information I had imparted to Winterstrike had caused the destruction of Caud's cruellest institution. But I just felt numb. The degree of devastation horrified me. This is what's known as growing soft, I thought. I couldn't feel ashamed of it, either. I shook myself free of plaster and scurried past the crumbling pillars to where I thought the main door was located.

Caud should have been under curfew by now – from the position of the constellations it was late in the evening – but light streamed in through the street. The main doors of the Mote – the official entrance, not the various means by which they took in prisoners – had been blasted open and now hung on their hinges. I squeezed through and out into the street.

I'd learned young that when you lose your focus, let concentration drift – when you think you're finally safe, if only a little – that's when terror really strikes. I should have known better. Maybe it was the unreality of what had just befallen the Mote that made me drop my guard – but I'd also been taught not to rely on excuses. Drop it I did and nearly lost my life in the process.

She came out from the shadows, faster than any I'd seen before. Excissieres are known for being quick and deadly, but they are human when all is said and done. This one moved like an animal, a flicker on the eye. I didn't even see her strike. Suddenly there was a stinging pain along my thigh and I looked down to see a gash in the leather, blood welling up through it. A second movement, a blur at the edges of sight, and there was another slice along my arm. A half-inch more and she would have hit the artery.

I'd like to say I fought, was brave. But let's not be stupid here: she was the best I'd seen and I was unarmed. I leaped backwards, running without looking, as I'd been taught, relying on senses that were on the very edge of panicked flight. The excissiere stopped, as if amused, her armoured head on one side.

She was almost naked, but her skin didn't look like human flesh. It had a sheen to it, a hardness, and the lights of the city reflected dimly from it. At the same time, she seemed faintly wet, a kind of eldritch glisten; I didn't know whether that was innate to her nature, whatever that was, or whether she'd just emerged from one of the canals. There was a flutter at her throat, something that might have been engineered gills, or a wound, opening.

'I don't speak your language,' I said. I glanced over my shoulder and saw that there was a wall of fallen masonry behind me, and all around. I'd have to leap high if I wanted to escape and fear started to rise in my throat. The excissiere grinned and I saw that her teeth had been sharpened. Her shaven head was as white as bone, and ridged, like some ancient helmet designed to deflect sword strikes. Her breasts were vestigial, with no sign of nipples. She appalled me. I said, 'Make it quick, then.'

The excissiere's head turned even further to the side, an odd, cocked movement: *Where would be the fun in that?* it seemed to say. She pounced, feinted, struck – I was in a foetal ball on the ground by now and I'd have died, without doubt, if the warrior-shape of the Library had not risen up between us. A great gaping wound appeared across the warrior's chest, from collarbone to crotch. It laid her open, revealing the neat, pallid mass of her internal organs. The Library looked down at her wound with slow contempt. The excissiere's lips drew back from her teeth in a smiling snarl. She struck again, laying open the Library's face. The warrior showed no sign of agony, only a remote disdain. I did not understand how she was even experiencing such wounds, unless – bizarre thought – she and the excissiere were communicating rather than fighting. I saw the warrior's ruined lips move, speak a word. A slice of ripped skin appeared down the length of the excissiere's body: she looked at it in amazement. Her mouth pursed into an 'O', a theatrical, exaggerated gesture. The warrior spoke again, a string of words I was not able to hear, but each one blossomed a wound on the excissiere's body. The artery of her wrist opened up, displaying a viscous flow of blood: it seemed that this, too, had been artificially slowed. I suppose she might even have been dead, technically speaking. But gradually, totteringly, her eyes glazed over and she collapsed onto the rubble, a broken, malignant doll.

By this time I was back on my feet and staring. I turned to the Library, to thank her. But the warrior was no longer there. Instead, there was only a small glowing thing on the ground, like an icy-hot coal, burning blue. I looked at it for a moment and then I recognized it: it was the sphere of the Library itself. It must have fallen out of my pocket. I picked it up, finding it quite cold, and put it back. Leaving the excissiere's shattered form behind me, I strode from the remains of the Mote and out into Caud.

SEVEN

Essegui Harn — Winterstrike

It was only when I got to the top of the crater that I allowed myself to stop and look back. The cold air burned its way into my lungs, making me wheeze, and my eyes were watering, but the main points of interest were still clear: the shattered bridge, the smoking hole in the snow where the ire-palmed section had fallen, the fortress still punching its way out of the crater like an upraised fist. The excissiere orthocopter had landed by now, thundering down into the crater as I huddled against the wall, hoping that my black coat and hair would stop me from being too noticeable. Just as I came over the crater lip, another craft hurtled overhead with the yellow-green flash of heavy bulb cameras: a news team. I would later learn that the Matriarchy had conveniently blamed Caud, and indeed, it might even have been true. I didn't stop to have my picture taken. As the news copter swung out over the crater, I grasped the upper rail with a shaky hand and pulled myself across the lip onto the slick stone of the plaza. Then I walked swiftly, but not at too obtrusive a run, across the plaza and past the Temple. The little aspith that had haunted me on the Temple steps was nowhere in evidence, though I kept a sharp eye out for her. Inside my head, the geise and speculation about the Noumenon warred for place, making genuine reasoning difficult.

I was trying to remember everything I'd ever heard about them: a morass of rumour and theory, very little of it based in fact, or so it had always seemed to me. But the feeling that it was here that answers were to be found lay in my gut like a stone. It seemed to me that I needed to go to the Noumenon to find out what had happened to my sister, and I had no idea how I was going to get there, not with the world in the state that it was and winter already firmly bedded in. Somewhere, a small cold voice told me that this was not even rational, but I didn't listen to that.

News of the strike on Caud was all over the newsboards just beyond the plaza, along with a continual gallery of images. No doubt they were manufactured; I paid no attention to them, but walked quickly on until I came to the northern stretches of Canal-the-Less. This was some distance from Calmaretto, a much less attractive district based around the docks, where ships came in from the Small Sea and the canals of the Plains, bringing a stream of cargo into Winterstrike. I'd always liked the docks, the smell of spice and chemicals and tea; the shouts and banter as the boats were unloaded. Now, in winter, the shipyards were quieter, with many of the cargo vessels ice-locked in the southerly ports of the Plains, waiting for spring. I debated whether to try to take a boat and dismissed the idea as unfeasible at this time of year. Instead, I skirted the dockyards and headed for the Great North Gate.

Winterstrike is built on classical lines, dating from the very early days of the city and following the dictates of Earth. That didn't last long: the wide streets and gracious avenues, the elegantly appointed civic structures, soon gave way to wars and botched experiments and earthquakes and air strikes. That enormous crater at the heart of the city was evidence enough, although there were those who felt that it had actually given Winterstrike more room, since as I'd just seen, people lived in the crater walls. The Age of Children, the Rune Memory Wars, all of these had started in Winterstrike and forced the city's contraction and expansion and contraction again, like some unnatural birthing process. But, somehow, the four quarters of the city had remained and the North Gate itself dated back to the Age of Dissonance, when Earth and Mars had been separated for generations and we had forgotten our origins, tried to forge ourselves anew.

The Gate was, correspondingly, a monstrosity. It rose up out of the dust and dishevelment of the docks like a great red trunk, two slabs of Plains marble, red and mottled black like most of the city, surmounted by a looming guardhouse that was supposed to protect the northern way out of Winterstrike, but which had suffered a kind of blight during the latter stages of the Age of Children, when stone-plagues were so rife. It bulged and blossomed, lumps of marble excrescing outwards from its originally smooth surface. Occasionally, they dropped off, injuring pedestrians and inviting calls for a public inquiry, which inevitably proved futile. The Matriarchy of Winterstrike did not approve of interfering with historical artefacts, no matter how repulsive or dangerous they proved to be.

The area around the Gate was surrounded by boarding houses, congregating there to deal with the mass of travellers. I went into a store and bought a makeshift journey pack for myself and then, after some effort, I found a room at the third boarding house I tried and took up residence. It was a dingy chamber, at the back of the house but with an angled view of a slice of canal. The rug, thrown onto bare boards, sent up puffs of dust whenever I trod on it and a thin yellow trickle came out of the tap above the basin. But it was still better than Calmaretto. I thought grimly of Canteley, still under the sway of our mothers. But sometimes it seemed to me that Canteley had done better than either Leretui or I.

Every time I thought about Leretui, it filled me with dismay. My little sister, whom I'd failed to look after. When we were growing up, it had always been Hestia and I and Leretui against our mothers: ranged against Alleghetta and Thea and my aunt Sulie, three against three. And now I'd let Leretui slip away. I shoved those thoughts aside.

Next door, there was a tea-house that served basic meals. Trying to keep myself muffled up in a shawl, and attracting as little attention as I could, I chewed my way through a tasteless Plains buffalo steak, my stomach finally allowing me to keep food down. I was certain that it was the distance from my home that permitted this. I bought a flask of tea and took it upstairs to the chamber, then drank it as the lights of the ships glowed down the canal and a red gibbous moon rose over the summit of the Great North Gate.

I watched the newscasts obsessively, seeing from another angle the collapse of the bridge, the segment falling into the snow. I did not see a small dark figure running across the floor of the crater: it was too shadowy, too black, and this came as a considerable relief. Blame of Caud was freely expressed, by a variety of commentators.

When I finally checked my personal antiscribe, the screen held several messages, all of them bearing the stamp of Calmaretto. I deleted each one without reading it. But there was one message with an unfamiliar stamp. If Leretui had managed to contact me, perhaps from a public 'scribe . . . I clicked the message open.

I expected to read a few lines. I didn't expect a channel to open up. A moment later, I was staring into the face of the majike.

I jerked back. My hand slammed down onto the control panel but nothing happened. The majike gave a thin grin.

'It won't work. Nice to see you again, Essegui. I'm glad you're all right. I've been worried about you.'

'I doubt that.'

'I know you're angry. I can understand why. I can't tell you that what we did was for your own good, Essegui, but it was for the good of your sister. You want to find her, don't you? Where do you think she is?'

'I don't know.' Her stare was almost hypnotic, but it wasn't that which made me add, 'The records spoke of the Noumenon. People used to disappear and reappear at will.'

The majike's gaze sharpened. 'So they did. I can give you some help, Essegui, if that's where you decide to go.'

'Well, what do *you* think? Do you know where she's gone?'

'I would say,' answered the majike, 'that the Noumenon is a very good choice. I'll arrange for you to have help. Now. You're at the North Gate, aren't you?'

'How did—'

'There's a pilgrimage leaving in the morning,' the majike continued serenely, without giving me time to finish my question. 'Link up with it and you'll find that they take you with them. Once you're out on the Plains, we'll try and arrange transport to the Noumenon. Well done so far, Essegui. I'm pleased with you.'

Then she ended the connection and I was left staring at the blank screen of the antiscribe. It was a moment before I realized that her approval had affected me and then, angrily, I sought my bed.

I dreamed of burning buildings until just before dawn.

EIGHT

Hestia Mar — Caud

Caud was in chaos. Perhaps with the destruction of the Mote and the occupation of its excissieres, the Caudi had decided to explore just how much anarchy could be perpetuated in a single night. I met bands of women running to and fro in their nightgowns, like flocks of shrieking geese. A gang of children looted an engineering store with silent efficiency. On the main canal, onto whose banks I was ejected by the crowd like a cork from a bottle, it seemed that someone had stolen a boat: quite a large one, probably a cargo ship come up from the Small Sea. The sails were rattling up and I could see fighting breaking out on the deck. Someone hit someone else over the head with a large jug. It was all rather like watching a play, although I think that my recent escape from imprisonment and a bloody death may have made me a little light-headed.

The canal seemed to be running higher than normal, slopping up and over the stone balustrade that kept the walkway from the water. I squinted downstream, trying to see. A girl in a trailing crimson veil sprinted past me, holding up her skirts as she ran; I recognized her for one of the acolytes at the Temple of Sem, one of the older cults of Caud. The veil gave me a start, however, reminding me as it did of Gennera. The girl was shouting something that I did not catch, in a strong local dialect. Moments later, an excissiere clawed her way up the balustrade on a rope thrown from a boat and ran after the acolyte.

I would never know, I thought. As long as they left me alone. If I was going to get out of Caud in a hurry, then the canal seemed like my best option. With all the chaos on the waterfront, the chances of an escaped prisoner being spotted seemed relatively remote, although I did not know how much there was to connect me with the prisoner who had, by default, been implicated in the murder of an excissiere. The scissor-women were said never to give up, if the matter concerned the death of one of their own. I repressed a shiver, as much to do with fear as with cold, but there was plenty of the latter. My clothes were winter gear, of course, but I'd lost my heavy coat in the Mote and now wore only a tight underjacket. The icebreakers had only recently swept the canal, as they did every evening, and the blocks of shattered ice bobbed and buffeted against the balustrade and the side of the boats. Striding along the riverbank, I scanned the water, looking out for symbols. Eventually I found what I was looking for: a painted eye, an ancient sign, denoting on this world a craft from the shores of the Small Sea. It was pulling out; I could see a figure on the deck, hauling at a rope.

A cry came from behind me and I turned, to see two excissieres sprinting along the dock wall. A glance over my shoulder showed that there was no one behind me: they were aiming for me. Cursing, I jumped down onto the dockside.

'Over here!' someone shouted. The figure on the barge was waving.

'Hang on!' I cried, and fled. I'd changed my accent as I spoke, turning from the clip of Winterstrike to the longer vowels of the Small Sea. 'Can you take a passenger, mistress?'

'Get on,' the woman said. I sprang aboard, narrowly missing the water, and immediately the barge pulled out, leaving the excissieres on the dock. They watched for a moment, then I saw them turn and head back. They'd have ways of recognizing the barge, but whether they were in a position to do anything about it remained to be seen.

'Where are you headed?' The pilot shaded her eyes against the glare of torchlight, looking upward. 'I'm going as far as Tauk, no further.'

'Good enough,' I improvised, 'I'm bound for Sheruk.' It was the village before Tauk, far to the south of the Crater Plain, and I knew that relations were good between them, unless things had radically changed since I'd last set foot in the Sea Matriarchies. The same could not be said of all the shore towns. The barge itself was a long low thing, bulky and blunt at the prow.

'Came up with a load of seacoal,' the captain said. 'This is my own boat, my mother's before me.' Easy to believe: she was as squat and blunt-nosed as her vessel. She did not have to tell me that I'd be working my passage. Anyone from the Small Sea would be expected to haul rope and do the same.

'I've spent too long here,' I said.

The skipper laughed. 'What, been here a day? I came three nights ago, won't be coming again. I doubt they'll be able to pay – had to argue for it, easier to wring money out of the coal itself.'

'Things have been difficult here,' I said. 'I came two years back. A teacher,' I added, to her unspoken question. She might not believe me, but I didn't really care. She'd let me on board and if she'd put any variances in accent down to the long stay in Caud, then that was well and good.

'Who's your family?'

Oh damn. But I'd been to Sheruk, at least. 'Montak.'

'I know of them. Don't know 'em well except old Rehet. Decent people, so I've heard.'

'More decent than this lot.' I gestured towards the canal bank, as the big barge slowly swung out into the stream. I could hear what sounded like weapons fire. I looked back and up at the broken towers, the flicker of street lighting running up into the hills but full of gaps, like missing teeth. From this vantage point, the once impressive skyline of Caud was a mess. As the barge swung out into the icy canal, I glimpsed the ruined dome of the library, and fingered the sphere in my pocket. I didn't know how badly the library had been damaged, whether the warrior would reappear. I hoped it hadn't been terminal, especially since she, or it, had saved my life.

'How long will it take?' I asked.

'A week,' the skipper said, adding rather suspiciously, 'But you'd know that.'

'I came on the train,' I told her. She swung the tiller out and the barge headed into the string of departing water traffic. Caud fell away, the shouts growing gradually fainter and the lights going out, one by one.

Interlude: Shurr — Malay, Earth

The entourage of the Centipede Queen reached the port at dawn, with a coolness in the air and a chewed half-moon hanging low over the harbour. Both sea and sky were a rosy grey in the morning light and Shurr took a deep breath, wondering when, and whether, she'd see Khul Pak again. She had travelled before, to the Rimlands of Cascadia, the islands of the Siberian Sea, but never to another world. Already she had a sensation of immensity, as though the universe was opening up before her and allowing her to slip secretly through.

The Queen's litter glided ahead: an enclosed shell on hovering stabilizers, like a coffin or a barque, its sides rendered opaque so that the Queen could look out but others could not look in. It preserved the mystique, the Queen had once remarked, for her not to appear except at the great festivals and, of course, at her ritual marriage, when that took place.

Shurr looked now at the litter sliding ahead through the

morning air and clenched her fists within the folds of her sleeve, making Segment Three slide restlessly up her arm. It had taken a lot of money to persuade the Matriarchy of Winterstrike to sanction this visit and there was still plenty of time for something to go wrong: Shurr could feel trouble ahead, like a fog bank, vague and yet ominous. But there was no sign of it yet. The harbour lay peaceful in the morning light, the great red ball of the sun rising up over the low-rise tenement blocks that ringed the city sprawl and gleaming through the smoke cast up by the industrial units to the north of Khul Pak. Shurr waited as the Queen's litter was guided down the steps of the quay to a rocking security sampan. Beside her, Ghuan murmured, 'Not long now before take-off.'

Shurr nodded. It took some getting used to, seeing Ghuan as a woman. The slanting eyes were the same, amusement-filled, and so were the delicate features – the same, and yet different, as if the cocktail of hormones had caused them to blue slightly around the edges. And there was something different in Ghuan's gaze, too: an unfamiliar anxiety.

'Are you all right?' Shurr asked, risking loss of face for them both.

'Mars is – a long way away.'

'I know. But you're female now. You've nothing to fear.'

'It's not all that friendly to women, from what I hear.'

Shurr laughed. 'It's a hell of a lot less friendly to men.'

The litter was now at the end of the sampan, locked into the boat's own system and surrounded by a faint glow. From the subtle lightening of the litter's walls, Shurr knew that the Queen had activated the viewing switch and was taking an interest in what was happening outside. She followed the litter down into the rocking sampan. The motor was kicked into action and Shurr, Ghuan and the other members of the Queen's party were whisked out into the harbour, past the teeming flotilla of boats which occupied the typhoon shelters and out into the wide open ocean.

The city fell behind. Shurr glanced back at Khul Pak and from this new angle saw the Palace of Light rising on its slight promontory in the midst of the maze of waterways and canals. She'd heard that Winterstrike was built on water, as was Caud, and the other cities of the Plain. A sudden excitement filled her: the prospect of a new world, where the Queen's lineage had once been revered and might be so again. Then the city was gone, lost in sunlight and water haze, and the sampan was shooting out across the sea to the platform.

On clear days, which were few, one could see the platform from the upper storeys of the Palace of Light: a spiky, attenuated porcupine shape far out to sea. Shurr had often stood on the balconies of the Palace, watching the sharp sparks of incoming and outgoing haunt-ships rising and falling from the platform, and had never ceased to wonder where each one was heading, or had come from. The choices were limited: Mars, Nightshade, the Moon, perhaps the strange rim settlements clinging to the rocks of the Belt or the scattering of vast post-orbital craft that glided between the worlds. And each one whispered to her: she could hear the voices of the dead channelled through the Segments she had carried, for this was part of their function, too; to listen to the Eldritch Realm and seek answers.

Segment Three must feel this now, for it stirred and quaked within her sleeve. Shurr ran a hand along the centipede's spiny body, murmuring reassurances. Ghuan turned an unsettled face towards her.

'Do you think that's our ship?'

Shurr followed his – no, *her*, she must get out of the habit of thinking of him as a man – pointing finger to where a dark shape was hovering over the edge of the platform. Shurr had only once before been close to a haunt-ship, and then as now, the thing had been difficult to see: blurred around the edges, with detail suddenly illuminated as if by lightning. As the sampan drew closer to the platform, the haunt-ship solidified, becoming a squat oval craft with gleaming metal sides and a bristling canopy at its

summit. As Shurr watched, a gape-mouthed form, barely recognizable as human, shot out from underneath the ship and
skimmed across the water, passing through the sampan and stirring Shurr's hair with an icy spectral breath.

'Looks like it,' Shurr replied.

NINE

Essegui — Winterstrike

The sound that woke me was so faint that at first I thought I'd imagined it, or was still lost in dreams of the fortress bridge, blazing. Around me, the dingy room of the boarding house was filled with a creeping light. The river birds which congregated around the gate were already shrieking and clucking with the approach of dawn and it must have been one of those that woke me – but then I heard the sound again, a slight stealthy scratching at the base of my door.

Very carefully, I sat up. There was something glistening under the frame of the door, as though oil was being poured through the gap. Something prompted me not to put my feet on the floor. The back of my neck was prickling with the recognition of something eldritch: the guest house was not, as far as I could tell, warded apart from some basic mechanisms around the front door, but this had the twitchy feeling of sophisticated tech.

And the majike, at least, had known where to find me . . . But she'd offered help, hadn't she? Somehow, I did not think this was it.

Standing on the bed, I reached for my pack and hauled it over my shoulder, grateful that I'd slept in my clothes. Then I climbed across to the windowsill, like a child playing a game, and perched on it while I unclasped the window. Glancing over my shoulder, I saw that the oil, or whatever it might be, was starting to coalesce into a greasy film across the rough parquet of the floor. As I sent the window rattling up, the oil flashed like white fire and a shape appeared in the centre of the room. It lunged at me, a toothed maw, but I was already out of the window and hanging onto the sill. I dropped ten feet into a snowbank and without waiting to catch my breath, ran for the gate.

I'd wondered how, without transport, I was going to get clear of the city. The majike had mentioned a pilgrimage, but I didn't like the thought of relying on information provided by someone who was, as far as I was concerned, an enemy. I didn't have much choice, though. The Calmaretto carriage was a useless machine, used only for formal occasions and short distances – the theatre, the park. On the rare occasions that we'd been taken up to the Harn country house – really no more than a cottage in the upland meadows of the Saghair, and thus unusable for the cold months of the year, which was most of it – we'd had to hire transportation. Anyway, after the events of the early morning, I was reluctant to draw further attention to myself.

Due to the outbreak of war, most public transport between Winterstrike and the region of Caud was on hold or severely compromised, although there was some canal traffic. It would, however, be difficult to get from Winterstrike to the mountains by water. Normally, there were trains into the foothills, but now these, too, had been placed on hiatus. I spent half an hour or so huddled in a makeshift tea-house within the lee of the gate, working out how best to hire a ground car anonymously.

The oil-thing had not come after me and this wasn't a surprise. I'd recognized it as a roaming ward: a portion of someone else's house defence hijacked and booby-trapped, sent out into the world to kill. It wasn't an easy matter, and that told me that whoever had sent it after me meant business. Not a comforting thought.

As I sidled out of the shadow of the gate, the geise nudging me at every step, I saw a procession coming down the street. This was motley, disorganized, and yet seemed to have an element of cohesion. A large carriage in the centre of the procession swayed from side to side, drawn by two horned, lowing beasts, and a crowd pressed around it, banging hide drums and playing the mournful flutes around which, in the south, entire orchestras are based. The whole procession was producing a doleful cacophony as it headed towards the red bulk of the North Gate. Oh, what the hell, I thought. I had to find my sister and besides, someone was trying to kill me. I needed to make a decision. I ran forward and caught the sleeve of a woman walking behind the carriage.

'Is this a pilgrimage?'

'Why, yes. We take the mantle of Ombre to the mountains, we walk in shadow.'

The mountains: that meant the Hattins, which were effectively the foothills of the Saghair. From there I might be able to get canal transport or a train to the region that surrounded the Noumenon, as the majike had suggested.

'Can I come with you?' I asked. The majike's idea had held some sense, however little I might like it. Going along with the procession would provide me with a measure of security – I could see guards walking by the carriage, weapons sheathed within the city walls but weapons nonetheless – and a reason for being out in the wilds.

'All are welcome,' the woman intoned. She did not sound happy about it. I wondered what private tragedy had impelled her out onto the road. Pilgrimages are rarely formed of the blessed. I'd heard of the Mantle of Ombre; one of the lesser cults that had grown up around the festival itself, but it wasn't one of the big state-sanctioned belief systems and I knew little about it.

'Thank you,' I said, and fell into line behind her. I had no

drum and no flute, but I followed the chants as best I could –
some were old hymns that I'd learned at my governess's knee. I
walked with the procession into the darkness beneath the North
Gate and when I came out again, Winterstrike was at my back
and the Crater Plains lay beyond.

An hour passed, then two. I realized how unaccustomed I'd
become to walking so far and my calves started to ache again after
the exertions of the day before. The pack I'd bought in the matriarchy store was filled with no more than cheap underwear and a
bottle of water, but it started to weigh on me more and more heavily as we walked on. Gloomily, I supposed this was natural, and
anyway it was so cold that the water must be turning to ice. But
the pilgrimage had its advantages. The incessant chanting, which
under normal circumstances would have infuriated me, served to
drown out the voice of the geise. It resurfaced from time to time,
a little less insistent than before, and although I wasn't sure
whether this was a result of the chanting itself or simply that I was
doing what the geise wanted, it was nonetheless a relief.

I also took the time to study my fellow pilgrims, as covertly
as I could. Most of them seemed to be from Winterstrike, to judge
from their pale colouring, but there were a few exceptions. I did
not know where the very young girl with the long hair striped in
red and black might be from: her skin was much darker than that
of someone from the city and she kept casting nervous – no, more
than that, frightened – glances around her as she walked. And
there were three women wrapped in brown veils, whose faces
could not be seen and who did not, as far as I could tell, join in
with the chanting. I moved a little closer to them, out of curiosity, but they remained silent and paid no attention to me. As we
passed one of the ruined towers that star the landscape outside the
city, however, one of the women raised an arm and pointed out
the tower to her companions. I saw something sinuous slide along
her arm, disappearing up her sleeve. A bracelet? But it looked as

though it had moved under its own power. I decided to keep an eye on the three brown-clad women.

The highest buildings of Winterstrike had become tiny by midday, far in the distance and no more than a series of blocks and domes. Here, heading north-west, the Plains themselves were still monotonous under their covering of snow. In summer they would become all red soil, black grass, thin waving fronds planted in the very early days of terraformation and proving impossible to eradicate. The towers, a legacy of some long-forgotten war, rose in vitrified obsidian splendour at intervals across the plain, each one bearing the face of a different demon, carved some twenty feet in height. One of them was inhabited: a forlorn black and white pennant snapped from its ruined summit and a scuttling at the doorway as the procession drew near suggested it was some hermit, perhaps one of the mad religious that haunt Winterstrike's further boundaries. None of us cared to find out more. In the distance, after we'd passed the tenth tower, a moving herd veered around and away, scenting us on the wind.

'Gaezelles,' one of the guards volunteered as I drew close to her.

'Really? This far north?'

She shrugged. 'They come up from the southern craters sometimes, if there's danger.'

'I'd have thought there was more risk here, near the city.'

'Perhaps it's worse in the south. Or maybe they're short of food: they come up if their prey fails.'

I felt a little uneasy. In the olden days, they'd been designed as herbivores. So much for that. I knew they'd been revived, and it seemed there had been revisions. 'Any likelihood of attack?'

'Probably not. But if they do – well, we won't have to look far for supper.' The guard gave an unpleasant smack of the lips.

By the time the sun sank down and cast the Plains into a russet shadow, I had blisters. The procession had not been permitted to halt apart from short breaks, but in the early afternoon a woman had gone among the crowd dispensing meat buns for a small amount of money. Though I was not used to a midday meal – at Calmaretto this was always considered vulgar, like so many things – I bought one anyway and ate it as I walked. But as the sun fell, I realized that the march-pace of the procession had been in order that we might reach shelter for the night, as I'd suspected and hoped.

There aren't many settlements between Winterstrike and the mountains. Unlike the south of the city, where the lakes lie and there are many small villages, this part of the region is still relatively deserted, apart from the towers and their accompanying ghosts. The place we now came to had been an oasis once, during the ancient desert days, and its name was Gharu. In the lost years, when this part of Mars had relied on beast-transport, it had been a way station and the old sinks and plunges were still there: pools of water beneath a thin layer of ice-trapped weed. The low buildings beyond were only the top layer of the town, which extended beneath the ground to preserve the place from the worst of the winter winds. The procession came to a gate, seemingly standing on its own: a rough black dolmen leading into nothing. At first, I thought it was some ritual structure, then realized that its appearance was deceptive. As the guards stepped up to it, the air shimmered beyond and revealed a winding flight of steps, leading down.

'Dormitories,' the guard explained.

When we went down the stairs, filing two at a time, I discovered that the whole place was geared towards pilgrimages. This must be the only way the occupants had of making a living. Rows of beds stood in nooks set into the walls, affording some privacy, and a hatch at the end of the long room dispensed basic meals. I claimed a bed, then queued with the rest and bought a mess of meat porridge. Everyone seemed subdued, probably from fatigue. I kept thinking about Leretui, wondering where she was now, how she was faring. We ate in silence. I found myself facing the three brown-veiled women: they conveyed small fragments of food to their mouths with deft movements beneath the veils, and drank hot tea through long metal straws. My own tea was too scalding to touch: I watched in awe as the women sipped. They must have metal-lined mouths, I thought. I kept looking at their sleeves, but nothing else moved in them. I started to wonder whether I'd imagined it. Then something glistened briefly at one of the women's throats. I raised my head to see that she was, apparently, staring at me. They finished their tea and simultaneously rose, then went to one of the slightly larger bed-booths, all three, and hung a blanket decisively over the entrance, blocking the booth from public view.

I wasn't the only one watching. The woman sitting next to me, an older person, turned to me and said in an urgent whisper, 'Do you know who they *are*?'

'I'm afraid I don't,' I said.

'They're a clone-group from the south,' someone else said knowledgeably from across the table.

'No they're not,' someone else replied. 'They're from Bale. I've seen people like that before.'

An argument, conducted in hushed voices, broke out around me as various theories were put forward and ruthlessly demolished. I finished my meal and debated whether to go outside for a breath of fresh air; the common room was stuffy and smelled of hot wool. Then I remembered what had happened in Winterstrike and decided that safety would be the more sensible choice. I couldn't rule out anything befalling me in the middle of the mass of pilgrims, but whoever was after me would find it harder to accomplish in a crowd than if I was on my own. I bought more tea and took it into my chosen bed-booth, electing to leave the opening uncovered. I stripped down to my underwear and took refuge under the blanket.

I didn't get to sleep until a couple of hours later. It's hard to sleep when people are singing and someone insisted on playing the flute, which whistled and mourned around the echoing common room like a wind over the marshes.

Eventually there came a shout: 'Can't you *shut up*?'

Another argument, resulting in a brief but vocally ferocious intervention by the guards, and peace reigned. Whoever was responsible for the common room dimmed the lights to a faint rosy glow and I slept, but not for long.

When I woke, it was colder. It struck me, fancifully, that I could feel the winter pressing down on the roof of the common room, hard and final as a fist. Someone was whispering, a quick, urgent sound. Then a figure flitted past the entrance to my bed-booth and in the lamplight I caught a glimpse of floating brown cloth. There was an almost inaudible chittering.

Infernal curiosity! But I thought I'd rather try to pre-empt an attack, after what had happened to me already. I slid out from under the blanket, bundled my coat around my inadequately clad self, then peered around the corner of the booth. Old, cold stone pressed against my face. The figure was heading quickly up the steps. Sliding out of the booth, I went around to the brown women's booth and lifted a corner of the blanket. The booth was empty.

It was none of my business, I told myself, but I still followed them, up the steps past the silent serving hatch and out into the covered courtyard. Heaters were blasting out warmth from either side of the courtyard, keeping the frost at bay, but there was still a bite to the air in between the gusts of heat. I kept back, hiding in the shadows. Ahead, I could see movement and hear a distant whispering. I moved closer, trying to catch what was being said, but when I reached the end of the column of pillars which supported the roof, I found that the voices were not speaking in the common dialect of Winterstrike, or standard Northern Martian, or indeed any language that I understood. A hissing, clicking language – I wasn't even sure whether it was an actual tongue, or some kind of code. But now that my eyes were adjusting to the dim light I could see the brown-clad women. They stood in a huddle like ancient witches, arms about one another's shoulders and heads close together. Something was writhing along their linked arms: a smooth, cool-looking body that at first I took to be some kind of snake, until it shifted position and I saw the myriad carpet of legs gliding underneath. A centipede.

It looked almost like some kind of plastic. I wasn't sure at first whether it was a real animal, or a machine. Then the head came into sight: stubby twitching antennae and formidably curved mandibles. I stood a step back and the thing raised its head as though listening. I held my breath and to my intense relief it resumed its movement around the linked bodies of the women. I melted back the way I had come and returned to my bed. A few minutes later, I heard footsteps and again the three forms flitted past.

I hoped they hadn't seen me. It was so hard to know what abilities people have these days, what technology. Nothing about the women spoke of haunt-tech. I closed my eyes and tried to sleep and forget what I had seen, and eventually I did so.

Fatigue must have caught up with me, for when I next woke most of the pilgrims were already up and about, and the air smelled tantalizingly of tea and frying meat. I crawled out of bed, wrapped myself once more in my coat and went to the washroom. A shower, blisteringly hot, woke me up, but as I washed the water stung my arm. I looked down at the bare skin. Something had bitten me, producing two deep holes about an inch apart on the underside of my wrist, embedded in raised bumps. Gingerly, I prodded the bumps. The skin felt numb.

I thought at once of the centipede and fought back panic. Had the women detected me, there in the shadows, and sent their familiar to deal with me? Would I die? It seemed ironic that I'd survived two apparent assassination attempts in Winterstrike only to meet my end as a result of my own stupid curiosity out here on the empty, barren Plains. I dressed, wondering whether to confront the women or complain to a guard. But what would I say, if it turned out not to be the case? There were all manner of insects living in the countryside: it might have been something else entirely that had bitten me.

When I went back out into the common room, however, the three women were nowhere to be seen. Already inclined towards paranoia, I saw this as suspicious. I asked a woman where they'd gone and she replied that she did not know, but someone had told her that they had left shortly after dawn in a great hurry.

This did not, I thought, bode well. I kept an anxious eye on the bite throughout my quick breakfast, but although the numbness seemed to be wearing off to some degree, the bite was not as painful as it looked and I felt much the same as before. But it was yet another thing to worry about. I was glad when we left the way station and recommenced our journey: it took my mind off things, although in a manner which was not altogether welcome. Since we had entered the way station the evening before, the weather had taken a turn for the worse, and now a stinging squall of sleet was washing down from the distant mountains and scouring the Plains before its lash. I bundled my coat closer and kept my head down as we left the huddle of buildings that made up Gharu and struck out on the open road. If I had not been so intent on avoiding the sleet, perhaps I would have seen what was coming for me, and avoided that, as well.

TEN

Hestia — Caud/Crater Plain

I'd noticed before how extensive Caud was, how far it reached beyond its city walls. The barge took me past interminable industrial estates, each with its own dock: some gleaming and newly framed, others rotting into the water. Occasionally the captain, whose name was Peto, pointed out areas of note and I pretended to take interest in them. I found that I kept looking back, as if at some level I couldn't really believe that I'd managed to escape the city, but it was more that I expected pursuit. The warrior of the Library had not returned, but in the Library's absence, the excissiere I had killed haunted me instead. I glimpsed her out of the corner of my eye, ghastly and unmoving upon the deck, propped up between boxes, or hanging from the stairs. I couldn't put these macabre visitations down to guilt, since I didn't feel any. I was damn relieved that the Library had managed to dispatch her when she had, otherwise I'd be dead myself. It struck me, however, that the excissiere might have managed to download some encapsulated element of herself into the Library's own functionality and the Library, herself contained, was projecting the excissiere outward in random stress. Peto, to my immense relief, didn't seem to see her, and this suggested that the appearance of the excissiere was peculiar to my own visual system.

Either that, or I was simply being over-sensitive as usual. I had no idea whether the excissieres were capable of haunting beyond death: they keep their secrets close and no one outside their Orders really knew what the hell went on in there. I didn't even think it was truly accurate to describe them as human any longer. And to think that people still avoided the Changed.

These thoughts occupied me as the bleak hinterland of Caud passed by and we came out onto a series of locks. Then I had no more time for speculation: the captain put me to work on the lock system and we descended, slowly, creakily, onto the first dark reaches of the Crater Plain.

It was still very cold, but it seemed to me to be a little milder than in Caud. At this time of year, really warm weather would only be found much farther south, towards the lakes. My hands, even in gloves, fumbled with the lock mechanisms and I could feel the breath freeze in my nose and mouth. I bit down on ice crystals. Finally, we reached the last descent and the barge glided out onto smooth water.

Civilization, if you could call it that, lay behind. Here, no torches illuminated the canal banks and the only light came from the faint splinter of Phobos, hanging red over the frozen grass-land. When I went to the place in the cabin allotted to me and tried to raise a signal on the antiscribe, I could not get any response out of it. I wondered fruitlessly what was happening back in Winterstrike. Now that I was away from the game, I had a chance to start thinking about whether I wanted to stay in it, and what the ramifications of leaving it might be. Spies who jump ship are not popular at any time, and even less so in times of war.

Peto leaped out and tethered the barge to a ring for the night and I slept a fitful sleep, surrounded by the cries of night birds and the rustle of winter insects in the grass along the bank, until I woke to the white and grey dawn.

When I forced myself to leave the comparative warmth of my bed and go out onto the deck, I found that I had been mistaken:

we were not alone after all. Half of Caud seemed to have departed with us, fleeing the recent strike. A makeshift refugee encampment stretched out across the icy grassland: plastic sheets strung on poles to keep out the winter wind, shelters made of bedsheets and towels. Dim lights moved between these temporary tents as early risers – probably unable to sleep – sought friends and relatives. The acrid smell of tea drifted across the plain. I felt suddenly privileged to have the protection of the barge, solid wooden walls and a kettle.

Peto was soon up, walking briskly about the deck as though she'd been awake for hours. She paid no attention to the encampment and I wondered whether she'd even noticed it; but the people of the Small Sea were known for paying little mind to other people's business; one of their more endearing traits, as far as I was concerned.

I'd have followed her example, if it had not been for an anomaly amongst the transient shelters: a series of slender spires, rising up in the middle of the encampment. Fragile banners in green and crimson and black fluttered in the early-morning wind. The spires were in the shape of cones, with a narrow, tapering top.

'What are those things?' I asked Peto, who shrugged.

'How would I know?'

'Do you mind if I take a look?' I asked. It might mark me as someone not from the shores, so I added, 'I've seen something like them before. Traders, from the far south.'

That sparked a flicker of interest in the captain's flat eyes. 'As you wish. But don't be long. I'm looking to set off in the hour. Don't know what other traffic might be coming down. We'll hit Sendar Locks before nightfall and if there's a clog . . .'

'That's fair,' I said. I didn't want to get held up any more than she did. 'I won't be long, I promise.' While she busied herself with securing any cargo that had come loose on the way down, I stepped onto the bank and strolled through the tents to the spires, with the frost crunching underneath my feet. It was exhilarating just to be out of the city and into what passed for freedom, though I took careful note of my surroundings, in case any excissieres had come with the refugees.

Those who had fled from Caud were varied, that was for sure. I passed a whole coven of acolytes, shivering around a meagre fire, a family with a flock of pinch-faced children, two little girls who seemed entirely on their own, a woman with a cage full of hens. As I drew near to the spires, they became even stranger: they looked as though the wood they were made of was moving, alive.

I stopped and blinked. No, definitely moving. Intrigued, I walked closer and saw now that the spires were attached to a long carriage, made of metal and what looked like bone, but which was probably some plasto-substance. It had wheels, small and with thick black tyres, but also a glide barrier, quite a powerful one, suggesting that the carriage had the ability to rise into the air and fly for short distances.

All of this meant money. There was a general air of opulence about the carriage, which had tinted windows set high on the sides – too high to look out, surely, and that usually meant that the occupants had camera access on the outside of the vehicle, to watch their surroundings from privacy within. I searched, and there it was, a shining obsidian eye set into the sinuous decoration that covered the sides of the carriage. I couldn't tell what this carving was supposed to represent: it looked like a silver spine, the vertebrae coiling and curving about the sides and up over the roof. That took my gaze up to the towers again and I saw that the thin struts were not moving at all. Something was crawling up them – many things, pallid, slender bodies with thousands of legs. *Centipedes*. Each one of them was at least as long as my hands, placed fingertip to fingertip.

The excissiere materialized behind me, so suddenly that I didn't have time to pretend I'd been looking somewhere else.

'What do you want?'

'I was interested.' Tell the truth, why not? I forced my voice to normality. I pointed to the towers, bending under the weight of their unnatural occupants. 'Those centipedes. Why are they here?'

The excissiere said, with pride, 'They have come with their Queen.'

'Their Queen?' Now that I was looking at her more closely, I saw that she was not, in fact, an excissiere – not of the kind I knew, anyway. The scars were there, along her wrists and inside the high collar that she wore, but her uniform was the same cream as the bodies of the centipedes, and segmented. A close-fitting helmet confined her hair, spined along the top and back. She had no visible weapons except a trident-prong, wired up for electrical impact. But I could see cleverly concealed slits in the sleeves of her uniform, suggesting that she had weapons modification underneath.

Now, the excissiere-guard nodded. 'The Centipede Queen. She travels south, from Caud.' Her face, all gaunt ridges of bone, contracted in an expression of distaste. 'Caud. We were sent to it by your orbital authorities, not to Winterstrike as we wished and planned. They sought to show her as a freak, not a visiting dignitary as we were promised. We were glad to see it struck, gladder still to leave.'

'Caud's not the most hospitable place, true.'

The guard squinted at me. 'You're from the south?'

'From the shores of the Small Sea.'

'Ah.' The guard nodded again. 'A long way from Caud, then, and from our home, too.'

'Where are you from?'

'From Earth.' Sound came from the carriage, a rustling, chittering noise, and the guard looked uneasily towards it.

I was fascinated, but I knew when to make a sensible exit. 'Thank you for the information,' I said. 'I wish you safe travelling.'

'And you, also,' the guard remarked. Her manners were better than an excissiere's. And she hadn't tried to kill me, either. At least, not yet. She headed off in the direction of the carriage, swinging the trident, and I walked thoughtfully back towards the barge. Interesting. If they'd come all the way from Earth, then no wonder I'd never heard of such a person as the Centipede Queen. I stepped onto the barge where the captain was impatiently waiting and we cast off without further ado. The refugee camp was waking up around us as the barge glided away, the air filling with steam from a thousand kettles, indistinguishable from the light morning mist.

'If I had a year of life for every plea I've had to "take me with you", I'd live to my third century,' Peto said as we pulled away.

'They're desperate,' I murmured.

We did not speak of the matter any further, being occupied in taking the barge out into the stream amongst the heavier water traffic. There was a lot of it, now – huge industrial barges travelling down, an icebreaker with its double rams taking up centre place in the stream.

As we headed south, the canal widened. I could still see the opposite bank, the high stone wall dimly visible through the layer of mist. Markers stood along it at intervals, ancient guard towers from when this was the main link between Caud and the Plains that it had once ruled. What must it have been like in those times, I wondered: when Martian origins had become a mystery and all contact with Earth had been severed? Times of great technological advance and great cruelty, times of stagnation followed by horrifying change. Times in which I should not like to have lived.

Not that the current one was a whole lot better.

It was at this point that Peto chose to share her travelling plans with me.

'I'm not going to take the Grand Channel all the way down to the Small Sea. Too many locks and there was talk over the 'scribe – this morning when you were off. Talk of searches.'

'By whom?'

'Don't know. Excissieres.'

I had a sudden weird moment of guilt. They wouldn't be looking for me – I'd finally managed to get through to Gennera and they knew exactly where I was, had grudgingly approved of my means of escape. They'd have sent someone to fetch me, so Gennera had said with what almost passed for apology, but they had their hands full at the moment and anyway, she didn't think I'd want to attract attention.

This was, I felt, the Winterstrike Matriarchy's way of telling me that I'd done my job, very well done and all that, now get yourself home and if something happens to you along the way, well, at least we won't be implicated. The work of a spy is, one might say, somewhat thankless at times.

I turned my attention back to what the captain was telling me, which was that instead of heading down to the great locks – those miracles of invention that had made the Grand Channel a possibility – we would be taking a series of smaller locks into the mountains. This would cut days off our journey and, though not without risk, was less likely to run us into trouble than sticking to the Grand Channel under present circumstances. After some thought, I agreed with her. The mountain route wasn't unguarded and in this part of the hinterland was ruled neither by Caud nor Winterstrike, but by a small and separate matriarchy, very ancient, called the Noumenon, the Shadow Clans. Once upon a time, these had been rebels, from Caud I believed, but had been ejected from the city and sought refuge in the hills, battling off men-remnants to take control of a jagged range of hills, the High Galar, within the range called the Saghair. There had been a very popular public entertainment series about it when I was a child: we had not been allowed to watch, due to its sexual content, but did so anyway, in secret. Essegui and I had learned a lot, not all of it historical.

'All right,' I said to Peto. 'Seems reasonable.'

'Good, you agree. We take a cut-off just after the next locks.

A good thing we left when we did – have you seen what's coming down behind?'

I took a look at the little radar screen. An enormous green blot was moving swiftly up the canal. 'What's *that*?' I asked.

'Don't know. Go and look.'

I went onto the deck. It was clearly visible, even from this distance. It was some kind of dreadnought, bristling with cannon and a high observation turret, which to my mind made it look as though it was about to topple over. Glide rafts along its sides served as stabilizers and given the depth of the Channel – which I knew to be considerable but not *that* considerable – were also serving to keep the thing afloat.

'That's not from Caud,' I said. The Caudi splatter their official craft with all manner of insignia to show everyone how important they are. Winterstrike is more restrained. But this thing had no symbols at all, no identifying marks, and that made me nervous.

'Never seen that before,' Peto said, coming to stand beside me on deck.

'No idea where it's from?' It might be privately owned, and that was even more worrying.

'No. But one thing's for sure.'

'What's that?'

'We'd better get out of its way.'

Peto took the tiller and I brought the radar console out on deck and started keying in coordinates. With a barge of this size, this was not strictly necessary in terms of steering, but Peto was careful about everything going into the log. I wanted to watch the dreadnought go by, so I sat with the console on my lap until Peto's movements grew increasingly frantic. The dreadnought was bearing down on us at a rate of knots. We came perilously close to banging into another barge; there were shouts. I snatched the tiller from Peto's hand, being younger, and hauled the barge round, feeling a hydraulic rush as the steering mechanism finally kicked in.

'Not there!' Peto yelled. 'To the side! *To the side!*'

I aimed the barge at a gap between a wallowing cargo carrier and what looked like a municipal ferry, crammed with passengers. It lurched from side to side and even if it didn't capsize, I was afraid that it might crush us in the narrowing gap. I revved the barge up to its maximum power, which remained underwhelming, and we shot forward into the gap. Standing at the prow – the narrowest part of the barge – I could still have reached out an arm and touched the vessels that flanked us. The faces of the ferry passengers gaped like something out of a comic drawing; children, and some of their mothers, were screaming. At that point the sides of the barge scraped the ferry with a noise like old iron being banged with a hammer.

'Careful!' Peto cried, but from the way she was glancing from side to side, I could see that she was thinking the same thing as I. We were not going to make it through the gap. I looked over my shoulder and saw the great metal wall of the dreadnought rising up behind me. I could have stood in each of the cannon mouths with my arms upraised. Shouts were coming from the dreadnought itself – there seemed to be fighting taking place on deck – and just as I realized this, the dreadnought's stabilizers roared further into life and the whole vessel rose upwards, wobbling. I was knocked backwards in the great draught of air, luckily onto the deck. The ferry wasn't so fortunate. It swung, righted itself, then rolled over, spilling shrieking passengers into the canal.

Peto leaped over me and seized the tiller. The barge was rocking to and fro, but I thought it was broad enough not to go over, even though enormous waves were washing diagonally across the canal. I scrambled to my feet and joined her at the helm; she was, as far as I could see, trying to avoid mowing down the overboard passengers. There was a great bubbling of air from underneath the capsized ferry: a moment later, its own stabilizers kicked in and it righted itself, carried up by a huge bladder, which subsided to let the ferry down onto the choppy water. Together with Peto, I grabbed hold of the swinging tiller and took the barge out into the middle of the stream, from which the dreadnought had so recently departed. Lifebelts were thrown and some passengers were already clambering back on board the ferry, but I'd seen at least three go under and not come up again. Had there been time, I'd have gone after them, but that would have meant the barge crashing into another vessel and probably costing more lives. I felt guilty and uneasy, all the same. Gradually, the churning surface of the canal returned to relative placidity and I looked up, to see the dreadnought flying south. It had extended a pair of vast wings on either side, which made it look like an unwieldy airborne beetle. People were hurling curses after it. I could not blame them. There was a pair of binoculars hanging on the cabin door: I slapped them to my eyes and saw that there was still movement across the dreadnought's decks. A figure went over the side and fell sprawling through the air, running in nothingness.

'Did you see that?' I called to Peto. 'Someone fell.'

'Pirates,' Peto spat. 'All as bad as each other.'

Perhaps she was right. I glanced around the canal and saw that the scrum of vessels was starting to resolve, with most people heading for open water and a degree of safe passage. I turned the binoculars on the horizon and saw that a line of mountain wall had appeared in the distance, with a low red sun hanging over it and casting it into indigo silhouette across the silvery expanse of the plain. From what Peto had told me, that meant we were not far from the locks and the cut-off: I'd be relieved to be clear of the main channel, if this sort of thing was going to happen. The dreadnought was now no bigger than a moth.

'Check the cargo!' Peto called, and I went down the stairs to the cabin at a run. But when I reached the bottom of the stairs, someone came out of the shadows in a rush and I was pinned against the wall with a razor at my throat.

Interlude: Shorn

When she looked back on her time in captivity, it seemed most of all like a dream. Faces moved in and out of sight, voices shivered the air. But when she thought about it, it wasn't as though anything before that had been very real. Only the earliest years, laced into her stiff dresses, tottering like a little doll about the maze of the house – that was real enough. She remembered the way the light fell through the stained-glass windows of the rooms and cast a fractured pattern of colour across the floor, the frost on the windows of the winter garden on the roof of Calmaretto. She remembered the burn of lamplight on wineglasses as she crouched on the stairs, gazing down on her mothers' dinner parties and glad, even then, that she was not old enough to be expected to join in.

Thea hiding something in the cistern; the guilt on her face as she turned to see the little girl staring at her. Leretui hadn't understood until much later that the thing had been a bottle. And she wasn't sure that she really understood, even yet.

Alleghetta storming about the house. The rage, when she'd been turned down for the council, time and time again. Alleghetta blaming Aunt Sulie, for spoiling her chances. Then success, rapidly soured by Leretui's disgrace. She would never forget the look on her mother's face, as realization dawned.

It had been different for Essegui, although they were so close in age. Essegui had always had that self-contained remoteness, the ability to shut everyone and everything out. Even when their mothers scolded her, which was often, Essegui would sit with a closed, still face and Leretui had the distinct impression that she simply wasn't listening, although she could always repeat back what had been said if required to do so, with a faint air of wonder that verged, always, on contempt. Leretui had admired that, but she knew she'd never be able to emulate it even though she tried.

And she did try: inventing whole countries, entire nations, inside the brittle cage of her own skull, conjuring alternative lives for herself, where she was not dull little Leretui, the quiet child, the scion of musty, dusty, Calmaretto, but an adventuress, a Matriarch, a warrior.

The last thing she ever considered was that it might come true. But then the Voice had come, on a golden afternoon in summer, as she ran down towards the weedwood trees on the edge of the canal. The Voice was wild, proud, free as an animal's voice, and it told her of many things, made many promises. She could be another person, if she chose. She could be anyone, if she only listened and waited.

Leretui did both and dreamed of escape. She spent hours poring over the big atlas: the one that showed all the worlds in various stages of their development – Earth, before its floods; Mars, in the earliest days of its terraforming, as far as they could piece together the lands before the Lost Ages. She read about the haunt-ships, the great transliners that carried the passengers through into the realms of the dead and brought them back to life again, all the ancient, half-comprehended technologies bequeathed to the modern era from before the Age of Ice and the Age of Children, the Age of Error and the Age of Pain.

And the Voice told Leretui things, too: how it was to live in the marshlands, in a burrow with one's sisters. How it felt to give birth to a brood, teaching them to swim and hunt, but not too well, in case they turned on their mother, as often happened. How it felt to live under a different sky, the sun another colour, closer; and to run through the great ruined cities of one's foremothers, ancestors very different to oneself, ancestors who could and must be blamed. The Voice whispered to Leretui about promises made and promises broken, on and on until her dreams were filled with the whispers and the Voice's corrosive bitterness seeped into her heart like acid and left it etched and stained, so subtly that she barely realized the damage it had left in its wake.

Then the years went by and Leretui grew up and the Voice went away. But then, one day, it returned. It sounded different and even stranger. The alien remoteness had gone from it: it was a Martian voice, it said, but it did not sound like any voice that Leretui had ever heard before. It told her to do something quite different from the study of an atlas. It told her to go to the bridge on the Curve at Ombre and there she would meet someone, the kind of person she had always wanted to meet, and her vague, odd longings would be satisfied at last.

It did not occur to Leretui to question the Voice, or to consider that it might be leading her into a situation from which there would be no return. Trustingly, she did exactly what it told her to do and when the vulpen skated out from beneath the shelter of the bridge and held out its unnatural hand she experienced a moment of cold and awful shock, and then complied.

If they had not been discovered, what would have happened? Leretui did not know. There were rumours about men-remnants, of course, and their perverted practices: the idea of penetration, which to Leretui seemed to embody violence and which was immediately abhorrent, and yet attractive at some deep level all the same. It was by these thoughts that she knew herself to be lost and this was why she had permitted her incarceration: to give herself time to consider how best to kill herself, because she could not be allowed to live, not after this.

There in the locked chamber, on the night of Ombre, she thought she'd succeeded, for the Voice had come back – the second one, not the sibilant, whispering original of her childhood.

I want to die, she told the Voice and the Voice had replied, *Why, so you shall.*

They punished me, Leretui said, still a bewildered child at the root of it all.

Of course they did. You're different. Better, stronger. You make them afraid.

The Voice had spoken with great assurance, so much so that

Leretui was unable to disagree with it even though she did not feel it to be true: why would anyone fear her, ineffectual as she was?

The Voice told her that death would be easy. All she had to do was to sit very still, and will her breathing to stop, and then to wait. Shorn, grateful, had done exactly as it instructed her, masked behind the costume of Ombre and therefore hidden a little even from herself. As her breathing slowed, the blackness behind the mask had fallen in upon her, pounding inside her head and bringing a sunburst of golden stars as she felt herself falling with it.

She hadn't died, though. She had a confused impression of movement, someone taking her by the hand with thin, strong fingers and leading her down a flight of stairs.

'Come along, Leretui,' the Voice said, coaxing. 'Come along.'

Then the cold, sudden outside, and snow crunching underneath her feet, the air freezing the spit in her mouth, and darkness and speed. Then, nothing. She'd woken up – not in the locked room, but here, in the high tower overlooking range upon range of mountains, a captive princess. The room was round and in it was a bed, and a table, and a jug set upon it. The jug was filled with water and there were strange white flowers floating in it, filling the room with a wild perfume, not altogether sweet. A narrow window looked outward and all of this, to Shorn, was a luxury after the year in dim captivity. No one to berate her, no one to come and tell her how badly she had let them down, how shamefully she had behaved.

During her earlier years, Shorn had told no one about the Voice: let them think her bad, if they must, but not madness and the blacklight correction that would follow – she'd brushed close enough against that in any case, and it was only that Alleghetta didn't want further scandal that had held her mothers back from full psychiatric correction. Here, there was only the bare room and its ancient carvings, faces from the Age of Children, an old tower abandoned long ago, and the view and the cold air that breathed through the window when she opened it. When she looked up she saw empty sky: nothing flew over this land and Shorn rejoiced in its remoteness. The window looked out onto a glacial wall and the high peaks beyond, which caught the sun in the evening and changed to a deep, translucent scarlet.

For three days she was alone. Food appeared on the table – basic stews of bread and grain, with an alcoholic aftertaste. Shorn didn't mind *basic*, after Calmaretto's over-elaborate meals, and there was plenty of water.

On the third day, the woman came. Shorn had spent a lot of time sleeping, and she was lying on the bed when the woman came through the door, with the wind whistling and calling through the window, singing into Shorn's dreams with its own clear voice.

'Wake up, Shorn,' the woman said. Shorn started up. She saw a tall person, perhaps in her twenties, with a narrow, pointed face, her hair concealed by a veil. Thin brows arched upwards and the skin around the woman's liquid black eyes looked bruised. She wore armour and a long coat over it, in the manner of the north, but it did not look quite like northern clothing, all the same. Shorn tried not to stare.

'Who are you?' she asked.

'My name is Mantis.' A deep voice, which tugged at Shorn's memory. The name meant nothing to her.

'How did I get here? I mean, thank you. I'm grateful . . .' Her voice trailed away.

'You should never have been locked up in the first place.' Mantis came to sit on the bed beside her, a little too close for someone of uncertain status. Shorn forced herself not to move away. Mantis reached out and drew a finger down Shorn's cheek. Mantis's flesh was icy and this time Shorn did flinch. There was an extra joint on each of the woman's fingers. Beneath the veil, Leretui glimpsed her hair, intricately arranged into small whorls.

'You're one of the Changed,' Leretui whispered.

Mantis smiled. 'It's all right. I'm not going to hurt you.' There was almost a hint of mockery. Something silvery moved in her eyes and Shorn thought of blacklight and promises. 'You're rather beautiful, aren't you? I've seen ideograms of the ladies of Calmaretto, from ages back. All the same – they must have standardized the birthing chambers at some point. White skin, black hair, grey eyes. Your sister's the same, isn't she? Like princesses from a fairy story.'

'What do you want?' Shorn whispered.

'Oh, this and that. You'll find out. In the meantime, enjoy yourself. I imagine you'll welcome some peace and quiet after all the stress and excitement.'

'Maybe,' Shorn said, and to her own ears her voice sounded very small. Mantis patted her hand with cold fingers.

'Good girl. We'll look after you. I'll be back in a while.'

She rose and went out through the door. Immediately, the psychic pressure lifted, but Shorn was left with one overriding thought.

That was my Voice.

ELEVEN

Hestia — Crater Plain

'Be quiet,' a voice hissed in my ear, 'or I'll cut your throat to match your mouth.'

I had no intention of speaking. The arm that had clasped me around the chest was like an iron band, and when I squinted down I saw that it was clad in black haunt-enhanced armour. Redness flickered in its shiny depths.

'Now,' the voice said, very low and chilly, 'answer me precisely, in single words. Do not cry out. Remember what I told you.'

I gestured assent past the constriction of the arm.

'Where is this vessel going?'

'Small Sea.'

'Ah. Good. Are you going there directly, or will you be taking the cut-off?'

'The cut. Through the Noumenon.' If I'd hoped to put her off, it was unsuccessful.

'Even better! Are you the pilot of this vessel?'

'No.'

'Then what?'

'Refugee.'

There was a laugh. 'How unfortunate it must be, to have a home. Whereas if you were a traveller, like me, this would be no more than an inconvenience. But you don't sound as though you're from Caud.'

'Small Sea.'

'Oh, I don't think so,' said the voice. 'That's not a Shores accent, though it's a passable imitation. Where are you really from?'

She was good enough that I thought it inadvisable to lie any further. 'Winterstrike.'

'That's better. And of a Matriarchy clan, from your tone. That's not the voice of a peasant. How interesting! So what are you doing all the way out here? Keep it simple. And don't lie. I'll know.' Across my chest, the armour flickered. 'I see you've been tortured recently.'

'Yes.'

'Why?'

'They thought I was a spy.'

'Are you?'

Good enough, but not that good? We'd soon find out. 'An industrial spy,' I said.

'Ah, but industrial spies in times of war are spies in the truest sense, aren't they? You needn't worry. I've no loyalty to those strictists in Caud. I don't like dour fanatics. Or flouncing aristocrats, in case you're wondering.'

'Then who are you?' I risked.

'Me? Why, I'm just a simple marauder.'

That didn't exactly surprise me. 'We have nothing here for you,' I said. 'The pilot dropped cargo off in Caud – these are just containers.'

Another laugh. 'I'm not interested in cargo. I'm interested in passage.'

'Let me go,' I said, 'and we'll talk about it.'

Rather to my surprise, she did. I backed away against the wall and turned to see a woman in stark contrasts of red and black. Her skin was like jet, shining as if oiled, but her hair was a dark, unnatural crimson, bound tightly at the back of her head. Her eyes, too, were dark red and the flicker of haunt-tech occasionally passed across her skin, moving from her armour to her flesh.

'My name is Rubirosa.'

'Should I have heard of you?'

'For your sake, I hope not. And yours?'

'Shenday. Marlis Shenday.'

The red eyes narrowed. 'Is that the name you were given at your naming ceremony? Or one adopted for your trip to Caud?'

'Does it matter?'

She grinned, displaying sharpened teeth. 'Maybe, maybe not.'

'Look,' I said. 'We could take you with us. Assuming you're not wanted by a pack of excissieres.'

'Ah. Yes. Well.'

'I can't speak for the pilot, but I can say with some certainty that neither of us wants trouble. That dreadnought that came down earlier – I saw fighting on the deck. Would that be anything to do with you?'

Rubirosa looked shifty. 'There was a small local disagreement.'

'And you want to rejoin your – companions?'

'Eventually.'

Again, that sideways look, a crimson flash.

'Look,' I said. 'I can't see the pilot being too happy about this. And you – wouldn't you be better off with a faster boat?'

'They'll be *looking* for fast craft,' the marauder said. 'This isn't my usual style.' She cast a disparaging glance around the dingy cabin. 'That makes it perfect. And *you* won't turn me in, will you? Because that would draw too much attention to you.'

I was silent. Telling Peto to turn the marauder over to the authorities would mean the captain asking awkward questions of myself, and I didn't want that.

'Besides,' Rubirosa added casually, 'I've put a bomb on your boat.'

'What!'

'Just as a small guarantee. It's only a small bomb. But it will put a large hole in it. As soon as we get to the Noumenon, I'll disable it, don't worry.'

I stared at her. She gazed back, with a kind of ruthless innocence. 'Just who did that dreadnought belong to?' I said.

'Let's just say it was someone very rich.' She gestured upwards. 'Your captain will be wondering where you are. Shall we?'

I was, not unnaturally, quite correct. Peto was not happy to find a pirate and an explosive device suddenly installed on her barge.

'It'll take a while, mistress, before we reach the Shadow Clans,' she warned. Her squashed face glowered in the direction of Rubirosa.

The marauder shrugged. 'I'd rather get there slowly than not at all.' She sat down on a container with a flicker of haunt-tech and examined an armoured arm. Something had scorched across it, leaving a rusty stain.

Peto said, 'I don't want that stuff on my boat. Bad enough that you've set a bomb on it.'

Rubirosa, having got what she wanted, raised a conciliatory hand. 'I'll have no need. You don't object to an antiscribe?'

'Do what you need to do,' Peto said, very sourly. 'But no funny business.'

There had, I thought, been quite enough of that already.

We reached the cut-off about mid-afternoon, when a sombre chill had descended upon the canal and the sun hung low over the plains. The capsized ferry, now righted, had kept pace with us, a little way behind, but hugged the bank with its remaining passengers. After what had befallen it, I couldn't blame the pilot for her decision: the keening sounds of mourning for the drowned occasionally floated across the water, chilling my blood and reminding me of the dreadnought, whose attacker we now carried.

I spent some time down in the hold, ostensibly checking the security of the containers, but Rubirosa watched me with a prey-bird's eye and I knew that she was not fooled. There was no sign of the bomb and I wondered whether she'd even had time to set one, whether we should call her bluff. Once I'd finished as much of the pretence as I could sustain, therefore, I went back up the steps onto the deck and sat in a patch of thin sunlight. I ran a small antiscribe borrowed from Peto, which had basic facilities for such things, and ran an anomalies check.

There was *something*. I couldn't tell what it was or where it lay, but the antiscribe showed me a hot-spot somewhere on the barge and that, most probably, indicated the presence of explosives. The way that the symbol fluttered across the screen meant haunt-tech, too, and was separate from the larger mass of Rubirosa's armour. Something independent, something *moving*, it looked like, and I knew from experience that this might be something very small and fragile, perhaps some kind of mesh. From experience, too, I knew how devastating such devices could be. I decided not to take any chances, but shared my findings with Peto.

The captain was, ultimately, pragmatic. 'So, she's heading for the Noumenon. So are we. I'll insist that she gets off just before the border, in case customs find her. If we're harbouring a criminal, you can't see us being welcome, can you?'

I couldn't. 'That reminds me,' I said. 'Do I need papers, for the Noumenon? All my documentation got left behind in Caud, it was such a rush to get out.'

'They'll usually accept bribes,' Peto said. 'You have money, don't you?'

'I've got a chip.'

'I think you'll find that they'll take whatever you've got.'

Somehow, this did not surprise me.

The cut-off was clearly visible now: a squat guard tower flying warning pennants of cross-canal traffic, a signal system that I did not fully understand but which was apparently familiar to Peto.

High in the guard tower there was a flash as someone's binoculars caught the late sun. Peto was squinting against the light.

'It's closed. We'll have to see if they're letting traffic through.' Her heavy face was frowning and I knew why: what action might our unwelcome guest take, if we were not allowed passage? I hoped she'd have the decency to deactivate whatever device she'd installed and go on her way. But decency wasn't common Martian currency these days, especially amongst Rubirosa's kind. Or, indeed, mine. It struck me that the marauder might simply take us down into the cargo hold and dispatch us, leaving no witnesses behind her. If so, I promised myself, I wouldn't go down without a fight.

When we came to the cut-off, Peto signalled a left turn and hauled the barge across the channel, heading for the series of locks that led down onto the Plains. I could see the cut-off canal clearly now: a silver line leading, arrow-straight, towards the mountains, which towered, deceptively close, above the wintry grassland. I knew how far they were and yet I could see the lines of glaciers snaking down through the rocks, all of it ghostly in the pale light as if sketched onto the sky.

We were stopped. Just as the barge came to a wallowing halt, Rubirosa's voice whispered in my ear, 'Not a word, now!' She sounded quite cheerful about it; doubtless she felt she held the upper hand. As indeed, she did. I turned to retort, but there was only a glitter of haunt-tech, vanishing into the shadows of the cargo hold.

Peto had to hand over a seemingly endless series of document chips, all of which were carefully stamped through a rudimentary blacklight device, but it appeared that it was the boat that mattered, not the personnel. Secretive though they were, the Noumenon didn't seem to have Caud's degree of paranoia and the barge was not searched. I remained on deck, watching as the ferry disappeared slowly down the canal, accompanied by the other vessels that I had come to regard as neighbours during our time on the Grand Channel. I wondered what had become of the Centipede Queen and her entourage, feeling the prickle of darksight that suggested I would see them again. It was one of the abilities that the Matriarchy had tried to train in me, but this one had remained largely useless. It gave me future glimpses of cups of tea, shop assistants, oncoming weather – rarely anything of real value or use. Whether my future meeting with the Centipede Queen would be among the latter, I did not know.

At last Peto was done. The door to the cargo hold remained closed. The first of the locks was activated from the guard tower and we moved through, leaving a queue of boats behind us. It appeared that we'd have company on our journey through the mountains; I wondered what that might bring.

TWELVE

Essegui – Crater Plain

On the second day, the pilgrimage took on a monotony. Without the presence of the brown-clad women to distract me, I found that I was becoming accustomed to the sonorous chants and the dismal tone of the instruments. The pilgrims had lost their mystery for me: familiarity had indeed bred if not contempt, then at least tedium. I should have been more alert, and I tried, but the attack in Winterstrike was already assuming the dimensions of a dream and I felt oddly hot. My arm burned where I'd been bitten and that made me anxious. If I collapsed . . . But I didn't feel faint, just slightly feverish.

The weather continued to be dreary, with a misting sleet drifting across the plains in veils and encrusting the ruins with ice. The road beneath us still had the old heating mechanism, glowing faintly at the roadsides: not haunt-tech, but something older and perhaps more robust, drawing on the internal heat of the deep soil and passing it upward. But in places it had broken down, so that we walked on bare tarmac and then ice.

The attack, when it came, was a rush and a confusion. We were passing one of the ruins, a more extensive complex of turret and fortifying buildings that surrounded it. In the chilly weather, it looked like a column of ice. The assault itself lacked subtlety.

The women raced out from behind the ruin on ground-bikes, bouncing easily over the frosty plain. They wore skin-tight white armour, much patched, and black goggles against snow-glare, which suggested to me – when I thought about it later, that is – that they were not local, but had come down from somewhere much colder. There were four of them and they carried glowing lances beneath one arm. The bikes themselves were equipped with shriekers: I clapped my hands to my ears involuntarily and I was not surprised to see the guards do the same, before they activated whatever protective mechanisms existed within their helms and started firing. One of the attackers was hit in the tank of the ground bike and it exploded in a bright thermal flare. I saw her cast up towards the ruin, a flying, burning doll. Then a hissing swift thing was bowling pilgrims right, left and centre as one of the ground-bikes dodged between them. Women screamed. The guard, hampered by the swarming mass of people, fired, but it went wide and sent up a tussock of grass in a fiery spray. The bike was heading straight for me and the shrieker was deafening, interfering with my balance. I stumbled, ducking to the side, which turned out to be a mistake: the bike did not hit me, but it rapidly became clear that running me down was not its rider's intention. She grabbed me efficiently by the waist and threw me over the front of the bike at its widest part. The shrieker howled in my ear and the rider slapped me across the side of the head. By doing so, she must have given me some kind of patch, because a brief chill spread around my ears and the noise of the shrieker was abruptly muted. Then we were heading off across the plain. I squirmed around, struck upwards at the rider and caught the glowing lance with my hand. It burned and I snatched my hand away. The rider laughed: I could see black polished teeth beneath the rim of the goggles. A mesh had worked its way out of the bike and now held me securely. The rider put both hands on the steering and kicked the bike into a flaring speed. I caught a last glimpse of the little dark shapes of the pilgrims in front of the tower and then we were over the horizon.

The rider didn't bother to stun me, so I got to see the whole of the trip, albeit face-downwards. Half an hour or so passed, hurtling through driving sleet and then snow. We were climbing. The wind stopped and the world took on a blanketing hush. Twisting my head, I saw trees: the black, conical spires of pin-wood. That meant we were probably up in the Hattins, a long way to the north-west of Winterstrike. Once, my ancestors had enjoyed country residences here, before the fashion changed to the more southerly lakes and winter hunting was no longer so popular. Common legend spoke of ruined mansions, deep in the forest and haunted by shrikes and cold-tropes, as well as the ghosts of the dancing, hunting dead. Looking at the dark trees as we shot by, I did not find this difficult to believe.

My position on the bike was, not surprisingly, uncomfortable. The uneven surface of the pommel was starting to bruise my ribs, so that every bounce and jolt sent a flare of agony through my chest, ricocheting from my spine. I had a quite remarkable headache and my vision had started to blur. The geise was mut-tering away in my mind but everything else was blotting it out, which was one mercy, at least. Throwing myself from the bike had long since been ruled out as an option: I couldn't wriggle free, and in any case, if I managed to fall off, I'd only be picked up again. And I'd have to find my own way back to the pilgrimage over sev-eral miles of rough ground. It seemed better to stay put but I chafed at the knowledge all the same.

The trees were thinning out now, and we were climbing. When I looked back I could see the long slope stretching behind us, with the cold sweep of the plains beyond. There was no sign of the tower from which the bikes had come. The rider gave my shoulder a shake.

'Not long now!' she shouted. She sounded quite cheerful about it, as though we were out on some pleasure jaunt. I mumbled something sour. The bike was slowing down as it wove its way through the trees, but the top of the rider's helmet touched a branch and shook down a great pile of snow. I spluttered and sneezed, hearing the rider laugh. Ahead, I glimpsed an enormous cliff face, many thousands of feet in height and ending in ice-locked crags that looked like teeth. Clouds wreathed the summit, smoking in and out of the rocks. The bike swung dangerously close to a thick tree trunk, veered away, and headed straight for the wall of ice that was the foot of the cliff.

'Hey, watch out!' I cried, but it was too late. The bike was speeding towards the wall and I shut my eyes. Next moment, we were into darkness and silence. For a second, I thought I was actually dead. Then I realized that the ice wall had, like a miracle, opened up in front of us and let us through. The bike stopped with a great scraping and rattling of gears. I was hauled off and thrown against a wall.

I was certain that I hadn't banged my head, but even so, things became very dim for a while, as if I'd slid into dreaming without the bother of falling asleep. The chamber swam before me – high rock sides and a roughly cut ceiling, clearly hacked out of the cliff wall. All these mountains outside Winterstrike were riddled with caves, the legacy of ancient floods, perhaps even before humans came to Mars. But this looked human-made. I could hear the steady drip of water and a hollow, echoing boom that I could not identify: later, I wondered whether it was simply the sound of my own blood, reverberating inside my head. A pair of eyes floated before me like lamps. A voice said, hissing, 'Yes, this is the one.'

'Who are you?' I thought I said, then wondered whether the words had really been spoken aloud. The voice did not reply. I felt myself drifting along, moving through corridors and channels. There was the lap of water by the side of my head, although I didn't remember lying down. Then the slap of oars and a light far ahead, gleaming off the water and sending reflections dancing across the ceiling.

Everything went dark again, but I was still conscious. Something was sparkling and glittering all around me.

'Where am I?' I said, but again, was not sure if I'd even spoken aloud. I didn't remember being drugged, there had been no sting of injection, no sudden puff of gas, but I felt completely blank, as if someone had switched me off. The eyes swam above me and I now saw that they were moons, the small moons of Mars circling high above the planet's orbit. Then I saw Mars itself, a round russet ball, white-capped. The plains and mountains were very sharp, as if etched onto the blank surface of the world with some galactic scalpel. Further out and now I could see the haze of Venus and the azure globe of Earth, swimming with cloud and its little satellite spinning around it. Sparks of light passed between the worlds and once the black sky cracked, revealing a flash of something between: a haunt-ship, jumping from life into death and back again.

I watched all this quite passively, unconcerned by the fact that I seemed to be leaving the solar system altogether. The gas giant passed by, then ringed Saturn, then the outer worlds: the mining colonies of the asteroids, the pilgrim places solitary and serene on the blasted surface of barely terraformed rock. I swung low over a temple, a huge place sprawling across the surface of Io, saw its pools and ice-locked waterfalls, its towering spires dedicated to deities of the outer reaches and unknown to me. Then on, past the farthest world of Nightshade and the cobweb span of Farlife.

And then . . . somewhere else. A shadow land, with high crags and a tower on a jutting crag, outlined in flame. A missile hurtled upwards and exploded in firework petals.

'What do you see?' said a voice, caressing and soft.

'I see—' Down into a landscape of fractured rock – except that it was not rock at all, but water, endless seas and a city rising from them. I glimpsed another high tower made of iron, rising out of the waves, and then an impression of black coiling tentacles.

'I see,' I started to say, but I could not get the words out and a cold clamping hand came down on my wrist and hissed, '*Tell me . . .*'

'Take a look,' I said and in some uncomprehended way I opened up my own head and let her stare inside.

'Ah . . .' said the voice. 'No. She's not really seeing anything. She's just picking it up from me.'

'Nowhere,' someone else said. With dim surprise I realized that it was I who had spoken. 'Its name is Nowhere.'

Then the place was gone and I was back within the comforting, confining cage of my own skull. Dark globes were gazing down at me: eyes, not moons, floating in front of a polished obsidian ceiling. The blacklight sparkle of haunt-tech was all around me and I realized that I was in a vertical vice, with my wrists and ankles securely bound. An electrical wind blew through the chamber, stirring my hair with static.

The eyes were black and milky at the same time and they belonged to a pointed face, surmounted by a trailing veil. A small mouth twitched. I glimpsed sharp teeth. There was the swish of robes as the creature took a step back.

'You're—' I said. I'd seen something like her before, in the streets of Winterstrike. I remembered the theatre, with the masked women dancing in front of it, then the thing I'd seen floating above the canal. But demotheas didn't exist.

'I am Mantis,' the creature said.

'Hello, Mantis.' I struggled against the bonds. 'Any chance of letting me go?'

'Not just yet.' Mantis reached out a hand and touched my pulse. Her fingers were cool, with an extra-than-human joint.

'Why did you take me?' I said.

'Ah, well, I wanted a closer look at you, you see.' She frowned. 'What's *that* inside your head? That whispering?'

'I'm under a geise,' I said.

'Who put it on you?'

'My mothers.'

There was a low whistle of surprise across the chamber. I craned my neck and saw the rider who had brought me in. She was still wearing riding gear and goggles; there was snow melting from her boots and pooling on the mirror-black floor. 'Not a happy family, then?'

'You could say that.'

The rider strode across the chamber and seized me by the neck. There was a twinge in my head and then I was saying, babbling almost, 'My name is Essegui Harn, ceremonialist of Winterstrike, a scion of the House of Calmaretto, sister of Shorn, once called Leretui, still called the Malcontent.'

'I know who you are!' Mantis said impatiently. 'I'm interested in Leretui,' she added. 'Imprisoned for consorting with a male, indeed. Shouldn't you be at home, instead of cavorting across the Plains with pilgrims?'

So she did not know that Leretui was missing – or was affecting ignorance in some elaborate double bluff.

'I am a ceremonialist,' I said. 'I observe Ombre. These are difficult times. I felt the need for spiritual succour.'

'Yet you went to the Temple of the Changed,' Mantis said. 'Then to the fortress. Why was that?'

Had she been there, listening among the shadows? I was becoming increasingly certain that this was the person responsible for the attacks on me. I thought of the little aspith, fleeing into the depths of the Temple. In my head, a bridge shattered and fell.

'I work there,' I said. 'Why shouldn't I go there?'

'We can blacklight you again, drag it from your head,' Mantis warned.

'If you do,' I said, knowing that it was the truth, 'I've had warning now and I'll just faint. And what will you listen to then?'

I looked into her dark-milk eyes, and knew that, for the moment, I'd won.

In spite of the haunt-tech laboratory, the rest of the complex was primitive, really no more than a series of underground tunnels and rough-hewn chambers hacked out of the side of the cliff, reeking of mildew and age. The rider who had originally snatched me now accompanied me down through a maze of passages, with a sting-prod at my neck. I did not care to test it out, having seen what lay outside, and I decided not to give her any trouble. She introduced herself perfunctorily as One, and introduced me also to a small cramped cell in which, she gave me to understand, I would be spending the indefinite future. This was all very well, but the geise was now battering at my senses, shouting at me to get a move on, and despite that quasi-sentience it seemed to possess it evidently did not understand that I was in no position to act out its wishes. Was Leretui herself here? I bit back frustration.

'You won't be able to get out, by the way,' One explained, somewhat unnecessarily, as I'd already seen the blacklight glitter running through the mesh. The cell door was wired up to the haunt system, and as an experiment I ran a hand across it, once One was safely out of sight. Immediately the system erupted into a shrieking ward that flashed across my head. I ducked, even though I knew it wasn't real, and the nerve-jangling it left in its wake reverberated through my head for a moment after it had passed through the opposite wall. But I was used to my mothers' systems at Calmaretto, too, though these were different. I wondered just how far Mantis was prepared to go. I sat down on the rudimentary bed and thought of flight.

THIRTEEN

Hestia – Crater Plain

Half a day and the mountains appeared no closer, and no further, either. My world and Peto's had shrunk to the distant glacial peaks, an icy green sky, the red ridges of the Plains as we progressed along the side cut of the canal. The only glimpse I'd had of Rubirosa in the last few hours had been a glint of eyes in the shadows of the hold. She was whittling something with a haunt-knife that whistled and whispered as the shavings fell away. I thought it might be a bone. I didn't really want to know.

So I sat on deck with Peto instead and took turns at steering and boiling tea on the little deck kettle. It was growing colder now, the comparative mildness of the Plains beyond Caud dropping away as we rose in a series of stages towards the Noumenon. When I looked back, I could still see the long straight stretch of the Grand Channel and some of the masts travelling down it. Along the bank, the grass grew sparser, replaced with a dense plant with shiny dark-green leaves, and the small birds of the lower Plains disappeared. Red-eyed predators appeared in their place, sailing high on fringed wings, catching the thin thermals.

Peto pointed out areas of interest: she knew this country. There were battlefields, barrows of the dead dating back to the Age of Children, scenes of great valour. It all looked the same to me. I couldn't tell what she was pointing at half the time. It had all been swallowed by the remorseless, still-transforming earth, though Peto also told me that the place was full of spirits, and this I did not find difficult to believe.

'Wait until night comes,' Peto kept saying, peering at me from the corner of her eye to see how I was taking it. 'Then you'll see.'

Something to look forward to, then. She did, however, manage to attract my attention with a phenomenon that was clearly visible: a ruined fortress on top of a great crag, seemingly all on its own before the beginning of the mountain wall.

'Temperire,' Peto said. 'It's said they invented haunt-tech there, when the Matriarch Mantis found a way to harness the conjured spirits of her torture victims.'

I felt a need to dismiss this in robust terms. 'Nonsense! Everyone knows haunt-tech came from Nightshade, from the laboratories there, and was given to the Memnos Matriarchy. Although I won't deny that some folk claim it comes from torture, all the same.'

'That's what some folk *would* say,' replied Peto, placidly enough. I sighed, although I couldn't deny that Peto had a point.

'What happened to Temperire, then?' I asked, to change the subject.

'Oh, there was a great battle. Ended in a siege and Mantis disappeared. Her enemies brought in their majikei, stripped the spirits from their enemies and sacked the castle. Stole Mantis's own technology and turned it against her: drove her soul into an engine and they say it grinds there still, down in the rocks beneath the ruin. You can hear it on winter nights, groaning and grinding away.'

I'd have loved to dismiss this as folklore, but it's hard to do that if you're Martian. 'What does this engine *do*?' I asked.

'It drives a mill and the mill makes creatures of blacklight and sends them out across the plains to steal other people's souls.'

'How delightful.'

'Well, that's what they say.'

We fell silent for a moment, then I said, 'And have you ever seen one of these creatures? You've been this way before.'

'Plenty of times,' Peto said, confounding me. 'But they can't touch me.'

'The boat's warded?' I'd already surmised as much. But it hadn't kept Rubirosa out.

'I've got my own stuff. My people's stuff. A mesh, in my head.' She gave me a sidelong look. It seemed that, somewhere along the way, we'd abandoned the pretence that I was from the same neck of the woods as she was.

'That's . . . sophisticated,' I said.

'You think it's only the city folk who have that kind of thing? My mother's mother's mother grew this mesh, from an old brain. Trapped spirits in the marshes, gave it its power. We each had a bit of it, my sisters and me. Just enough to protect us.'

'What does it do?' An intrusive question, but I was fascinated.

'Likely you'll find out,' Peto said, with what I hoped was neither warning nor threat. Conversation died after that and I took refuge in the excuse of making more tea.

Although other vessels had followed us through the cut, they now sailed far behind. Peto thought that the first one had encountered some administrative difficulty, because it was an hour or so after we'd got through that the next vessel showed up on the radar. So the barge glided on up the lock skein in solitary splendour. We left Temperire on its crag, and the locks increased in frequency: we were rising. At last I looked up from the tiller and got a shock, because far from the hovering sameness of distance that they'd displayed all day, the mountains now looked as though they were hanging right over my head, gilded with sunset against an arctic sky.

'They say Mantis went mad because of the view,' Peto said, appearing suddenly at my elbow and making me jump. 'Looks like they're going to come right down on you, doesn't it?'

It did. 'So, what happens now?' I asked. 'More locks, and then
– what?'

'It's actually not as close as it looks,' Peto admitted. 'There are
step locks from now on – you can let the boat handle them, they're
remotely activated. All you have to do is keep steering straight, so
that's why we're going to pull in for the night. You needn't worry
about being hit. Everyone else will do the same and if they don't,
they'll just have to wait.'

The stream was wide enough still for more than one boat. 'Are
you stopping in mid-channel, then?'

'Yes.'

'Why, because of wandering spirits?'

'Yes.'

So that was that.

We slept down in the cabin, along with Rubirosa. Peto had
clearly activated some kind of ward, for when I went back on deck
for a final check, the air was filled with a silvery humming and
the air around the barge glistened. I touched the coal in my pocket
and it felt less cold, almost comfortingly warm, in fact, but there
was still no sign of the Library. I watched the air for a moment all
the same; I found that I missed the warrior's grisly presence.
Besides, she might be able to tell me what the hell was happening in Winterstrike. I'd tried, as surreptitiously as possible under
the dual suspicions of Peto and Rubirosa, to contact Gennera
again, but the coder had stayed silent and there had been no reply.
The only stuff on public channels was allegedly morale-boosting
propaganda, utterly useless unless one happened to have been
born an idiot. I chafed under the lack of information, but I
couldn't do much about it. I suppose it was sad that, even with a
wired-up-and-about-to-explode boat, wandering ghouls and flying dreadnoughts, my life right now was calmer than it had been
for some time.

Time for a change. I needed a way out of this game, needed
to break free.

A low moon was hanging over the mountains, glowing yellow, and as I watched, the other climbed up above the glacier rim. In the west, Earth was a lamp. I remembered my cousin Leretui, poring over the atlas that depicted the changes of Earth, her longing to go there. Maybe I could go to Earth, too. I hoped they'd let Leretui keep her books in that cruel imprisonment. Knowing Alleghetta, probably not, but I trusted Essegui to sneak things in to her sister, just as she had done when they were children. She and I.

It was growing colder. Water slapped gently against the sides of the barge, interfacing with the wards and producing an occasional electric hiss. I went back down the stairs, to find Peto and the marauder staring at each other like a couple of cats.

'Is all well?' Peto asked.

'As far as I can tell. It's pretty quiet up there. Your wards are holding.'

'Good,' the captain said. She wrapped herself in a blanket and lay down to sleep. I did the same, fully intending to keep a secret watch until Rubirosa, too, fell asleep. But my last memory of that evening is of the marauder's red eyes in the lamplight, watching me instead.

When the disturbance came, however, Rubirosa was as startled as Peto and I. There was a sudden, thunderous bang from the deck. We all leaped from our beds, senses conditioned to immediate action, however unwise. Rubirosa and I knocked heads like some comedy act. We both swore. Peto was already running up the stairs, armed with an ancient scimitar that I hadn't even seen before.

But when we reached the deck, nothing was there.

'What was that?' The marauder's armour was glittering as though wet, and her wrists bristled with weaponry. She turned from right to left, swinging with swift, economical movements. Peto was hunched over the sword. I prowled around the circumference of the deck, looking for incursion. The only anomaly was a long scorch mark close to the bow, as though something had tried to enter and been fried by the wards. 'Peto!' I called. 'Look at this.'

The captain's face was dour as she surveyed the damage to her deck. 'Ghosts,' was all that she said.

'All right,' said the marauder, looking from side to side. 'Where are they now? There was more than one of them. My armour tells me that.'

We peered cautiously over the side of the barge. The water seemed untroubled, but I thought I glimpsed something moving in the depths, far below.

'What was that?' I started to say, and then all hell broke loose. There was a cannon-like boom as the wards on the starboard side activated and then fused, with a shriek that knocked me against the railing. Something shot overhead, a white gleam against the frosty stars. Beside me, Rubirosa cursed as her armour shorted out with a high-pitched whine. She started stripping the cuffs, trying, I presumed, to get manual access to her weapons.

'That won't do any good!' Peto snorted. I turned. The captain's face was aglow. She'd told me that she'd had a mesh implanted. What she hadn't told me was that it penetrated the entire dermis: her square face and stubby hands sparkled with a quick, unfamiliar haunt-fire, a wet marsh gleam. High above us, a thing like a white bat rattled down through the sky. It wrapped its bony wings about it as it fell and as it came below the mast, it turned into smoke. Peto's mouth opened wide and inside, it too was glowing. She swallowed the smoky thing and shut her mouth with an audible snap. I couldn't see why she'd even bothered with the scimitar, which now hung listlessly from her hand.

'There's more where that came from,' she said.

We looked up. A swarm of the things was flying at us. Rubirosa gave a yell and swung upwards with a knife: not an ordinary blade, but one that was filled with red fire, as though she held a flame in her hand. One of the white things lashed through it and disintegrated into smouldering fragments on the deck.

'Watch out!' Peto cried. I turned. Three of them were whistling towards me and before I could duck, dodge or defend myself, they were passing through me as though I did not exist. An unpleasant stinging sensation started to pass through my gut, but as soon as it had begun, it was extinguished. Abruptly, I felt something in my mouth. I put up my hand and removed three little fragments, like splinters of burned wood, from the surface of my tongue. The remaining swarm was off and up into the darkness, to be swallowed by the shadows of the mountain wall.

This time, it was the turn of Peto and Rubirosa to gape at me.

'How did you do that?' Peto asked. 'You have no mesh. I saw nothing.'

'And you have no armour,' Rubirosa echoed. 'My own system read nothing in you.' She sounded more offended than alarmed.

I smiled. 'Oh, I have my own kind of protection,' I said, and swaggered past them down the steps to below deck, leaving Peto to resurrect the wards of the barge. In fact I had no idea how I'd done it. The only anomalous thing about me was that I still carried the Library. I fingered the sphere in my pocket, but it was the same temperature and consistency as before.

'I wish you'd tell me what's going on,' I whispered under my breath, but the Library was silent. The warrior did not come to me, and I did not dream of her for what remained of that night.

In the early hours of the morning, however, I woke up again. Even in the relative safety of the cabin, my breath steamed on the air. Peto was fast asleep, wrapped in a huddle of blankets. The marauder sprawled in a chair and at first, with a start, I thought she was awake, for her eyes were open. But when she made no attempt to look at me directly, I realized that she was still unconscious. In sleep, her face had lost a little of its ferocity and she looked as peaceful and as fragile as a statue.

I was not, however, deceived. Rubirosa's armour gave an

occasional flicker, signalling that its haunt-capacity was once more working and would probably warn her if I made any move. I did not do so. Instead, I put my hand down to where an uncomfortable sensation had awoken me. Inside the folds of my pocket, the sphere was icy.

I thought: *very well.* I pushed aside the blankets and made my stealthy way back on deck. Peto had done a good job with the wards, for they were once more up and running. Ahead, the mountains floated on the morning shadow. Venus hung bright in the east. I took the sphere out, holding it in a twist of material, trying not to juggle it. At its present heat, I'd probably drop the damn thing in the canal. I was surprised it didn't burn its way through the cloth.

When I looked up again, I saw with a leap of the heart that the warrior was standing there. My relief at seeing her took me aback, but she was much more fragile than she had been, transparent, like a real ghost. The sinews and veins of her exposed skin followed the distant striations of the mountains, as though she had been enfolded into the landscape.

'I'm glad to see *you*,' I said. The warrior looked at me without recognition for a moment, then she took a deep rasping breath, more like one who experiments than one who truly needs to breathe – for of course, she was not real.

'Ah,' she said. '*This* is where we are.' Something like satisfaction flickered across her dead face. 'I remember this place.'

'You've probably got books about it,' I said.

'In *life*, I knew this place. I fought here. A sad sour place.' The warrior frowned. I did not see how she could really remember, being no more than a simulacrum, but maybe the Library contained some implanted memories to add to its verisimilitude.

'It's not the happiest,' I agreed. 'The ghosts, or whatever they were – did you get rid of them?'

'They gave me energy.'

'Well, that's good. At least you've come back.' I paused. 'Why?

Is it just because I'm the one with your projector, or whatever it is?'

'I've been asked to help you,' the Library said.

'By whom?'

'I am under orders not to say.'

'That's not reassuring.'

The Library's frown deepened. 'I can't help that. They're looking for you. Also, did you know there's a bomb on this barge?'

Two pieces of bad news, not that either came as any great shock. 'They. Who? The excissieres?'

'Yes. I've been shielding you, and thereby, myself. It's taken a lot of energy.' The warrior's form fluttered, as if about to dissipate into the morning mist.

'Hey, don't go,' I pleaded. 'I might need you around.'

'I'm still here,' the warrior said. Then she gave another breath like a sigh and disappeared, leaving me staring at the empty air.

FOURTEEN

Essegui – Crater Plain

The effects of the haunt-tech that Mantis and One had used to extract information from me – or whatever that alien vision had been – lasted for most of the night. I was exhausted, and slept a fitful sleep even on the hard mattress they'd provided. I kept having broken dreams – of Calmaretto, of my cousin Hestia, who now looked at me across a great span of land with sad dark eyes and mouthed words that I could neither hear nor understand.

Then, towards dawn, the effects of the tech and the drug ebbed away and I found myself awake and startlingly clear. I got off the bed, and although I was shaky, was able to stand without holding on to anything and, shortly, to move about. I made a thorough investigation of the cell, which reminded me uncomfortably of searching Leretui's locked room, back in Calmaretto. And like Calmaretto, there was no sign of any way out. I could not have slid a razor's edge between those slabs of honed stone and the floor was a seamless sheet of rock. The only opening was the grille in the door, and that was far too small to clamber through. I sat back down on the bed, temporarily defeated.

The air shivered. For a moment, Alleghetta was standing before me. She did not look pleased. She said something I couldn't hear and I could see the wall through her body.

'Mother, what—' But she was gone.

Then something knocked on the wall, a sharp, deliberate sound. Having little to lose, I knocked back. The sound came again, a quick tapping that, after a moment of incomprehension, I recognized. It was the pattern of the bell of Ombre, the same precise rhythm that I had rung out across Winterstrike only a few days before. When it ended, I tapped it back again.

A pause. I wondered if this was going to continue indefinitely: it was the only code I knew, after all. But the knocking stopped and I heard an odd, half-familiar rustling. There was movement at the grille. I saw a long, segmented body glide through the grille and down the wall.

I'd last seen that thing, or something very like it, disappear up the sleeve of a shrouded woman on the road out of Winterstrike. Involuntarily, I clapped my hand to my bitten arm. Next moment, there came a hissing voice.

'Stand away from the door,' it said. 'Let it do its work.'

The centipede dropped down onto the floor with a rattle. Its body broke into separate parts, neatly disjointing. The legs of each segment carried the body under the door in a sideways scuttle. There was a moment of stillness, then the bottom of the door started to glow. I watched, fascinated, as the lower half of the door, then the whole thing, crumbled into ash and fell apart. I stood in the centre of the room, staring out at the woman who stood on the other side of the door.

I'd seen her in a shroud, behind the brown veil. Now, the veil and her long sleeves had been pushed back and she stood revealed: slanting brown eyes in a skin that was not far from the colour of her veil, the shade of mountain earth. Her cheeks were scarred, contoured in a series of spiny patterns and stained indigo, and the scarring continued along her arms. She smiled, baring small pointed teeth, and said, 'Well, so here you are.'

'Who *are* you?' I said.

'A servant of the Centipede Queen,' she said. She looked

sidelong. A companion came out of the shadows, a smaller, older woman bearing similar facial scarring. 'We ought to go. They'll be waking soon.'

The woman reached out and clasped my hand. Knowing what was up her sleeve, I took it gingerly. Her fingers closed over mine with a strength that hurt. I tried to free myself and couldn't. She pulled me through the door and out into the musty corridor. We ran along stone, under beams – some half-fallen – and through arches leading into endless rooms. The warren seemed to go on for ever, but my rescuer appeared to know where she was going: I had no idea how. There was something faintly ignominious about being rescued. *Never mind*, I thought. *You're being saved. So shut up.*

But saved from what, exactly? And saved *for* what?

The darkness grew until I could not longer see in front of me. The hand that clasped mine twisted strangely and I felt the tickle of spiny legs against my wrist. Next moment there was the rush of cold fresh air against my face and I was abruptly released. We were standing on the hillside, among trees, with a cold moon above.

'Come on,' the woman commanded.

I followed her down the hillside, stumbling through untrodden snow, until we came to a ground car. It was an ancient object, rocking on its stabilizer jets, embellished in an ostentatious black and gold trim. Most of this was flaking off.

'Where did you find this?'

'We borrowed it,' the servant of the Centipede Queen explained. 'It is the belief of the Queen that all property is hers by right.'

'I see.' How convenient. I climbed into the ground car, which was dusty and smelled of musk. The other women were already seated in it, one of them at the controls. She touched a panel and the car glided away through the trees. I expected the bikes to come roaring out after us at any moment, but behind us the forest remained dark and still.

'I'm afraid I've never heard of your Queen,' I said, as much to fill the silence as to gain information.

The woman waved a hand, dismissing my ignorance. 'Few people have, on Mars at least.'

'And elsewhere?'

Again the smile. 'On Earth, of course.'

'Of course?'

'The Queen is from Earth and so are we, her servants.'

That explained why I hadn't recognized the accents, but not why these people from Earth were going out of their way to effect my rescue. Unless they had something else in mind. 'Which part?' I asked.

'Khul Pak, in Malay. The north, from the islands.'

'But what are you doing on Mars?' Of course, people travelled between the worlds, but very few that I had met, even in the sheltered luxury of Calmaretto. It took money to travel so far. Money and a very good reason.

'The Queen is – looking for someone. An old enemy, returned.'

'Do you mean Mantis?'

'Yes and no. Mantis has taken an interest in you, however. She's tried to capture you twice before.'

'You've been watching me? Was that why were you on the pilgrimage?' I looked around. 'Is one of you the Queen?'

Sly looks and shy laughter. 'Why, no. The Queen is in the west, not far from Caud. She sent us to—' the woman paused.

'To spy,' the older woman said.

'Fair enough.' I suppose it was sad that this seemed so reasonable.

The woman shrugged. 'It is a time of war. The Queen was concerned. We joined the refugees out of Caud, as a cover, telling folk we'd arrived there by mistake.'

'So where are you taking me now?' I asked.

'To the Queen. She wants to meet you.'

'Why?'

'That's for her to tell you.'

'And what will she do with me?' I was not sure I wanted to know, after Mantis.

'Just to talk with you. Nothing more.' The woman must have seen what I was thinking in my face, for she spoke reassuringly. As reassuringly as someone can when they have a foot-long centipede sliding about in their clothes, anyway. I couldn't help wanting to scratch.

The sky was starting to lighten above the trees. I didn't understand why we hadn't been pursued. It was beginning to dawn on me that I had become – in some way I did not understand – a valuable commodity. Given what I'd just experienced, I didn't think this was at all a good thing.

FIFTEEN

Hestia — the Noumenon

Obviously, I didn't mention the Library's reappearance to Peto or Rubirosa. Everyone was rather dour that morning, still suffering the after-effects of rogue haunt-tech and disinclined for conversation. We reconfigured the barge's stabilizers in silence and set off towards the mountains. The surface of the water was lightly iced over, not enough to require a sonic ram, but enough to make it crackle as we moved.

As the barge glided on, Rubirosa finally spoke.

'Last night. What was that all about, do you think?'

'What do you mean?'

'Who drew those things to us?'

'They were stray haunts,' I said. 'Plains remnants, bits of old histories, nothing more.'

'Yes, but things like that usually avoid human contact,' Rubirosa pointed out.

'Do they? I thought they were common enough.'

'Not the winged forms. I don't think you realized this, but they're very rare. I've seen them only once before, much further south. One of my contacts had managed to catch a flock of them to power a – let's just say it was a device, never mind what kind. She was stupid enough to get in amongst them; she thought she could cope. I saw what they left of her. She was no more than a shell by the time they'd hollowed her out.'

'Good thing you didn't tell me that last night,' I said after a pause. 'I might have been put off.'

'There wasn't time,' Rubirosa said, ignoring my attempts at wit. Her dark, delicate face was sombre as she stared out across the mountain wall. 'I don't think that was a random incursion of loose haunts, my spying friend. I think someone was trying to kill us. Peto,' she hesitated, 'seems a placid enough sort, even if she does have some intriguing defences. That leaves you and me.'

'You amaze me. I should think the only difficulty will lie in which number they are on the list.'

Rubirosa's lips twitched. 'Not popular, are you?'

'Any more than you. Let's face it, Rubirosa, *you* might be trying to kill me. If we're looking at lists, how about starting at number one and working down from there?'

'You think that was my doing, last night?' Rubirosa asked. She did not seem offended by the question. 'No, if I had decided to do away with you, I'd have had much less complicated opportunities. Given the bomb, and all.'

This was unflattering but probably true. The marauder placed her hands on the railing of the deck and leaned out over the ice-splintered water. 'Well,' she said. 'If we really want to find out who's trying to kill us, all we have to do is wait.'

Unfortunately, I thought she was probably right. Peto came on deck at that point and I made myself busy with the early morning duties of the barge, but it was already apparent that we were nearing some semblance of civilization. A scatter of low-roofed compounds – thick-walled dwellings around a central courtyard – began to appear along the canal bank, and from one of them spilled a handful of children dressed in bulky red clothes, like stuffed dolls. All of them had milky blue eyes. They ran down to the edge of the bank as soon as they saw us coming and began to hold out baskets of various things for sale – fruits and wool.

Peto waved them aside but they clamoured on, making shrill wordless cries. Rubirosa had departed for below deck and soon the children fell behind, but more buildings appeared. Here was a tall temple, shaded by trees with leaves that resembled white froth. A woman walked under the avenue they formed, an elegant creature in fur-rimmed hat and boots, with a trailing brocade coat. Two gaezelles, their horns clipped and bound with gold, strutted behind her on a leash.

'I thought that was illegal,' I said.

'Maybe in Winterstrike.' Peto's face was expressionless; I could not tell whether or not she disapproved. 'Up here? Things are different.'

'We must be on the edges of the Noumenon,' I said.

'We are.' Peto indicated the temple. 'That's the temple of the High Lost Matriarch, the one who's said to have founded this country.'

'Why is she lost?'

'I think someone kidnapped her and didn't give her back.'

'Ah.' I'd have made some remark about quaint country customs if the *mores* of Winterstrike had been beyond reproach. Unfortunately, this wasn't so.

Peto pointed ahead. 'Look. You can see the city wall.'

The canal was taking us straight to a gap in the mountain and the gap was entirely filled by a battlemented bastion, extending several hundred feet up from the valley floor to the summits of the interrupted ridge. Flags fluttered from towers at the top of the battlements and I caught sight of the flash of binoculars, turned in our direction.

'We'll have to go through customs,' Peto said. 'Then through the Noumenon itself, and down onto the other side. Shouldn't take more than a couple of days. I don't think the place is that big, but there's quite a lot of water traffic.'

I shrugged. 'It'll take as much time as it takes.' I did not feel as nonchalant as I was trying to appear. I planned to make inquiries once we entered this mysterious matriarchy and see if alternative passage to Winterstrike could be obtained. Once I got back – well, we'd see what happened then. I didn't like the idea of handing in my resignation at a time of war, but I was sick of being manipulated. Maybe I could serve the city in some other way.

Nor did I like leaving Peto with Rubirosa and the marauder's bomb, but I had a task to carry out. If I could find the device and defuse it before then, I would do so: I felt that I owed a debt of gratitude to Peto. Even spies strive for occasional honour.

I had very little idea as to what relations between the Noumenon and Winterstrike might be. Peto had spoken of neutrality and the Noumenon had kept itself strictly apart until the strike on Caud, but things change fast, and even faster in times of war. I'd already been out of Caud for days, and with no concrete information as to what had been happening in my absence, I was reluctant to predict matters.

We were almost at the gate. The wall rose above us in a series of massive smooth slabs, half-fused in consequence of some ancient struggle. The gate itself was a hundred feet high, to let masted craft through, and carved in the old style with glowering faces.

Again there was a lengthy and tedious wait while details were painstakingly recorded on an antique antiscribe by a woman with a face like a fanatical bird of prey. She insisted on searching the boat and I admit to being just a bit smug about this, and a bit hopeful. But Rubirosa was nowhere to be seen and neither, apparently, was the bomb. Chagrined, I could find no way of alerting the guards to her presence and anyway, the same issues applied as had held me back at the start of the cut-off.

The barge glided into the tunnel that ran beneath the wall. This extended a long way, with an arch of light at the end of it. As we slid through, there was a faint thud on the deck behind me and I turned to see Rubirosa standing there. Her haunt-armour picked up the reflections of the lapping water, turning her into a thing of mutable shadows, interlaced with red fire. A moment later she was gone – down below deck, I assumed. When I looked back, the light was growing stronger and we were almost through the tunnel.

The Noumenon: a tumble of cliffs and ravines, crammed with buildings that rose on top of one another, as though the city had already partially collapsed. The whole city was encased between two sharp mountain ranges, their glacially encrusted peaks visible high above, but dreamlike against the green winter sky. Easy to see why their ancestors had chosen this cleft as a refuge: readily defended and with the canal running through it. But the place surprised me. From what I'd heard of the Noumenon, the Matriarchy had once been a thriving queendom, the centre of its own small empire of the Plains, but ruin had come to it during the wars of the Age of Children and now, so I'd been told, the Matriarchy was no more than a huddle of villages clinging to its mountain. This, however, was an extensive city. Maybe my informers had been wrong, but research in my own section was painstaking: it had to be, for our own safety.

From the looks of them, the people of the Noumenon had conformed to the geographical restrictions of their nation. They too were elongated and narrow, with long suspicious faces. I now saw that the guard at the customs post was not atypical: in fact, she was probably considered a beauty. Sallow skins, somewhat grey in tone, were commonplace, along with pale, pebble-like eyes under elaborately conical hats.

Peto was watching the passers-by with an expression I couldn't interpret. 'I suppose you get like that,' she said 'Growing up in the dark.'

'Like mushrooms.'

'Exactly.' Here at the base of the valley, the sun must rarely penetrate. There were lamp globes along the length of the promenade, casting a pale radiance through the gloom. Snow still lay in patches along the lee of walls and the shadows through which the barge passed were cold. I couldn't see far ahead: the canal entered a series of bends, angling around the sharp edges of the cliffs.

We pulled into a small mooring place cut into the side of the canal, and were joined by most of the water traffic that had been following patiently in our wake over the last few days. Above us, the sky was deepening in colour; here in the cleft it was almost dark. Someone touched my arm and I turned to find Rubirosa at my elbow.

'Had a word with Peto,' she murmured. 'Seems we're staying overnight.'

'There's no other mooring between here and the end of this stretch, apparently. So it's here or nowhere.'

The marauder frowned. 'I don't like this place. There's something odd about it.'

I nearly laughed. 'That's Mars for you.' But I was being flippant. She was right. There was something strange about this sombre matriarchy, with its cold corners, more sophisticated than it should be. The uneasy feeling that had been with me ever since we passed through the gate now sent chilly ripples up the back of my neck. It reminded me of the feeling whenever I used my own abilities: the chill that crept over me whenever I stole someone's soul. I glimpsed figures from the corners of my eyes, seeing ghosts, as usual. I thought it was down to the haunt-tech they must be using: the Noumenon felt like the plain where we'd encountered Mantis's tower and the ghosts. The scene slipped and bled.

'You're not in armour, of course,' Rubirosa said. She detached the narrow collar of her gear and placed it around my neck. The gesture had an oddly symbolic quality, as though she'd conferred some honour upon me. Or placed me in a shackle. 'Now try.'

The borrowed haunt-tech filtered up through my senses, affecting each one in turn, and finally meshing with my own training-enhanced abilities. I grew colder. There was a gunpowder taste in my mouth and a burnt odour in my nose. I heard whispering at the edges of my hearing, as though people were talking about me, just beyond my view. But the greatest difference was in my sight. Whereas the vista of the Noumenon had previously been merely monochrome and bleak, with shadows congregating in the corners, it was now plain that most of the buildings were actually ruined. Shattered stumps of turrets, their battlements crumbling, squatted on the heights, and down by the waterfront the wide promenade was cracked and stained. The people themselves were shades, flitting by.

'Half of this isn't real,' I said.

'No,' Rubirosa murmured. 'But it used to be.'

'Yes, it did. I was told this place had been devastated years ago, never really recovered. So what are we seeing? Some kind of projection?'

'Maybe. I don't know. I've never seen anything like this.'

Neither had I. But there were other issues biting at me. 'I need to find an antiscribe,' I said. 'A proper one.'

'Mind if I come with you?'

'Yes.'

Rubirosa grinned, displaying her pointed teeth. 'I'm coming anyway. I fancy a night off this boat whatever I'm going into.' Myself, I thought she enjoyed the prospect of adventure.

'What if you're recognized?'

'Unlikely. But if they do – well, we'll just have to see. I haven't got any other clothes.'

'Neither have I. And Peto's too short to borrow some from her.'

That seemed to be an end of it. I gave the collar back to the marauder and the city of the Noumenon returned to its gloomy illusion. I told Peto what we were doing, but said nothing about the city's changes. Dishonest perhaps, but I didn't want to alarm her, or come back to find that she'd gone on without us. I knew she'd take the opportunity to search for the bomb, although I didn't hold out any real hope. If neither of us had located it by now . . .

'Do what you need to do,' was all that Peto said. 'And be careful. This can be a – curious – city.'

'I'd noticed.' So perhaps I hadn't needed to say anything, after all. She was probably grateful to have her two guests off her boat for a while, I thought.

Rubirosa and I strolled together down the promenade, endeavouring and failing to look like tourists. I kept thinking of what lay beyond my actual vision, the layer of the world revealed by Rubirosa's haunt-armour. No one stared at us directly, but I was aware of sidelong glances, and the back of my neck burned.

'I think we're causing a stir,' Rubirosa murmured. She took my arm, mincing slightly, and ogled a whey-faced girl with her crimson gaze.

'Stop it. You'll get us lynched.' I was, all at once, a little too aware of her touch. When had *that* started to happen? It had been a while since I'd been involved with anyone, I told myself, it was doubtless simply a matter of proximity.

'They're supposed to be a people who mind their own business. You've seen why.'

'*Their* business. Not the business of others, forced upon them. They can't possibly imagine I'm your girlfriend!'

'Why not?' the marauder asked. 'You're not that ugly. Bit pale, perhaps, but I don't mind that.'

I detached her hand from my arm. 'Stop provoking people. Whatever they are, I have work to do.'

Eventually, we found a tea-house with a series of public antiscribes set into the wall. Rubirosa lounged on a couch while I ordered local tea in a desperate attempt to appear inconspicuous, and logged on. The episode with Rubirosa had unsettled me, and my hands were unsteady over the console. I forced myself to concentrate.

As I'd expected, there was nothing from Winterstrike apart

from the usual stale pap of propaganda, but I was eventually able to access Gennera.

Her pasty face popped onto the corner of the screen so suddenly that it was almost frightening, a spectral apparition. Or perhaps my nerves had been wound to a pitch by what I'd seen. The dissonance between the tea-house, so ostensibly normal, and what I'd glimpsed was starting to rub raw at my senses.

'Where are you?' she hissed.

'I'm in the Noumenon.'

'What in the name of the Bell are you doing *there*?'

'You *know* what happened. I told you. Caud erupted,' I typed, clicking off the voice link and rendering my message in code. 'I had to run. Took a barge out. This was the way we had to come – I told you when I'd reached the plain. The canal was closed.'

'No, it isn't. It's still open.'

'What? But the pilot told me it had closed. I checked.'

A cloying dismay had begun to settle around me.

'They closed it for a day, no more. Then it opened again.'

'But the barge, the pilot – I just got on at random.' I sounded like a child. People can be bribed.

'Get out of the Noumenon,' Gennera said. 'Get out now.'

'I'm trying!'

'Do so,' Gennera said, and logged off.

But there was another message waiting for me and it came from a surprising source: my aunt Thea. 'Leretui missing. Please come home. We need your help. E gone after her.'

I stared at the antiscribe in dismay, typing back, 'Where has E gone? Do you know?'

Oh Essegui, I thought. Spies should have no ties, but I thought of my cold-faced, warm-hearted cousin, the features I saw every time I looked in a mirror, and all those shared secrets . . .

I turned back to where Rubirosa was reading a paperback novel of the kind much admired in Winterstrike forty years before, and attracting covert glances from the rest of the tea-house's customers.

I wondered what they really thought. I wondered what they really *were*.

'Finished your messaging?' the marauder said, without looking up.

'It would appear so.' I went to sit by her, at a safe distance. I was still thinking about Gennera's instructions. 'We'd better go,' I said.

'Agreed.'

When we left, the strip of sky overhead had become dark and starry. The Noumenon was filled with the glow of lamps, all the way up the heights of the cliffs. I wondered who had – and who still – lived at the summit: perhaps government officials, or would they live at the safety of the base, a society geographically reversed? Rubirosa and I made our way through cramped and narrow streets; it was like travelling back in time to an earlier Mars, or perhaps even Earth – some strange day when technology was unknown. A ground car, gliding overhead, dispelled this illusion somewhat, but even that vehicle had an antique air about it. I thought of ruins, of a people glimpsed like shadows from the corner of the eye. I felt an electric tingling through my eldritch senses, like the activation of haunt-tech. From high on the cliff above the rooftops came a great burst of light, a soundless shower of sparks that, from this distance, must have been burning material that was several feet across. A moment later, the cliffside rumbled.

A bomb? And then, across the street, a storefront exploded. Both Rubirosa and I were already diving for the ground, smacked there by the force of the blast. Above us, a plexiglass window flexed, bent outward, flexed again and collapsed against its own pressure. I covered my head with my arms as pieces of the window fell in. Someone was screaming. There was an intense, unnatural heat but I couldn't hear the roar of fire. Cautiously, I raised my head. I couldn't see much beyond the window, only a white wall as though the snow had blown up, or someone had changed a programme to static. As I watched, a face bubbled out of the wall, mouth agape, eyes staring. And through its eyes, all I could see was stars.

Interlude: Leretui

She would enjoy it, Mantis told her with a brittle gaiety. It was a return to the ancient times; she must have read about such things, perhaps even seen videocasts, old and flickering. Leretui need not be afraid, because she would be high above the action and well protected.

Mantis would make very sure that she was protected. Leretui knew that, didn't she?

So why, Shorn thought, did she continue to feel so strange?

There were other emotions mixed in with the fear, however. Mantis fascinated her. It was the way that she thought about things, so alien, so *different*.

'You see, Leretui,' she said, sitting in the chair in the chamber while Shorn sat on the bed, hugging her knees. 'Things have been out of balance on Mars for far too long. The original matriarchies – progressive social experiments, that got out of hand. After all, Earth still has males.'

'In a subservient role,' Shorn argued.

Mantis shrugged. 'Perhaps. But things could change. The oldest legends tell of cycles: how first women dominated, and then men, and now women again. We need to get past that kind of thinking. We need equality. That's what the Age of Children was all about, you see. Equality between the genders. Equality between different human species.'

Shorn was silent. She did not see how equality could be possible, after so long. And Mantis was the first member of the Changed she'd ever really talked to at close quarters: you could not call the vulpen 'human'. Yet something still skated through her mind, the long face, the bony fingers clutching her own.

'You mentioned this – test,' she said.

'A chance for the vulpen to prove their skill,' Mantis said. Her eyes shone, first dark, then pale. She spread her oddly jointed hands. 'They demanded it, not I.'

Shorn did not see how this had anything to do with equality, or any of the theories that Mantis had propounded to her. The woman seemed to want a confessor, or at least, an ear. This proposed test sounded more like the sort of things excissieres went through, so wasn't it just a case of males mimicking females, without any real understanding of what they were doing or why?

But the thought of seeing vulpen again – she didn't understand how she felt about that, couldn't seem to pin the feelings down.

'You'll enjoy it,' Mantis said again, and she sounded very sure of it. So Shorn said, doubtful, 'Maybe I will.'

She was looking forward just to getting out of the tower room for a while. The long view had paled, and it had become too reminiscent of the year she had spent locked in the heart of Calmaretto. She found that her thoughts had taken to spiralling endlessly around, like birds around carrion, dwelling on the past, on shame and humiliation. She tried to turn them away from the subject, but could not. So Shorn let herself sink into it, until the time came for Mantis to lead her down.

The tower was not, after all, as ruined as she had thought. At some point in its long history – more recent than not – someone had gutted the interior and replaced musty stone and rotting wood with a plastic shell, in plain muted colours. The floor beneath Shorn's feet sparkled with shot light, running through the tiles, and occasionally faces appeared in the walls, eyes empty, mouthing words.

'Who are the haunts?' Shorn asked. Her hand was tucked into

the crook of Mantis's elbow and held there firmly. Under her fingers, the arm was unnaturally hard, like bone.

Mantis laughed. 'Trapped souls, nothing more. I suppose I should have done something about them, but – well, it lends atmosphere, don't you think? Besides, some of them are men, you'll have noticed. I thought it's an interesting reminder – what we were, and what we've become. So I decided to leave them.'

'Do they ever – escape?' Shorn asked, thinking of Calmaretto and its multiple wards.

'Only occasionally. They don't do anything, can't be used for anything, either. Too diffuse. A shame, really. It would be interesting to question them, but they're just images. Any content is long gone.'

But Shorn could hear something up ahead now, a distant, pervasive murmuring. 'What's that?' she asked.

'Ah, those are your subjects, my lady.' Her grip on Shorn's hand tightened. 'Don't be afraid, now. You know they can smell it?'

And will I see – him – there? The one beneath the bridge? The one who changed everything for me? Shorn did not say this aloud. How would she *know*? she thought. They were said to look all alike, clones and shifts, like the female versions of the Changed. Then they turned a corner and she was standing in a great domed chamber, filled with long white faces like ghosts. All of them were turned towards her and the sudden silence was deafening.

This time it was her own grip that tightened on Mantis's arm. Her breath sounded loud in the hush.

'Don't be afraid.' Mantis's voice was very solemn, as if trying not to mock. She led Shorn up a flight of stone steps and Shorn stared straight ahead, not looking down, wanting and yet not wanting to meet those inhuman eyes. Their gaze bored into her until she felt as full of holes as a sieve. Mantis led her into a rickety iron cage, dangling above the crowd. Once inside, she was ushered onto a red velvet seat. She perched there gingerly, as the cage swung. Eventually she forced herself to look down. The floor of the cavern was covered with a glassy oval: from the chill that rose from it, she recognized ice.

'What's happening?' she whispered to Mantis, who still had hold of her hand. Her fingers were growing numb.

'A contest. They like to prove themselves.'

One of the vulpen skated out onto the rink, the blades of its – his – feet whistling across the ice. He wore black and white robes, a swirling chequerboard pattern, blurring into a blizzard as he moved. Shorn gasped. The long feet flashed beneath the hem of the robe, carving temporary patterns into the ice. He carried a pole of glinting metal, marked with long barbs. On the opposite side of the ice, another vulpen skated forth, wearing black and red. The barbs on his weapon were also red: a flaring crimson. Shorn craned her neck, trying to see if either of them looked familiar, but of course she could not tell: they all looked the same, with those pointed faces and small inverted ears, the arching brow ridges and bony skulls. The combatants hissed, displaying triangles of teeth. Black-and-white spun, whirled, whipping the barbed pole over his head and kicking out with one serrated foot. Red Warrior ducked, dived, skidded in a moth-flurry of robes across the rink, rebounded to his feet. A thin trail of blood followed: Shorn watched it, fascinated, the little drops marbling as they froze.

Beside her, Mantis laughed. 'Nothing like blood,' she said.

'Will one of them kill the other?' Shorn asked.

'Perhaps.' She did not sound as though it mattered.

White Warrior whisked over, stabbing down with the barbed pole. Red rolled, trying to avoid the stabbing point, which stopped just short of the ice. White's skates cut graceful arabesques across the floor. Mantis pointed, said sententiously, 'It's as important to be beautiful as it is to be strong.'

Shorn would have liked to disagree, but the patterns that were forming before her were mesmerizing: black, white, red; blood and ice and the sad darkness of an eye. She leaned forward, forgetting Mantis's grip on her hand, and watched the combat. She thought, for a moment, that she could feel Mantis's smile.

Red and White were now both back on their skating blades. They rushed towards each other, poles forming wheels in the air and sending upward a draught that stirred Shorn's hair. It was a dance as much as a fight, she understood, and yet the fight lay at the base of it all, the brutality underneath the beauty, and that was what made it exciting.

She'd seen violence before, of course. She was of Winterstrike. There had been the bloodgames played by the excissieres, running through the streets during Misrule. Shorn and her sister and cousin had not been allowed out of the house, but they'd watched anyway, hiding behind the windows of the winter garden on the roof and watching the silent violent dance in the snowy street below. The masques held by the coquettes – Shorn had been to a few of these and they'd almost always ended in a fanning, the razor-edges flickering out across a face. That was normal, just another side of life, but this was different, a different smell in the air, catching hold of her senses and twisting them in.

Red Warrior leaped, rising high above the rink and kicking down. White fell, throat torn out. The scent of blood struck Shorn like a blow. She watched, avid, as the vulpen clustered around and began, delicately, to feed on their fallen companion.

SIXTEEN

Essegui — Crater Plain

I wanted to sleep, but it wouldn't come and so I stayed wide awake and stared out at the changing landscape as the ancient ground car sped along. I half expected to see Alleghetta standing out there amongst the scrub, but she didn't appear either, which was a relief. Being haunted by one's still-living (as far as I knew) mother was, I felt, coming close to the final indignity.

We came down from the mountains and out across the plains once more, whistling through the icy grass. It was still very early in the morning, with the stars speckling the sky. Occasionally we started flocks of hunting birds up from the grass and they flew upwards in spirals, like smoke. I had that early-morning sense of the world made new, that time when the planet seems to belong to you and your companions, and no one else.

This time, however, it was my companions' disconcerting presence that was probably stopping me from sleeping. I hadn't paid much attention to the bite on my arm after my capture by Mantis's rider, but now it started to itch and burn, whether from mental association with the centipedes, or because the haunt-tech episode had dampened it down, or simply because I now had the leisure to think about it, I did not know. I pushed back my sleeve and looked at the bite: no point in trying to pretend it wasn't there, I thought, seeing that the thing that had given it to me was probably lurking in someone else's clothes right now.

And indeed, one of the women leaned forward and examined the bite with interest. It had become raised into a shiny knot, the flesh oddly twisted around a central core, like a mutated boil. I stared at it with revulsion.

'It's reacted quite well,' the woman said, with approval.

'Oh, well, that's good, isn't it? One of your familiars sinks its pincers into my arm and it comes up in a great oozing lump – fantastic.'

The woman did not appear to notice any sarcasm. 'Shurr, look at this.'

'Sometimes there's a very strong reaction,' Shurr said. 'Your immunity must be quite good. It can be painful.'

'Why did I have to undergo it, in that case?'

'It's a tracking implant,' the woman explained. 'It's how we found you.'

'Let Three take care of it, now that we have more time,' the other woman said. She tapped her sleeve and the centipede slid out of it. I didn't like to ask what had become of the one that had liberated me from the cell: it must be dead, but I wasn't sure that they were alive in the first place. This thing had a gleaming white carapace, unmarked except by a small silver dot near the head. It moved with smooth mechanical precision.

'Is it real?' I asked. 'That is, I mean is it a machine?'

'In part. A bio-engineered organism. Rather like your excissieres, I suppose.'

'I don't know much about how things are done on Earth,' I said, 'but aren't those very expensive?'

The woman smiled as the thing slipped onto my lap. I tried not to flinch. 'They belong to the Queen. They are hereditary, very ancient technology.'

'I see.'

'Don't worry. It won't hurt you again. Let it do what it must with the bite.'

I watched as a glistening droplet of moisture seeped from the centipede's jaws and ran down one sharp pincer. It fell directly onto the bite and there was a numbing sensation, then a coolness, not unpleasant. The centipede withdrew until, to my great relief, it was no longer visible within the woman's robes.

But with that drop of moisture came images.

There was a palace, a colonnade of stout stone columns. A vine climbed up them, bearing crimson and gold flowers, and the windows of the palace blazed with light. Voices came from within: it sounded like a party and reminded me of Calmaretto and the balls my mothers had hosted when we were growing up. Water flickered over the surface of a canal but it did not feel like Mars.

Then, dense jungle with a temple in the middle of it, all ruined and shattered, but clearly once a large construction – a ziggurat, carved around its base with figures in erotic configurations, and at its summit a round bowl of plexiglass, also ancient, I thought, but still much later than the temple. A thought came to mind: this is the Queen's observatory.

Then I was standing on a boat and coming in to a long shoreline, edged with buildings under a hot blue sky. Everything was azure and gold and white, the buildings high-rise and shining, and I took a quick breath, because I knew that this was Earth. A light, bright place – but then the boat on which I was standing skimmed over choppy water and I looked down through the clear depths to see buildings far below. Earth the Drowned, and that made me realize that what I'd just seen was real.

The scenes flicked out like a dead broadcast. I said, 'I had a vision.'

'It stores memories. Sometimes there's a little bleed.'

'Was that Malay?'

'Most probably. Its recent memory selection will be of Mars.

I downloaded, but possibly not all. You need a good clean, don't you?' she added to the thing inside her sleeve.

From the front, the driver said, 'We're almost there.'

I looked over my shoulder at the receding mountains. We'd passed the main road out of Winterstrike – the one on which the pilgrimage had come – some time before and now were crossing the greater plains in the direction of what I estimated to be the Grand Channel, not far from Caud.

'Caud's at war,' I murmured, just in case they'd forgotten.

'We know.'

More traffic was appearing now. We passed a big government vehicle trundling along a commission way, bearing city colours. Caud, not Winterstrike. It only increased my unease. Then other vehicles started coming into view, lots of them, of all different kinds, straggling out across the plains. Refugees, fleeing the stricken city. The old ground car wove its way between them, deftly avoiding the heavier traffic, the thundering long-wheel-base trucks and buses without air capacity. All of them looked crammed full: I'd be surprised if there was anyone left in Caud.

Shurr spoke rapidly into the comm, in a clickety language that I did not recognize. A moment later, a reply crackled back.

'They're not far away,' Shurr reported. We were in the thick of the refugees now but I could see the gleam of the canal in the distance. Then pennants and a tall construction. All the women in the car gave a little shout, like a ritual exclamation.

'I take it we've found them?' I said.

'That's the jaggernath, yes. The Queen's waiting for you,' Shurr said.

I could have found it by myself, I thought later. It did not look at all Martian, being covered with signs and symbols, with the delicate tracery of haunt-wards that looked nothing like those you found on Mars. The air around it seemed clearer than the surrounding plains, as though it was accompanied by its own atmosphere. Tall poles and banners clung to it. The ground car shuddered to a halt not far away and a girl ran out of the construction and clung to the step of the car. The woman in the back opened the door and let the girl inside, speaking to her in their own language.

'Am I to meet the Queen now?' I asked.

'First, preparation.'

I didn't like the sound of that, but it turned out to simply mean a wash. If I'd been the Queen, I suppose I'd have objected to meeting grubby Martians, as well. A truck followed the Queen's own vehicle, and in it I found a makeshift sonic washroom with a change of clothes, slightly too large. I decided against these, apart from the underthings, and remained in my black-and-bone. Then I waited, was brought tea and bread, and then more tea, and waited some more. We kept moving all the time, travelling at a snail's pace parallel to the Grand Channel. I amused myself by trying to identify passing ships, without great success. The geise snapped at me from time to time, but the centipede's antidote, or whatever it had been, seemed to have put a dampener on that, too. I can't say I wasn't grateful.

Eventually Shurr reappeared and announced that the Queen would see me shortly: she'd had some unexpected business to take care of. We were to follow the jaggernath and wait until called. So I walked out onto the plain and followed the vehicle of the Centipede Queen, with the cold grass lashing against my legs and the watery wind from the canal on my face. It was one of the last peaceful moments that I remember from that time.

But it did not last long. Shurr and I had been walking for perhaps fifteen minutes when an awning at the back of the vehicle rattled up to expose some steps and a narrow doorway. We were beckoned inside by a tall, slim person who immediately struck me as *wrong*, although I could not have said what was the matter with her. A round face and plum-black eyes, with similar ritual scarring to the others.

When I stepped through the doorway, it took my eyes some

moments to readjust to the low level of light. There was a lamp high on the wall, emitting some kind of smoky substance, and the air smelled heavy and drugged. I had to struggle not to cough. Several people were standing in front of me: two of them I knew from the pilgrimage and my rescue, but the third – who was similar – was unknown to me. They all bowed, as if I was an honoured guest.

'The Queen will see you now,' the third person said, and stepped aside.

She isn't human. That was my first thought. The thing that looked expressionlessly up from the couch was as lovely as a doll: almost naked, with skin as white and hard as the carapace of one of her centipedes. Her arms appeared boneless, but then she shifted position and I saw spines moving underneath the skin. Her face was oval, with huge dark eyes and a sullen mouth. Black hair fell smoothly from a central parting and was then caught up again in a complicated topknot. I could not see, but I strongly suspected that her spine was as ridged as the back of her arms. Her breasts were bare and lacked nipples, and her crotch was protected by a black metal patch that looked as though it had been inset into the skin; similar patches were set along her shins and around her wrists. From the look of them, they were probably some kind of haunt device, but I knew very little about Earth tech.

And I didn't really want to find out.

'Your name is Essegui Harn?' She spoke with wondering slowness and I became almost certain that she was drugged.

'Yes. Matriarch,' I added, just in case. No one had told me how to address her, so I opted for standard courtesy.

The Queen patted a cushion and something slid deeper beneath it. 'Come and sit here by me.'

I didn't want to obey, but didn't like to refuse, either. I did as she asked, feeling that it would be a considerable social solecism to squash one of the Queen's bio-eng pets. Nothing reacted, fortunately.

The Queen immediately put up a hand, much faster than I'd have expected of someone in her apparent condition. Four white fingers and a thumb, as hard and smooth as glass, attached themselves to my face. I pulled back but the hand came with me until the back of my head was flattened against the seat. The pressure was unbelievable, coming from someone who looked as fragile as the Queen. She looked straight into my eyes and I could not look away: it was like staring down a well.

'Don't be afraid,' she said. Too late for that. I felt like some little animal caught in a predator's snare. The bite started to throb and ache, the previous numbness now quite gone.

'I'll try,' I said out of a dry and nearly speechless mouth.

The Queen opened her lips and breathed. It was like being trapped in Mantis's haunt device. The Centipede Queen took from me all the visions that Mantis had conjured, and there was one more, too: one that had nothing to do with alien planets and drowned landscapes.

Instead, I saw my sister.

A fairy tale: a princess is imprisoned in a tower. She sits sadly by the window, her long black hair unbound and wild, her hands knotted in her lap, gazing out across a mountain range, at dusk. There are stars above her head and one of them suddenly falls, shooting out of the sky and burying itself with a smoulder in the stony earth. The princess gasps. There is someone at her shoulder. She reaches up and holds out a faltering hand. Someone takes it, someone who is *wrong*, just as the woman at the door of the jaggernath was also *wrong*. Someone – a thin dark woman in clothes the same colour as her hair – bends down and whispers in her ear. Then the window closes, shutting out the stars and the night, and the princess, from outside view.

Just a fleeting snatch of image, but of course I knew her. It was Leretui, known as Shorn, looking different. Looking mad.

'She's alive,' I heard myself say. Inside my head, the geise leaped and twisted like a fish on the end of a hook.

'Who is she?' The Queen's voice was rasping, hypnotic.

'She's my sister,' I said. 'She's missing. But I don't know where she is. I don't know how I saw what I saw.'

'Missing from a locked room,' another voice said, across the chamber, but my head felt too heavy to lift and look. I felt something tickling the back of my hand and forced myself not to glance down. 'How interesting.' She leaned forward and opened her mouth again. I could see right inside it: not pink like a normal human's mouth, but quite white and glassy, with a small spiny tongue and sharp ridges of teeth. She breathed once more and this time I found myself possessed of an unnatural and unfamiliar clarity. There was a strong fresh smell in the chamber, cutting through the musk.

'Better?' asked the Queen, with an arch of eyebrow.

'Thank you, yes, I think so, I'm not sure,' I said, all in a rush. The Queen smiled.

'Someone will bring you some tea. A good idea? Yes.' She answered her own question. 'So, now we know what you are.'

'And what's that?'

'A sister.'

'Well, yes.' Obvious enough, but the Queen went on, 'Do you know what a whisperer is?'

'Someone who whispers?'

'A whisperer is an old word for someone who hears things. Whispers, in the night. Long ago, they maybe thought they were hearing spirits, or demons, or gods. They are not. Now, of course—' her mouth curled indulgently '—we realize how foolish and primitive such notions are, for we understand the nature of death, its animations. But then they did not. And later, equally foolish, they thought that the voices that they heard were evidence of madness.'

'So what are they?'

'Transmissions.'

'From where?'

'Let's say – from the past. From things that should have died out long ago, and yet did not. Things who possessed the ability to speak mind-to-mind, through the medium of the dead world, the Eldritch Realm. I think you are sensitive. I think you can pick up things from other people, perhaps broadcast them.'

'What do you mean, the past?'

'Ah,' the Queen breathed. 'You know how it is, these days. The time of the bleed, my people call it. Ghosts are everywhere, the dead return through the aid of machines, those who are supposed to be long gone live on. Mars and Earth have had their day, Essegui Harn. Everything's breaking down.'

I said nothing.

'And some people can hear the voices of the dead. Maybe your sister is one.' A sly glance, as if she knew much that I did not.

'I see.' I remembered Leretui, folding to the ground beneath the weedwood trees in the summer light. But I thought the description applied more to Hestia, with her ability to steal souls and glimpse the future.

'You said you heard whispering in me. That's not from the past. That's something my mothers did to me, and a woman called a majike – do you know what that is?'

The Queen gave an indulgent smile. 'A sorcerer. Yes, I can hear that you're cursed. But there are other whispers in your head. Echoes.'

'I don't understand,' I said.

The smile grew sweeter. 'Neither do I. I wonder if your sister does. You're an echo of her, you see.'

'Why are *you* here?' I asked. 'And how do you know about this?'

'My family has ancient texts, from before the Drowning. They give codes of contact, emblems that have reappeared. Symbols that were used by certain of the Changed, once upon a time.'

'What if someone else has just – well, stolen them? The original species might have died out by now.'

'No one steals from the None,' the Queen said.

'The None? Who are they?'

'The dead-who-speak. It's what they call themselves.'

'What does everyone else call them?'

The Queen smiled. 'Everyone else just calls them *destruction*.'

I was escorted back to one of the accompanying wagons. The group would, so the Queen had told me, release me soon and I would be free to resume my search for my sister. Shurr would be sent with me, to assist. I asked why they were prepared to help me, pressing the point, but the Queen would not reply. She asked me to tell her the story of Leretui's disappearance and I did so, but I did not get the impression that she really understood the nature of my sister's crime. When I mentioned the vulpen, and the act of transgression that Leretui had committed, the Queen's gaze slid up to meet that of the dark-eyed girl, and of course it was then that I realized.

The Queen had seen me looking. 'Yes, he is,' she admitted. 'Although to come here, a physical change was necessary.'

'She's – he's – been modified?' *He*. How odd that sounded, that archaic Martian word, uttered without vilification or even revulsion. Despite my sympathies for Leretui, I had to stop myself from bolting out of the room; it was worse than the centipedes, in a way. And from the look in the young man's eyes, the relationship between herself – *himself*, I corrected – and the Queen was not platonic.

Unnatural. But not, it seemed, on Earth.

Now, back in the swaying wagon, I thought of Leretui and of the dead and of men. I'd asked the Queen more about the None, but she hadn't known, or claimed not to: it was a name from the far past, the lost long ago, a name around which terror still clung. It had been hard to make much sense out of the

Queen's ramblings. Something ancient had returned, or seemed to have done, and Leretui was connected with it in some way, but I could not see how.

They'd said they could help me find Leretui, but they hadn't told me how this would be done, either. The Queen had seen what I'd seen, that fairy-tale vision, but neither of us knew how to interpret it. I didn't even know if it was Leretui's real location, or a metaphor for something: such things had happened before. If only she'd been looking out at a public monument . . .

I was so lost in my thoughts that it was a few minutes before I realized that the wagon had stopped moving. What amounted to a refugee convoy had progressed in fits and starts, so I thought this was just some inevitable hitch. I got up and went over to the window hatch, nonetheless.

Outside was a sea of vehicles, stretching across the Plain. People were shouting and calling to one another, more than the usual subdued hubbub. There were cries from up ahead and the place where we'd come to a stop was strangely dark, though faint sunlight washed over the rest of the Plain. I went quickly to the back door of the vehicle and jumped down. Outside, I cannoned into Shurr, who was running round the side of the wagon. Her dark face was a distorted mask. She cried, 'The Queen! The Queen!'

'What's wrong—?' I started to say, and then I looked up.

It was enormous. It was green and gold, like a beetle, shot with amethyst. From its gleaming carapace hung a thing like a huge hook, bristling with wires and sparks of electricity. It brushed against one of the pylons of the Queen's vehicle and a shimmering radiance washed out into the air, penetrating the shadows in which we stood. Shurr was already running towards the Queen's wagon, brandishing a small slim weapon, but the whole vehicle now was enveloped in sparkles of light, like the sun on water. I remembered the blue place I had seen, the place on Earth: Khul Pak. A terrible, desolate cry came from the interior of the wagon.

The hook jerked and then the thing that hung above us was shooting upwards, a squat upper-atmosphere craft that quickly became a bright star in the heavens and was gone.

Shurr threw open the doors of the Queen's wagon. The young man sprawled unconscious, or perhaps dead, at the threshold. But the Centipede Queen of Khul Pak was nowhere to be seen.

SEVENTEEN

Hestia – the Noumenon

Rubirosa got to her feet. I'd have followed her, but I was still trans-fixed by the spectral faces that were seething out of the white wall in front of me. I recognized a couple of generic types – these were women of the Southern Plains Matriarchy, that oval-faced girl with the sharp bones was surely from Ord. Haunts, used to power something and possibly connected with the bomb itself, and now released into the atmosphere. They shrieked upwards like rockets, trailing a smoky mist behind them.

Someone was shouting: 'Get out! Get out!' I dragged myself away from the released ghosts and followed Rubirosa among the maze of awnings and fallen plaster. The shine of the marauder's armour led me through the dim regions at the back of a tea-house and then we found ourselves in the kitchen.

I straightened up. 'What the hell was that?'

'Listen,' Rubirosa said. She put out a warning arm, stopping me from going forward. Outside the tea-house, there was a high, painful whine.

'Something's coming down!' A moment later, it hit. The tea-house shook and more plaster fell from the ceiling, but the beams held.

'The whole place is under attack. Anything to do with you?'

'Not that I know of.' The marauder turned to me with a frown. 'I don't think either of us is *that* important, are we?'

Another hit and the tea-house would be down around our heads, I thought. I rattled the kitchen door, which had stuck, and wrenched it open. We fell back out onto the street, into a sea of panicking people.

I shoved through the crowd, heading in the direction of the barge. A haunt screamed past me like a gunpowder rocket. Rubirosa grabbed my arm. 'Look!' She pointed upward.

Something was descending through the cleft of the mountains, something familiar. It took me a moment to recognize it, then it turned and I saw the dreadnought I'd last glimpsed out on the plains, rising up from the Grand Channel and capsizing a ferry in its wake. Haunts were being sucked up toward it like moths to a flame, sizzling out against its flickering sides. A blast of light from its port bow sent fire shooting out across the valley and briefly illuminated a building at the summit as it erupted into flames, but I did not think it had been aiming at the building itself. A shadow passed over the peaks: another aircraft. Fragments of burning material rained down and one thin strand clung to my sleeve. I knew better than to brush it off: that was a good way to become possessed. I dodged under an awning, Rubirosa close behind, and we dived down a flight of steps. If I'd got my geography right, the mooring was not far away, but I wondered at the wisdom of returning to the barge: not the world's swiftest craft, especially with a bomb on board and a captain I couldn't trust.

'The thing you put on the barge!' I shouted to Rubirosa. 'How sensitive is it?'

'Not sure.'

'So all this haunt activity might set it off?'

The marauder gave me an uneasy glance. 'I don't think so.'

'But you're not certain?'

Another blast from the dreadnought swallowed Rubirosa's words. We ran for the mooring, arrowing through angled streets and leaping over fallen masonry. Then I leaped for what I took to be a low wall and fell heavily: the wall was low, but only on one side: the floor had caved into a cellar and I now sprawled on the rubble. Rubirosa's face appeared over the top of the wall, looking somehow inhuman.

'Are you all right?'

I was winded but not, I thought, seriously hurt, though there was a sharp ache in my ribcage when I breathed in which suggested bruising or a crack. 'Yes.' But then the shattered walls around me started to shimmer and break apart. A huge lump of rock came loose from the main wall and hurtled towards me. I tried to roll out of the way, but then it struck . . . and passed straight through. I had a sudden glimpse down into a gaping chasm, right through the middle of broken walls and floors, all the way down to what looked like a black pool. A moment later, I was lying by the side of that pool as the city broke down around me.

I didn't understand what had happened. Rubirosa's face was nowhere to be seen but the stars above the city were very bright. I got to my feet, with a stab from the rib, and hobbled around the perimeter of the pool. It wasn't until I reached the opposite point, halfway round, that I realized there was someone there: standing motionless in the shadows. I stopped dead. Beside me, the Library suddenly shimmered into sight. She said, whispering in my ear, 'Do you see her?'

'I see.'

The figure was shadowy and wore a long hood that concealed her face. For a moment she shivered and I saw the outline of the wall behind her. 'She's a haunt,' I said. 'Or a hologram.'

'She registers as real,' the Library said.

And she was real enough when she stepped forward and a sharp stinging constriction came around my throat. The figure raised a hand and pulled me in; I went stumbling, like an animated doll. Her hand closed over my face, I tried to fight but could not. Behind me the Library cried out, or so I thought, but this was not like the battle with the excissiere. From the corner of my eye I saw the Library collapse inward, folding down into herself, and then there were only shadows.

I can't say I was unconscious. I was dimly aware of what was going on, but it was vague and inchoate. I was led through a myriad of rooms and passages, some of them modern – all metal and polished stone – and some antique, no more than channels in the earth. For a few minutes I thought I walked across the surface of the planet as it had been before humans ever came, before there was any life at all except the thin smears of bacteria deep in the ice-locked caverns. I could breathe but the cone of Olympus reared up over me, pressing me down. My boots scuffed in red dust. Above me, the sky was a pallid ochre. It was very cold, colder even than Winterstrike in the depths of Ombre, but just as I was about to faint from it, a chilly wind blew and green curled up in the dust under my feet. Soon I walked through a landscape of needle pine and pitchwood, the early engineered conifers, saw the glint of water ahead. Olympus was still there, shadowy at the edges of my sight, but now its huge summit was white with snow and I could see lights on its slopes. I thought of spirits, of the old stories of the haunted hills, and shivered.

Then cities were rising up around me, the old cities of the Crater Plains and the start and heart of the Martian mythos. Yere and Shua, Tokamay and Khalt, cities of the saltmarshes and the deep deserts. A woman rushed past me, gaunt and tall, armour-clad with black hair streaming. Her mouth gaped, her eyes stared; I remembered the mad matriarch Mantis and thought of ghosts.

'There she goes,' a familiar, creaky voice said. I blinked. Old Mars was gone. I lay on a pallet bed, a blank cracked ceiling above me. Thin air was trickling in around the warped frame of a window, a breath upon my face. The Library stood looking out, feet braced, her back towards me.

'Who—?' I remembered the woman. 'That was Mantis? Where *are* we?'

'You've seen it before,' said the Library.

'This is Temperire? Mantis's tower?' I got off the bed and went to the window, instinctively moving to shoulder the warrior aside and nearly stumbling as I passed through her. It was almost dark, but there was a last gleam of sun low on the horizon and in its light I saw the canal, with the lamps of ships slowly passing up it to the Noumenon. The shadows of the rocks lay squat and black, scattered over the plain.

A tall door, almost too high and narrow for a normal person. Our ancestors were different, after all: experimentation, resulting in the Changed. The door was locked and though I rattled it, it would not budge. There was none of the feel of haunt-tech and yet the place felt infested, all the same.

'It's not a mechanical lock,' the Library unnecessarily informed me.

I sat back down on the pallet. I felt bruised; my rib burned and the confusion of the last half hour was overwhelming. All I wanted to do was to lie down and close my eyes, but I had to think. Had the Noumenon fallen? I wasn't even sure.

That weapon I'd delivered to Gennera. What exactly did it do? I fought back dismay.

Like the door, the window was bolted shut, but in this case the bolt was rusty and old. After some minutes of determined tugging, the whole thing gave way in a shower of rotten wood and ancient nails. I breathed in snowy air. The sill was narrow, but a short distance away was another window. The only difficulty was the drop, which I estimated to be in the region of a thousand feet or so. It was now dark enough that I couldn't see what lay immediately beneath, but it was probably rocks.

'Are you going out there?' the Library asked. I thought I detected a familiar note in her engineered voice: the sort of tone that reminds you of your mother.

'It's the only way out,' I said. 'I don't get vertigo.' Well, not much. I hauled myself up over the sill and stood, teetering over nothing. Flattening myself against the wall, I stepped out and caught a handhold on the frame of the next window. As I stood on the sill, the Library hovered disapprovingly beside me in mid-air.

'It's all right for you,' I said. I squinted in through the window. Another small room, but this was empty and the door was open – in fact, it didn't look as though there was a door there. I kicked the window in with the heel of one foot and it bounced on its frame. Next moment, I dropped into the room.

Whether or not the ruin used haunt-tech was irrelevant. The room was full of ghosts: I could hear their whispering spirits trapped in the old walls, which breathed out damp and must and despair.

'Very busy,' was the Library's only comment.

'Is that Mantis?'

The warrior frowned. 'I don't – I should not say her name, if I were you.'

'Very well.' I was beginning to conceive an unreasonable fear of Mantis, long dead but somehow, I felt, still here and still mad. The vision of the woman with the streaming hair was forcibly to the forefront of my mind. I told myself that I was infected with fairy stories, the legends dredged up by Peto on the barge as we crossed the plain.

'What brought me here?' I whispered to the warrior.

'Someone who isn't human.'

Not very helpful, even if accurate.

'Do you mean a haunt-engine? Do you know why?'

The Library shook her head. 'I can't read this place,' she confessed. 'Not well.'

'Yet part of you is from the same epoch?'

It was a guess, but a ripple passed over the face of the Library, a shimmering alteration that, brief as it was, left her looking concerned. The flayed brow furrowed.

'I think that's true. I can't remember.' Her gaze turned inward, as if processing. I gave up. By now, the passage had taken us deeper into the ruin, ancient layers of stone and metal, buckled out of shape as if by fire. The stone itself looked vitrified, but that was common in much of Winterstrike itself, a relic of earlier days.

Most of the doors had gone: blasted off their hinges, from the look of the tangles of metal in the side of each frame. The air smelled of gunpowder, like the fireworks they set off along the Great Canal at every festival except Ombre. Something huge and silent fluttered against my face and I nearly cried out, thinking it to be a haunt, but then I saw that it was only a moth. Its wings shone with phosphorescence and it blundered into the wall and clung to the stone. I watched it crawl upward, a blind thing as large as my outstretched hands.

And then I heard voices. They were coming from somewhere up ahead, but they were so faint that I couldn't tell whether they were really there, or yet another product of this haunted place. 'Listen,' I said to the Library. 'Can you hear them? Are they real?'

'By "real", do you mean human?'

'Yes.'

'I cannot tell.' The Library's face rippled once more, as though she stood in a wall of heat. 'Something is interfering—' And then she was gone. At that point, I wasn't sure whether the Library was more of a help or a hindrance, in any case. I went cautiously towards the voices, but as I turned a corner I saw someone and dodged back behind an outcrop of stone. It looked as though this corridor had been subject to some kind of bombardment; the stone was pitted with thousands of tears and holes, so that it resembled lace. I remembered the Mote in Caud, turned into a ruin in an instant. I peered through a gap.

Two people were walking along the corridor. One of them held the other firmly by the arm, and there was something familiar about this drooping figure: she wore a long black dress, of a style in fashion in Winterstrike a year or so ago. Its hem dipped to her ankles, a swathe of material trailing behind. This was no ghost of long ago, but someone real.

Her companion wore leggings and high boots, a long-tailed jacket. Her hair was hidden by a long veil in the manner of some of the southern cities: Eremis, perhaps. I could not have placed her in any particular time. She moved with a jerky, elegant angularity, a mincing walk that reminded me of some of the Changed.

As they turned the corner and disappeared from view, I slipped after them. Their footsteps receded, knocking hollow on the stone flags, and I took care to be quiet: this was a palace of echoes. Periodically I halted, just in case someone was following, but the passage behind me remained quiet.

When the attack came, therefore, it was all the more shocking. The vulpen dropped down from the ceiling in a flurry of robes, a whirling white shape. The razor-edged staff that he held snapped out, striking the stone wall as I dodged away. Sparks filled the air. I glimpsed the long bone skull, the ridged hands: a thing that had once been called *man.*

I struck out, aiming for his knee, and felt my kick connect. The vulpen staggered, the white robes swirling, and I found myself looking down into the pallid face. He hissed. I glimpsed razor-sharp teeth and a pointed tongue, forked like a serpent's, flickered out. It lashed across my hands with the burn of poison. I was already leaping back and cannoned against the wall. The vulpen grinned. I kicked out again, the vulpen dodged, striking out with a clawed hand. I jumped and this time my foot connected with the vulpen's jaw. The head spun round, more than a human's should have done, and the thing collapsed. It looked like a broken puppet; I thought its neck had snapped, but I didn't want to risk bending over it to check. Instead I ran, in the direction that the two humans had gone.

A murmuring roar filled the caverns, rustling like the sea. Two figures stepped out of the walls – not a niche in the structure, but from the walls themselves. I cried out as they grasped my arms and led me forward.

The hall was huge, a domed cavern that had been hollowed out of the rock. I could still see the stubs of stalactites, protruding like broken horns down from the roof. From the distance I had come, I thought we were probably in the foundations of the castle, though it made me queasy to think of all that rock and mortar sitting on top of this great gap. But I was queasier still at the sight of the crowd in the cavern.

Many were vulpen. Some were the Changed, but female remnants rather than male. I saw aspiths, nothing like the little thing at the temple, but feral and snarling. There was something else, too: a being that was snake-limbed and snake-haired. Mottled black and white skin gleamed in between the straps of a harness, an elongated medusa with a simpering oval face and eyes that shifted from dark to light. What the hell was *that*? She reminded me a little of the masked women outside the theatre, long ago, and the thing I'd glimpsed dancing on the surface of the canal outside Calmaretto – but demotheas weren't real. Were they? There were others, too, more beings I did not recognize: some no larger than children, their bones clearly visible beneath stretched skin.

And they were shouting. 'Send her in! Send her into the ring!'

I was shoved ahead. 'Library?' I whispered, but the warrior did not come. One of the child-sized things minced forward, stepping on high-arched feet. It carried a flail. Its small mouth curled upwards, grinning. Its eyes were yellow and when it blinked, there was a roaring in my head and the world changed.

We were standing on a red plain. Not far away rose the walls of a city, all squat russet turrets, and I thought I recognized the ancient settlement that would one day become Tharsis. Flags fluttered from the gateposts and below them sat skulls, mounted on the stonework. They didn't look particularly human.

'Yes,' my opponent said. 'This is the Age of Children, when the world was young and Earth forgotten. This is when things begin again.' It had a high, lisping voice. Neither its mouth nor its tongue looked the right shape for human speech. It tucked a wisp of hair behind its ear and swung the flail. I dodged away. The flail struck a rock and left a long deep groove in its side. Not equipped with a weapon, I was disinclined to be choosy. I picked up a stone and threw it as hard as I could. The child-thing dived away, but not quickly enough. The rock glanced against the side of its skull. It shook its head like a wet animal and drops of black blood spattered the ground. The child-thing's curling mouth smiled wider. It spat, and a burning welt appeared across the back of my hand as its saliva struck. The pain stung me into further action: I bent down, snatched another rock, and as the child-thing ducked away in anticipation, I rushed forward instead and beat the rock down at its head.

The child-thing collapsed. After the previous injury, I expected a lot of blood. But this did not happen. Instead, the child-thing melted away under my assault and I was left standing alone on the plain outside old Tharsis. The moons had risen now, and hung pale in a rosy sky, just over the long ragged ridge of mountain that separated Tharsis from the mass of the Demnotian Plain. The gates clanged open and I turned as if in a dream, still clutching the rock in my hand, and a figure on a galloping animal shot out of the city towards me. A reptile, moving on long loping legs, the animal sped towards me and a moment later it was upon me. It passed straight through me and I realized that I was the ghost, not the world itself. Then the cavern rose up again and the baying crowd was back.

I looked up. A fragile cage made of thin struts of metal hung over the fighting pit. A woman stood in the centre of it, the same woman I'd seen before in her Winterstrike attire. She was staring down at me and I saw the shock of recognition in her eyes. It was mirrored in my own, because this was my cousin Leretui Harn, now known as Shorn, free of her imprisonment in the city and here at large outside the Noumenon.

I was not allowed to speak to Shorn, though I saw her turn in the cage and address the veiled woman with urgency. The woman smiled and shook her head. She reached out and put a finger to Shorn's lips, a playful gesture. By Shorn's side, a vulpen leaned over and nuzzled at her ear. I watched with revulsion, but Shorn didn't seem to mind: she closed her eyes and swayed towards the vulpen, her lips parted. Then the shadowy figures returned and took me by the arms. I struggled, but their hands were steely and they ignored my efforts to free myself as though I was nothing more than a moth. They took me away into a maze of passages and small cells, and there they left me.

I had no idea what was going on. As for what had occurred outside Tharsis, that had been simply bizarre: I knew I'd been *somewhere*, because the welt on the back of my hand still burned and stung, but where? I could only assume that there was some kind of holographic game overlying the reality of the combat pit. Perhaps it had different historical settings. That must, I thought, be the most logical explanation.

But whatever had actually befallen me, two things remained. I wanted to find out what Shorn was doing here. And I had to get out.

This time, however, the cell was sealed. I explored every crack and crevice, without result. Some time later, a person appeared with a bowl of soup. She was not one of the shadowy figures and she looked quite solid, but not entirely human all the same. The bones of her face were the wrong shape. She reminded me of the little aspith at the Temple of the Changed, but she didn't have the fierce aspect of the ones I'd seen earlier. I didn't know whether trying to steal the soul of one of the Changed would work, so I did not try. The aspith said, in a rapid whisper, 'They told me I was to feed you.'

'Am I going back in the pit?'

'Not tonight. I don't know when. But you will go back.'

Since she seemed disposed towards conversation, I said, 'The girl in the cage. The one who looks like me. Do you know who she is?'

'She's Mantis's protégée.'

I frowned. 'The Matriarch Mantis?'

'Yes. She's come back to us.' The aspith beamed with pride.

'How? She died long ago.'

The little jailer glanced nervously around. 'They say it was through black science. But I don't know for sure.'

'Is Mantis human?'

The aspith looked shocked.

'Oh no. She's a demothea.'

'A demothea!' When I'd thought her reminiscent of the women outside the theatre, it was a notion, nothing more. 'They're not supposed to exist.'

'But they do. Mantis said once that everyone thinks they've died out but it isn't true. There are others. Mantis is—' The aspith hesitated, then lowered her voice as if making an indelicate confession. 'Mantis is not pure-bred. She's part human.'

'Is that possible? To mix human and demothea?'

'It must be, if Mantis is here,' the aspith said with simple logic.

I stared at her. She did not seem to think she had said anything extraordinary. But then, my closest friend right now was a Library. I leaned closer, trying to grasp her soul as I'd clasped the soul of my excissiere jailer, back in Caud. But she was looking away from me, her eyes downcast. 'Listen to me,' I said, urgently. 'The girl – Mantis's protégée – is my cousin. I have to talk to her. Will you help me?'

The jailer blinked. 'Why should I?' she asked, reasonably enough.

'We're rich,' I said. 'One of the foremost houses of Winter-strike. My family will reward you.'

'With what?'

'Money?'

'I don't need money. Mantis gives me what I need. She gives all of us what we need. And she gave us a place here, where every-one else cast us out.'

A thought struck me. 'How long have you been living here?'

'I was born in the mountains. And my mothers before me. That was long before Mantis came back, of course. Things were different then.'

'In Winterstrike,' I said, pitching my voice low, 'there is a temple for your kind. You're right. Things *were* different then. Your people are no longer persecuted. They're allowed to move freely throughout the city.'

The jailer looked uncertain. 'You're lying to me.'

'No, it's true. If Mantis told you otherwise, then she's the one who's lying. Look. If you take me to Shorn – to Mantis's protégée – then she'll tell you the same.'

The jailer's small face became even more uncertain, like a child tempted with a sweet. 'I should like to see that temple,' she faltered.

'Then let me go.'

With a swift, sudden movement, as if she did not want to give herself the chance to change her mind, the jailer reached out and touched the lock. It disappeared, melting into the metal cage that imprisoned me. Before she could protest, I was through the door. 'Where's Shorn?' I said.

She took me back up through the maze of passages, higher and higher into Mantis's tower. The ghosts were silent, perhaps sated by their glimpse of blood. Someone in the ancient days of Earth had once described ghosts as hungry, but as a child I had never understood this: they were part of the technology around me, and it made no more sense to say that a spirit hungered than to say that a kettle did, or an antiscribe. But out on the haunted vastness of the Crater Plains, or here in this rotting ruin of a dead queen's fortress, I knew what the ancients had meant. I could feel the hunger all around me and though the spirits that generated it slept, the hunger continued, seeping out of their dreams.

'We're almost there,' the jailer whispered, 'but if she's with Mantis, or someone else—'

I'd been trying not to think about this. I'd never known what to think about Shorn's alleged perversion: in a world where merely being seen in the company of a male creature was regarded as evidence of moral decay, I'd not been sure whether she'd sought the vulpen out or whether, as her sister Essegui had claimed, it had sought her. Shorn had been lucky to live in Winterstrike, a city seen by some as epitomizing a dangerous liberalism. In the old days in Caud, or in modern Tharsis, she could have been put to death. But perhaps it might have been kinder. Yet here was Shorn, inexplicably, in a haunted castle in the company of vulpen.

We had paused outside a door. No sound came from inside it.

'If Mantis is there . . .' the jailer said. She shot a fearful look at the door.

'I can't hear anything,' I told her. I put my ear to the wood. Nothing. 'You're sure she's in here?'

'This is her chamber.'

Very carefully, I touched the lock and the door swung open. So Shorn wasn't a prisoner, unless the lock only worked one way. At first I thought the room was empty. There was a bed, but it was not occupied. Then I saw that there was a figure sitting with its back to the door. She was half-hidden by the curtains that ringed the bed and gazing out of the window. Over her shoulder, I could see stars and the chewed orb of Deimos.

She said, and it was Shorn's familiar voice, 'You came back.'

I didn't think she was speaking to me. 'Leretui,' I whispered.

The figure on the bed gave a start and turned, clutching at

the curtain. In the unlit room, Shorn's face was as pale as the little moon's. '*Hestia?*'

'It's me,' I said. I beckoned to the little jailer, who was still hovering at the doorway. 'Can you keep watch?'

'Yes.'

'What are you doing here?' Her hands grasped the curtain like an anchor. 'I saw you in the pit, I didn't—' she faltered into silence.

'I could ask the same of you.'

Shorn looked confused. 'I – they let me out for Ombre.'

'And you escaped?' Thea had said nothing about this in her message. I'd assumed that Shorn had still been locked up.

'No. I went back to Calmaretto. They shut me up, of course.' The bitterness was clear. 'And then I came here.'

Mantis. But why would a cloned ancient queen bother with an outcast like Shorn? The only connection I could see was that this was clearly a stronghold of the vulpen and Shorn had met one . . .

'How did you get here?' I came to sit by her on the bed. She smelled odd: an acrid overlay, like fear.

'I don't remember. I think she—' she hesitated.

'Do you mean Mantis?'

She turned on me with sudden fierceness. 'She's been kind to me!' Defensive, too, though I didn't think it was merely the fact that Mantis had apparently become a friend; there was something else, too. I didn't think I'd imagined the fear. 'After what my mothers have done . . .'

What a sorry state of affairs, I thought, that one of the Changed should have been kinder to her than her own family. But knowing Calmaretto, I wasn't entirely surprised.

'Leretui, I know they locked you away, but—' What could I say to her? That they couldn't really have done anything else, under the circumstances.

Next thing I knew, my little cousin was up off the bed and at my throat. I grabbed her hands and forced them apart, but she was strong, far stronger than she looked. Leretui stepped back and I barely recognized her. It was like looking in a distorted mirror, the black eyes milky, the bones of her face standing out in angular ridges.

'Leretui, what—'

'This is what they made me!' she hissed. I still didn't understand. 'Mantis is my sister.' She started to laugh. 'A real family affair, wouldn't you say?'

'Your *sister*? But Mantis has demothea genes.' Then I looked at her and saw. 'What the hell?'

Leretui looked smug, as though she had an advantage that I did not. 'Did you never wonder how Alleghetta got as far as she has in the Matriarchy? She made a bargain.'

'With whom?'

'With a majike called Gennera Khine.'

I felt as though the floor of the tower had opened up underneath me. I sat down on Leretui's bed.

'Gennera commissioned Mantis and me. And more of us, probably. She told Alleghetta to bring me up in exchange for power, to see what I became. If it was a successful experiment, she'd give Alleghetta a place on the council. But when the vulpen came for me, they disowned me, shut me up, on Gennera's instructions, I suppose. Showing my true nature, you see.'

'Leretui,' I said, 'what is your true nature?'

'Can't you tell?' she said. 'They don't call us the Changed for nothing. And I'm changing.'

There was a sound from beyond the door. This was bad, and I needed time to work out all its ramifications, but for now, we had to get out of here.

'Shorn – *Leretui* – listen to me. I've got to get out of here. Come with me.'

'Why should I?' It was the voice of a small girl, made to do

179

what she did not want to do. But I listened to my intuition and said, 'Because you're afraid of Mantis, aren't you?'

'Where would I go, now?' Shorn hissed. 'Back to Winter-strike? Back to Calmaretto to be locked in my room until I rot and die, or stuck in one of Gennera's labs? Out onto the Plains to be eaten by ghosts? I've seen what's out there now, Hestia.'

It was on the tip of my tongue to say, 'I'll look after you,' but I wasn't sure that was even close to the truth.

'This is the only place that will have me,' Shorn said. 'They treat me like a matriarch.'

'You were in a *cage*, Leretui.'

'That was to keep me safe.'

Maybe she was right. I crossed over to the window and looked out across the mountains, faint and white in the light of the moon. Earth was rising, a blue spark over the mountain wall.

'What about Earth?' I said. Essegui had spoken of taking her sister to Earth once, when we were quite certain of not being over-heard. Up in the winter garden on the roof of Calmaretto, hiding from my aunts, while a blizzard whirled white outside the win-dows and hid Winterstrike, too, from sight. But Essegui hadn't been in a position to act then, for their mothers would never have let Shorn out of Calmaretto. Now she was free, at least free of her family, and it was I who was caged, by the bonds of duty. Caged, but maybe not for much longer.

Shorn looked at me with a mixture of scorn and hope. '*Earth*? How would we get there?'

'There are ways, Shorn. Disguise, a soul-mask. I've got con-tacts.' This was true, although what I didn't say was that those contacts were criminals. She'd realize that, if she had any sense. But I wasn't sure now how much damage had been done to her, whether there was really anything of the old Leretui left, or whether she was simply Shorn indeed. And Shorn wasn't human.

'You'd do that for me?' Now she just sounded unsure.

'You're my cousin, Leretui. And besides . . .' *I think they've treated you monstrously. Maybe they felt they had no choice, but all the same, if what you say is true . . .* I didn't really know what to think.

Shorn gave a rapid nod. 'All right, then.' She stood and I took her cold hand and led her to the door.

Outside, the tower loomed over us like something out of a nightmare. I kept expecting to encounter vulpen, but the jailer had informed me in a whisper that they slept in a pit beneath the building; I had a vision of a huddled, naked mass. The thought disgusted me. I couldn't understand how Shorn had been able to bear their close proximity, but perhaps this also said more than anything else about how she had been treated at Calmaretto. And why she'd become an outcast in the first place.

The jailer led us down a series of steps cut into the wall of the tower. These were steep and often broken and I do not like to recall that long journey down, treading carefully on crumbling stone while the yawning drop spun beneath us. There was no handrail and I was forced to clutch at the wall of the tower, pressing myself against it.

When we reached the bottom, I paused to catch my breath. Far away, above the mountain was a dim glow: the lights of whatever remained of the Noumenon. I could hear water somewhere close, rushing and gushing through the rocks; a far cry from the slow slap of the canal. It raised my spirits.

'I can't – I have to go back,' the little jailer said, with a nervous glance over her shoulder.

'What about the temple?'

'I'd like to see it one day. But I—' she was afraid, faltering, and then she was gone, back to what she knew. I hoped her loss of nerve would not result in a betrayal of us, but I couldn't trust in her discretion.

'Come on,' I said to Shorn, but she stood rigid, staring at a figure that had stepped out from beneath the shadow of the tower.

'Hello, Shorn,' Mantis said.

There was no sign of any of the vulpen. Mantis stood alone, silhouetted in the glow of moonlight on water. But Shorn's fingers tightened around my hand and she tugged at it. 'Hestia!' she breathed. 'Run!'

Mantis stepped forward and immediately it was as if a net had closed around me. Without hesitating any further I turned and sprang onto the rocks after my cousin, ignoring the chasm that opened up below the outcrops and the thunder of water beneath. Shorn moved like a mountain goat, quite different to the languid, fragile child she had been, and I wondered whether it was fear that lent her the motion, or something else. But I didn't pause to see if Mantis was behind us; I simply ran. There was a psychic tug at my senses, immensely strong, like the haunt-tech that had been applied by the excissieres. Halfway up the rocks Shorn lost her footing and stumbled, but regained her balance. I glanced up and saw that a semicircle of vulpen had appeared on the summit of the cliff, their gaunt faces ghostly pale. Behind me, I heard Mantis laugh. It didn't sound human at all.

'No!' Shorn cried, and I felt something blast out around me, similar to the psychic net cast by Mantis but even darker and stranger in feel. The rocks shifted under my feet and I fell, but the moment of brief horror that I experienced as the river swung up to meet me was knocked out of me in the next minute as I hit solid earth. That shouldn't have been possible. When I raised my head, what I saw wasn't possible either.

There were lights all out across the plain and not far away I could hear the murmur of voices. Someone stumbled into me and I started, until I realized it was Shorn. She clutched my arm.

'Where are we?'

'This is the canal,' I said, recognizing the rim of mountain against the livid twilight sky. It wasn't winter any more but there was a storm on the wind; I could smell rain and iron. 'There's the Noumenon.' I pointed to the cliffs, where the shadows of buildings clung to the rocks. Turning, I saw the tower perched on its crag, but it was much further away than it had been a moment ago and the course of the river was different, too, though I was still able to hear it. Lamplight shone from the upper windows and I realized, with a bolt of shock, that it was no longer a ruin. This was a functional fort, with a keep and a gatehouse and the glint of armoured women high on its battlements.

'Never mind *where*,' I said to Shorn. 'It's more a question of *when*.'

Shorn looked at me, eyes wide. 'We've travelled in time? How?'

'If you can move in space,' I said, 'maybe you can move in time as well.'

Shorn shook her head. 'I didn't move myself. Mantis helped me.'

What concerned me was that there was a familiar smell in the air and it was the burnt odour of haunt-tech: familiar technology, used for unfamiliar ends.

'I don't know what's going on,' I said. 'Let's move away from the camp, at any rate.'

We skirted the rows of tents that dotted the plain. I heard snatches of conversation from within and it was definitely Old Martian, that rasping, grasping speech, spoken forward in the mouth, as if reaching out to devour what lay in its path. We'd learned it in the schoolroom but I'd never heard it spoken beyond, and it took me a moment to realize that I could understand it, at least in part. Tactics, the day's battle. Mention of 'Her', and I thought I knew who that might be, at least. From the design of the tents – round fungi-like things, with blood-red spirals decorating their eaves – I was becoming more and more convinced that this was the original Mantis's day.

Interesting, but also appalling. And where was Mantis herself, in either of her incarnations? Had she come after us? Trying not to breathe, Shorn and I moved onward. Soon, the tents clustered so thickly that we were unable to avoid the encampment and had to move among it, weaving our way with care over the tent ropes and the thick pegs that anchored each mushroom to the ground. At this time of year – what I estimated to be late summer and a traditional time for war in this less advanced period of Mars – the earth, which had been bare when Peto and I had made our way up the canal, was covered with thick sage scrub and its fragrance rose up to meet us as we crushed it under our boots.

We hoped to be unobtrusive, and indeed, it seemed as though the camp was settling down for the night. Not far away, figures moved amidst fires and I glimpsed a vehicle rumbling over the scrub and disgorging a contingent of soldiers. Their voices floated across the plain, describing recent skirmishes, and their ornate breastplates glittered in the firelight. I'd always wondered what it would be like to visit the far past, and now I knew.

There was a shout. A great bolt of fire shot outwards from the summit of the tower and struck the ground not far away from us, sending tents hurtling into the sky and spattering Shorn and myself with hot soil. We threw ourselves to the ground just as another bolt came down and gouged a furrow in the earth like some supernatural plough. Mad Mantis was, it seemed, battling back. Cries of fury came from the camp and the vehicle started up again, spinning its wheels in a violent turn and hooting back the way it had come. Cautiously, I looked up, but the tower was again silent and waiting. From across the encampment, there was a noise like a huge snapped wire and something shot through the sky, falling short of the tower – except that I couldn't see how it had done so, given its trajectory. A shimmer of the air around the tower and a fleeting glimpse of a shadowy form suggested that they'd erected haunt-defences. I knew how they'd fought in these distant days: with haunt-tech still in its infancy, each side had sought to inflict the maximum damage on the foe and enrol the deceased casualties for its own war engines: a depressing thought, that you couldn't get free of the army even if you died in the course of your military service.

A vehicle was rumbling back through the encampment: a juggernaut, with the huge ridged tyres that suggested it was for use in the deep desert, further yet than Tharsis. I glimpsed a figure standing in the bubble turret on top of the vehicle, black-clad, her head encased in a helmet that reminded me of a giant insect. She was pointing at the tower. Fire spattered over our heads and Shorn and I ducked.

'Shorn!' I shouted. 'Over there!'

A gully ran alongside the encampment, one of the dry waterways that crossed the Crater Plain. In winter, they were prone to flash floods and I was not enthusiastic about going down there; we kept high on the bank of the gully, slipping and sliding on the loose shale, but heading away from the camp and the fire. A burning figure stumbled in front of me and I cried out, before realizing it was a ghost. A moment later, it was gone. Shorn was shaking. As we followed the twists and turns of the gully, she said, 'We're heading back to the tower.'

'I know. But there's nowhere else to go.' I glanced back to where the gully was blocked with washed-down boulders. It was upstream or nothing.

Shorn said urgently, 'What if Mantis is there? Where did she go?'

'I don't know, Shorn.' I couldn't tell whether she asked out of fright or longing, or perhaps both. 'Did she say anything to you, about moving between times?'

She shook her head. 'She didn't say much about that. Only about what we were.'

There were voices up ahead, speaking low and urgently. Shorn and I crept between the boulders, keeping low. I wasn't even sure whether we could be seen, but I didn't want to take any chances. We drew nearer to the voices.

'Where is she? Where has she gone?' I felt Shorn's cold fingers close around my own and I clasped her hand as we crouched in the lee of a boulder.

'I don't know.'

'They're talking about me,' Shorn hissed.

'You don't know that. I went missing too. Now be quiet.'

The voice was frantic. 'If she's decided to go out there – you know how she is.'

'She's mad, not stupid.'

'There's a difference?'

'She's here.' The voice was strident, and it came from above us. I squinted up to see an armoured figure standing on the summit of the boulder, legs braced. She carried a haunt-bow, which hummed and sang to itself. A black plume fluttered from her helmet, caught by the night breeze, and in the light of the moon her armour was the colour of blood. I could not see her face. She raised the bow. Something spat over the rocks. The second figure in the shadows of the tower cried out and reeled back, clutching at her face. The first speaker melted back into the shadows: a wise move, I thought. This had to be Mantis the Original. She leaped down from the boulder, landing a few feet in front of us. A glance over her shoulder revealed a pair of glinting black eyes in the depths of the helmet, but she gave no indication that she'd seen us. I held Shorn firmly by the arm, all the same. She was skittish enough to do something foolish.

'Matriarch—' the soldier faltered. Mantis walked straight past her and said, 'So, they want a siege, do they? Then let's give them a siege.'

A black gaping hole opened in the side of the tower. A voice, unexpected, said into my ear, 'Go in.' I turned to see the spectral shape of the Library, ghostly pale and insubstantial, by my shoulder.

'You're joking. What for?'

'I've just remembered,' the Library said, 'that there's something in there I want to take a look at.'

Inside, the tower was much as it was in its future incarnation, but with more tapestries. Battles appeared to be a dominant theme, and hunting. But one of them, hanging from floor to ceiling, depicted Earth: a lovely, luminous globe, worked in silver and blue. I saw Mantis's gauntleted hand flick out as she passed it in a gesture that might have been superstition, or might simply have indicated greed. Shorn and I followed her up a flight of stairs, surrounded by her fluttering lieutenants, and into what was evidently some kind of war room. Narrow slits of windows showed fires across the plain.

'This will not do,' Mantis hissed. She turned to the woman on her left, an older, pinched face under a helmet that did not fit properly. 'Why isn't it working?'

'I told you, Mantis.' The woman sounded weary, and I noticed that she hadn't added Mantis's honorific. 'The engine isn't configured properly. It's too old.'

'It's got to work.' Mantis reached up and took off her helmet. She looked, of course, like the woman I'd met, but could have been anywhere from twenty to sixty, all bone and pale parched skin. 'You said you could make it work.' The plaintive tone of a small child with a broken toy, it reminded me of Shorn. I didn't envy the inhabitants of the tower, having this for a commanding officer.

'When we found it, you remember, it was in pieces. We've done well to make it reach the point that it has. I can't do any more.'

'It needs more blood, then,' Mantis insisted. 'Take the captives in the lower dungeon. Feed them into it.'

'More won't mean better,' the lieutenant said. But from the look on Mantis's face, I didn't think she particularly cared.

It was not a process that I liked to watch, but for the sake of the Library we followed Mantis to the engine room. This lay at the heart of the tower, and I thought it might be the cavern that now formed the fighting pit, in which case the engine had long since been dismantled. From the look of the thing, it was Nightshade-made and very old: its sides were pitted and scorched and it still bore the uncanny alphabet of its native world along its sides. A huge thing, blackened, with stumps and spires and wires jutting out from its sides like something assembled by a deranged inventor. It hummed, like Mantis's bow, and unlike most haunt-tech, which had the sense of death, I had the inexplicable impression that it was alive, just as, in some manner, the Library was alive. And with that thought, I turned to the Library herself and mouthed a question.

'Why are we here?'

The Library was staring intently at the engine. She pointed a mailed finger at it, like someone casting a spell, and the engine's hum grew to a sudden roar. Across the room Mantis spun around, open-mouthed. I saw a spark of light flicker from the engine to the Library's finger.

'What did it do then?' Mantis demanded.

'I don't know.' The adviser looked baffled. I shot a glance of enquiry at the Library but her face was intent and preoccupied. Mantis gave an angry shrug and turned away.

'Set them up.'

We watched in silence as three pinch-faced women were brought from the dungeons and strapped into a blacklight matrix: a primitive device by modern standards, bearing great coils and curlicues of ebony and silver wire. A flickering array of circuitry lay behind it, sending spiral messages across its face. The women made no sound as they were strapped in, though their eyes burned as they stared balefully in the direction of Mantis. I wondered why they didn't speak. Perhaps they couldn't.

The matrix crackled into life and at the beginning of the array, the first woman's head snapped backwards, straining against the array. She died quickly; I felt her spirit go into the haunt-engine. The second one took longer and I did not want to watch; I turned away. Mantis seemed to lose interest, and with a click of the fingers left the rest of the work to her advisers. She strode from the chamber and I followed. The Library lingered for a moment, then came behind.

Mantis went upwards, climbing a spiral stair with rapid, clicking steps. She reminded me of a large insect; some kind of ticking wall beetle. As she passed along a narrow corridor, she began stripping off her armour: first the helmet, then the band which confined her hair and made it look as though her forehead was striped with blood, then the breastplate, until when she reached a door at the end of the room she wore only a series of body straps, breeches and boots, rather like an excissiere. Her skin was very pale, almost a luminous blue in the dim light, and looked hard in texture.

A demothea cross-breed. I could believe it, watching her now.

She stepped out into fresh air. The sudden breath of it on my skin was startling, after the confinement of the fortress. I sidled after her, and gasped.

The dreadnought was hanging in the air above the fortress. I'd last seen it sailing over the Noumenon, and before that, careering down the length of the Grand Channel. The faces of the drowning women were still with me, as though the dreadnought carried the souls of its victims with it, like barnacles. Perhaps it did.

It looked exactly the same: beetle-green in the moonlight, with its emplacements dangling and coiling from it, as if whipped by a wind that I couldn't feel. Mantis was shouting something but her words were lost in the roar from the dreadnought.

A ladder was falling down from the bottom of the craft. Mantis ran forward, leaped as it struck the battlements of the turret with a rattle. Down on the plain, someone was firing, but the bolts fell well short of the dreadnought's flanks, harmless as pinpricks from this distance. Mantis seized the base of the ladder and was hauled up into the sky: the dreadnought was already lifting up, blacklight sparkling across its sides and shorting out down the firing path of one of the bolts. Down on the plain, I saw a flicker-burst of darkness and there came a cry.

Above the dreadnought, a crack was opening up in the air. The dreadnought was heading straight for it and it was reaching down to us: this was what it was like to journey through haunt-space, when you're faced with the moment of your death and then falling into it. I'd only done it once, and never between worlds. Behind me, I heard Shorn cry out and realized that she'd joined us on the battlements. There was a flash, so bright that I cast my arm across my eyes, and then I was stumbling. Shorn and I were thrown against the side of the battlements and when I was able to see again, we'd moved. We were still on the summit of the turret, but it was once again ruined. Something was falling down through the afternoon sky, travelling meteor-fast. It was a ship, but it wasn't the dreadnought. It went down behind a spire of rock and I braced myself for an explosion, but none came. There was a thin, high whine and a distant thud, sending up a cloud of dust. I wanted to get off the tower: if we were back in our own time, that meant Mantis and the vulpen weren't far away. I motioned to Shorn and she followed me down the metal-runged ladder that picked its way across the ancient stone. I felt we were going round in circles: up and down, round and round through time, like some nonsensical game. But I was glad all the same when my feet touched rock and the turret once again towered above me. In its lee, with Shorn at my heels, I made my way to the rocks and looked down.

The ship was small, unfamiliar, and bulbous. It sat in a bowl of dust, surrounded by the rocks. I leaned further over and paused. Directly below me stood a figure. Next moment, I grinned. Time to repay a score. I dropped lightly down the few feet that separated the ledges and snapped an arm around the figure's neck. She jerked, but I was holding her fast.

'Surprise!'

Rubirosa sagged slightly in my grip.

'I've been looking for you,' the marauder said. Shorn's timid face appeared over the edge of rock.

'Hestia?'

Rubirosa looked sharply up. 'Who's that?'

'My cousin.'

'Ah.' The marauder's expression grew sharper and my suspicions blossomed into life, like weedwood flowers. 'Wasn't coincidence, was it? You descending on Peto's boat? And I'd put good money on there never having been a bomb.'

It was, it appeared, the marauder's turn to grin. 'Peto's . . . an agent. She wasn't sent to pick you up, though. Took a day or so for her to realize who she'd got on board her boat.'

'An agent? Of whom?'

'Of the Noumenon.'

'Peto?' I'm rarely accused of naïveté, and few things surprised me any more, but that struck me as incongruous, somehow.

'Not a willing one,' Rubirosa said. 'She was coerced. The Noumenon might seem to keep themselves to themselves, but they've got long tentacles and a long reach. When I found out, I came along for the ride.'

'But I saw you fall—' I stopped. I knew better than this. I'd seen someone fall. Rubirosa's knowing smile told me the truth.

'So if you're not a pirate – who are you?'

'Who said I'm not a pirate?' Rubirosa asked. 'I'm for hire. For the moment, I'm working for Gennera Khine.' The shock of that name hit me as though someone had thrown icy water in my face. The marauder was working for Gennera, who had commissioned

Shorn's making, according to my cousin. Had Gennera told Rubirosa about Shorn?

The marauder looked up at Shorn, who had come a little way over the lip of the rock and now stood on a ledge, listening. 'So that's the missing cousin. Looks like you found her.' I couldn't detect anything except mild curiosity in her voice.

'Found a lot else, as well.' I lowered my voice. 'Why didn't you tell me you worked for Gennera?'

'I wanted to see what you'd do,' Rubirosa said. 'Wasn't sure you could be trusted, to be honest. Don't take it personally. Anyway, Gennera's arranged transport. We're going back to Winterstrike.'

'Very well,' I said. I didn't buy her explanation for a moment. It was surely Gennera who didn't trust me, who had sent Rubirosa to spy on her spy. Rubirosa turned and headed for the ship.

'She's working for the majike,' Shorn hissed over my shoulder. 'I heard her say so.'

'Try and trust me,' I said. Shorn wavered, but I gripped her hand. 'I'll get you out of here,' I said. I found I'd made a decision. 'And we're not going back to Winterstrike, either.'

Rubirosa was settling herself into the pilot's seat when I clambered on board the little craft, with Shorn behind me. I struck the marauder once, behind the ear. She crumpled over the console and with Shorn watching, her expression unreadable, I took the ship up and into the hills.

EIGHTEEN

Essegui – Crater Plain

After the Queen's disappearance, I was immediately confined. I spent the evening chafing against the bolted door and picking at the latches of the little window. Halfway through this process, without any warning, we started moving again. It was growing dark, and eventually the lights came on amongst the refugee caravan. My fidgeting with the window latch was finally rewarded by a breath of cold air underneath the pane: I tore at it with my nails until it gave way. Catching the pane before it banged against the sill, I glanced round. There was no sign of Shurr or the others. I hauled myself up onto the sill and squeezed through the window, dropping to the ground. It was further than I expected. I landed with a grunt and a gasp, but the ground was solid underneath my feet; curious how accustomed I'd become to the swaying, shifting vehicle in the short time I'd been incarcerated in it. Still no one, and I ran – but around the corner of the caravan, I came face to face with Shurr.

In the lamplight, her face was a startled mask. I struck out, catching her across the cheek. She stumbled and immediately the ground was a writhing mass as a great centipede dropped out of her sleeve and fell to my feet. It lashed out; a pincer caught my boot and stuck in the leather. I kicked up with the thrashing creature attached to my toe, a pantomime performance. I stamped on its head with my free foot and felt it crush. Shurr gave a howl of fury and rushed forward, her veil billowing out behind her. I snatched at the veil and twisted it in my hands, pulling her further in. Then I dodged her strike and whipped the veil around her neck, throttling her until her hands went up and clawed.

I'd never strangled anyone before and this must have presented a lurid tableau: the vehicle rumbling on, Shurr crumpling to the icy ground, myself curved above her and the centipede still palely thrashing in its death throes. When Shurr had gone limp – not dead, but unconscious – I tore the veil from her head, wrapped it into a bundle and ran in earnest, heading for the canal bank and what I hoped might be freedom. No chance of asking anyone to take me in: I was too obviously from Winterstrike and I thought the Caudi refugees might take advantage of the presence of an enemy scapegoat in their midst.

I stumbled down the bank, at first trying to avoid the barges that were moored along the water's edge, but further upstream decided to take a risk and struck out onto the canal itself. The water traffic was so thick at this point that the boats formed a bridge over the canal; I thought I might have a better chance of escape if I took to the opposite bank. I wrapped the brown veil about myself: if anyone saw me, they might take me for a servant of the Queen, or at least, might not recognize the alien garment.

The journey across the canal seemed to take for ever: a cold breeze blew down from shattered Caud, smelling of gunpowder and ice and making the lamps rock so that reflections splintered across the surface of the water. I could do this, I tried to tell myself. I'd survived two attempts on my life and a kidnapping. I wasn't just the sheltered child of Calmaretto. *Hestia* could do this sort of thing. And maybe Shorn already had.

I avoided those boats that might be fitted with alarms, keeping instead to the poorer-looking craft. I saw few people moving about on deck: most were huddling in the shelter of their cabins, and that suited me. I crawled, clung, leaped across the barges for an hour or more, until the lamps of the refugee train grew dimmed by the rising mist and the further shore swam up ahead. When I jumped down from the last barge onto the opposite bank, and clambered up the steep stone barricade to the land above, I realized what I had done. I had left both Caud and Winterstrike behind and ahead lay the lands of the Plains, and then the hills of the Noumenon. The geise whispered in my head. I thought of my missing sister, took a breath, and walked on.

By mid-morning, I was a long way from the Grand Channel, though not far enough to satisfy my longing for safety. The ground was rising, giving a sweeping view back over the plain, and the icy rubble was broken up by great boulders, lacy spires and pillars of rock, legacies of early terraforming when this land had been nano-blasted into submission. Ahead, the mountains were visible, and I remembered a superstition that a governess of ours had once told me: *All things go to the mountains. Everything ends up there*. And now, it seemed as though I would, too.

Whereas the Hattins, the foothills, were a relatively low range, these mountains, the Saghair, were immense, roaring up into a green sky. The rocks were the colour of flame, and underneath my feet, between patches of snow, the sand was red as rust. Once, all Mars had been like this, until the alchemical transformation wrought upon it by Earth had changed it to the shades that now dappled its surface.

A buzzing sound, almost subliminal, brought my attention towards the horizon. Something was coming, a dark dot just above the skyline. I ran for the rocks, crouching down in a crack between two of the tumbled boulders. Seconds later, the thing roared overhead: an excissiere craft, needle-narrow, but with no indication of whether it came from Caud or Winterstrike. I didn't care to chance it. I kept my head down, hoping they weren't looking for me, and the craft was gone, twisting down over the mountains. The reverberation left by its passing echoed among the rocks for a moment and then all trace of it had disappeared.

How much power did the Queen's retinue possess, here on Mars? It wasn't something I wanted to test. I stayed between the rocks for a quarter of an hour, and then when I was quite sure that the vessel wasn't coming back, I went on my way.

There was a track leading up into the jagged rocks of the foothills. At first it wasn't clear to me that it really was a road: it was nothing more than scuffs in the dirt, something that could have been made by an off-road vehicle. Then, a little way on, the soil thinned out to reveal tarmac. It looked old, pitted and pock-marked and scoured by wind and ice. The geise shivered in my head when I laid eyes on it, making the back of my neck prickle. As I walked along it, I started to feel that I was walking out of my own time, into the far past: if I had seen an early spacesuited set-tler, from the days before terraforming, I would not have been at all surprised.

The road wound up into the mountains. I looked back once, to see the empty plain stretching out behind. The masts of the boats that thronged the canal were needle-small. So I kept walk-ing.

City girls don't hunt. I wish I could tell you that I'd proved myself in those hills: made a makeshift bow, brought down some small but nutritious vermin. But I couldn't find any suitable pieces of scrub for making a weapon or a trap, and I didn't see any vermin anyway. I just got hungrier and colder as the day wore on and I began to think that it might have been wiser, after all, to take my chances with a band of Caudi refugees, or to have braved it out with the entourage of the Centipede Queen. My mothers should have hired an excissiere to find Shorn, not me. And as if thinking about her had conjured her up, I saw Alleghetta again. This time, she was very faint indeed and wore different clothes: her dressing wrap. She shouted something.

'I can't hear you!'

Alleghetta looked distractedly around and vanished. Stay that way, I thought.

I did manage to find water, though I had to break ice to reach it, and to light a fire with the sparkpack I used for lighting the old-fashioned lamps in the bell tower. I missed the tower: somehow, over the years, it had become more of a home than Calmaretto. I wished I too had been able to simply disappear, just as Shorn had.

Moments later, I wished it even harder.

The voices floated through the air like moths. I hid in the rocks as soon as I heard them, trying to tell whether they were coming closer. But it sounded as though the speakers were somewhere up ahead, and in one place. Cautiously, I made my way through the boulders until I could gain a vantage point.

There were four of them, and three were ghosts. They were truly spectral – I could see the rocks through their robes, which drifted in a wind I could not feel – but motionless, unlike the weir-wards of houses, which are almost always moving. Their clothes suggested that they were from the Noumenon itself: robes of fawn and grey and black, like the old illustrations I'd seen in books. One of them was human, or appeared so: she was, at least, more substantial than the rest. She wore armour, a leather harness, which flickered. I thought she might be an excissiere, but she wore no identifying emblems. She was speaking in animated tones, gesturing, but I wasn't close enough to hear what she was saying.

One of the ghosts, a tall woman in grey, shifted restlessly. She spoke in turn, pointing towards the mountain ridge that lay ahead of us. Here, if I had got my directions right, lay the Noumenon.

They turned and began walking. I hesitated, then followed. They were, at least, likely to lead me to where I wanted to go. Yet they were ghosts, and the woman moved with a lithe stride that suggested danger to me; she was clearly armed. And there was something familiar about her . . .

The armed woman stopped and paused. She pointed, into the sky. Concealed behind an outcrop, I couldn't at first see what she was gesturing at. Then I noticed a tiny speck against the mountain wall, twisting and turning as it descended. It was coming in fast: seconds later it resolved itself into a familiar shape. It was the dreadnought that had stolen away the Centipede Queen.

NINETEEN

Hestia — Crater Plain

Rubirosa's armour was cumbersome at first, but I rapidly got used to it. In the old days, so I'd heard, haunt-armour was haunted indeed, but this simply whispered to itself, then fell silent, as I stripped it from its mistress and put it on. Then Shorn and I strapped the unconscious marauder to a passenger chair.

'What if you don't come back?' Shorn asked. 'I never learned to fly a ship.'

'If I don't come back,' I said, 'then it's over for both of us. Give me three hours. After that — make your own way, Leretui. I'll have done what I can.'

After a moment, she nodded. 'Fair enough.' I left her staring dubiously at Rubirosa and left the ship. I hoped she wouldn't take it into her head to do anything drastic while I was gone, like dispatching Rubirosa. It wasn't that I had *feelings* for the marauder, I told myself. She'd be a valuable source of information, that was all. I was trying not to think about Gennera, aware of how far I'd already crossed the line. Shorn might not have been telling the truth, after all, but I'd gone ahead and acted on it anyway. If what Shorn had said was true, I'd have gained a lot of kudos from turning her in to Gennera.

Fuck that, I thought. I might have a duty, but Shorn was my

cousin and Gennera had distrusted me enough to send a spy after me.

Besides, I needed to know what was going on: who, or what, Mantis really was. Who had engineered the attack on the Noumenon. What the weapon was that I'd delivered from Caud. I was sick and tired of acting from ignorance. So, moving fast in my borrowed armour, I headed towards Mantis's turret. I kept expecting to turn and see the Library striding alongside: I missed her. I wondered whether we'd left her marooned in the past, or whether temporality had any meaning for someone who wasn't even real in the first place. But the sky was starting to darken over the mountains, highlighting the faint lamps of the Noumenon and causing the column of smoke that still spiralled up from the chasm of the city to become thinly etched against the clouds. I was still high up, climbing through rocks that looked as though they'd never known terraforming.

And there was the turret of Temperire ahead. Three hours, I'd promised Shorn, and it might be a promise I could keep. I didn't want to be another one who'd let Shorn down, but I might have to, even so.

On that fateful night of Ombre, I had not been in Winterstrike, but down in the south, near Tharsis. But I hadn't tried to rescue Shorn either, although I'd tried to negotiate with my aunts, who had proved predictably obstinate. Alleghetta was furious about the council post, of course, and in any case disinclined to listen to me. Talking things through wasn't the same as getting the girl out of there, however. It struck me again with some force that what I might actually have done was to save Shorn from the wrong enemy. *Mantis has been kind to me.* I repressed a shiver.

Whatever the situation, it had left me with a spy mistress whom I could no longer trust. I could have felt betrayed, but instead I felt like a free agent for the first time in a decade, and now Temperire was towering over me again, the haunt-armour revealing flickering shapes along its ruined battlements. I headed for the rocks around its base and hoped the haunt-armour would protect me.

At least our previous adventures had given me some idea of the layout. I avoided the lower reaches of the turret, vulpen-thronged as they were, and headed back up the stairs. The haunt-armour kept talking to itself, murmuring and muttering, occasionally tingeing my vision with crimson flashes. It unnerved me until I realized that the armour was trying to mesh itself into the haunt-arrays of the turret itself, rendering me unseen, and then I was grateful. I had no idea whether it had achieved it, however, when it finally fell silent.

By this time we were on an upper landing, close to the chamber where I'd found Shorn. I could hear conversation and drew closer.

'She's scared,' Mantis was saying. 'You can't blame her.'

'You need to find her.' An unfamiliar voice, deeper than Mantis's, and weirdly accented.

'Of course I need to find her,' Mantis snapped. 'For her own sake. If our maker catches up with her, she'll be put back in a laboratory. Don't you think I don't know what that's like?'

'I know you know.' The voice, caressing, sympathetic. And I thought to myself, without understanding how I knew: *that's a male voice*. I edged closer to the chamber door and looked through the crack.

Mantis was sitting on the bed, straight-backed, like a skin-and-bone doll in her leather harness. Her coiling hair was tightly braided and haunt-energy flickered over her skin like lightning. I'd seen her as an ancient warrior, and also as one of the Changed, and now I saw her for the first time as an excissiere. Whatever Gennera had done to her – if she had – she'd been designed as a warrior.

A vulpen sat at her feet. It – *he* – wore a billowing black robe, pooling out over the floor like ink. All hollows and shadows, I thought, almost too fascinated to feel repelled. Almost. His head was more like a beaked skull, as though the engineers of the Changed had decided to dispense with the soft flesh, paring down to edge and blade. His long fingers held Mantis's hand, gripping tight, their curving nails meshing together.

Lost children, and deadly.

'Have you spoken to the Queen?' the vulpen said, and my ears pricked up.

'Not yet. She'll be a valuable ally if I can persuade her to join us.'

The vulpen hissed. 'I told you. Why are you wasting your time with her? She's not the same as us: she is many, we are one.'

'She has a matriarchy of her own. She is Changed, so are we.' Mantis sounded stubborn.

'Her kind have always gone their own way. Besides, they're not even Martian.'

Mantis said stiffly, 'She came here to find us, didn't she? She came after Leretui.'

'She came to take her back to Earth. Your Gennera experiments on demotheas. So does the Queen. Why else are her people hiding in the marshes of Ropa, looking for your kindred?'

'Looking for alliances, I'm sure.'

'Mantis – you are so loyal,' the vulpen said, and there was definite affection in his voice. 'You believe we're all the same, that we can all be one happy clan.'

'I think we can,' Mantis insisted.

I hadn't moved, but Mantis's head went up all the same.

'What was that?'

Time for me to go, I thought. I slid away from the door. The haunt-armour kicked in at once, whispering advice. There was a room around the corner, in which I could hide. I wasn't going to turn down free information. I dodged behind the door as Mantis and the vulpen strode by, and then I made my way out of the turret and into the night.

Ropa. That was on Earth, one of the drowned western conti-
nents. A long way from Malay – because I had no doubt that the
Queen to whom Mantis had referred was the Centipede Queen
herself. And it had sounded as though Mantis had access to her:
was she out on the Plains still, or here in the tower?

When I got back to the ship, I found that Rubirosa had
regained consciousness but not her freedom. And even though I'd
locked the craft up, Shorn was nowhere to be seen.

'Oh, it's you,' Rubirosa said, very sour. 'Any chance of setting
me free?'

She'd obviously been trying to escape her bonds, from the
state of her wrists. I grinned.

'I don't think so. Where's Shorn?'

'I don't know. She was speaking to someone, in the back. I
couldn't hear what she was saying. Then she got the door lock
open and bolted. I don't suppose it would be too much trouble
to give me my armour back?'

'Yes, it would. Sorry.'

'Look,' she said. 'There's something you'd better know. When
I told you about Gennera, I wasn't being entirely honest.'

'There's a surprise.'

'Gennera thinks I'm working for her.'

'And are you? She sent you to spy on me, didn't she?'

'Yes. But I'm reporting back to someone who's watching her.
Someone in the Matriarchy.'

'And who would that be?'

'Her name's Sulie Mar.'

'My *mother*?'

'Your mother's a powerful woman, Hestia.'

'I'm not doubting that,' I said. 'I didn't think she was that
worried about me.'

Rubirosa snorted. 'She's not worried about *you*. You were inci-
dental to all this. She's worried about what Gennera's up to.'

'You can prove this, can you?'

'Talk to your mother.'

'I will.'

'And in exchange, how about some information from you?'

'Very well. Gennera's been breeding demotheas,' I said.

'What? They don't exist.' Her look of surprise could be genuine, or it could not.

'It seems I just left you locked up with one.' I hesitated. 'How would you like a trip to Earth, Rubirosa?'

'I think you'd better explain,' she said.

So I did.

Interlude: Shurr — Mars

Segment Three was nipping at her wrist. She felt a sudden cool surge through her body, memories and images flooding in along with antiseptics, rejuvenators, anti-spasmodics, as the bioengineered segment did its medicinal work.

'Shurr! Are you all right?'

She raised her head. The Martian sky wheeled above her and the odours of sage and cold came as a shock. The wagon stood a short distance away and her companions crouched by her side. The Queen was not among them. They were alone on the plain; the refugee convoy had moved on.

'The woman – Essegui—'

'She's fled,' Mhor said.

'She attacked me,' Shurr said, sitting up. She was aware of an all-encompassing sense of failure. 'Ghuan—'

'Ghuan is dead. We'll grow another one,' her companion, Mhor, said reassuringly. She put out a hand and lightly touched Shurr's head.

'But the Queen—'

'There's been a message. Come inside.' Mhor helped her to rise and led her back inside the wagon. The Queen's perfume hung heavily in the air: Shurr might almost believe that she was still there. The pheromone-enhanced scent soothed her.

'Sit,' Mhor instructed. Shurr did so, and Segment Three slid onto her lap. Shurr held out her wrist and the centipede bit. The Queen appeared, superimposed over the empty couch, and smiling.

'Shurr. If you live. I hope so. Don't come after me. Our enemies have found me now, but don't be concerned. They won't hurt me and even if they do, I have left instructions at the palace. A new queen's being grown.' The Queen leaned forward, her beautiful, empty face compassionate. 'Don't be angry with me, Shurr. I'm where I need to be.'

Then she faded, shimmering against the air. Shurr made a small, inarticulate sound and immediately Mhor was there, an arm around her shoulders. Segment Three coiled about her wrist.

'She's left instructions,' Mhor said. 'She's recruited locally, she said. We're to return to Earth without her.'

'But—'

'All will be well.' Mhor's face was serene, but Shurr could not sustain that level of faith, even though she knew it to be a betrayal.

'They're not like us,' Mhor said, when she voiced this thought. 'They work from a different perspective.'

'I know that, but all the same—'

'You know the Queen isn't as you see her,' Mhor said. 'Remember, when the old Queen died?'

And Shurr did remember, how could she not: the lovely face and perfect body cracking open, the shell breaking to reveal the mass of squirming symbiotes within, tiny organisms except for the massive central spine. Remembering how Khant had reverently picked up the fragments of the spine as it came apart, placing each one in frozen stasis apart from the pincered head with its faceted diamond eyes, the processing core which would form the memories of the new Queen.

'We're here to do their bidding,' Mhor said, with only the slightest hint of reproof.

'I know.' And Shurr was a little more content then, though a trickle of forbidden thoughts tugged at the very edges of her mind: who put us in thrall to this organism, this hive mind? Where does it come from? Did it evolve, or was it made, or did it come – as she had heard whispered – from the far stars? But those thoughts were not permitted and they soon faded, like dreams, or like the smiling image of the Queen herself, gone into the shadows of the alien day.

TWENTY

Essegui – Crater Plain

There wasn't time to run, from where I was hiding amongst the boulders. The ship glided over us, coming low, just as it had over the Caud refugee camp. I felt, impossibly, my shadow snatched by the shadow of the dreadnought, as though it was a physical extension of my own body. I was pulled in its wake, like someone caught in a riptide. I had a swimming, incoherent view of the landscape below me, then a moment of blackness as if I'd passed out, though I didn't think I had. My feet touched metal and I staggered back against a wall, banging my elbow. The pain gave me clarity. I was in a hold, a huge arching chamber beneath metal struts like the ribcage of some mechanical beast. My elbow hurt but this wasn't all: my soul felt bruised, as if it had been beaten with some unnatural hammer, and even the geise seemed to crouch, whimpering, in a corner of my mind. At the end of the chamber, a wind was roaring in and I saw the tips of the red mountains, parallel with the doorway: we were rising. The floor tilted as the ship lurched, sending me onto my knees; I grasped at a strut and only just stopped myself from rolling out of the hatch. Steely fingers closed around my wrist. I tried to wrench my hand away and failed. I looked up and to my horror Mantis was standing over me. Something stung my arm and the world blurred. Mantis said something I didn't understand, but I suspected it was: *You're coming with me.*

In the cell, I passed the time by counting the number of people who had now attempted to kidnap me. So far, I made it about a dozen, including the excissiere who now sat hunched on a chair outside the cell, filing nails that were more akin to talons. Occasionally she glanced up, rarely in my direction, apparently focusing on something I could not see and speaking to someone I could not hear. Spirits, or something in her head? Impossible to say. I asked for water and was ignored. Eventually one of the red-robed women came in and spoke in a low voice to the warrior, who rose and strode out. I was left alone in the cell, but not for long.

'Essegui Harn?' someone said. I spun around. Another ghost stood behind me in the cell: a woman with a flayed, grinning face. The image was so ghastly I took a step back.

'I'm a friend of your cousin's,' said this thing. 'I'm the Library.'

'Sorry?'

'Hestia?' the ghost said, patiently. 'Your cousin? We met in Caud. I tagged along.' She tried to look self-deprecating and failed.

'What *are* you?'

'Well,' the ghost said, sitting down on the bench that served as a bed. 'Technically speaking, I'm not the whole Library. I'm a particular archive. Don't need to go into that now.'

'So what's an archive and a friend of my cousin doing here? And what is this thing we're in?'

'It's a relic. Like me, I suppose. Have you heard of Mantis the Mad?'

'I've met her.'

'She used to be a figment of fairy stories. In the country districts, people used her to frighten their kids. They were right. This is her ship.'

'But she can't be that old.'

The Library inclined her ravaged head. 'She's a clone. I met the first version, long ago.'

'But you said you were a Library.'

The Library frowned. 'Yes, and yet, I have memories . . . Mantis and I were contemporaries. I think.'

'Caud wasn't more than a – what? A settlement, at that point?'

'Caud *started* as a library,' the warrior said. 'A building in the secret hills, holding texts rescued from the cities of the plain when society began breaking down.'

'I'd never heard that.' I shot a look at the chamber beyond the cell. The stanchions bore the metal faces of demons, only subtle distortions from the faces of the Changed themselves, probably a superstitious attempt to protect the ship from whatever waited for it in haunt-space. I couldn't even remember whether they'd had haunt-tech in Mantis's day.

'So why are you here? What have you got to do with Mantis?'

'A vested interest,' the Library said. Her image flickered. 'Your cousin's in trouble.'

'You know what Hestia's doing?' Realizing that the Library might in some way be connected with my cousin made my spirits rise.

'Yes.' A grim smile. 'You're closer than you know. Mantis has gone after her. And so has the one who's after Mantis.'

'What?' But then the dreadnought shuddered under my feet and I realized we'd changed course. I had a sudden dizzying sense that the huge ship had plummeted.

'Excuse me,' the Library said. 'I've got things to do.' And she was gone into thin air. But not before she'd reached out and opened the door of the cell.

I fled through it before anyone had a chance to come back and stop me. Running through the corridors of the ship was itself like travelling through some ancient castle: Mantis must have found it a home from home. Everything was of a dull burnished metal, rimmed with rust. That didn't inspire me with confidence: it seemed all too likely that the ship might simply disintegrate if put under too much strain. The twisted faces of the demons stared out at me from every corner, making it seem as if I moved through a haunt-infested realm. After a while I stopped noticing them.

This particular bay of the ship had, unexpectedly, a viewport. It was rimed with frost and heavily stained, but I could look out through its small bulbous eye and see the mountains swinging below. That city – clinging to its steep cliffs above a snaking river – must be the Noumenon. Then the ship veered up and I saw a little craft shoot out from below the curving side. I thought of the Library: was that my cousin in there?

'Hestia,' I whispered. But I didn't want to risk discovery while I was gazing out of the viewport. Then the geise twinged inside my head, making my hands go to my forehead. I leaned, panting, back against the wall, then glanced out of the viewport again. The little ship was gone and we were moving away from the Noumenon, the city falling behind as the dreadnought glided out into the red sunlight. The Crater Plain stretched beneath and I saw Olympus reaching up into the aquamarine sky.

Around the corner, I caught up with Mantis again. She was bending over a console, a thing like a bronze pedestal, growing out of the floor. Hiding behind a stanchion, I could see what looked like an early version of a map array flickering over the surface of the console, and realized that Mantis was punching in coordinates. Seen from this viewpoint, her angular frame reminded me somewhat of the gaezelles of the Crater Plain: knobbed vertebrae along the curving spine.

The ship was descending. I didn't know whether we were coming down onto the Plain itself, or whether we had turned back. I wished the Library would return, my only objective source of information. And then I felt something tickling my wrist. I jerked, almost betraying my presence: Mantis's veiled head snapped up to stare in the direction of the stanchion, but then she turned back to the console. I looked down at the tiny thing looped around my wrist. It was a centipede.

TWENTY-ONE

Hestia — Noumenon

I looked towards the place where the Noumenon lay: at the ghostly houses with their spectral occupants, at the column of smoke rising into the morning sky and at the still-dim expanse of cold land into which my cousin had vanished.

My mother had confirmed Rubirosa's story. Over the antiscribe, her face was as cold and carved as ever, and I couldn't help wondering whether there was all that much to choose between Gennera and Sulie. But she'd got us passage out, and for the moment I could live with that.

The launch site itself was on a high spire of rock, perhaps natural, perhaps not. It was reached by a bridge, strung on pylons that reached horizontally from the walls of the gorge so that the bridge looked as fragile and frail as a spider's web. It reminded me of the bridge that led to the tower in the heart of Winterstrike, where Essegui tolled the festival bell. I eyed it with unease.

'Conspicuous.'

'It's early,' Rubirosa said. 'And the Noumenon has other things on its mind.'

'That isn't reassuring,' I said. 'They wanted me enough to threaten Peto, didn't they?' And send haunts out across the Plain, though I wasn't sure yet whether that could be pinned at the

Noumenon's door. And had they been after me because of my connections to Gennera, or Calmaretto, or my mother?

'This isn't a Noumenon outpost,' Rubirosa said. 'It's neutral.'

'I've heard that before.' From the look on her face, Rubirosa didn't believe her own words either.

Early it may have been, but there was still traffic going out across the bridge: a delivery truck sending cargo out by air, a long car marked with the insignia of one of the southern matriarchies, with tinted windows and florid trim. We crossed the bridge on a sidewalk; I looked down once, to see the chasm falling away below into a dizzying precipice, as yet untouched by the light of the sun. Where was Shorn now, in all that dappled land? And was she where she wanted to be?

At the far end of the bridge was a guardpost, decorated in the unnecessarily ornate manner of a couple of hundred years before. A pair of attenuated statues stood on either side of the doors.

'I've arranged things,' Rubirosa said. 'On your mother's instructions.'

'You bribed someone?'

'I see you're commendably familiar with the customs of your society.'

When we reached the guardpost, a bored woman was sitting slumped over a popular novel, read out in a dreary voice from her antiscribe.

'I spoke to you earlier,' Rubirosa said, producing a slip from her pocket.

'Oh, yes.' The woman brightened imperceptibly. She had a typical mountain peasant's countenance, at once narrow and flat, not unlike the faces of the Noumenon and yet clearly different. She held out a docket and Rubirosa inserted the slip. A minute later, we were through onto the little concourse and the tones of the antiscribe were once more reading out romance behind us.

From this angle, through the tall windows of the port, the

Noumenon was visible: I could even see the canal and the gate-house through which Peto and I had come. I didn't like being so close to the shadow city, not after that attack. When it became clear that we would have a short wait before the craft arrived, I borrowed the little 'scribe from Rubirosa and checked the news. Caud had attacked the Noumenon, if one believed the Winterstrike newsfeeds. What the hell? I thought. Why would Caud do such a thing, preoccupied with the war with Winterstrike as they were? Reading the Caudi press, it was of course the other way around – *Winterstrike* had attacked the Noumenon, they claimed.

As if we didn't have enough to contend with. And I kept wondering about the weapon I'd found in Caud; what had that been, and where had it come from? Even worse, what had it actually *done?*

A roar from outside the concourse told us that the ship was coming in. We headed for it. I hoped they'd let us board quickly; if there were excissieres about, I didn't fancy hanging around.

Then, when we got outside into the chilly day, I realized I'd been wise to be vigilant. There were two excissieres out there already, weapons drawn, watching the craft come down. We ducked back behind a pillar.

'They're not from Winterstrike,' I said. I didn't recognize the armour. As we watched, they were joined by a smaller figure in a grey robe.

Rubirosa turned a red-eyed gaze to me. 'Do you know who they are?'

'No.'

'Well, I think that woman is from the Noumenon.'

'How do you know that?'

Rubirosa looked modestly at the ground. 'Because some of them were after me.'

'I have news for you,' I told her. 'They still are.'

The excissiere was sprinting across the landing strip, taking huge strides as her exo-armour carried her along. Wounds flickered as she ran and she fired without breaking pace. A piece of the column next to my head broke off and splintered to the ground. The ship was now down. Rubirosa's arm went up and she fired in return, a red bolt of energy, but the excissiere dived below the bolt and it struck a long-faced statue on the face of the concourse. The statue rocked for a moment, as if thinking about things, then crashed to the floor.

'Lock on!' Rubirosa commanded her armour, and handed me her gun. I went down on one knee and fired, shearing the excissiere across the knees. Like the statue, she fell, toppling slowly forward.

'Well done,' the marauder said, sounding somewhat surprised. Dodging, we raced across the plaza in the direction of the ship. I heard shouts and found myself face to face with one of the excissiere's colleagues as we came around the side of the vehicle. I dispatched her before she had time to do anything serious. Then I sprang up onto the landing ledge and into the vehicle. It was unpiloted, a remote array flickering out of sight as we boarded.

It wasn't like anything we had in Winterstrike, although the controls were similar: manual control panels and a haunt-array, very finely decked out in golden lace wire.

'Can you fly this thing?' Rubirosa shouted behind me.

'I can try. What about you?'

'Don't know,' the marauder murmured. She peered at the control panels. I slammed the landing hatch shut behind us.

'See if there's anyone else in here. I don't want one of them springing out of a closet.'

Rubirosa disappeared into the back of the craft and I touched the manual array. We shot upwards. The landing strip, with a small host of scurrying figures, disappeared behind us. I had a dizzying view of the Noumenon below as we hurtled up past the buildings on the cliff wall. I even saw the mooring, outlined in lamplight, but we were already too high and it was too dark for me to glimpse the barge.

There was an exclamation from Rubirosa. I checked the navigational array, saw something vast drift into electronic view. The dreadnought was back. I experienced a sudden image, almost a visionary flash, of Mantis's face at the controls.

I heard someone shouting, 'Turn around! *Turn around!*', realized it was myself. My hands touched the array and the little ship swung.

The shadow cast by the dreadnought glided over us; it was like being swallowed. Then, looking at the navigational data, I understood the truth: the dreadnought had veered and was coming after us.

Moments later, Rubirosa was at my elbow. 'Must have realized we're on board.'

'Can we outrun her?'

'We can try,' Rubirosa said, dubiously. We were out of the cleft now and rising. The curve of the world rimmed the distant plains: both the Grand Channel and the cut-off were visible, paths of silver light. At the horizon's edge, the sky shone blue in the oncoming Martian day. The haunt-array was flickering now, trying to grab my attention as we edged atmosphere. But I could see that we had interspace capability on this squat little craft and the dreadnought, still in pursuit, was nonetheless falling behind: an insect shadow far below.

'Let's see what we've got,' I said to Rubirosa, and kicked the haunt-array into action.

Interlude: Shorn

She hadn't recognized him, down there in the unhuman crowds of the pit, but somehow she had known he was there, known he would come. Her flight with Hestia had been a reaction to it, a last-ditch attempt to salvage Leretui from Shorn, but she'd known at the last that it wouldn't work. Hestia would take her back to

Winterstrike, whatever she claimed, and turn her in. Back to Calmaretto, back to her mothers, back to oppression.

So while Hestia was gone, Shorn had worked the lock of the ship and run, back into the failing day, and as soon as her feet touched the stony soil she'd realized it had been the right thing to do. She reached the tower a short while after that, almost gasping with relief, and found Mantis in an upper chamber.

'I've come back,' Shorn said, and to her own ears her voice sounded stronger, different.

Mantis wheeled around and her gaunt face lit up. 'Shorn!'

'She was family,' Shorn said. 'But I chose to go. I chose not to stay.'

'I'm so happy to see you,' Mantis said. She drew Shorn towards the window. 'Where did you go?'

'The past. I saw you there.'

Mantis's eyes widened. 'The past?'

'What *is* this place?' Shorn whispered.

'It's not the place,' Mantis said, smiling. 'It's you. You are a door, Shorn, and also a key. Like me.'

'I don't understand,' Shorn said.

'Not yet. You're too young. You're only just starting to understand what you can do.' Mantis stroked her hair. 'Look, Shorn.' She opened the window. The same scene as before – the high peaks under the dying light, the glitter of stars and snow – but now that Shorn had chosen it, it felt like home.

'What am I looking for?' Shorn asked.

Mantis pointed. 'Out there, across the Crater Plain, lies Winterstrike. We were made there.'

'I was born there,' Shorn agreed.

'I meant, the Changed. In the laboratories of Winterstrike, at the beginning of the Age of Children. We were supposed to be the inheritors of the human race. And now look at us. Clinging to ruined towers and ruined temples like vermin.'

'But the Matriarchy rules Winterstrike now,' Shorn said. 'What are we to do about it?'

And Mantis replied, 'Take it back.'

Later that night, Shorn sat on the edge of her bed, waiting. Mantis had said little more after that, remarking only that Shorn needed to rest. She'd been grateful to be left alone. She felt strange, as if something was expanding inside her skin, a sensation like the cramp you sometimes feel in the calf of your leg, as if you need to stretch and stretch. As if something was trying to get out.

And her vision seemed odd as well, sometimes darkening until she could barely see, sometimes flashing so brightly that Shorn cried out and put her hand to her eyes. The room looked different after it, unfamiliar angles and dimensions, with furniture that did not belong there imposed upon it like a holographic image. Shorn blinked and the room was as before. She looked down at her hands. They looked the same – the thin fingers and pointed nails – but they did not feel familiar. Shorn stared at her hands for a long time, until she heard the door open.

She didn't need to turn around.

'It's you,' she said. There was no reply, and at last she did turn, and saw the vulpen. His robes were blood-red. The skull-face gleamed in the moonlight that fell through the window. She thought of Canal-the-Less, the long curve, and stepped forward. In her head, she was skating swiftly, and he came to join her. Inside her body, something alien flexed and stirred. There was the taste of blood in her mouth. Her jawbone creaked and she felt a sudden pain in the bones of her face. The vulpen smiled, displaying sharp teeth.

'Shorn.'

She put her hand to her mouth and it came away red. The vulpen bent his head and his tongue flicked out, licking. Canal-the-Less was gone: her mind was filled with a memory of a dark burrow, something moving inside it, writhing. She felt her spine bend and arch. And Leretui was gone.

TWENTY-TWO

Hestia — haunt-space

The haunt-array of our stolen craft howled into activation as soon as I touched. We were beyond the atmosphere now, Mars lying below, the dreadnought dimly visible as a speck of shadow far beneath us. Ahead loomed the maw of the Chain, linking Mars with Earth via the Eldritch Realm. The spines of its inner workings looked unpleasantly like teeth.

The marauder leaned over my shoulder. 'Ever done this before?'

'On simulations. What about you?' This last may have been uttered at rather higher volume than I'd intended.

'Once or twice. Better let me take over.' Rubirosa's hands flickered over the console, making adjustments as we grew closer to the Chain.

'I hope you know what you're doing,' I said.

'So do I.'

A woman appeared on the far side of the cabin, hair streaming, dressed in a long white robe that looked somehow wet. She was revolving, slowly.

'Altitude: 700 and rising. Temperature: minus 120. Minutes to Chain entry: nine. Navigational coordinates remain unplanned.

I am requested that you submit navigational coordinates immediately, for relay to Earth-station seven.'

'Request denied,' Rubirosa snapped. 'Can't you get rid of her? That sound's getting on my nerves.'

It was true that our on-board system was accompanied by a subliminal moaning, often a defect in older haunt-systems. I flicked a switch and the ghost vanished.

'Much better.'

'Except that they probably will start firing unless we tell them who we are and where we're going.'

'Aren't there any priors?' Rubirosa asked.

'Well, have a look.'

She starting running through the flight records, examining a host of destinations, none of which made any sense to me.

'These are all on Earth,' she said. 'Your mother must have set this up.'

'We can't just—' I started to say, but then the array fluttered and I saw something remarkably large coming into view off the starboard bow. It made the dreadnought look like a dinghy. Rubirosa's mouth fell open.

'What the hell's that?'

I didn't have a clue, but it was coming towards us at a rate of knots, slamming round the small crescent of Phobos. Flower-bursts of light showed around its perimeter and a moment later, our little ship rocked.

'They're firing!' Rubirosa sounded more offended than anything else. There was a watery gleam across the cabin and the manifestation of our haunt-array was back. This time, her face was bloodied.

'Damage sustained to arc-side stabilizers,' she said. The wailing which had previously accompanied her was now considerably more pronounced.

'Chain security,' Rubirosa proclaimed.

'That's it,' I said. 'We're leaving.' I punched in the first of the destination codes and we shot towards the Chain.

When you travel through haunt-space, you die. I can't say it doesn't hurt. It's like having the air torn from your lungs, the breath snatched from your mouth. All moisture flees: you are desiccated, mummified. Catch a glimpse of yourself on the journey and you will see your own nightmare self, eyes wide and staring, hair astream, hands clawed. I gather it's fashionable to do this, among certain social circles. Mine wasn't one of them.

Rubirosa and I watched our own swift demise in the reflective window of the viewport as the array hurled us into hauntspace. Since neither of us were trained pilots in this particular realm, all we could do was remain in our chairs, paralysed, dead, as the aftergone of the Eldritch Realm swirled around us. We shot through entire histories: mutant faces from the Memnos Matriarchy and the Age of Children, hands clawing at the sides of our craft as we passed by, beings striding beyond the perimeters of vision, unguessable, unknown. Sometimes, I knew, they became weary of the constant transgression and seized a ship: there were a lot of lost vessels in haunt-space. But we were not one of them. With a shudder and a gasp and a cry we hurtled out of the other end of the Chain. Rubirosa and I were reanimated under Earth's moon and Earth lay below.

As we reappeared, so did the representation of the array. She emerged with a shriek, spinning wildly. Her limbs were contorted and blood arced out into the air, to spatter through me. I didn't need her presence to tell me that the ship was in trouble. Earth swung up below, a wheeling azure ball. A scatter of lights skeined down darkside. Rubirosa swore.

'Moonstation requesting add-on destination codes!' the array shrieked, and tore her hair.

'At this rate,' Rubirosa unnecessarily informed me, 'we might as well give them all of them. Since we'll be coming down in bits.'

'We need to head for Ropa. My mother should have sent the coordinates through.'

I was still trying to process everything that Sulie had said to me and it didn't make easy processing. *Go to Earth, to Ropa. There are people there, servants of the Centipede Queen. Tell them she's missing, if they don't already know.* And when I'd asked – Who are these people? What are they doing there? – because I'd known that the Queen had come from Malay, on the other side of the planet from drowned Ropa – she'd told me that they were a research team.

And they'd been hired to look for demotheas. Matters were beginning to knit together, into a pattern that I did not like the look of.

I didn't have time to think about this now. The ship was starting to shake, a deep through-the-bone shuddering that I'd felt once before, on a flyer stricken above the mountains just outside Winterstrike. We'd crashed then, but we'd been flying low and over trees. This time, after all, I'd only just been reanimated, on our re-entry from haunt-space. I didn't fancy going back into the aftergone quite so soon.

The array was still screaming. I slammed a hand down onto the console and shut her off, taking the ship back onto manual. It was no comfort to know that I'd only ever done this before on simulators from this altitude. I hauled the ship around out of the path of a satellite station, looming up in front, keyed in a hopeful-but-optimistic re-entry angle and took the ship down. There was a ripping sound from behind me, and a moment later I saw a fragment of nacelle fall away and spin planetwards.

Someone said, 'Best let me do it.'

Rubirosa said, 'Who the fuck are you?'

I turned, to find myself staring into the flayed face of the Library.

'You're back!' – to the Library. And to Rubirosa, 'And you can see her!'

'Haunt-space,' the Library said modestly, 'seems to agree with me. You can see me because this is a haunt-vessel. I'm linked into its array. What's left of it.' She passed a sinewed hand over the console and the manual array flickered in its wake. Rubirosa was still gaping.

'But my armour—' she began.

'I reasoned with it,' the Library said.

I said, 'This is the Library of Caud.'

'What, all of it?'

'No,' the Library said, modestly. 'Just an archive.'

'Some archive,' Rubirosa said, impressed.

Earth was a lot closer now. We were flying in over darkside and the ship was still screaming and shaking, but at least it was remaining intact. The Library's hands were a blur: representation only. Her essence was inside the array; I could see the codes whipping through her half-solid flesh, like the wounds displayed by an excissiere.

I was familiar with Earth from viewcasts, of course, but it was the old atlas at Calmaretto that came most readily to mind, the skeins and patterns of islands, the fractured lands between. There, a patch of white that had to be the Thibetan island shamandoms, running all the way up through the Siberian Sea. Here, the ridges of the Americas, barriering the Atlan Ocean.

I turned to the Library. 'Where are we due to land?' Might as well be optimistic.

'There,' the Library said, and pointed to a shimmer of white peaks.

'Isn't that Ropa, there?' Rubirosa asked. 'The whole continent's nothing but a swamp.'

'Fine with me,' I said. Swamps sounded soft. We were out of darkside now and flying lower, curving around the world. The ochre splash of the Dahomey lands was beneath us, the mountain cones rising out of shallow seas, scattered with the white spires of the great cities of Afrique. Possibly just as well that the Library didn't plan to land us there; I wasn't sure where the Afriquenne Matriarchies stood with Mars.

But politics weren't my main preoccupation right now. Earth was coming up fast. The Library said, 'Excuse me,' and vanished in a rush of data into the array. We shot over sandbanks and long, snaking rivers, over deserted shorelines and low ranges of hilly islands that looked as if another tide would submerge them completely. The viewport was partly obscured by smoke and I realized this was coming from us.

The Library reappeared, no more than a shadow.

'Controls!' she ordered. 'Go to manual!' and I grabbed the flight control and tried to glide. This was not completely unsuccessful. We spun, once, causing curses from Rubirosa and a stream of instructions from the Library that, unfortunately, I failed to understand. We flipped again, hung briefly over the uprushing world and then crashlanded, right side up, in a morass of reed and water and peat.

The silence was deafening and brief. A moment later, the haunt-array kicked back in with a shriek. The Library strolled over to her, walking easily on the tilted floor, and took the spirit by the arms. Then she folded her neatly down into a little smoking pill and swallowed her whole. I think this unnerved me more than the crash.

'That's better,' the Library said. 'They don't like releasing information, sometimes. Had a hard job getting it out of her on the way in.'

'Where are we?' Rubirosa asked. The viewport was too mired in black spatters of peat for me to be able to see out, so I disentangled myself from my seat and lurched down to the hatch, holding on to the console as I did so and discovering several new areas of injury: bruised ribs, a banged shin and several cuts where my knuckles had met the surface of the array. I could not have cared less; I felt lucky to be alive.

The hatch was stuck. I kicked it, and nearly fell into the marsh.

'How safe is this thing?' I shouted to the Library. From the pungent scent of burning, not very. Rubirosa joined me at the hatch and together we helped one another down onto a reed bed. The ship shuddered: it was starting to sink. A thick column of black smoke was rising from its side and spiralling up into a pale grey sky. Rubirosa and I hobbled along the reed bed as fast as we could. My concern now was not just that the ship might blow, but also the kind of attention we'd attracted on the way down: I didn't have a clear idea of Earth's regulations but *unauthorized ship, lack of proper permits, forced re-entry, crashlanding* did not inspire me with confidence. It didn't bode well for the ultimate success of our hastily planned mission, either.

'Bit bleak,' said Rubirosa, leaping nimbly across to a causeway. She was right. The saltmarsh extended as far as the horizon: a labyrinth of reed beds and causeways, which might or might not have been human-made. As far as the eye could see lay a wilderness of silver-grey water, the reeds bleached fawn, with frothy plumes like smoke, and the black crumbling earth rising low out of the water. The air smelled of salt and wet and rot. There was no sign of any habitation.

'How long does this go on for?' Rubirosa asked the Library, clearly underwhelmed.

'A thousand miles, maybe? Perhaps more. This has changed a little since I last took data in.'

'This is the north of the northern hemisphere, yes?'

'Yes. A great centre of civilization, once. Cities and spaceports and all.'

I balanced on a narrow strip of earth and looked down into the swirling water. Not far away, a startled flock of birds flew up from the reeds, black against the pale sky. From the position of the sun, which was low, this felt like mid- to late afternoon, but I could not be sure. 'And of those cities, now?'

'They say their bells toll under the waves,' the Library said. 'That if you look down at low tide, you can see roads and towers. There's the ruin of a great city a little further to the north. But the tides took almost everything, over centuries. Folk moved east to the more developed lands. Here, they were too proud, so it's said, to take action. In the east, people were more accustomed to disaster.'

I stared into the water and thought of cities. 'Is anyone likely to come after us?' I asked. *Apart from Gennera, that is.* 'We must have violated any number of laws.'

'I'm not aware of any broadcasts,' the Library said. 'But whoever was after you is unlikely to give up.'

'We'll have been pretty visible,' Rubirosa agreed. She looked back to where the roof of the ship was still visible, but only barely. The smoke was finally dissipating, smearing the air.

'Better keep walking,' I told her.

By early evening neither the ship nor the smoke from the crash was visible. I was growing very tired of saltmarsh. But the sky had stayed empty: only a very faint contrail, far above, as some vessel sought orbit. No one had come looking, but that didn't necessarily mean anything. I hoped they'd assume we'd died, but if I'd been in their position, I wouldn't have assumed a thing.

I was also growing more and more certain that the causeways had been made by sentient beings. They seemed too regular, too straight. The Library, when consulted, confessed that she did not know. I pointed out the interwoven mesh of reeds, so tightly and carefully twined together that it made a strong floating base for the causeway. 'That isn't natural,' I said.

'Doesn't mean a human made it,' Rubirosa pointed out.

'What else?'

'Earth is full of the Changed.' The marauder spoke with an authority that irritated me. 'Many water people – the kappa, the deinah, the phine. A big thing in engineering, once – they wanted to make sure people would cope with the water levels.'

I thought back to my own dry Mars and shuddered. There, the Small Sea was the largest sea and all this water made me feel weak at the bone. I said as much. And I couldn't help thinking about demotheas, too.

'Do any of these amphibious folk live here?'

'I don't know,' Rubirosa said, uneasy. 'But this has to lead somewhere.'

And indeed, it did.

TWENTY-THREE

Hestia — Earth

It was as though the village manifested out of thin air: one moment the saltmarsh was empty apart from the desolate call of birds and the slight slosh of water, the next, we were on the edge of a settlement of round huts. I pulled Rubirosa behind a wall, which seconds before had resembled a bank of reeds. The Library walked on, fading as she did so. I could smell smoke over the salt-and-bullrush odour of the marsh.

'Where's she gone?' Rubirosa murmured. Her hand showed the tips of weapons.

'I don't know—' but a minute later, the Library was back, striding stiffly out of the air.

'There,' I said.

'Where?'

'I'll speak to your armour,' the Library said, with what might have been a sigh. A moment later, Rubirosa took a step back and said, 'All right, I can see you now. What have you found?'

'No one's home.'

'What? Nobody?'

The Library shook her grim head. 'It's deserted. Can't have been that long ago, though.'

'There's smoke,' I said.

'More than that,' said the Library. 'There's food on tables.'

Cautiously, we followed her into the settlement's one and only street: a narrow lane between the huts, ending in a perimeter wall that, curiously, ran along only one side.

'Maybe they're all out hunting,' Rubirosa said, doubtful.

'Maybe they're hiding,' I said aloud, and wished I hadn't. Whoever had built the settlement had done so with some degree of expertise: the walls of the huts were tightly woven from reed and the roof beams, which were a mixture of wood and metal, fitted snugly. But they were still primitive in design. A central hole lay above a firepit in each hut and the furniture was basic, consisting mainly of low tables, also woven, baskets, and blankets that seemed mainly to consist of reed pith and feathers.

'Know anything about the people here?' Rubirosa asked the Library.

'Nothing at all. They lived like this on Earth, in the ages before the ages. Before the Flood. Or so it's told.' Which meant 'no' too, when all was said and done. I glanced out of the doorway behind us.

'I don't think we should stay here. It's not far from dark.' Already the sun was a low yellow smear over the marshes and the air was humming with insects. I slapped a biting fly away from my face and more took its place. If we did find somewhere else to camp, I thought, we'd have to light a fire or be eaten alive.

'I agree,' Rubirosa said. 'It's all very well for *you*.' She nodded in the direction of the Library. '*You're* not real.'

The Library's face might almost have betrayed hurt. 'I am as real as you!'

'I just heard something,' I said. Rubirosa and the Library fell silent. A thin, distant scratching came from beyond the hut.

'Beetles?' Rubirosa said.

'Go. Now!' But we were too late. As I stepped through the doorway of the hut, shapes were rising out of the ground in the twilight, short squat forms which did not move like humans, or smell like them.

'Kappa,' the Library said. Damp webbed hands caught me by the wrists and twisted back my arms with surprising strength. Rubirosa's armour flared and, hissing, extinguished itself. The kappa were all around, murmuring in soft, angry voices. Someone struck me in the face with what felt like a handful of wet moss, a pungent, astringent odour. My knees buckled then, and I went down.

When I came round again, it was completely dark and my wrists and ankles were shackled. After a moment, my eyes adjusted, but all I could see was earth, a low peat ceiling. I could hear the kappa not far away, talking among themselves: the Library might have been able to understand them, but I could not. At that thought, the Library was at my side.

'Sorry,' the warrior said. 'Can't do much with low tech.'

'I don't expect you to,' I whispered in reply. 'Where's Rubirosa?'

'In another room. We're underground, in case you hadn't worked that out. Of course, the kappa live primarily in burrows. I should have remembered.'

'It would have been helpful,' I said, but I found it difficult to blame her.

'There's not a lot I can do,' the Library repeated. 'They're scavengers, as far as I can see. Bits of passing ships seem to be incorporated into the architecture.'

'Bits of wrecked ships, you mean.'

'There's an old antiscribe,' the warrior went on, as though I had not spoken, 'and a couple of devices I'm not familiar with. Might be weapons. Might be food-mixers. I can't activate either of them, in any case.'

I sighed, nodding in the direction of my bound limbs to indicate that I'd make a start in trying to free myself. The Library melted away. I tugged and twisted and achieved nothing. One of the kappa came to stand over me. There was no expression of triumph over an enemy in its large, liquid eyes: only a melting sadness.

'What's your name?' I asked. 'Can you free me? I am a friend of the Queen.' Not strictly true, but worth a try. I'd made a stab at the patois tongue of Earth, but the kappa just continued to stare at me, uncomprehending. Then there was a sudden sound from outside the chamber, a kind of rippling wail. The kappa stumped off, leaving me alone in the dim room.

I started working at the bonds again. Squinting down, I thought they were reed pith, a stretchy, tough substance. Angling myself up against the wall, I pulled my bound feet through my arms, so that I could get at my wrists with my teeth. Several minutes of determined chewing ensued. The pith tasted disgusting, like rotting weed. After a while, a bitterness seeped out over my tongue and my mouth became numb, which was a mercy because it meant that I could no longer taste anything properly. I kept listening as best I could. There were faint sounds from beyond the chamber, rustling, and voices.

Finally, with a tug, the bonds separated and my wrists were free. I set to work on the shackles around my ankles, tearing at the pith with what was left of my nails. At last this, too, came free and I got off the bed and stood up. There was nothing in the room that would serve as a weapon, but there were two blankets. A hasty arrangement gave one of them the vague impression of a huddled figure, not that I thought this would fool the kappa. The Changed on both worlds were different, not stupid, no matter what many folk believed.

Cautiously, I peered around the door. The chamber led into a rough earth corridor, with white roots snaking through the ceiling. Primitive, but it was dry and did not smell unpleasant. I suppose there were worse boltholes. I slipped down to the next doorway and found Rubirosa stripped of her armour and pinned to a bench, rather as I had been, with bonds of plant material. The door was open. I went in and freed her hands.

'They've taken the armour,' Rubirosa hissed, once she'd got rid of the gag that blocked her mouth. She sat up, dressed in a thermal tunic and leggings, also dark red. 'Bloody stupid. They can't know what to do with it. They can't know what it *is*.'

My feeling was that they probably knew only too well. For these kappa, lost in the middle of their marsh, anything that came their way could be used as a weapon. Especially a weapon itself. With my lips to the marauder's ear, I whispered, 'They don't know about the Library.'

'I suppose that's something.' Rubirosa was grudging. 'But without technology, the Library can't do a whole lot.'

As she spoke, the warrior appeared behind her. 'Good!' she said, all approval. 'You're free.'

'For how long, though?' I said, since Rubirosa, deprived of the haunt-armour, could not see or hear the warrior. 'Can you find us a way out of here?'

The Library sighed. 'This is a maze. I've explored some of it. You should see what's down the corridor.' She gestured.

We followed her down the passage, ears cocked for movement. But though the low sound of voices went on, the kappa themselves remained out of sight.

The Library would not tell me what lay beyond, perhaps fearing that we might be overheard, or perhaps – with nearly human glee – wanting to keep it a surprise. She was partly a teaching mechanism, after all. I was expecting anything from ancient palaces, buried beneath the rising flood, to undersea caverns. But what we walked into was a munitions dump.

'How *old* is this?' Rubirosa asked, wandering around boxes and crates marked with the old skull symbol, a grin for danger.

'This is a latent explosive,' the Library intoned. 'Deliver it, and it can take months to activate, burning through its half-life. The crates are shock-proof.'

'It looks like they're using it as a shrine,' I added, relaying this to Rubirosa. I was standing in front of one of the boxes, which had been pulled slightly forward from those above it in order to make a shelf. On the shelf stood a row of what looked like dolls: some of them as squat as the kappa themselves, but some attenuated, with twig bodies and limbs made of reeds. Tufts of red and blond wool created hair. Rubirosa came to stand beside me.

'That's sad,' she said.

'Why so? It's the custom of primitive peoples.' But I didn't think the kappa *were* that primitive, all the same.

'Latent Life destroyed cities, when this was an empire,' the Library said. 'Londress and Hagen, Dam and Vennen. Paris, the nearest city to this place. All gone now, underneath the waters. But they were dead before they drowned.'

'I've never heard of those places,' I said.

'They lived thousands of years ago. I have only fragmentary references to the wars that devastated them. Much was lost.'

'And this has been here all the time?'

'Just think what you could do with this,' Rubirosa breathed. Her marauder's face betrayed the avarice of the warrior.

'If it's still active,' the Library said. 'It may not be.'

'Maybe the kappa are the best guardians,' I said. But I was more interested in where the cavern led than in what it contained, although I filed the information away for future use. I'd already delivered one weapon to the Matriarchy, however. I wasn't particularly enthusiastic about delivering another.

At the back of the shrine was a door. It opened easily enough and there was no sign of a lock, which struck me as odd. I was the last one through and checked the room behind, but it remained empty. I got the impression that the kappa, having captured us, had not really known what to do with us.

Narrow stairs and walls made out of pitted concrete, slimed with damp and earthstain. The Library paused, causing me to walk right through her.

'Don't do that!'

'Sorry,' the Library said, with faint surprise. 'It doesn't affect me, you know. There's someone up ahead.'

We proceeded with caution. The Library was right: I could hear someone shuffling about, muttering and mumbling. I didn't recognize the language, but it had to be one of the kappa.

'If there's only one,' Rubirosa whispered, 'we can tackle her.'

'Agreed.' With the Library close behind, we hastened ahead. The muttering was growing louder. I stepped through a doorway into dim light and stopped dead. The kappa had not been behind us all this while. They had been ahead of us. They stood in a semicircle, whispering to themselves, around someone who sat in a small pool of light in the centre of a huge hollowed chamber.

TWENTY-FOUR

Essegui — Crater Plain

The centipede's feet were sharp against my skin, like pins. As they scratched, information came to me: the vessel was descending, which I already knew, and the location lay within the mountains. And also, I was given the whereabouts of the Queen: a chamber not far from here, a series of left turns. I didn't have anything to lose, I thought. I waited until Mantis had finished her work at the console and moved on, then followed the directions I'd been given.

The door was locked from the outside, an old-fashioned punch-lock. The centipede was too small to activate it, but when I touched it, it obediently swung open.

The Queen lay on a divan with her back to the wall. The air had that same curious smell of musk, a heady narcotic drift. Since her captors were unlikely to have provided her with an actual drug – unless she had talked the equivalent of One into giving her something – it seemed that this was some natural secretion of the Queen. It made her seem even more alien.

'Hello?' I said, pushing the door to behind me but making sure that it did not lock. Slowly, the Queen turned her head.

'It's you,' she said, with a mild wonderment. Her words didn't seem to be entirely in phase with her lips.

'Yes. They captured me, too – at least, I'm not sure if they know that I'm on board.'

'They may have picked you up through our tracker,' the Queen said. 'They have something which locks onto my people. They plan to use us.' Her beautiful face reminded me of a porcelain doll that one of my aunts had given me as a child. I'd never liked it. I laughed.

'I don't know what use I'll be to these people, I'm sure.'

'I spoke of *us*,' the Queen said, patiently. It took a moment to work out what she meant: herself in the plural, not herself and me.

'I see,' I said carefully, though I did not. The Queen smiled.

'It's happened before.'

'Someone's kidnapped you?' She'd had an exciting life, for so young a woman.

'No. I mean, to my lineage.'

'Why? How do they try to use you?'

'In many ways,' the Queen said. She yawned. She seemed remarkably unconcerned about being captured and imprisoned and I wondered again about drugs.

'We need to try and get out of here,' I said. 'When this thing lands.' My shadow, outlined by the dull lights of the Queen's cell, gave a twinge of pain.

'No,' the Queen said, placidly. 'I wish to stay. I want to find out what they want, who they are.'

'I can tell you who they are,' I said. I related to her what the Library had said to me. The Queen leaned forward with the first signs of real animation I'd seen in her.

'Mantis is a queen? From the past? How exciting!'

'I'd far rather have a quiet life, myself,' I said.

Another gentle smile. 'You are not a Queen.'

I wondered whether all of them were mad, then thought of Alleghetta, who hadn't made Matriarch yet but who'd be a Queen if only she could. That would be a *yes*, then.

'You must do as you please,' the Queen said, as though we were on holiday. She waved a pallid hand. 'I should not keep you here, if they don't know you are aboard.'

But there were footsteps behind the door and the sound of voices.

'Over here,' the Queen said, her voice suddenly sharp. She undulated from the couch and drew out a long drawer: it looked as though the room had been used for storing bodies. Perma-sleep for space flight, or simply a morgue? I darted across the room and lay in the drawer. The Queen shoved it shut.

I could hear, but the darkness was oppressive and stifling, making my head ache along with the geise. Mantis's voice said, 'Have you reconsidered?'

'I have not done so. I don't think I'll join you.' She sounded as though she was talking about a party: I could imagine her examining her fingernails as she spoke.

'Why not?' Mantis sounded astonished, and angry.

'It isn't our history,' the Queen said.

'You think you're better than us, don't you?' Mantis's anger was growing. 'They created you, just as they created us.'

'Perhaps,' the Queen said. She did not sound as if she greatly cared.

'They must be overthrown,' Mantis hissed. 'We've suffered enough.'

'*You* have suffered. But I am a Queen. We are worshipped, we give guidance to our people. We are the mothers, not the children.' She spoke with a distinct condescension; I couldn't entirely blame Mantis for becoming annoyed. I wondered who Mantis meant by 'they'. I had a feeling it might be anyone who wasn't of the Changed.

'Then you can be mothers alone,' Mantis snapped.

Lying there in the dark, in the sudden charged silence, I thought Mantis had a point. The Changed had, after all, been created by the ancient Matriarchy of Winterstrike with the expectation that they were to be an evolved form of the human species. It hadn't worked out that way. The men-remnants were debased, bestial. I thought of the vulpen and shuddered. The female species were fragile, often weak, often simply mad. If you knew this, and your people had been reduced to a menial, marginal position in human society, why wouldn't you rebel? But that didn't mean I had to become a fellow traveller: these issues dated from the old days, they were nothing to do with us . . . Whatever my familial issues with the current Matriarchy of Winterstrike, I needed to let them know about this.

Light flooded in and I blinked. The Centipede Queen was staring down at me and in the swimming sensation caused by sudden illumination it seemed as though something crawled behind her eyes.

'We're landing,' the Queen said, and blinked.

I couldn't stay in the drawer, because if they came for the Queen, there would be no one to let me out. The Queen, I'd decided, could pursue her own agenda: she clearly had one, and I was under no obligation to rescue someone who didn't want to be rescued. Besides, as the geise told me in whispered reminders of increasing insistency, I had an agenda of my own.

So I slipped out of the Queen's chamber, making sure that no one was in view, and found a lockless storage unit in which to wait out the landing. The centipede came with me. It might, the Queen said with her customary vagueness, prove useful. I suspected it was a way of keeping an eye on me, and – remembering the bite – a means of control. But I saw little point in returning the thing: it was so small that it could easily slip back into my clothes without my noticing. So I accepted the Queen's doubtful gift and made my way back into the depths of the ship.

The dreadnought had obviously been a high-tech craft in its day, but times had moved on. Despite the speed with which it was clearly capable of moving, its descent was bumpy and I had to brace myself against the sides of the storage unit, eventually sitting down with one arm wrapped around my knees and another gripping a nearby wall-bar. We shuddered to a bruising halt and the whole ship rang: it was like being back in the bell tower and I felt an acute and painful nostalgia which took me by surprise. At least life at Calmaretto had been predictable. Until my sister's transgression, anyway.

Once the ship had stopped moving, I cautiously let myself out of the storage unit and found the nearest viewport. This revealed a high, bright sky and a quantity of red crags and gullies. Olympus's cone rose far across the plain, visible at the end of a wash. We had not, in fact, come all that far from the point at which I'd been abducted, but were still up in the Saghair, not far from the Noumenon. From the position of the sun, it looked as though it was mid-afternoon: a bright winter's day.

I hastened down the corridor, listening for any signs of life. The ship appeared deserted and there was a breath of fresher air across my face, making me realize just how stale the atmosphere of the ship had become. I followed the freshness, seeking a way out. After ten minutes or so, I found it: a hatch set into the wall of the craft that was ajar. Checking to see that there was no one around, I swung it open and climbed down the steps.

The ship sat on a plateau of rock, sloping down into the wash but surrounded on all four sides by the high rim of an extinct crater. The red walls completely concealed the dreadnought from all sides, apart from the end of the wash itself, but from the angle of the ship I didn't think it would be visible. That was saying something: the dreadnought towered above me, a huge curving shell of green-bronze, its sides pitted and scarred with patches of rust. From this close outside view, it was at once both less and more impressive: I had time to note the baroque detailing on its flanks, the intricate care with which the rims of viewports and gun emplacements had been ornamented. But the decay was also highly evident: it was clearly a very old ship.

When I went around the side of the thing and looked across the plateau, a small procession of people was making its way to the slope of the wash. From here, I saw that there was a structure high on the crags on the far side of the wash: some kind of tower. It looked like many of the ruins that were scattered over the face of the Crater Plains: as ornate and twisted in its way as the dreadnought itself. The procession was making for it and I thought I glimpsed the dark, sleek head of the Centipede Queen. Mantis's veil was a shadow in the sunlight.

I followed the procession, taking care to skirt the edges of the plateau where the rocks provided some concealment. If anyone might be watching from the ship itself, they'd have a pretty good view of my movements, but I had to take the chance: I couldn't skulk in the shadow of the ship until nightfall, in case it took off again, in which case I might be killed or sucked back into it. Neither appealed. Besides, it was good to be back on the ground, even under such doubtful circumstances: to feel the cold wind on my skin and the red dust beneath my feet. The air smelled dry, of nothing, apart from an occasional sweet-musty scent of sagebrush from deeper within the wash.

The procession soon took itself out of sight. It was a little later than I'd thought; soon, the shadows of the crags were lengthening and my own danced long in front of my own steps. I went down into the cool dimness of the rocks, leaving the plateau and the ship and heading into the wash itself. I hoped nothing dangerous was living down here: it would be ironic to escape death at the hands of several kidnappers only to be devoured by vulpen or awts in the mountains. But there was no sign or smell of anything down here, only the dust and the sage. Thinking of the vulpen, however, prompted thoughts of Leretui. Where was she now? Was she even alive? If I couldn't find her, I decided, I'd work passage to Earth and find a majike there to treat me, where no one would know me, or be likely to inform my mothers.

These thoughts were interrupted by a hail from the tower,

which now lay ahead around a fold of rock. It sounded like a horn being blown, an ancient, atavistic noise that made the hair on the back of my neck stand up. It was answered by a cry from up ahead, and then I saw them.

I'd been wrong to worry about wild vulpen living in the rocks. These were a party of four, robed and somehow stately as they walked out from the folds of rock to greet the procession, which had now come back into view. One of them held a long staff and their faces gleamed in the shadows like lit bone. I saw Mantis run forward, a sinuous gait, and greet the staff-bearer with enthusiasm. She even touched him and I repressed a shudder. The Centipede Queen was looking around her with what might even have been interest and I wondered what spiny minions she was sending out into the landscape. I glanced down at my wrist but this time there was nothing there. The wound had almost healed, but not entirely: a faint mauve stain on my skin, seeping a little.

The vulpen clustered around the procession, drawing them closer to the tower. I lingered in the shadows of the rocks, waiting until the women and the men-remnants had disappeared, and then I followed them.

Vulpen. I thought of a figure, skating swiftly round a bend, reaching out to take a woman's uncertain hand. The texts in the bell tower of Winterstrike had told me that answers, if there were any, might be found in the mountains of the Noumenon and now here I was, with the red crags arching up behind me and the ruins ahead. I walked down through the wash, weaving through the boulders, towards the tower.

TWENTY-FIVE

Hestia — Earth

For a moment, I didn't recognize the thing that sat in the centre of the chamber, surrounded by the kappa. It took me a moment to realize that it was actually caged: the walls of its cell were vitriglass and so clear that only a stray reflection betrayed their existence.

There on the banks of the canal at the end of the lawn of Calmaretto, under the weedwood trees, dancing on water and fractured light . . .

It was a demothea, but it looked old: the tangle of tentacles that framed its head were drooping, released from the tight knots that coiled them in, and the huge eyes were dulled in its elegant, bony skull. It looked listlessly around, head moving from side to side, almost as though it did not see the throng of kappa, or as if it did not care. I suppose I should refer to it as 'she', but there was something sexless about it, something so inhuman that normal gender terms did not apply, and as such, it reminded me more of the men-remnants than anything else, of the vulpen with their white countenances and bony, spiny hands. The demothea's skin was like wax; the eyes the colour of polluted milk. Its long hands twisted together in its lap, as a woman might express regret in some ancient play, but somehow the gesture did not seem to have the same meaning. It was as though the demothea was engaged in some kind of private communication. Skeletal feet, with an unnatural arch, protruded from the edges of its robe. Its toes tapped erratically on the floor, beating out a staccato rhythm. Its mouth, a small, prim oval, occasionally twitched.

I stepped back, passing inadvertently through the Library. Rubirosa was frowning. We withdrew around the bend.

'What's she doing here?' Rubirosa hissed. 'That's a demothea, isn't it?'

'I don't know if you noticed,' the Library said, 'but some of those kappa were armed.'

'A private army?' I suggested. But the demothea had looked too listless, too infirm. 'They were holding it prisoner,' I added.

'But why? They're all the Changed, aren't they?' Rubirosa said.

'Well, not all the Changed get *along*,' the Library said didactically. I relayed this to Rubirosa. 'There are factions and divisions, just as there are in the human world. We just don't get to hear about them.'

The Library put out a warning hand. 'They're coming back.'

The kappa were filing out of the room. Followed by the others, I ducked into a storeroom, which turned out to be filled with boxes of roots. An earthy, musty smell, not unpleasant, imbued the air. I could hear the kappa talking quietly amongst themselves in their own language. Then there was silence.

I wanted to know why it was here. The thing I'd seen on the canal at Calmaretto had, I realized now, never really stopped haunting me. The ethereal re-creations outside the theatre had born no relation to this hunched thing. I said, 'I'm going to take a closer look at it.'

'What if it sees you?' Rubirosa asked.

'I'll make certain it doesn't.'

The marauder looked doubtful but she gave no further protest. I slipped out of the root store and made my way back to where the demothea's cell had been. The door was closed, but there was a small, roughly cut panel in it, set with a grille. Through it I saw the demothea, slumped on the seat. Its head drooped. A trickle of viscous blood ran down its pale face. I kept well back, but then the Library was there, stepping out of the air in front of me. The warrior said, in old Martian, 'Can you understand me?'

The demothea's head came up slowly, as if it moved under water. So she could see the Library, then.

'A Martian. Who are you?' Through the grille I saw a spark of curiosity in the huge eyes.

'I'm – here by accident. Yourself?'

The demothea grinned, startling on that narrow face, with that small mouth. I glimpsed thin ridges of teeth.

'They captured me. Are you going to set me free?'

'That depends,' the Library told it. 'What were you doing here?'

'That is my own concern,' the demothea said. Its head came up abruptly and met my eyes in the shadows. I felt a sudden, sucking pull, as though I'd been caught in a current of a river. I ducked my head to one side and felt that something physical had given way.

'Be careful,' the Library said, unnecessarily. But it was almost too late. Dizzy, I stepped out of the room.

'I looked into its eyes,' I said to the Library, who had followed me.

'Soul-stealers,' Rubirosa murmured, coming up behind.

'Is that what's said of them?' It's what they said of me.

'Who knows what they can do?'

I could hear it in my mind, whispering. *Free me, free me*, like the hush and rush of the sea.

'I think we should go,' I said. My interest in the demothea had evaporated into fear: I did not like to think of what it might do to me if I hung around. The thought of travelling with that thing whispering and muttering at me was not to be borne.

We left it there in its dim prison and made our way back towards the root store. I could smell fresh air, Rubirosa agreed, and when we followed it we found a hatch in a wall that led onto the outside world.

'Surely they've realized we've gone by now,' Rubirosa said. But either the kappa had not realized, or they did not care. There did not seem to be anyone around and this struck me as eerie: that we had only just seen a crowd of the kappa and now the little settlement felt as though it had been uninhabited for years, just as it had done when we first set foot there.

'If they're the Queen's research team,' I said, 'we need to find them. If only to see what they're doing.'

We made our wary way back onto the causeway and the track that led into the marsh. The moon sailed out from behind a wisp of cloud, illuminating patches of scrub, treetops that rose up out of the water and in which something was hanging. Then the moon was gone again and the glimpse with it. I didn't consider it wise to stray too far from the causeway.

'Get an hour or so away from the village,' Rubirosa said, as if she read my mind, 'and then camp.'

'Agreed.' We'd deal with it in the morning, I decided. I was by no means convinced that the kappa settlement housed the research team: it just seemed too primitive. But I also wasn't sure what else they could be doing there, with a captive demothea. I did not, however, feel like tackling the kappa tonight.

The air was settling into a clammy chill and there was a faint sea mist rising up off the salt flats. But then our plans were abruptly overturned. A drawn-out, keening cry came from somewhere off to my left, among the flats. It didn't sound like anything human. Rubirosa's hand shot out towards my arm in an instinctive clasp and was as swiftly withdrawn.

'What was that?'

'I think that's the kappa,' I said.

'Must have discovered we're missing.'

'This is the only obvious track out,' I told her. My heart was sinking. The kappa knew these marshes, as we did not, and were surely accustomed to the pathways through them. Slow and blundering they might be, but they had the advantage of knowledge, and that was likely to prove our downfall. We could run now, but we couldn't run for ever. And I didn't know how powerful the kappa's sense of smell might be. Rubirosa and I started to jog along the track, hampered by the lack of light and unfamiliar terrain. I stumbled once, followed shortly after by the marauder. We helped one another, muttering curses. The cry came again, this time from up ahead.

'What if they've got hunting beasts?' Rubirosa asked.

'Then we're in trouble.'

The kappa were not far away now; I could hear them, their whistling voices and the sound of their feet splashing through the low water levels. We were level with a patch of the submerged trees: I took Rubirosa firmly by the arm and indicated a rudimentary shelter.

The trees were vast: a central twisted trunk from which depended an arching canopy, sending branches back down into the water and forming a ball of root and branch, with as much below the waterline as above. We edged out onto a narrow strip of the causeway to reach the shelter of the branches, then stepped under the canopy itself. The branches were springy and gave a little under our feet, but they held. I was conscious of my feet becoming wet. The Library was an insubstantial presence among the ball of roots, apparently standing on the surface of the water.

'Here they come,' Rubirosa whispered. Clutching tightly onto the canopy, I watched a group of five kappa hasten by. They carried basic spears and one of them had a thing like an electric prod. They whistled to one another with urgency as they passed. None of them looked in our direction.

'Maybe they're not after us,' Rubirosa said, hopefully. I thought that was too good to be true, but then there were cries from the other side of the causeway and a second group of kappa came over the ridge. They, too, brandished spears.

'What's that?' I said. I could see something through the branches of the canopy, something light and drifting over the water. A moment later, a glowing ball of phosphorus floated by, becoming momentarily entangled with the branches and breaking apart, only to coalesce back together again. Beside me, I felt Rubirosa relax.

'Only marsh gas,' the marauder said. 'I've seen it on the edges of the Small Sea.'

'That was marsh gas,' I said, nodding in the direction of the ball, 'but *that* isn't.'

It was as I'd seen it so many years ago on the canal beyond Calmaretto, like and yet unlike the hunched, debased thing in the cell, like and unlike Mantis, too. The demothea drifted over the surface of the brackish water, its tentacles coiling and drifting around it. The robes that it wore were the same as the ones I'd seen on the imprisoned creature back in the settlement, but this thing had a face filled with light, ethereal in its beauty, and its eyes glowed like moons.

'It's escaped,' Rubirosa breathed.

'Or they let it out to hunt it,' I said. 'If it's the same one. I don't think it can be.' Next moment, it was clear that I was partly right: a spear whirred through the air and splashed into the water, just beyond the canopy. The demothea hissed and disappeared, going under in a shower of glistening spray. There were shouts from the kappa, who now waded out into the water, fanning out so that they formed a semicircle in front of the canopy.

'Stay where you are,' the Library instructed, into my ear, but I didn't need telling. The kappa might seem faintly laughable, with their stocky bodies and waddling gait, but the spears were real enough and so was their intent.

'Where did it go?' Rubirosa whispered. 'The water can't be that deep if they're walking through it.'

She was right, but I could see no sign of the demothea: it had vanished as completely as if it had never been there. I wondered whether it had just been an illusion, but the kappa didn't seem to think so. They were coming forward and one of them was striking the water with a long pole. Perhaps there were underground tunnels that the demothea knew . . . Then, suddenly, it was back, rising up from the water inside the canopy with such speed that Rubirosa and I nearly fell off our branch. The kappa cried out and pushed through the canopy and then we did fall: I stumbled into the dark water and found myself up to my knees. The kappa ignored me, even though they were all around. They pushed past me, shoving me out of the way as if I was no more than an inconvenient branch, and closed in on the hissing demothea.

It might not be armed, but it wasn't without defences. Something lashed out from it, a long black tentacle like a shiny whip, and took a kappa's legs from under it. The kappa crashed into the water, flailing. The tentacle whipped out again, curling past the branches and aiming at the leading kappa. The water sizzled as it struck: some kind of localized field. The kappa doubled over and the whip struck again, catching the prod that the kappa had held, but not gripping it. The prod flew through the air and I reached out and caught it. I had no time to think about my decision. I lashed out and activated the prod just as the tentacle came towards it.

A shudder ran the length of the tentacle and the demothea screamed. It went into a writhing, blurring coil of motion, thrashing the water around it so that the spray shot upward, silver in the moonlight. The kappa gave a great collective shout. The demothea's whip lashed to and fro, then abruptly drooped. The thing folded in a tangle of robes and sank into the water. This time it did not disappear. The kappa surged forward and picked it up, making a hammock of its own robes, then wound it into some kind of net.

The one who had held the prod turned to me.

'Are you hunters?'

'So you can speak Martian,' I said.

'Only I. I was not there when you were taken. The others cannot. I learned for the demon.'

'The demon?'

The kappa nodded towards the bundled form of the demothea.

'I see. No, we're not hunters. We're travellers. We – came from the Queen.' In a manner of speaking.

'From the Queen?' If the kappa had possessed eyebrows, they would have risen. 'Did she send you?'

'No. She's been abducted. My enemy is a demothea. I came because I thought you could help.'

'I know that the Queen has – gone away.' She didn't sound unduly concerned. 'You have a ship?'

'We crashed. The craft was destroyed,' Rubirosa said, with minimal truth. 'We escaped with our lives.'

The kappa turned and spoke to her colleagues, presumably translating. They murmured among themselves.

'Do you think,' I asked, 'that we could go somewhere less wet?'

A tall order for a saltmarsh, but we managed it. The kappa led us back to the village, this time as guests, not prisoners.

'My name is Evishu,' the Martian-speaking kappa said. She listened to our names with a frown, memorizing unfamiliar syllables. The Library walked alongside and remained unaddressed: evidently the kappa could not see her.

'Your village,' I said. 'I wasn't sure if we'd got the right place.'

'It's not a village. I think it was a military installation, from some time long gone, though we built the huts. We came here in pursuit of demotheas.'

'Where I come from, they're a legend,' I said. 'There are none to be seen.'

249

'That's because you don't know they're there. Do you have marshlands?'

'Yes, around the Small Sea to the south of the Crater Plains.'

'Then you will have demotheas,' Evishu said.

'So what are they? Why were they made?'

'They're military. They cope well with water, as you've seen. They have the power to create illusions around themselves. The whip is obviously the weapon and they emit a localized form of electricity, like an electric ray. They were designed as killers. Very probably, where you come from, the people did their best to exterminate them, during the time after the Age of Children. You can see why.' The kappa might be the Changed, I thought, but Rubirosa had been right when she'd spoken of divisions and rivalries.

'So if they were Martian,' I said, 'why are they here on Earth?'

'We don't know. The most likely explanation is that a group of them were sent here for some military purpose and never went home. Ropa is huge, you can see that from any map. After the floods, there was contamination – an engineered disease. No one comes here any more.'

'No one except you,' I said. *And us.*

'We were sent here by the Queen.'

'What does the Queen want them for?' asked Rubirosa, evidently sharing my paranoia.

'We don't ask that sort of question of her,' Evishu said, placidly enough.

'So you just do what you're told?'

'That's what *we're* for,' Evishu said.

I gestured towards the bound form of the demothea as the kappa carried it along the path. It looked as though the thing was beginning to regain consciousness: it twitched and writhed in the hands of its captors, who plodded along unheeding.

'What are you going to do with it now?'

'Let the Queen's people know that we've had a partial success,' Evishu said.

'Partial?'

'There are more, in the marsh. We already have one, but it's dying.'

The notion of more of these Martian-grown monsters in this limitless landscape, cold under the moon, made me shiver. And this was what Mantis and Leretui were. 'Do they ever band together?'

'They hunt alone. But they come together once or twice a year. We think,' Evishu added, 'that you'd best spend the night with us. They may come for her. It isn't safe out here.'

I looked out over the expanse of the moonlit marsh, the thick banks of waving black reed and the distant glitter of the swallowing sea, and agreed.

TWENTY-SIX

Essegui – Crater Plain

I was glad when the last of the vulpen disappeared into the base of the tower, taking the Centipede Queen with them, but that also meant that I was alone out here among the rocks, and twilight was coming.

But where there were vulpen, so might there be Leretui.

I crept closer to the base of the tower. It squatted on top of its tumble of rocks like a dishevelled bird of prey. It wouldn't have surprised me if the whole thing hadn't suddenly toppled off in a shower of mortar and stone: it looked derelict enough.

But there had to be a way in. I'd seen the vulpen disappear. I explored the rocks around the tower, feeling it loom over me, as though it was watching. The light was fading quickly now, the short winter day coming to its swift close, and the shadows around the rocks were deepening. I had to make a decision, whether to stay out here and find a bolthole in the boulders, or keep trying to find a way in. I kept looking. The Queen's little pet crawled out of my sleeve as I searched and nipped the back of my hand, making me jump. The image was of a hatch, leading down. The Queen must have come this way, and transmitted the information to her creature.

Among the rocks, at the far side of the base of the tower, a scuffle of ribbed sand betrayed what I was looking for. I swept the sand aside, and found the hatch. No haunt-tech, not even a bolt. The hatch had a heavy metal ring, which twisted when I hauled on it. Open, the thing revealed a dark hole and steps leading down. I listened. There was no sound from within, but there was a dim light, enough to see by. I pulled the hatch closed behind me and went down the steps.

They did not lead far. After a short descent, I came out into a narrow passage with a stone-flagged floor, winding into the base of the tower. The walls had been smoothed and lights set into them at intervals: from the illumination, and the almost dustless condition of the floor, it looked as though this tunnel was regularly used. There was also a strange, strong smell, unfamiliar to me, but I thought it might be vulpen. The idea made me nauseous, but I kept going. I could hear a sound: a distant roaring like wind on a stormy night. I started to go towards it, before realizing that it wasn't external at all: it was the sound of the geise inside my own head. It cried out my sister's name.

Then I turned a corner and my mother Alleghetta was standing under one of the lights on the wall.

'Essegui!' she snapped, in the tone one would use to a disobedient child. 'Where are you?'

'Can't you see?'

'I've only just managed to find you again.' She sounded as though I'd got lost in a shop. 'Where have you *been*?'

'Looking for my sister,' I said through gritted teeth. 'Just as you wanted me to.'

'Well, and have you found her?'

'Not yet. But I think I'm close.'

'You'd better get on with it,' Alleghetta said. 'I need her back in Winterstrike.'

'Why? I'd have thought you'd be glad to get rid of her, under the circumstances. Haven't you got your Matriarchyship coming up?'

A shifty, furtive expression crossed Alleghetta's face, one I'd seen many times before, usually in the course of discussions about politics.

'I have my reasons,' she said, just as she'd said so many times, too. 'Bring her back, Essegui. As soon as you can.'

And so I would, I thought, as her figure faded and something twinged inside my head. Dark science could rot the soul, so they said, and I believed it.

The little centipede twitched inside my sleeve and there was the sudden sense of a growing excitement, not my own. I took this as a sign that the Queen was nearby. She'd helped me before, I thought; perhaps she could do so again. And then I heard her voice.

'This is the one,' someone said, a low voice with a familiar timbre to it. Mantis.

'I've told you before,' the Queen said. 'I won't help you. Besides, aren't you an abomination?'

'Who is this woman?' That was a woman's voice, clear and high, and of course I knew her. Leretui. I'd found her.

'I told you,' the low voice of Mantis said. 'An ally, from Earth.'

'I'm not your ally,' said the Queen, and for the first time there was a touch of anger in her tone. I couldn't blame her; I wouldn't have liked to be ignored, either. But the voice went on, 'Leretui, it's time to go. Would you like to see Earth?'

'You know the answer to that,' my sister said, almost purring, and a long-held suspicion that I hadn't wanted to entertain was confirmed. My sister hadn't just disappeared. Somehow, against all odds, she'd run away.

I followed their footsteps as they receded up the stairs of the tower. Alleghetta's voice echoed in my head: *Where is she? Where are you now?* Stop badgering me! I silently cried, but her hectic voice went on.

Up and up. There was no sign of the vulpen, though I could still smell that odd, rank odour. Turning a corner, I caught sight of them: Mantis and my sister. I ran down the passage, in time to see Mantis speak to Leretui, invisible now behind a door, and go on ahead.

I waited a moment until I was certain that she wasn't coming back immediately, then knocked on the door.

'Leretui!'

'Who is it?' my sister's faltering voice asked.

'It's me. It's Essegui.'

The door opened immediately and Leretui's pale face peered through the crack. 'Essegui!' I couldn't interpret her expression: as much dismay as anything else, replaced swiftly by a kind of calculation that I didn't recall seeing in my sister's face before.

'Did our mothers send you?' That wasn't quite what I was expecting, either. 'You've come!' or 'Thank heaven!' would have been more like it.

'They tried,' I said. Partly true: they'd succeeded, as well. 'Can I come in?' Standing out in full view of whoever might come down the corridor was making me nervous.

'I suppose so,' Leretui said. I didn't give her a chance to change her mind and stepped into the room.

The light was better in here, and the room might actually have been described as well appointed. I closed the door behind me. Leretui looked different: no longer the timid girl, nor the bitter Malcontent. There was a glitter in her eyes which reminded me of my cousin Hestia, when she was in the middle of plotting something.

'You've come for nothing,' my sister said, and that sounded more like Shorn than Leretui. 'When Hestia was here—' I jumped at the name, as though she'd pulled it out of my head '—there were things I didn't understand. Now I do.' She looked smug and the note of self-importance wasn't one I'd heard in her voice before, either. She turned to the window, to the single shining moon, tossing her hair back over her shoulder. She sat down on the bed with her back to me.

'Did you leave of your own accord?' I asked.

'Of course not.' Scornful, without turning round. 'How could I? You saw how they kept me. You *helped*.'

I started to say *I didn't have a choice*, but the words died on my tongue.

'I know how strong they are,' Leretui said. 'Our mothers.' There was the note of condescension in her voice now, also unfamiliar. 'I know how hard it is to resist them.' *But you didn't even try.* I wasn't sure whether I heard the accusation in what she did not say, or whether it was my own guilt, speaking.

'How did you get out?' I asked.

'I don't really know.' This time, she sounded unconcerned, without even the wonderment one might have expected. For her, it was clear, the episode was past and gone, with only the bitterness remaining.

'You must have *some* idea,' I insisted.

'Why does it matter?' Finally, Leretui turned. She gave a small smile. 'I'm here now.'

'Is Hestia still here?'

'I don't know.' Leretui looked even more smug, as though she'd done something particularly clever, and I wondered where my timid little sister had gone. Perhaps we ourselves had killed her. 'She asked me to go with her. We went to – other places. But I ran away. Couldn't trust her, you see. Her friend was planning to take me back to Gennera and I couldn't have that.'

'Who is Gennera?' I asked, and that was when she told me what my mothers had done.

When she fell silent, I stared at her. I'd have found it hard to believe, but I could see it in her face: the likeness to Mantis. And I knew what the majike – Gennera – had done to me. I didn't know what to say. I took a step back and Leretui smiled.

'Where was Hestia headed?' I asked, trying to regain some control. 'Did our mothers send her after you, too?' It would have made more sense, I thought, than sending me: Hestia the Matriarchy spy had abilities that I did not.

'I told you. I don't know.'

I didn't want to hear the answer to the next question, but it forced its way out. 'What about the vulpen?'

'What about them?'

'This is a vulpen stronghold, isn't it?'

'*You*—' she spat the word out, 'you and my mothers turned me into a pervert. That's what you said I was, a deviant, because I was seen with a male creature for less than a handful of minutes. You took my name away and you shut me up in that house and so now, why should I not take a male as my lover and be what you have made me? I know what I am now, so get out, Essegui. Get out of my room and my home and be thankful that for the sake of the childhood we had, I haven't turned you over to them.'

I really meant to go. She was right, it seemed to me. Even if she was not, then whatever dreadful circumstances she found herself in now – among men-remnants, among outcasts and exiles – seemed better than what she had left. The geise was shrieking in triumph in my head and it had Alleghetta's voice. A flicker of movement caught my sight and I looked across the room. Alleghetta stood there, more solid than before, and smiling.

'What are you staring at?' Leretui asked.

'Bring her back!' Alleghetta commanded.

'She doesn't want to come,' I said aloud.

'Who are you talking to?'

'It doesn't matter whether she wants to or not,' Alleghetta said. She made a quick gesture and her gaze flicked off to the side. 'She'll come. Tell her to open the way.'

'I don't—'

'Tell her!' Alleghetta demanded, and the geise rose up in my head, singing in a high-pitched humming buzz that made me clap my hands to my ears.

'Alleghetta—' I whispered.

'What is it?' Leretui got to her feet and took me by the shoulders, shaking me. 'What are you doing?' Then she looked up. I felt the geise detach itself from my soul, taking part of it away. I think I cried out. I saw the geise flicker between Leretui and myself and knew that its ability to remove itself depended on the physical contact between us: we made up a circuit along which it could travel. I tried to push Leretui away but her hands were gripping my shoulders with the force of rage and I could not break free. It sparkled as it flew, a little blacklight matrix glittering in the air. It entered Leretui's left eye and she screamed, clapping a hand to her face, but it was too late. Something was opening up behind my sister: a rip in the air, expanding fast. Beyond it, I glimpsed the Eldritch Realm, haunt-space, and we were falling through.

'No!' Leretui cried and the loss in her voice seemed to tear the air even further. 'No!' But the gap was closing. I lost consciousness for a moment, dying, and when I opened my eyes we stood in sudden silence in the mansion of Winterstrike, with Alleghetta before us and someone else standing triumphant.

She reached out and grabbed Leretui by the hair. My sister screamed and at once I was back in our childhood, with Alleghetta raging at Leretui, at Hestia, at myself. Hestia and I had known early on to avoid her, to run and hide in the greenhouses or the cellars or the winter garden, but Leretui had always been slower, dreamier. It seemed, however, that she'd learned something from the vulpen. She snapped round and sank her teeth into Alleghetta's wrist. It was my mother's turn to yell. I stepped in, seizing Alleghetta by the arm and forcing her round.

'Let her go!'

Someone stepped forward and dragged Leretui off. For a moment, seeing a dumpy figure, I thought it was Thea, then realized it was the majike, Gennera Khine. Her black garments fluttered as she touched something to my sister's neck and Leretui slumped to the floor, dazed but not unconscious. Alleghetta's wrist was bleeding heavily: surely Leretui's teeth weren't that sharp?

'Essegui, leave us,' the majike commanded.

'I don't think so,' I retorted. 'How did you bring us back?'

The majike looked smug. 'I wasn't expecting it to work.'

Even though a fragment of my soul had gone with it, the relief left by the departure of the geise was enormous, eclipsing everything else. 'She didn't want to come back. Can you blame her, after what we've done to her?'

'You stupid girl,' Alleghetta hissed. I wasn't sure which one of us she was speaking to. 'You think you were being punished?'

'What else could you call it?' Leretui answered. Her face was white and blazing, barely human. 'Shutting me up out of sight, keeping me from everyone and everything? What else could it be but punishment?'

'Actually,' Alleghetta said icily, 'one might call it "protection".'

Leretui stared at her. 'From what?'

'What do you think? From what you did and what you found.'

'Alleghetta,' I said. I stood and faced her, though I found that I did not like to turn my back on my sister. I wanted confirmation. 'What is Leretui?'

A sly look crept over my mother's face, one that I had seen a thousand times before. And free of the geise, I slapped her.

I'd always stopped short of physical violence before now, though I'd come close. Duty, if not love, had held me back, because she'd certainly merited it. Alleghetta grew perfectly still. The mark of my hand burned red on her white cheek. Leretui watched, avid. This should, I thought, have happened long ago. Then Alleghetta said, very politely, 'Essegui, would you come with me for a moment?'

My sister surged forward and seized Alleghetta by the arm, as if my act had permitted her own motion. The majike stepped forward again, but held back. 'You're not going to shut me in again!'

Alleghetta gave her a long, considering look. 'No,' she said. 'I don't think I will.' Leretui stepped back, surprised. 'But I do need to speak to your sister alone.'

A day before, I'd have told her that whatever she had to say could be said in front of Leretui as well, but now I was not so certain. I kept silent, wondering where Thea was. After all, we had two mothers, however ineffectual Thea might be.

'Very well,' Leretui said, stung into concession. She wrapped her arms around herself and walked out into the corridor. We followed.

'My study, please, Essegui,' Alleghetta said. It actually sounded like a request, not a command: perhaps the slap had done some good after all. Leretui was standing by one of the tall windows on the landing, looking outwards. Glancing over her shoulder, I saw that it was mid-afternoon, with a drift of snow floating down over the city and the lamps already lit. A barge slipped quietly along the canal, a black block between the leafless branches of the weedwood trees. Whatever had been done to me here, whatever remained to be done, this was still my home, a long way from the Crater Plain and that sinister ruin, and suffused with unexpected relief I followed Alleghetta down the hall, our heels tapping on the marble like the tick of an ancient clock.

Alleghetta's parlour was a wide room on the first floor, looking out over that same view of lawn and canal and weedwood grove on one side, but on the other facing the northern part of the city. The bell tower was sometimes visible in a direct line of sight, when it wasn't snowing. Now, all I could see were a neighbouring mansion and the dome of the Winterstrike opera house, which rose in a black lamplit curve through the falling flakes. I watched the snow come down. I could sense Alleghetta watching me and forced myself not to turn around: I didn't want to give her the satisfaction.

Eventually, Alleghetta said, 'Essegui?'

'What?'

'Where did she go? What was it like out there?' There was an odd wistfulness in her voice, and for the first time it struck me what a constrained life Alleghetta must have led: consumed with duty and appearance and formality. It was only at the summer-house that she'd ever seemed close to relaxation, in a stiff sort of way.

'We were in the Crater Plain,' I said. 'A tower, a ruin. Close to the Noumenon.' Instinct warned me away from any discussion of the vulpen, or my cousin, but it seemed that Alleghetta was forewarned, for she said, 'The men-remnants. Were they there?'

'Yes.'

'As I feared,' Alleghetta murmured, half to herself, I thought. 'Like calls to like.'

I turned to face her, putting my back to the snow. 'I repeat: what is Leretui?'

'What did she tell you?'

'That you were paid by that majike to have her created. That you'd raise her in exchange for a position in the Matriarchy, if the experiment worked. Is it true?'

'I certainly wasn't expecting her to turn into a deviant and vanish into thin air, if that's what you mean.'

'And what about me?'

'You were a usual sort of child. There was nothing special about your creation, put it that way. Thea wanted a baby and of course we needed an heir, so you were it. If something had befallen you, we'd have had you replaced.'

'It's *so* nice to be wanted.'

'There's no need to be sentimental. Look at what you'll gain from it, when Thea and I are gone.'

'What are you going to do with Leretui, now?' It struck me that Alleghetta might simply try to have her done away with. After all, everyone would now know that the Malcontent of Calmaretto had gone missing, and apart from Alleghetta and myself, no one knew she'd returned. That familiar, shifty expression came back to my mother's face.

'She won't be confined – not in the room, anyway. But you do see that she can't be allowed to leave the house? For her own safety.'

'Who is she in danger from, exactly?' I myself had been the recipient of several attempts on liberty and life. I wanted to know who I was dealing with.

'I don't know.' Alleghetta was lying, I thought. 'The Matriarchy was very insistent that I should keep her confined, for her own sake. I know what you thought. But it was all for her own benefit.'

'If she's already managed to escape from a sealed room, I don't see how you propose to keep her in the house.'

'Don't worry about your sister,' Alleghetta said, with a return to confidence. I felt her hand touch my shoulder and tried not to flinch. 'She need no longer be your concern. I'm actually very pleased with you, Essegui. You carried out your task.' If I'd waited for her to apologize for placing me under the geise, I'd still be standing in front of that parlour window.

'What about my soul?' I demanded. 'There's a piece missing, and I want it back.'

'I'll speak to Gennera,' my mother said, and I knew she lied.

'Do that,' I said.

'You can go now,' Alleghetta said. 'I'm sure you need your rest.'

It was a dismissal, not a suggestion. I left the parlour without looking back and sought the relative sanctuary of my own room. Leretui was gone from the passage window and I had a duty to myself, as well.

Once in my chamber, I stripped off my dusty, dirty skirts and ran a bath. The steaming water, immediately available, was more of a luxury than I could have imagined. I sank down into it and tried to submerge my anxieties in its depths. But they kept floating back to the surface. Someone had tried to kill me. Several people had been responsible for my kidnapping. I couldn't believe that this would just – *go away*, now that Leretui was home. Maybe she was the target and not me, but one thing was clear: Leretui was wanted, by all manner of factions. Going back to life as it had been was no longer a viable possibility. I got out of the bath feeling cold, despite the humid warmth of the room, and dressed quickly. Time to find out what my mothers were really up to.

By the time I headed down the hall, it was dusk. I was hungry, after several days of self-imposed rations. I wondered how the Centipede Queen was faring: somehow, I'd had the impression that she didn't need to eat. It wasn't that I owed her any loyalty, but the Queen had intrigued me, and she'd helped me, too, which meant a lot. She might even have saved my life. She'd told me to go, but I still felt a twinge of guilt about that.

I wasn't prepared to go in search of supper until I'd located Leretui, but in an anticlimactic moment, I did so in the dining room.

'Ah, there you are,' said Thea, as though I'd merely stepped out for a constitutional stroll. She was seated along the table, sipping something sticky and yellow that smelled of fruit: my mother liked her sweet cocktails as well as her sherry. 'How are you feeling, dear?' Her smile was as sickly as her drink.

'How do you *think*?'

'You must have something to eat, dear,' Thea said, anxiously. I didn't trust myself to speak. Instead, I nodded and sat down at the opposite end of the table from Alleghetta, who might have been carved out of stone.

'Where's my sister?'

'In her room,' Alleghetta said.

'Well,' Thea added quickly, 'isn't this nice? All the family together again. It won't be long before Canteley's old enough to eat with us, too.'

'Oh, do stop babbling, Thea,' Alleghetta snapped.

'Where's Canteley?' I asked. The meal already had a dream-like quality: this morning, I'd been out on the Crater Plain dodging vulpen. 'I haven't seen her yet.'

'She's been at her lessons all day. She's doing very well. Won't you have some soup, dear?' Thea looked as though she was on the verge of collapse. One of our silent serving maids wafted in with a tureen. A thousand meals in this very dining room, a thousand thin soups served out of this same tureen of faded ancient china. It made me depressed all over again. I started thinking about Earth to cheer myself up: I still hadn't relinquished that particular dream.

'I'll have a little soup,' I said. We ate in silence: all through the soup itself, and then the meat in fruit sauce, then a sorbet which tasted as cold as the dusk outside looked, and then tea. It was all remarkably tasteless – strange, after the erratic meals of the last few days.

I would be surprised, I thought, if Leretui was still here in the morning. I didn't think anything we could do would be enough to keep her within Calmaretto's walls. But as usual, I'd reckoned without Alleghetta.

Excusing myself abruptly, I headed for my sister's chamber. They'd put her in her old room, not the Malcontent's sealed prison, but I couldn't see this as evidence of any softening on Alleghetta's part. But when I knocked on the door, there was no answer.

'Leretui?' I was beginning to get déjà vu when my sister's voice snapped, 'Go away!'

'Are you all right?'

'*Yes.* Now leave me alone.' The same sort of conversation we'd had growing up. Some things never change. At least she was still in there. But although tiredness was starting to beat down on me in waves, I did not seek my bed. I crept back downstairs, feeling like the child who'd tried to eavesdrop on her mothers' dinner parties: that fascinating, golden world of adult conversation which, once I'd joined it, turned out to be merely dull. I wished Hestia was here. But Hestia was gone, who knew where, and Leretui had turned into Shorn, and I was alone.

Except for Canteley. My little sister ambushed me halfway down the passage, eyes wide.

'Essegui! You've come back! What about Tui? Is she with you?' A torrent of questions, all falling over one another.

'Yes, and yes. She's in her room – the old one,' I added hastily.

'But where did you *go*?'

'Somewhere very far away. But we're home now.' I felt my tongue stumble over the noun.

'You were very brave, to follow her,' Canteley said. I didn't disabuse her. Our mothers wouldn't have told her about the geise, and although the servants gossiped, it didn't seem to have reached my sister's ears. Or perhaps Alleghetta had been more prudent than I'd thought, and news of the majike's visit had not got out.

My little sister lowered her voice. 'Did you see – *him*?' Her eyes grew even wider with the transgression of uttering the forbidden pronoun and my heart sank. Romanticism could be dangerous and never more so than now.

Gently, I said, 'No. No, I didn't. He – it – didn't rescue her, Canteley. She rescued herself.'

And as far as I knew, it might even have been the truth.

I made Canteley go back to bed. There were voices coming from Alleghetta's parlour. I kept an eye out for weir-wards, but the only one I glimpsed was a faint, screaming soul that saw me, recognized me for one of the household, and drifted away. I suppressed a grin: Alleghetta would have done well to have reconfigured the house to react to me, too, but perhaps that would have been too troublesome. It was always my mother's weakness, I thought, to underestimate her children. I put my ear to the parlour door and listened.

'. . . don't now know what to expect.' That was Alleghetta, speaking tightly.

'Of course not.' A woman's voice, not Thea but familiar. It spoke in smooth, reassuring tones and there was a twinge inside my head, at once and unlike the geise. The majike, of course. The little centipede – which I'd missed when I undressed and bathed – crept from my sleeve and sat on the back of my hand, rearing up as if listening. I didn't know how to discourage it and besides, it might be that the Queen had a right to know. I left the creature where it was.

'How could you know, when they have not told you? But I understand your suspicions.'

'We've *seen* them.' Thea spoke urgently, and all at once I realized where Canteley had got her manner of tumbling speech. I'd never noticed it before.

'In the house?' the smooth voice said.

'No. Not as close as that.' There was an unfamiliar note of relief in Alleghetta's voice. 'But in the garden, on the canal. They seem to float.'

'It's an illusion. They're good at that. They exude mental alterators, it was part of their design specifications.'

'That may be so,' Alleghetta said, and it seemed to me that she shared my unease. 'But it isn't natural.'

'Nor is disappearing,' Thea said, still rushing, as if they were trying to keep her silent. 'She vanished out of a locked room, right under our noses, and came back the same way.'

'I doubt that,' the majike said. I pictured her squatting in the middle of the parlour like a toad. I could almost feel Alleghetta, staring.

'What do you mean?' Alleghetta said.

'I think it is much more likely that on that first occasion, your daughter was in that room all the time. You just didn't see her.'

'Impossible. My other daughter was the first to find her missing. She searched the room. Although Essegui has not always been the most obedient child—' I could hear her mouth turning downward, too, and thought: *too bad*. '—I do not suspect her of any collusion.'

'I'm not suggesting that, either. Didn't you hear what I said? That they can create and control illusions?'

'You mean she made Essegui think she wasn't there?' Thea said.

'Yes. And then someone came for her. But now – her abilities will be growing.'

Alleghetta was silent. I imagined her mulling over the majike's remarks, trying to assess what manner of thing she was dealing with, in her daughter and her adviser both. At this point, I thought I heard a faint sound behind me. I spun round but there was no one there. I told myself it was only one of the weir-wards, briefly active.

'But a – a demothea?' Thea said. Ironic, I reflected, that the word contained part of her name, as if the clue had been staring us in the face all the time and none of us had grasped it.

'Leretui was an ordinary enough child,' Alleghetta said slowly, 'if frail.'

'Are you so sure?'

'She suffered from fainting spells. That's all.'

'Demotheas are slow to mature,' the majike said. 'That was one of their flaws, perhaps the reason why so few survived. Many of them were wiped out in their hatcheries when the Age of Children came to an end.'

'If what you say about my daughter is true,' Alleghetta said, 'then what now?' *My daughter*. Never 'our', as though Alleghetta had herself given birth to Leretui in some archaic manner, not merely lifted the mix of DNA from the vat.

'Well,' said Gennera Khine, as if amused. 'It won't be entirely your decision, believe me.'

'We've done everything you asked.' Alleghetta sounded sour again.

'You have indeed,' the majike said, soothing, 'and I won't cast you adrift. Don't worry. I'll take care of things.'

'I cannot afford to lose any more status.' Alleghetta sounded agitated. 'The ball is in a few days' time – I'm to be encouncilled then.'

'I know. And so you will be. We'll concoct a story. Leretui's disgrace was a matter of public record, little could be done about it, even by me. This is different.'

I didn't like the sound of that. Leretui might have changed – literally, from what the majike had said – but she was still my sister.

There were sounds from inside the parlour, indicative of movement. I backed hastily along the corridor and ran up to the landing. Soon there were footsteps on the stairs below. I looked down at the sleek black head of Alleghetta – now devoid of her Ombre curls – the untidy blondish one of Thea, and the majike's hat. She was pulling on her gloves as she walked. The lights from the canal suggested that a sledge was waiting for her.

'Thank you for coming,' Alleghetta was saying, stiffly, as if forced.

'We're old friends, aren't we?' Gennera Khine said. There was a cosy note in her voice which made my skin creep. 'Don't worry. All will be well.'

I watched, covertly, as my mothers escorted her down the stairs and into the main hallway, moving across its black and red tiles like pieces in some ancient game. There was a blast of cold as they opened the river door and through the coloured glass I saw the shadow of the majike moving down the path to the canal.

In spite of my exhaustion, however, I still couldn't sleep. The geise might be gone, but my soul was still incomplete. At last I got out of bed and went to the window, throwing aside the heavy drapes. The majike's sledge had long gone and so had the bulk of the daytime canal traffic. Beneath its blanket of snow the garden looked peaceful, and I had to remind myself that this was still a city at war. I'd looked up the newsview a little earlier in the evening, but it had held nothing of great interest: it seemed that my own journey had taken place in a lull. It wouldn't last. I tried to imagine Winterstrike under weapons fire, perhaps even occupied, but the attempt failed: the city still held the stifling sense of continuity that it had always done. I wondered whether they'd repaired the bridge to the bell tower, and went over to the antiscribe to take a look. If I couldn't sleep, I might as well read.

There were a few headlines about the bridge. Caud had been blamed, and had not bothered to issue a denial. Repairs had already started, but the bell tower was off limits. Just as well. As I was scrolling down the latest report, the scribe chimed with an incoming message.

'Accept,' I told it.

'Esse?' My cousin Hestia's face appeared on the screen, curiously fractured and pixellated.

'Hestia? You're very faint. Where are you?'

'I'm on Earth. We—' Hestia glanced over her shoulder at a background of static.

'I didn't catch that. What are you doing on Earth?'

'. . . to get out of the Noumenon. I—'

But her image was gone. I tried to put a track on it, which ended in a jumble of numbers: no address that I recognized and one that would not allow incoming messages. I sat staring at the scribe in dismay, thinking *What now?*

It was very late. I hadn't thought I'd been lying there for all that length of time. I switched off the mainscreen of the scribe, first asking it to alert me if there were any more messages, and went back to the window to draw the drapes.

Someone was hurrying down the path. I caught sight of a figure, swathed in a heavy coat, disappearing between the weedwood trees, and I recognized her walk. It was Leretui.

So, I thought, she'd got out after all. I threw on boots and my greatcoat over the shift and hurried down the stairs.

The river door was still bolted shut and a blacklight crackle showed that the weir-wards were in place. I knew where Leretui had gone: the little cellar door that had once led below the building and now opened out onto a short flight of steps. It was warded, but as a child, Hestia had discovered the ward key and all of us knew how to turn it on and off. It had been years since I'd used the cellar door; I'd imagined that the codes would have been changed a long time before, but it seemed they had not. Sure enough, the door was ajar. My sister's footsteps led out across the snow like the trail of a mouse. I followed.

I couldn't hear or see anyone. I thought of a sledge, gliding silently down the curve of the canal, taking my sister away for ever. I never thought I'd have entertained such an emotion, but I was aware of a sudden sympathy for Alleghetta.

And after what had happened to me already, I didn't feel safe out here. I was just about to turn back when movement caught my eye. Someone – Leretui? – was standing at the very edge of the canal. I slunk between the trees until I could see more clearly.

Then the figure turned its head and a cold rushing shock went through me. It wasn't Leretui. It was a vulpen. I could see its skull gleaming in the lamplight. The inhuman head turned to and fro, moving slowly, searching the length of the canal. Then lamplight caught it and I realized: it was Leretui after all, wearing the vulpen's mask from Ombre. It was almost as great a shock as the first. I had to fight the impulse to run down the bank and wrench it from her head. Relief and anger warred, and relief won, but not for very long. What did she think she was doing? I felt that Leretui had been playing some weird game all along: as if we were the experiment, not she. The thought made me even colder. I'd believed I'd grown up alongside my sister, ourselves arrayed against our mothers, and now I was wondering whether I'd ever really known her at all. Little Leretui, her big atlas in her lap, bore small relation to this masked thing.

Leretui raised a hand. There was, I saw for the first time, someone standing on the opposite bank. It was tall, wrapped in a draped coat against the cold. Its head was bowed and it gave no sign that it had recognized Leretui, or even seen her. I had the impression that its hands were clasped before it, an attitude of modesty that seemed uncalled for. Leretui gave a strange low whistle, not something that sounded as if it came from a human throat. At that, the figure's head came up and its hood fell back. I saw a narrow head, a face as white as the snow surrounded by writhing black hair. It was a demothea, and as I watched, it sent out a field of blacklight, sparkling over the snow and the icy surface of the canal. Leretui held out her hands and the blacklight disappeared into them as if she had absorbed it.

I nearly called out to her, but bit it back. The confidence of her gesture appalled me. The demothea was gone as if it had never been. I shrank back into the meagre shelter of the weedwood trees as Leretui spun on her heel and strode back to the house. She had pushed the vulpen mask up over her head and I saw that she was smiling; a smile that had once seemed shy and now appeared sly, instead. I waited until she had vanished into the old cellar entrance and then, cold to the bone, I followed her, taking care to stay out of sight of the opposite bank. I didn't like to think of what might be watching.

When I entered the house again, Leretui was nowhere to be seen, but there were snowy footprints leading a pattering dance up the stairs. I went slowly back to my room, and when I reached it, the first thing I did was to peer out behind the concealment of the heavy curtains. The garden was empty, and nothing was standing on the opposite shore.

TWENTY-SEVEN

Hestia – Earth

In the morning, I went outside shortly before dawn. A cold wind was scouring the face of the saltmarsh and land was a mass of bleak shadows. Suddenly I longed for Mars in this dim, monochrome world: for the depth and richness of its colours. Then the sun came up over the rim of the sea and the marsh was flooded with silver light, the shadows banished to subtleties of grey and pearl. A beautiful place after all, until one remembered what was living out in those banks of reed and the walls of the sea ruins.

'Morning,' the Library said, appearing at my shoulder and making me jump.

'The demothea we captured,' I said. I jammed my hands into my pockets, trying to generate some warmth. 'Is it still here?'

'Yes. I've been watching it all night. It hasn't moved. I think it's in some sort of trance.'

'Maybe it's injured,' I said.

'Some of the Changed can will their own death,' the Library informed me.

'If its purpose was military, it might very well have some kind of suicide mechanism.'

'Someone's coming,' the Library said, and faded into the morning air. Evishu bustled out from behind one of the huts.

'Ah, it's you,' she said, peaceably enough. 'I thought I heard someone.'

'I couldn't get back to sleep,' I explained. I didn't want to tell her that my dreams had been full of water and writhing blackness.

'Hard, in a strange place,' Evishu sympathized.

'Now that you have your demothea,' I said, 'what will you do?'

'Some of us will stay. Myself, I will take the creature back. I suggest you come with us. Your own ship can perhaps be salvaged, but best you leave that to us.'

I nodded. We couldn't stay here, and the ship was useless.

'When are you heading out?' I asked.

'Today, if you're willing.'

'I'll talk to Rubirosa and—' *Don't mention the Library.* '—and I think so.' I was already getting restless. I looked out to where the sun was climbing, sending white shards of light across the choppy water. There was no warmth in it. I went to find Rubirosa.

The marauder was sitting on a bench in the hut that had been allotted to us, sipping something from a bowl and grimacing.

'Tastes like hot pond water.'

'It probably is.'

'If it's all the same to you, we'll be leaving later on. Evishu wants to get the demothea back to her base.'

'Sounds good to me,' Rubirosa said. She glanced out of the door of the hut, to where a light drizzle was starting to fall. 'This is a shithole,' she added, gloomily.

I found it hard to disagree. 'At least the thing hasn't escaped in the night.'

'I suppose that's something.'

'Evishu implied that it might die.'

Rubirosa gave an exasperated sigh. 'Maybe it will. Apparently the other one has. No loss, if you ask me. At least they could dissect it.'

Privately, I thought that was the best way to treat them. Yes, species ought to be preserved, and if I was still back in Winter-strike, maybe I'd be able to have the luxury of a compassionate view. But something about the sinuous form of the demothea had repelled me so much that I found it difficult to care. When Rubirosa next said, 'Let's go and have a look at it, shall we?' I had to battle with myself not to refuse.

The demothea lay in an adjacent cell: bound tightly in some kind of netting. When I laid eyes on it, I thought that Evishu had probably been right and that it was dying. The lustrous skin looked dull and dry and the tentacles that emerged from it seemed to have shrivelled and withered.

'Not pretty, is it?' Rubirosa said.

The demothea's eyes were closed, or at least, not open; it did not appear to have proper lids. It looked as though its eyes had sunk back into the surrounding flesh to leave blank skin, with a tiny hole at each centre.

'It's disgusting,' I said.

'Evishu said they could create illusions,' Rubirosa said. 'I don't think we want to spend too much time around this thing.'

I agreed, gratefully. Perhaps Rubirosa, too, shared my revulsion. We left the demothea lying there and went back to the hut. Shortly after that, Evishu appeared and announced that we would be leaving at noon.

Apart from the small, narrow boats, I hadn't seen any evidence of transport, so when it arrived it was something of a shock. I heard it before I saw it: a low humming, out across the marsh. At first, I thought the sound was a wave and had to fight down panic. Then I saw the dragonfly shape skimming over the reeds.

When it came in over the camp, it was bigger than I'd thought, too. Some kind of military orthocopter, with massive blades and a deep body, all vitrinous so that whoever travelled in it would have a 360-degree view. And it would look as though you were sitting on nothing, too.

'Malayan,' the kappa explained. It had an emblem on the side and on the big water runners that now swung down from the body of the craft. When it landed, fragments of reed lifted up from the roofs of the huts and whirled away on the wind. It looked far too technological for the hunched figures of the kappa and their little huts.

Two of the kappa brought out the demothea, strapped to a stretcher, and the pilot, a human woman, helped them to load it on board. I could see the demothea through the glass and it seemed to be twitching.

'Has it regained consciousness?' I asked Evishu.

'Somewhat. But it's hard to tell.' Evishu looked uneasy. I couldn't blame her. Rubirosa and I were invited on board and belted in; Evishu and another of the kappa followed. Looking through the glassy walls of the orthocopter, I spotted the Library looking back at me. Gradually, she faded.

'Hold tight,' the pilot said and the blades started up again. The roar in the long cockpit was immense. We swung up over the settlement and I could see, now, how tiny it really was in all that expanse of reed and water. The striped sandbanks I'd seen as we came in were still prominent and there were shadows in the shallows. I wondered what kind of buildings they had been; who had lived here all those centuries before when the shallow seas rose up and took the land. They would be as alien to me now as the kappa themselves, perhaps more so. The settlement was soon lost behind us. We turned south in an arc and I strained to see the place where the ship had come down, but couldn't make it out. The craft turned again. Clouds had come up now, sweeping across the ocean, and soon the orthocopter was enveloped in mist. It was not, I noticed, a haunt-craft.

We had been flying for perhaps half an hour when I first became aware that something was wrong. It started as an indefinable sense of unease, a hollowness at the pit of my stomach. Looking round, I saw what must have been a similar expression to my own on the face of Rubirosa.

'Evishu?' I heard her say. My vision went momentarily dark. and when I looked out of the front of the cockpit I saw a vast black cloud rising up before us. The pilot cried out. All of a sudden I was reminded of the weir-wards at Calmaretto, the instinctive fear that they were geared to instil, and I did the meditative exercise that had served me so well in the Mote. The fear ebbed, leaving my vision clear again.

'Evishu!' I shouted. 'It's the demothea!' The kappa was already making her way to the back of the craft, holding a stunner. We plummeted, dropping like a stone. The kappa, swept off her feet and dropping the gun, grabbed a stanchion and clung. The pilot, responding to something that only she could see, flung her arms up in front of her face. Rubirosa swore. When the orthocopter briefly righted itself, I hurled myself at the front of the cockpit. The pilot struck out, blindly. I saw panic in her face.

'It isn't real!' I shouted, but she wasn't listening. I dragged her out of her seat and Rubirosa grabbed her arms. They wrestled as the orthocopter dived nose-down into a murk of cloud. I snatched at the controls and the orthocopter came up again. I could feel what the demothea was trying to do now, and it was the same thing as a weir-ward: the same summoning of impressions and forces from the beyond. But I knew how to deal with that now, and while the demothea continued to throw illusions at me, I took the vehicle on into the rain.

We seemed doomed not to escape the swamp, I thought, as I searched the geographies for hard ground. Most of it looked like sandbank, but there was something just on the edge of the scanner, a round rim of shore . . . I headed for it.

The craft lurched as we broke through the cloud. There was a cry, abruptly cut off, from the back of the orthocopter but I didn't dare look round from the unfamiliar controls to see what was happening. Rubirosa had left the pilot in a heap on the floor. Cloud streamed past us and I could see the shore below: waves breaking white on a long curve of rock – no, wall. It looked too regular to be natural and I could see the remains of what had once been a massive barrage reaching out from it. I remembered what the Library had said about a city.

Now that we had found land, my problem was finding somewhere on it to set us down. The wall itself was too broken; years of battering by the sea had reduced it to a series of teeth. Behind it, I could see further structures and what might be a roof. It was flat, anyway; I'd just have to hope that it could take the weight of the orthocopter. It looked solid enough as I took the craft down through a veil of rain. Once the orthocopter was safely landed, I turned.

Evishu was pressing herself against the wall. A flicker of blackness whisked in front of her face. Rubirosa and the second kappa were flat on the floor.

'It's getting loose!' Evishu shouted. The tentacle snapped like a whip across the body of the second kappa and the kappa stiffened and did not move again. Next moment it struck the pilot and she, too, dropped.

'Rubirosa! Get back!'

The marauder rolled under the bench, the whip missing her by inches. I threw open the hatch and Evishu disappeared backwards onto the roof. The smell of rainy air was invigorating and I realized how stuffy the interior of the craft had become. Next moment, the demothea rocketed out of the holding cell. It clung to the ceiling for a moment like a spider, and its oval head swivelled from side to side. Its skin was still dry and flaking, but its eyes were huge. A thin tongue flicked out and tasted the air, then the demothea was gone through the hatch, arrowing like a squid.

Evishu was shouting, but there was a high wind blowing outside and I couldn't hear what she was saying. I paused briefly to check the body of the fallen kappa, but as far as I could tell she was dead, and so was the poor pilot. I didn't know what the demothea had done to her – electrocution? – but it had certainly been lethal. Rubirosa was already out of the hatch and I followed.

It was pouring with rain. The kappa was a small blur at the far end of the roof and we ran to meet her. She was looking down into what had once been a street: pale stone buildings, their windows reinforced against wave action, stood in a canal of grey water.

'Where did it go?' I asked.

The kappa pointed. 'Down there.'

'All right.' I glanced back at the orthocopter. 'Better make sure that's secure if we're going after it. Is that what you plan to do?' I rather hoped the answer would be *No*, but that left the question of what would happen to Rubirosa and myself: I doubted that the kappa would be willing to drop us off somewhere more civilized.

'It's been tagged,' the kappa said. 'We can track it if we wish.'

Rubirosa looked uneasily down into the canal. There was a reek of salt water and weed; the whole city stank of the sea. It might have been a fine place once. I thought of cold Winterstrike, swallowed by its own canals, and repressed a shudder.

'This is supposed to be a haunt of demothea,' I said. Evishu gave me a level look. 'Yes, it is. Are you willing to proceed? Two of us are already dead. I can't force you to go with me.'

'I'll go,' I said. I'd come too far to turn back now – not that I had much to go back for, except a court martial from Gennera and probably worse. 'But I don't want anything stealing our only way out of here.'

'I'll go, too,' Rubirosa said. 'Makes more sense to stick together.' She smiled at me.

'Very well, then,' Evishu said, an unlikely general. Her webbed feet made a faint sucking sound on the concrete as we went back to the orthocopter and secured it. Then, with Evishu carrying the rescued stun gun, we set off.

The name of the city had been lost, the Library said. We went down a flight of stairs, the carpet long since rotted to faint stains on the stone, and through a gloomy hall. Paintings hung on its walls, almost indistinguishable under blots of mould, long-dead human faces staring out beneath their blemishes. Some of them were men and their painted gaze made my skin crawl as we walked between their ranks. Maybe they'd been rulers here, or maybe it was just a family. Calmaretto's family portraits, I reflected, were in the most part the same face.

At the end of the hall Evishu paused to check the tracker. 'It came through here,' she said. 'It's somewhere further down in the building.'

'Is it still moving?'

'No. Sometimes they hole up and wait for prey.'

'What do they eat?' I asked. The thing had been so alien that it was hard, somehow, to see it being open to animal needs.

'Anything they can,' the kappa said. Cautiously, we pushed open the door and came out into a long corridor. The light of the kappa's torch played dimly over the walls, which were covered with rotting wood: the remnants of old panelling. 'If it's gone into the cellars,' the kappa said, 'we might not be able to follow it. At least, you might not. They're bound to be flooded.'

'Look, if that turns out to be the case, we're going back to the orthocopter,' I said. 'I'm not going to try to catch that thing in water.'

'It would not be wise,' Evishu agreed.

Halfway down the next flight of stairs, the kappa's torch went out. Rubirosa bumped into her and swore. There was an odd, pungent smell, like burned hair, overlaid with something less tangible and more familiar.

'Someone's got haunt-tech here,' I whispered.

'These ruins are pre-haunt,' the kappa said.

'Nevertheless.'

It was growing stronger, making my skin creep. There hadn't been the same smell when the demothea had attacked us in the orthocopter; this was different and made me think that it might be coming from another source. I hoped so.

The kappa nudged me. 'It's underneath. Look.' On the little

antiscribe that she held, a red dot hovered below us. When we got to the next flight of stairs, the smell was stronger yet, but this time it was accompanied by sound: a thin, increasing hiss.

'Wait,' I said to the kappa. I stole down the short flight of stairs, to where a ruined wall rose out of dark water. It didn't make me feel any more secure about the foundations of the structure. I looked through a gap in the wall and couldn't see anything, but I could hear it: many things, whispering. Gradually, my eyes adjusted a little. Writhing motion, black upon black. Not one demothea, but a multiplicity of them. I scrambled back up the stairs and told the kappa.

We didn't risk staying long after that. We went through the hall as fast as possible.

'Perhaps my superiors will see this as cowardly,' Evishu said as we hastened.

'At least you're alive.'

'They will not necessarily regard that as a plus.'

'You did your best,' I said.

Evishu turned to me and I saw, if not despair, then a profound concern in her round amphibian eyes. 'You see, now, what we face? What's been breeding here, perhaps evolving?'

'Evolving?' Rubirosa echoed.

'The Changed were bred with swift genetic codes,' I said, 'to deal with swiftly changing environments. Hardly surprising if new conditions bring out the worst in them. It made them weak, but adaptable. I'm sorry,' I added with belated tact to Evishu. 'I know you're one of them.'

'We're used to it,' the kappa said mildly. 'I take it as a compliment, even, that you don't see me as so very different to yourself, that you can forget. We were engineered for a specific purpose, however, and later than the rest, so that the mistakes that were made in the early days had become more obvious and could be avoided by the time it was our turn.' She gave me her wide smile. 'The kappa have a reputation for gravity, slowness, ponderousness. And that's being charitable.'

'Better that than murderous and mad,' I said.

'As you say.'

The rain had blown itself out into the rides of the great Ropa Sea and there was a pallid stretch of sky in the west, as blue as an eggshell. To my great relief, the orthocopter was still where we had left it, but that didn't mean it was safe. I wanted it thoroughly checked for lurking life forms before we took off.

Evishu was looking at the scanner. 'She's on the move again,' she murmured. I wasn't pleased, remembering that writhing coil of life in the cellars. The meeting had broken up, perhaps.

'But we don't know if it's on its own,' Rubirosa said.

'We can't take the chance,' I added.

'I agree,' the kappa said, with regret. 'But perhaps if we can see . . .'

'Also I wouldn't put it past that thing to hand the tag on.' Rubirosa's mouth turned down. 'It's as intelligent as we are, allegedly.'

'They didn't build this city, did they?' I asked. 'This *is* human?'

'Yes. The demothea don't seem very interested in buildings. Out in the marshes, they live in burrows and the hollows of trees.'

We made as thorough a check of the orthocopter as we could, both inside and out. We had to hurry, mindful of what might already be sliding up the stairs, but I didn't want to find that something had been clinging to the roof when we were in the air. The kappa kept checking the tag.

'She's moving away from here,' she said. 'Fast, along the street down there. She's probably swimming.'

'All clear here,' Rubirosa said from the ceiling of the orthocopter. She slid down to join us on the roof. 'As far as I can tell.'

'That illusionary thing,' I began.

'Don't start,' said Evishu, spreading webbed hands. 'Once you get going with that, you're never free of paranoia. And dealing with these beings, that's no bad thing. Keep your eyes out and your head as clear as you can.'

So this is what we did, whirling the orthocopter back up into the air. Evishu had tidied her colleagues' bodies under the seats, not wanting to leave them for the demothea. They made extra weight, but it didn't seem right, she said. I could not blame her. We agreed, however, to take the orthocopter over the city and see if we could glimpse our escapee. The demothea's capacities apparently did not extend to air bombardment: their defences were biological rather than technological and it was, at least, something to be grateful for.

At the heart of the city, rising out of the floods, was the top of a great iron tower, like a cage or a pylon.

'What was that, do you think?' Rubirosa asked, leaning forward.

'Some religious structure, no doubt. Some cultures put their dead out for the prey birds: sky burial, they call it. They do it in the Thibetan shamandoms, so I've heard.' The kappa spoke with authority and I wished we'd had more time to talk to her. Now that we'd made it to Earth, I had a hankering for more sightseeing than the endless dreariness of the Ropa seas. The rain was sweeping in again, driving a wall of mist before it.

'Where's our quarry?' I asked. The kappa consulted the tracker, which showed a red bead moving swiftly into the heart of the city.

'There.'

'I can take us lower,' Rubirosa said. The orthocopter swung down through the veils of mist, taking us over pale buildings, dappled with mildew as the water claimed them. Then the mist broke away and I saw a long avenue beneath us, wavelets breaking across its surface. Once, the people who lived there had put water doors in their homes, just as we did on Mars, but now the levels had risen and only the tops of the doors were visible, some of them decorated with signs and symbols whose meaning I did not understand, but at which I could guess. Superstitions had been rife, once it became clear that the seas were here to stay.

In the middle of the avenue, creating a small white wake of its own, arrowed a dark shape.

'Got her!' Rubirosa said.

'Not yet.' I turned to the kappa.

'There's a netting device at the base of the orthocopter,' Evishu said. 'It's not much use out in the marshes – the reeds and the treetops catch it. But here, without a lot in the way . . .'

'It's worth a try,' I said. I motioned to Rubirosa to take the craft lower and we glided downwards. I thought, though I could not be certain, that the demothea's oval head moved up to look. Then it dived, and I was sure. I swore.

'It's gone.'

'Not for long,' the kappa said. 'They're amphibious, not aquatic. She'll have to come up sooner or later.'

And a moment after that, she did: like a fishing bird break- ing the surface. I saw the smooth arch of body, a tentacle curl, and then the demothea was shooting forward.

'We're almost at that tower,' Rubirosa said. I'd been so busy concentrating on the demothea that I'd missed the passing scen- ery. I glanced up and saw that the tower was rising before us, its massive rusty legs striding out of the water. Weed had crawled up it, giving it a green glisten, and birds had nested in it. The untidy heaps of reeds starred its joints, and as the orthocopter whirred closer, a long-necked white form uncurled itself and glided down over the water. More followed, disturbed by our proximity, until the air was filled with wings.

'Can't see a damn thing!' Rubirosa shouted.

'Mind the tower.' If we hit that, you could say goodbye to any plans of returning to Mars. Rubirosa veered the chopper around but there was no sign of the demothea.

'We've lost it,' the kappa said.

'Not yet,' I said. I could see something at the base of the tower: the demothea, swimming. Then it coiled an arm around a strut and pulled itself up. Determination seized me.

'Open the hatch,' I said.

'What?' Rubirosa turned, open-mouthed. 'You're not going out there.'

'Give me the stun gun.'

The kappa was struggling with the hatch. I suspected this had less to do with compliance with my instructions, and came more from a feeling that I was probably dispensable. She thrust the stunner into my hands and I fitted it to my belt, grasping the handle by the hatch with one hand. As the hatch opened and Rubirosa took the orthocopter dangerously near, I stepped down onto the tower. I could see the demothea clearly now: its upturned face and the lamp-like eyes far below me. I thought, though could not have sworn to it, that there was a flicker of something in those eyes as it looked at me. Recognition? Triumph? My own imagination? I could not say for sure, but the demothea started to climb.

TWENTY-EIGHT

Essegui — Winterstrike

Next morning I woke stiff and sore, feeling as though I'd run a marathon. I'd been dreaming about my sister, a ruined tower, a demothea . . . and then I realized that all of it was true. Dismayed, I crawled out of bed and dressed in that winter uniform of leather skirt and silk blouse: the uniform of the bell guardian. It made me feel less disoriented, as if life was normal after all and not the nightmare tangle it had become. I studied my face in the mirror. My white countenance, combined with the straight dark hair that fell in wings on either side, reminded me too much of the demothea, and of Leretui. I went thoughtfully downstairs.

If my mothers had been silent yesterday, they were not so today. The dining room was an agitation of printed-out newsfeeds: something had happened in the night, when I'd been cavorting about after Leretui, or fitfully sleeping.

'They've declared war on both cities,' Thea was saying.

'Don't be so stupid. How could they?' Alleghetta said.

'Who?' I asked. Thea waved the paper at me.

'The Noumenon. There was a strike on the city this morning – some new kind of haunt-weapon. There are ghosts in the streets, ones that no one has seen before.'

'Are you sure it's the Noumenon? Not Caud, pretending?'

285

'They've issued a statement.'

'What kind of ghosts?'

'Men-remnants,' Thea hissed. 'And the Changed. Things no one has seen for generations.'

I'd like to have said: *What harm can ghosts do?* But I knew all too well how badly weir-wards could affect people, disrupting spirit and body alike, and the little pieces of my own missing soul were also there to remind me with their lack.

It was, however, almost refreshing to have something else to worry about. No one mentioned Leretui, and so neither did I. I went with Thea into the study, to scan the antiscribe for public announcements.

These were numerous, and characteristic. The Matriarchy of Winterstrike expressed outrage and shock. The Matriarchy of Caud spoke of their rage in being betrayed, though since the Noumenon had never been an ally of Caud, I could not see how.

'Maybe it'll bring us closer together,' I said, and wished I hadn't.

'Winterstrike needs no assistance from Caud,' Alleghetta snapped.

'Mother, this is an entirely pointless war. Started over what? Some snippet of the Crater Plain that no one really wants, surely?'

'Mardian Hill is ours by right,' Alleghetta said, and told me why, all over again. I stopped listening halfway through. I was thinking about ghosts.

'They say it isn't safe to go out,' Thea quavered.

'Nonsense! We have the *ball*, had you forgotten?' She turned an outraged glare on Thea, who quailed.

Winterstrike at war, and all Alleghetta was worried about was her position. I supposed that was typical, as well.

'You'll be coming with us,' Alleghetta informed me.

'What about Leretui?'

'She'll be quite safe here,' my mother said, and swept out, leaving me gaping in her wake. After all the precautions and paranoia, as well as what had so recently happened, I couldn't believe that Alleghetta had slid so easily into this new insouciance.

'She's very worried about your sister,' Thea said, reproachfully.

'Well, so am I! How do you think I feel?'

Thea recoiled; I might just as well have struck her.

'There's no need to snap,' she said.

I went over to her and leaned forward, putting my hands on her shoulders.

'Leretui was living in a nest of vulpen, Thea. She was living with a man-remnant. She didn't want to come home. How does that make *you* feel?'

Thea's plump face twisted. She didn't cry, but I thought it cost her not to. She slumped in my grip and I felt a mixture of pity and irritation.

'I just wanted another daughter,' she whispered. 'And then Alleghetta got to know that – that woman, Gennera Khine. And the next thing I knew, we were involved in some government experiment. I didn't know what she was going to turn into!'

There were tears in her eyes after all, but more for the loss of her domestic dreams than from any real sympathy for Leretui, I thought. They were both as bad as each other. I let her go. I wanted, for an instant, to tell her that everything would be all right, but it so patently would not that the words died in my mouth.

'Maybe it would be best to send her back,' I heard myself say. 'The Matriarchy created her, after all. Let them clean up their own mess. You'll still have me and Canteley.' If I stayed at Calmaretto, which was seeming more and more unlikely. And there was another question, too.

'Thea,' I said. I found my gaze burning into the panelled walls of the study, boring a hole through the polished wood. 'What is Canteley? Was she another gift from the government.'

There was a very small, still pause, and at last Thea said, 'I don't know.'

'What do you mean, "don't know"?'

'Alleghetta oversaw all that. She was the one who ordered Canteley.'

'That surprises me.'

'It surprised me, too,' Thea said with sudden heat. 'I begged and begged for another child after you, and when she gave in and we had Leretui it was – well, you know now what the conditions were. After that, I didn't think she'd ever agree to another daughter and then, all of a sudden, she came up with a set of making documents – I wasn't even here. We'd gone to the summer house, all of us, and Alleghetta had stayed behind in Winterstrike.'

I remembered that summer, up in the hills: as close to carefree as we'd ever been. A short, fine summer, endless days sliding down into the brief, bright nights of the north and the grass burning golden on the hillsides. There had been parties on Lake Rule, which we'd been just old enough to attend.

'When we came back,' Thea went on, 'Alleghetta had sorted it all out and Canteley was already being grown. I never asked her why, I was too afraid.'

'I think you'd better ask her now,' I said. 'And if you don't, I will.'

But Alleghetta was nowhere to be found. When I questioned her maid, Jennai told me that my mother had gone to an emergency meeting of the Matriarchy. So I went in search of Leretui instead, more to see if she was still there than because I had anything to discuss with her.

Seeping under the door of Leretui's room, there was a small puddle of water, staining the rug. It stank.

'Leretui?' I said. I knocked on the door. And as I'd almost expected, there was silence. 'All right,' I said, aloud. I had the key to her room on the ring at my waist: Calmaretto kept to a combination of the old-fashioned and the modern, and the key whispered its haunt mantra as I inserted it into the lock. The door swung open and I knew what I'd find when I stepped inside: an empty room, a missing sister.

But she wasn't missing. She was still there, or what was left of her. Wet black threads filled a quarter of the room, hanging from the poles of Leretui's bed like a web. She lay cocooned in the middle of it, strands curling out from her outstretched fingers, which were already starting to break down. Her eyes were staring wide and filmed with cataract. Her mouth, too, was slightly open and I could see a thin black thread moving about inside it, as if searching for something.

Liquid oozed over the floor towards me with a purposeful motion that it should not have possessed, and I took a quick step back. Leretui was beyond any discussion, that much was plain – she was beyond *human*. I swallowed panic, locked the door behind me and ran downstairs to find Thea.

Alleghetta's 'scribe had been turned off: presumably because she was in a meeting. Thea was of little use, wringing her hands and entering a meltdown that rendered her as uncommunicative as her daughter. 'You have to fetch Ghetta,' she kept saying. 'She has to know.' Which I interpreted as 'pass the problem on', Thea's usual way of dealing with unpleasantness. I suspected the sherry would be taking a heavy hit once I'd left her, but for once, I really couldn't blame her.

I thought that it wasn't just Alleghetta who needed to be informed, but also Gennera Khine. Whatever she might have done to me, she was still the closest thing to an expert that I had and, anyway, there was still the issue of my broken soul. I told my lamenting mother that I was going to find Alleghetta – drag her out of her meeting by the hair if I had to – and take her to the majike. If they removed Leretui from the house, well and good. From the look of it, we'd become a demothea's breeding ground, and if that was the case, I told Thea, war or no war, I was going to take Canteley and find a hotel.

She didn't reply, so I left her wringing her hands in the study, pulled on my greatcoat and left. On the surface, little enough seemed to have changed in Winterstrike: the decorations from Ombre hung limply from eaves and lamp-posts. Street vendors sold snacks – patties of meat, fragments of fried dough – out of steaming pans. But people were hurrying. A woman herded her group of schoolgirls in front of her with flustered anxiety, hustling them into a gateway and slamming it behind her. I caught a glimpse of her white pinched face as the door closed, sealing her into a snowy garden. Bitter cold: as I drew closer to the gilded dome of the Opera, its weather vanes drifting as the breeze changed, more flakes of snow started to fall, starring the leather of my skirt and the hem of my coat.

The outer wall of the Matriarchy now curved before me: a rough red semicircle, darkened by snow. Even though it was still relatively early in the morning, the winter gloom meant that lamps had been lit along the top of the wall, casting swirling shadows down into the street. An old fortification, this, built in the Age of Children but looking more like some castle from the distant past of Earth. I almost expected to see slits for arrows, like some of the fortresses in the south of the Crater Plain, but the wall presented a blank face to the outside city, keeping its secrets hidden.

When I reached the main gate, which was haunt-bolted, I held up my pass to the reader and my eye to the gate, a double precaution of bureaucracy and soul. I had a moment of doubt, there – what if the missing fragments of my spirit caused the lock to fail to recognize me? But after a moment it whirred and let me through.

Inside, the hall was full of people, all rushing about in a tight silence, many whispering into antiscribes or clutching leather-bound portfolios. I pushed my way through the throng to the main desk. Here, an elderly woman with a close helmet of lacquered hair beneath an iron-coloured snood sat peering into a screen.

'I'm sorry,' I said, with polite insincerity, infusing my voice with a note of command that I'd learned from Alleghetta. 'I need to speak with my mother, on a matter of urgency.'

She looked up at that. 'Your mother? Oh.' It was her turn to apologize, but the look of suspicion didn't leave her eyes, all the same. 'I'm sorry, mistress Harn. I didn't recognize you, for a moment. Your mother's in a meeting.'

'I'm aware of that.' She waited, but I did not continue.

'I can't just interrupt her, you know.' A note of reproach.

'I'm aware of that, too. I'm afraid I wouldn't try to interrupt unless it was extremely important. There's an emergency at home.'

'I see.' She didn't – how could she? – but I could only wonder at the rumours that must have been flying around the Matriarchy over the course of the last year. The look of suspicion had now been replaced by curiosity. 'Well, if it's really an emergency—' she sounded doubtful and I couldn't blame her. We were, after all, at war, and here was I claiming attention for some domestic difficulty. But I saw her put a message through all the same. Then she looked up.

'I don't know if she'll come . . .'

'Perhaps I should wait somewhere else,' I said. I glanced over my shoulder at the crowds bustling through the hallway. My own snow-trodden footsteps were fading on the red marble, forming a wet line to where I stood. The receptionist looked dubious all over again. I leaned down and said, conspiratorially,

'Is there a waiting room?'

'I suppose you could sit in the back office,' the receptionist said, involuntarily drawn into my intrigue. I didn't want everyone seeing Alleghetta rush out to berate me, or, conversely, not come at all and leave me standing at the desk. There had been enough covert glances already.

In the end the receptionist let me into a cubbyhole situated a little way down the corridor, away from the echoing vault of the main hall. Here I perched on a leather chair like a child, waiting for my mother. But when she swept into the room, I rose.

'Essegui! What in the world—?'

I stepped forward, grasping her arm and murmuring urgently in her ear, 'Is this room secure? I doubt it.'

Alleghetta might have been psychotic, but she wasn't stupid. She gave my face a single searching look, and whatever she found there must have convinced her, for she said, loudly, 'You're obviously not well, Essegui. Let's get some fresh air.'

I followed her through the sombre corridors of the Matriarchy, red marble and then black granite as we drew closer to the inner, older vaults. I'd been here before, on various matters, and I found the place oppressive, without the individuality of the bell tower, or its charm. I always felt as though I was falling over invisible secrets, stored in racks along the hallways. I was glad when we turned a corner and there at the end of the corridor was a set of tall, fragile glass doors. Alleghetta put her eye to the lock and we stepped out into the chilly day. The terrace we stood on looked out over the inner courtyard of the Matriarchy: black-branched trees in overly formal configurations, laced with heavy snow, interspersed with shapeless stone sculptures. Once, I'd been given to understand, these had represented human forms: perhaps the first venturers to Mars, but time and weather had worn them down into lumps. Behind it rose the ringed walls of the Matriarchy. It was not an appealing view, but I was grateful to be outside.

'Now,' Alleghetta said, rounding on me. 'What?'

'Leretui's changing,' I said. 'I went into her room and she was unconscious, in the middle of some kind of cocoon. She's breaking down, Alleghetta. To turn into what?'

Alleghetta's grey eyes were wide. 'Changing?' She sounded both furious and intrigued.

'You got a demothea cross-breed,' I said. 'I think you're ending up with a pure demothea.'

Alleghetta seized me by the shoulder. 'Have you told anyone about this?'

'No. Thea knows, and I can't speak for the servants, by now. I thought you needed to know, as soon as possible. And probably your majike does as well.'

'She'll have to be removed,' Alleghetta said, to my relief. 'She can't stay at Calmaretto. If she does change, there's no telling what she might do. We might all be slaughtered in our beds.'

'The Matriarchy made her,' I said. 'Let the Matriarchy take her back.'

'Thank you for this,' my mother said, surprising me. 'You've been a good enough girl, Essegui, in spite of – well, never mind that.'

I tried not to smack her. 'What are you going to do now?' I asked.

'I can't leave without telling them why.' Alleghetta brought her hand down onto the low wall of the terrace in frustration, dislodging a small fall of snow. 'Can you go to Gennera, Essegui? If I tell you where to find her?'

After a moment, I nodded. 'As you wish.'

I was heading for a laboratory at the back of Olympus Street, an address that, my mother had informed me, did not officially exist. She'd given me a password to use, and when I came to a gate in the wall I whispered it with only a little hope, and not a little apprehension. The gate opened, letting me through into a garden that, in summer, would be substantially more pleasant than the one that lay at the centre of the Matriarchy. A frozen fountain stood in the middle of it, and I saw the silver forms of fish gliding beneath the ice. When I rang the old-fashioned bell that hung from the veranda, the sound pealed through the garden, causing an icicle to crash and shatter. A moment later, the door opened.

Gennera Khine stood there, wrapped in voluminous black: a

garment at once religious and practical, with tight sleeves and a high neck.

'Hello, Essegui,' she said, without surprise.

'Has Alleghetta spoken to you yet?'

'Not today.' Her pasty face wore a look of bland enquiry. 'Is there a problem?'

'Yes, you could say that. Can I come inside? It's cold out.'

The majike opened the door a little wider. 'Come in.'

Alleghetta had said that it was a laboratory, but the room in which I found myself had no banks of equipment, no haunt-ranks. It looked more like an ordinary parlour.

'Sit down,' Gennera said. I did so, on an overstuffed chair; it was still too chilly to remove my coat.

'She's changed,' I said. It seemed to me that we were beyond secrets.

The majike leaned forward in her seat, bending at the waist like a doll. There was a bright and fevered interest in her face. 'Leretui, you mean? How? Tell me.'

So I did and she listened, avid. 'But this is marvellous,' she said when I'd finished. 'I must come back with you. No one's seen this process before – it will make scientific history!'

'If you think you can tell anyone about it.' But from the smug-ness in her expression, I thought there would be plenty in the Matriarchy who would be just as fascinated as she. 'You'll have to take charge of her,' I added. 'Who knows what she'll do if she's left where she is?'

'It might not be possible to move her by now,' the majike said. 'In the beginning – maybe.'

'So you *do* have some idea of what's happening to her.'

Gennera sighed, more out of frustration than any other emo-tion. 'There are some very old records, dating from the Age of Children. Incomplete, some barely legible. A handful, nothing more,'

'But enough for you to use, eh?'

She nodded. 'Enough for us to *re-create*.' She leaned over again and clasped my hand. Her fingers felt cold and greasy around my wrist. 'Your family is part of a great process, Essegui.'

And you owe it to me, for bringing her back. 'You owe me my soul,' I said. The coldness spread from her fingers until a shiver ran through me. 'What will you use her for?' I went on. *When she's fully changed.* I didn't expect her to tell me, but instead, she stood up.

'Come with me.'

I followed her through the long parlour and out onto a snow-covered veranda. She took me down the length of the house and through a set of double doors. It looked like an ordinary panelled room, furnished with carved chests and cabinets, but the touch of haunt-tech set my teeth on edge as soon as I stepped through the door, a blacklight hum which touched the empty pieces of my soul like prodding the hollow of a missing tooth.

Behind a panel of reinforced glass in one of the cabinets at the far end of the room stood a jar. It was dimly lit, but I could see that the glass was itself held by a force field. Inside the jar, something black writhed. We stood in front of it, in silence. It was sinuous, with a tapering tail. It had little black eyes. It was perhaps a foot in length.

'Embryo?' I asked.

'One of the few that survived.'

'What happened to the others?'

But the majike just smiled. 'Little sisters . . .'

'So will you bring Leretui back here?'

'We'll have to think about that. I told you, it could be damaging.'

'You do know I'm the heir to Calmaretto?' I said. The majike looked at me directly for the first time since she'd imposed the geise.

'Your mothers aren't old. And there's still young Canteley.' And I still have a fragment of you, her look said.

'Who idolizes Leretui. Who's not entirely stable.' It might not be true and I knew I was betraying her, but I had to try. 'And my mothers aren't young, either. Neither are you. Your own successors might need . . . support. We do support the Matriarchy, you see. Especially when Alleghetta joins the council.'

'Let's go and see Leretui, shall we?' It wasn't a suggestion, nor even a concession, but I felt as though I'd gained a small victory all the same. When we went outside again, through the frozen garden and the door in the wall, there was a vehicle waiting, as white as the snow itself. The majike, bundled in her garments, crawled into the back seat and I followed. Inside the car it was stiflingly hot, smelling of leather and secrets.

'Calmaretto,' Gennera said, and the car sped off through the silent streets. It was by now early afternoon and the usual crowds that clustered around the fast-food braziers were much diminished. We swung past the wall of the Matriarchy and I wondered whether Alleghetta was still inside, or whether she'd gone home. I checked the antiscribe, but there were no messages. As we pulled up at the back of the mansion, I looked fearfully up at the house as though our secrets might even now be spilling out of its windows, but Calmaretto was as closed and shuttered as ever. The majike was looking at me.

'Just wondering,' I said. She didn't say anything. She touched the seat panel in front of her and the car slowed to a halt. We got out. It seemed to have become much colder, but maybe it was just the contrast with the car. Thea bustled out of the parlour as we came into the hall.

'Ghetta still isn't home, I don't know what can have become of her, I—'

'We're at war, after all,' the majike said, removing her gloves. 'Where's Leretui?'

'Upstairs, where else?' The whites of Thea's eyes were showing, like a nervous animal.

'Show me,' Gennera said.

I didn't want to go upstairs, didn't want to see what Leretui had become. I wanted to be far away from here, and simultaneously never to leave the house again. Hiding in the winter garden, sometimes a childhood option, was beginning to seem highly appealing. But I went up the stairs all the same, conscious of the majike wheezing at my heels.

As we approached Leretui's room, the door began to alter before my eyes, changing dimension, now huge, the doorway to galaxies, and now tiny as a mouse's door. The majike's voice spoke in my ear.

'They generate illusion. Ignore it.'

Easy to say. I tried to put one foot in front of the other, but there was a moment when the whole floor seemed as though it was falling away from me, sliding down into a great red desert. I screamed and stumbled. Gennera caught my arm, but when I glanced at her face it was pale and damp.

'Not so easy for you, either, is it?'

'I didn't say it would be easy. But isn't it interesting? So new, and already this is what she can do!'

'I hope you've some way of counteracting this,' I said.

'Possibly.'

Thea hadn't come with us, I realized, and I wondered why. Possibly she was afraid, of Leretui or of consequences.

'Open the door,' the majike said. I reached out and took hold of the handle, then jerked my hand back. The handle was red-hot. I looked down at my palm but no burn mark was there.

'Illusion,' Gennera said firmly.

'*You* do it, then,' I snapped. But she hesitated, and in the end I reached out and snatched open the door.

Inside it was quite dark, though on my previous visit I'd noticed that Leretui hadn't drawn the curtains. The darkness wasn't natural. It was streaked with red, as if bloody, and silver shapes shot and swam within it.

'Leretui?' I said. My voice was muffled: I felt that the darkness had eaten it.

'Where is she?' the majike said, briskly.

'You tell me. She's in there somewhere.' My eyes were adjusting a little and within the swirling black I could see a pool of greater shadow, a silhouette outlined on the dark. It was moving, undulating like weed under water, and quite silent. Something that could have been a head, sleek and oval and wan, rose up and I knew we were being watched.

'Get out,' the majike said. We fell through the door and I banged it shut behind us.

'There's nothing left,' I said. Gennera looked more shaken than I'd expected: perhaps she hadn't quite realized what her experiment would become, after all.

'What's going on?' I turned to see Alleghetta, still in her long outdoor coat and fur hat, striding down the corridor. It was, I thought, a fairly rhetorical question by now.

TWENTY-NINE

Hestia — Earth

Clinging to the iron struts of the tower, I watched as the demothea climbed. It did so swiftly, hand over hand, its tentacles writhing around it. Beyond the tower hovered the orthocopter, with Evishu standing in the open hatch. Using the net might be impossible, but I had the stunner and as soon as the demothea came within range, I planned to use it. I was keeping a careful eye on the water below the tower, just in case the swarm I'd seen in the cellar had decided to come after their fleeing sister, but there was only a tidal churn. Given their amphibian nature, I thought I'd have seen them if they were there. Unless there were tunnels under the tower. Unless . . . You had to consider such possibilities, but they were still capable of driving you mad.

'Be careful,' the Library said cheerfully, appearing on the strut beside me.

'Oh, you're back, are you?'

The Library pointed to the clambering thing below me. 'It's down there. Are you ready for it?'

'I've no idea. Let's hope so. Otherwise that device that projects you will be lost in Earth's waters for ever.'

The Library shrugged. 'I'll be a sea ghost, then. Could be peaceful.'

'Could be dull.' I straightened up. The demothea was about twenty feet below, within whip-tip range. I swung the stunner down and fired.

The weapon didn't behave as I'd expected. It cast a crackling web of light down through the struts of the tower and the stinging recoil through the palm of my hand nearly made me drop it. The demothea had flung itself backwards as soon as it saw what I was doing, and it now hung upside down from a lower strut by a tentacle, drawing itself in like a squid. I cursed, jumping down to one of the struts below and firing as soon as I landed.

This time the whip-tip shot past my ear; it was longer than I'd thought. But the impact of the web through the strut the demothea clung to had knocked it off again: we were going back down the tower. I heard the hum of the orthocopter, turning, and hoped the kappa had a back-up plan. The waters seethed below.

'All right,' I said aloud. 'You want me, then come and get me.' Chasing the demothea hadn't worked well, so let's see where subterfuge got me. I started climbing back up the tower as quickly as I could, a little panicky, as if the failure of the stun gun to secure my prey had unnerved me. The demothea came after, moving as fast as I did, but keeping its distance in case I turned and fired again. I did not. Instead, I climbed higher and higher, until the city itself broke through the mist and I was up into blue air, with the white turrets all around me and, to my left, the eggshell dome of what was perhaps a temple. Beneath it, a window shone the colour of rose in the sudden sunlight, black-gapped where its panes had been broken. The tower was sloping inwards now, narrowing. I looked back only once, checking that the demothea was still following me, and went on, waving a splay-fingered hand to Rubirosa circling below and hoping that she'd understand what I wanted her to do. The Library was still present, her grim figure occasionally lost in the rainbow spray of mist as she drifted by.

I glanced up and saw that the top of the tower was visible: a sharp point bisecting the rainy skies. I'd have to make a decision

soon, in any case – the air was freezing and I didn't want to take
the risk of my numb hands slipping on cold iron and sending me
to a watery death. So I stopped, as if winded, and let the demothea
catch up.

I hoped it would work. I hoped Rubirosa had grasped my tentative plan. The orthocopter was now orbiting the tower in tight
circles, some distance below, and I thought she'd understood what
I wanted her to do. If not – well, at least there would be the nov-
elty of dying on Earth. The demothea was only a few feet below
me now, pausing with its alien head on one side. I could see the
close-knit whorls and shells that covered its head, that from a distance gave the illusion of intricately coiffured hair. No way of
knowing what purpose they served – radar? Telepathy? In the rain-
swept light its eyes had an opalescent gleam. It was waiting for me
to make the first move and I did. I brought the stun gun up
abruptly and as I did so, the whip-tip flicked out. But instead of
trying to fire, I threw the gun off to one side. I'd planned that the
demothea's swift reactions would be her undoing. Instinctively,
the whip followed the trajectory of the gun and as it lashed away
from me, I dived. I caught the demothea around the waist, grasping the root of the tentacular whip, which was under one arm,
and kept it from striking back at me. The demothea gave a
whistling scream, more of surprise than fear, and we both hurtled
down off the tower.

I have a confused memory of falling down through the rain,
the wetness lacerating my face. The demothea's body, clasped in
my arms, was at once slippery and hard, with an unpleasant yield-
ingness in certain places. It smelled strange, not distasteful, just
odd, like chemicals. I caught sight of a pearly eye, rolling in the
direction of my face, and then the orthocopter was roaring overhead, blotting out the demothea's scream, and the net whisked
out around us. We shot upwards, the demothea struggling and
fighting in earnest now that it found itself captured. I hung on to

it until we were over the lip of the hatch and onto the merciful hardness of the solid floor.

The kappa didn't waste time on congratulations. She held a device to the side of the demothea's lashing head and pressed. I felt the shock go through it and nearly blacked out, but the demothea went limp. Shakily, I disentangled myself and got to my feet.

'Well done,' Rubirosa said from the pilot's seat.

'Wasn't sure if you'd got the idea.' My breath seemed to have gone. 'Couldn't have done it lower down. Not enough room.'

'I damn nearly missed you,' Rubirosa said, reprovingly. I didn't want to think about that.

'Well, you didn't.'

Evishu was bending over the demothea, binding it securely. 'I don't want her breaking out again,' she muttered. Then she straightened up and looked at me. Her round eyes were expressionless, but she was smiling. 'That was well done. You risked your life.'

'We got it,' I said. Suddenly I needed to sit down, and collapsed into a seat, uncomfortably aware of the dead kappa's body underneath. Rubirosa turned the orthocopter and I saw the tower recede into the distance until its sharp tip was lost in the clouds. As a little warmth flooded into my hands, I hoped I'd never see it again, but it wasn't the memory of the climb that made me shiver. The nightmare of those writhing bodies in the cellar would stay with me for a long time. I looked down at the motionless body of the demothea and thought about tracking devices. I wasn't sure that the only trap had been the one we ourselves had set.

THIRTY

Essegui – Winterstrike

Alleghetta and I stood outside the door of Leretui's chamber, peering through the crack. By now, my sister had completely broken down: a kind of writhing soup filled the bed.

The majike had returned to her laboratory, saying that she needed some equipment. We were under strict instructions not to enter the chamber, and I, at least, had no intention of disobeying. Alleghetta was a different matter. I'd already had to stop her charging into the room: to do what, I had no idea. Probably to tell Leretui to stop it at once.

'Disgusting,' Alleghetta hissed now, but I could tell she was fascinated.

'That's your child,' I said, coldly. 'Or was your child, at any rate.'

Alleghetta gave me a stare of equal iciness. 'Leretui stopped being my child when she consorted with her fellows under that bridge.' *And when she nearly wrecked my chances with the Matriarchy.* Alleghetta's subtexts were not hard to interpret.

'She didn't consort,' I protested, but more from habit than any real conviction. Leretui and the vulpen: who had led whom into disgrace?

'Then tell me what's happening now,' Alleghetta pointed out.

I was silent. My mother gave a death's-head grin. 'Gennera will take care of it.'

'I don't know if—' I started to say, when downstairs, someone screamed. 'That's Thea!' I'd expected any shrieks to be coming from the two of us. I pulled Leretui's door closed and raced down the hallway to the stairs.

I couldn't tell quite where the scream had come from. We'd left Thea prostrate in the parlour, but I'd thought the sound had come from the other side of the house, from the long dining room with the windows opening out onto the lawn, where my mothers had held so many of their social-climbing dinner parties. I headed for the dining room, therefore, with Alleghetta panting at my heels.

Thea, ashen-faced, was backed against the far wall of the dining room, clutching the sideboard. At the other end of the room stood a familiar figure. Mantis was grinning. 'Why, it's the sister. Nice to see you again, Essegui Harn. Sorry we couldn't keep you for longer, but I suppose that doesn't matter now.'

'Essegui!' Alleghetta barked. 'Who is this?'

'Her name is Mantis. She's associated with the Noumenon.'

Mantis's grin widened. 'You'll meet them soon.'

A plague of ghosts, from a city of spirits, allied with the Changed. It made a certain kind of sense.

'The weapon that your cousin found in the library of Caud has been very useful,' Mantis said. 'A weapon that can break down the barriers between the world of the dead and the world of the living. Once that had been used, it left a crack for the Noumenon to seep through. So we owe everything to your family, really.' She strode forward and the lights from the chandelier caught on the barbs of the hooked weapon that she carried. Light flickered and flashed along the haunt-armour that she wore. Alleghetta took a step back.

'What do you want?' I asked, as if I didn't know.

'What do you think? Or "who", I should really say.'

'They've come for Leretui,' I said.

'No.' That was Alleghetta. Thea gaped like a fish and I nearly said, 'Take her.'

Alleghetta stepped forward, bristling. Seeing them together, I was suddenly struck by the resemblance between Mantis and my mother: they did not look physically alike, for Alleghetta was the product of years of Winterstrike engineering and Mantis was what she was, but the psychic similarity was remarkable.

'I don't think you could stop me,' Mantis said. 'Where is she?' she added to me. Her voice was caressing, almost hypnotic. 'You want to get rid of her, don't you?' she said. 'I can see it in your face.'

'Don't,' Thea's voice trembled, and it was this rather than Alleghetta's barked 'Essegui!' which made me, against my better judgement, say, 'I won't tell you where she is.' I stepped to stand in front of Mantis, between herself and Thea. But Mantis, instead of betraying annoyance, smiled.

'Not to worry,' she said gently. 'Looks like you won't have to.'

There was a sound behind me. The demothea that had once been my sister stood in the doorway. Leretui was still recognizable: something about the shape of the face, the angle of the eyes, and her long black hair. The small mouth opened and a trilling sound emerged. Mantis was staring, as much as myself and my mothers, and I saw something cross her face that might even have been a distant horror.

'Hello, Shorn,' she said.

The demothea's mouth worked. I could see components inside that were not remotely human: Leretui's transformation had been swift and effective. She extended a long hand to her friend, the fingers more like tentacles, but it was a graceful gesture, a lady asking her beloved to join her on the ballroom floor. After a moment's distinct hesitation, Mantis reached out and took it.

'Well, goodbye,' she said, mockingly. 'I'll make sure she

writes.' Alleghetta made a convulsive move forward but they were gone, through the French windows and down to the canal in the fading light.

We waited until the majike returned before investigating Leretui's abandoned nest.

'I think their genes must have been spliced with eels,' Gennera said on our way upstairs. 'Those things that live in the marshes of Earth, that stun their prey. The military were keen naturalists, when all this began.'

'She won't change back now, will she?' Thea quavered.

'Doubt it.'

The smell was apparent as soon as we stepped onto the landing.

'Like death,' I said, retching. 'It wasn't this bad earlier.'

'Let's take a look,' the majike said.

Leretui's room was now filled with a clustering mass of dark threads, trailing from the ceiling and across the bed. It wasn't clear where the smell was coming from until we looked into the pit at the centre of the bed itself. Tangled in a mass of sheets was a decomposing form: something small and twisted.

'It's a child,' I said. 'Where the hell did that come from?'

'A little older than a child, I think,' the majike said. 'It's shrunk.'

When we looked at it more closely, we found that it was a young woman, and when the majike lifted her head to display short red hair, I recognized her as one of the more recent servants, Jhule.

'How long has she been here?' I did a quick mental calculation. It wasn't long enough for true decomposition to set in, as far as I understood the process; that meant that this decay had somehow been accelerated. 'Did she use the girl to *feed*? Propel her transformation?' I sat down in the least contaminated of the chairs, feeling sick.

'I can only assume so. You can rest assured that this won't get out. I'll deal with it.'

'I'm not concerned with Calmaretto's reputation!' Not entirely true, but it seemed to me that we'd gone far beyond any questions of social status. 'Someone's been killed!'

'She's gone,' Gennera said, evincing some frustration. 'It's unlikely she'll be coming back.'

It was useless to ask her where she thought Leretui might have vanished to: I had a better idea of that than the majike did.

'We'll get this cleaned and tested,' Gennera added. 'I don't suppose you'll be wanting to use this room for a while in any case.'

I shuddered. 'If ever.'

Back in the parlour, I told my mothers what we'd discovered. Thea, predictably, went into hand-wringing panic. Alleghetta, also predictably, was dealing with fright by spitting nails.

'That she can just walk in here and – who is this Mantis, anyway?'

'I told you.' More or less. I sank wearily into an armchair. It was by now quite dark outside, the short winter day coming to its close. The majike had departed for her laboratory. I realized suddenly that the little centipede, the Queen's informative pet, didn't seem to be in my sleeves or anywhere on my person. Irrationally, I missed it. However strange she might have been, I felt that the Queen had been able to provide answers, somehow. I hoped she still lived.

'Essegui?' That was Alleghetta. 'I asked you a question.'

'Sorry. Wasn't concentrating.'

'I have as much on my mind as you, Essegui.'

I sighed. 'What was it?'

'When did Gennera say she'd be coming back?'

'Later this evening. With a team.'

Alleghetta bristled once more. '*More* people invading the house.'

'I don't think it can be helped, Mother.'

'And what am I to tell the serving agency?'

'That your daughter changed into a monster and ate one of their personnel?'

'This is no time for levity!'

'Mother, people will go missing.' I hated not to assume responsibility for this, even if it was a relief of sorts to have the majike taking care of things. 'We've been invaded by an army of ghosts. You can blame it on that. Did you even know what the girl was called?'

'I can't be expected to remember *everything*.'

I got up. 'We'll have to give the servants some sort of freedom, you realize that?'

'I don't see why,' Alleghetta said. My mother had always taken a rather grand view of staff: the assumption that they should show a proper gratitude for the great favour of being employed by us. Given how much they were paid and how they were treated, I'd never thought this was realistic.

'Because we're at war! We can't protect them.' We couldn't even have protected ourselves, if Mantis had decided to attack. And the incursion showed how effective the weir-wards were against certain persons. 'They have to be free to make their own choices as to whether they stay or not.'

Alleghetta's face showed what she thought of this idea.

'Look, I'll talk to you later,' I told her. It felt more like midnight than teatime. I went down to the kitchen, avoiding the servants' eyes. There was a palpable tension in the air: hardly surprising. I decided to take matters into my own hands.

'If the mansion's attacked,' I said, 'you're to do what you think best as regards your own survival. No one will be prosecuted later for desertion if you decide not to stay.'

'I won't leave Mistress Thea.' That was the cook, who'd been there for years.

'It's up to you, Shia,' I said. I could tell from the expressions of the younger servants that they'd be bailing out at the first opportunity if it came to it.

'Mistress Essegui?' someone said. 'I think Jhule's already gone. She wasn't in our chamber this morning and I haven't seen her for a couple of days.'

'She's probably fled,' I said, ashamed. I knew exactly where Jhule was. I wished the majike would come back, sweep all traces of Leretui from our home, leave us in peace. But peace obviously isn't an option in war.

I was coming back up the stairs when a group of people swept into the hall: Gennera, returning.

Alleghetta and I once more hovered as the majike and her little team of whispering excissieres stripped Leretui's chamber. Jhule's body was the first to be removed, and that lessened the stink, to some degree. I'd expected them to do tests, as Gennera had said, and they did, but they also removed all the furniture, including the wall hangings and the rugs. Leretui's childhood books were taken from the bookcase and piled into sterile crates. I watched them go numbly; she wouldn't be needing them now. It all took less time than I'd supposed, to get rid of a life. The majike gave me a penetrating look as she came through the door.

'Now you can start to grieve,' she said, with a sensitivity that I wouldn't have expected of her, or would not in any case have expected her to express. But I thought that I'd started grieving a year before, when the Malcontent had come home from Ombre.

'Thank you for everything you've done,' Alleghetta said, gushing. I tried not to wince.

'If we need further assistance, I'll call you, of course,' the majike said, with the faintest trace of warmth. Her gloved fingers pressed mine like claws. 'There's nothing more for you to worry about.'

Except invasion and war and my sister, changed. I saw her out of the house and sought my bed.

THIRTY-ONE

Hestia — Earth

I woke from an unsettled sleep to find that we were landing. Stiff, but warmer, I climbed down out of the hatch and saw that we'd come down onto a huge platform. The sun was sinking in a lemony sky and the heave of waves was clearly visible. After the chill of the ruined city and the saltmarshes, the humid heat struck me like a big warm fist.

'Where are we?'

'The edge of Ropa,' the kappa informed me. She pointed to what might have been a distant line of land. 'Pan-Asia beyond.'

'And this?'

'A refuelling station. For ships as well as aircraft. Owned by the Tukriya.' She pointed to where several figures were scurrying around a tank. 'I've arranged payment.'

'Will it be enough to get us to Malay?'

'No. We'll need more fuel later. In the shamandoms.'

That sounded more exciting than the platform. I walked to the edge of it with Rubirosa while the orthocopter was refuelled, but could see nothing except the slow churn of the waves. Small boats clustered around the base of the platform, riding out the night.

'A dreary planet, so far,' Rubirosa said. 'And wet.'

I was obliged to agree. We returned to the orthocopter, not wanting to leave the demothea alone for too long, although Rubirosa had told me that the kappa had stunned it again.

'Can't take the risk of it regaining consciousness.'

'No,' I said. I wasn't sure why it hadn't used its illusory powers on me when we were on the tower: perhaps it was simply a matter of overconfidence. It had thought it had the whip hand, after all. Literally.

But the demothea was still unmoving. Evishu had put it back in the holding cell and I watched it as we took off and the platform fell away, watched it as we sailed into night over the chop and froth of the Ukrainean Ocean and islands appeared and vanished again, a scatter of lights against the shadows. The orthocopter flew on and still the demothea did not stir. Nor was there any sign of the Library. Gradually, we caught up with the sun again and it broke over a range of mountains as high as those of the Crater Plain, except Olympus herself. In its cell, the demothea gave a convulsive twitch and Evishu reached forward and touched the gun to its whorled head once more.

'Too much of that, and it could die,' Rubirosa said from the pilot's seat.

'I won't take the risk of it breaking out again. A dead one's better than nothing at all.'

'A dead one's better than a live one, if you ask me,' I said. I didn't like this change of heart within myself: I'd always tried to support the rights of the Changed, even if I hadn't contributed greatly to the various political efforts on their behalf. And it wasn't just that the demothea had personally attacked me – people had tried to kill me before, out on the Crater Plains, and I hadn't come to detest other humans because of it. It was the level of difference that had caused the change in me, and I didn't like that, either. Rights for demotheas? Yes, in theory. I didn't want to have the mad insularity of Caud, their paranoia about other peoples. It wasn't the demothea's fault that they'd been made as they had, but here they were, and with my destruction as one of their admittedly more minor aims. If I'd been the kappa or her mistresses, I'd have left the demothea to their marshlands.

I passed the watch over to Evishu, who had been sleeping, and went to the cockpit to see the Thibetan islands rising up out of the water. The cliff sides were sheer, with only a tiny fringe of shore around them, and as we flew over the first islands in the chain I saw that their summits were rosy with snow. Strange to think that these must once have been landlocked mountains.

'Where's the landing pad?' Rubirosa shouted.

'In the second chain.' Evishu briefly abandoned our captive to point over her shoulder. 'There, do you see it? Halfway up the mountainside.'

There was a settlement there, too: a series of long, low, white buildings with scarlet and purple flags snapping in the breeze. We flew over a forest of poles and banners.

'It's the religion here,' Evishu said, but did not explain further. And when we landed and walked out into a cold that was close to Martian, I saw that they were also men. Once you got over the shock, the difference wasn't so marked: they were bundled up in layers of wool, their hair covered up by tasselled hats. Doe-eyed faces peered out and they smiled when they saw the kappa. One of them greeted her by name and took her webbed hands in his own. I thought of my cousin Shorn, imprisoned for so much less, and reminded myself that this was a different world.

The kappa, generously, insisted that Rubirosa and I eat while she kept watch on the demothea. We went into the hall of what was apparently a monastery and were given bowls of meat broth. I was conscious of sidelong glances as we took our seats at a window with a spectacular view of the coast. They might not have known we were Martian, but we were certainly foreigners and that would attract attention. We were hardly unmemorable, after all. I told myself that it might not matter, but I preferred unobtrusiveness.

'We're surrounded by males,' Rubirosa murmured. It was the first time I'd seen her truly unsettled.

'Just ignore them.' In their colourful woollens, they could almost have been women. I didn't want to pay too much attention to them, in case we attracted more of it ourselves. I concentrated on my broth, wondering how the kappa was faring. We did not linger, but went straight back out to the landing pad. The orthocopter was waiting. I turned up the collar of my coat as we walked to it; the banners rattled in the wind. We took off in a rising gale as Earth's uncertain climate drew the winds over the islands.

'How long till Malay?' It would be Rubirosa's turn to rest soon, while I took over the controls.

'Six hours or so.'

I found the orthocopter easy enough to fly and fell into a rhythm as the seas rose and retreated below, the high spines of islands occasionally rising up. Even though I'd seen images of Earth, and maps, it startled me how little land there was. Or maybe it was simply that I was used to Mars and its lack of seas.

Eventually the kappa came up front to tell me that we were close to the coast of Malay. I could see it now, a long string of lights, some rising high into the heavens, betokening cities.

'Khul Pak,' the kappa said, with satisfaction.

THIRTY-TWO

Essegui — Winterstrike

When I woke and switched on the little night lamp the shadows fled racing into the corners of the room, clustering and lingering like weir-wards. I looked at the clock. It was just before dawn. There was no black oil seeping under the door, no hint of menace. Everything was as it should have been, but I'd woken with a start, all the same.

Going back to sleep was out of the question. I wrapped myself in a robe and went to the window, drawing the drapes aside. The lawn of Calmaretto was stark under the snow, a bare white blanket. Further snowfall the day before had smoothed over any footprints that Leretui and I might have left. There was nothing hovering over the icy surface of Canal-the-Less.

I put on a skirt and blouse, and laced a jacket over it. When I opened the door, the hallway was peaceful. It was still too early for the servants to be up. We might be under invasion, but it was very quiet: unnaturally so, it seemed to me. Shouldn't I be hearing the sound of distant bombardment, shouts and cries? But what would they bombard? It was as though Calmaretto had been removed to a different Winterstrike, some sidelong dimension.

Without the barbed presence of Alleghetta, the parlour was a pleasant room, lined with books, although my mother had only

ever read the ones she thought she ought to. I clicked on the antiscribe. The rumour boards of the city were humming: stories of
ghost soldiers in the streets, things that hadn't been seen for hundreds of years walking arm in arm over the surface of the frozen
canals, people visited by long-dead grandmothers, and through it
all the undercurrent of paranoia and fear. I shared it. I'd seen a
demothea stroll through my home as if none of the weir-wards
had even been there. When all this was over, I thought – assuming there was anything left – Calmaretto wouldn't be unusual any
longer. Because vulpen had also been seen: in broad daylight, skating along the arcs of the canals, disappearing under bridges in a
swirl of robes, and they probably hadn't been ghosts, either. The
Changed were coming back to Winterstrike in force.

Just as I thought that, a siren started to wail, making me jump
out of my seat. Moments later, Calmaretto was awake. Alleghetta
came striding down the hallway, shouting orders to anyone who'd
listen to make sure that the wards were working.

'What's going on?' Thea was at Alleghetta's heels.

'I don't know. There's some kind of alarm. Mother?'

'I've heard nothing from the Matriarchy,' Alleghetta said. We
raced upstairs to look out of the attic windows. There was a dull
glow just beyond the Opera House: a pallid, unnatural light.

'What is it?' Thea breathed.

'Don't ask me.' There was no sign of fire or flame, just the
glow. 'Ire-palm?' I speculated.

Alleghetta was looking at the 'scribe. 'There's nothing here.'
She sounded irritated, as though the Matriarchy had elected not
to inform her.

Perhaps you're not important enough to be told.

'Perhaps they don't know,' I said.

'How can they not know?' Alleghetta snapped, and then I
realized exactly where the glow was coming from.

'Alleghetta, those are the Matriarchy buildings. Look – there's
the roof of the Opera and you can see those trees behind it.'

There was no colour in Alleghetta's face to begin with, but her skin was the colour of wax. 'It's been hit,' she breathed.

'By what? I didn't hear anything and we're close enough, if it was a missile.' But maybe it wasn't. I didn't understand this war, the nature of it. Invisible weapons and ancient technology.

'I have to find out,' my mother muttered and started punching furious messages into the antiscribe. I opened the window onto a great blast of cold and leaned out, trying to see across the city. There was another glow in the east and I felt even colder, then realized it was dawn.

'I'm going up on the roof,' I said, and was heading for the stairs before they had time to protest.

The glow was still there and I'd been wrong: it wasn't the Matriarchy. I was high enough now to be able to see beyond the Opera roof and I'd snatched up a pair of binoculars as I came up the stairs. The northern wing of the Opera was a melting mass of icy vitrification. It looked like a dripping cake.

Slowly, I let the binoculars fall. They'd been aiming at the Matriarchy, obviously. I didn't know whether its personnel had been in night session – it seemed likely, under the circumstances. In that case, given the proximity of the Opera, anyone around the vicinity of the building, outside the Matriarchy, might well be dead. I thought of Sulie Mar, Hestia's mother and my own aunt.

I shot back down the stairs, brushing through the pallid winter garden and hurtling headlong down the staircase. I found Alleghetta in the parlour, once more bending over the 'scribe. Someone had lit a fire in the grate and it burned blue and comforting, an illusion of winter normality.

'Alleghetta,' I said. 'Half the Opera has gone. They were aiming at the Matriarchy.'

'I know.' A whisper. 'I spoke to Sulie.'

'She's all right?'

'She left before the session ended. Stormed out, apparently.

Didn't like what was being said, but that's typical of Sulie, always taking offence.'

Even under the circumstances, I smiled. Hestia's mother and mine were mirror images: one of the reasons there was such a connection between us. Alleghetta detested Sulie; it had always been mutual. I was amazed they'd managed to bring themselves to speak to each other, even given what had just happened.

'She's lucky,' I pointed out.

'Well, of course she is.' Alleghetta sounded as though Sulie had survived on purpose. 'She was halfway down the street when there was a flash. She was thrown into a snowbank. When she got up and could see again, half the Opera House was gone.'

'That weapon Mantis was talking about—' The Opera had looked *aged*, a ruin. Could a weapon that opened a gap into the Eldritch Realm be used to kill *buildings*? An odd thought, but in this age of haunt-technology, where places were infested with ghosts . . . Could there be a weapon that slew spirits?

'I should go down there—' Alleghetta began.

'Mother, don't be stupid. You've no idea what's happening out there. You might be killed. We need to stay indoors until we find out what the situation is.'

Rather to my surprise, Alleghetta followed my suggestion and remained at Calmaretto. The strike seemed to have reached her where the transformation of her own daughter had not: her face, always taut, now looked old and she looked as though she had shrunk in upon herself. Once, this would not have alarmed me as much as it now did – a diminished Alleghetta would have been no bad thing. But now we were all in this together and the collapse of one seemed to betoken the collapse of all.

When I went down to the kitchens, there was a suspicious silence. I checked the little rooms in the basement in which the servants slept and all of them were empty, with evidence of hastily seized garments. It looked as though the staff had taken my advice to heart, and fled, even the loyal cook. I couldn't blame them. I made the tea myself and carried it back upstairs. No use telling Alleghetta right now – she was where I'd left her, sunk into a chair with a hand over her face. At some level, I thought, she was enjoying the drama.

THIRTY-THREE

Hestia — Earth

First the arch of the Earth, dappled white and blue, then a silent fall through thick clouds. When we came out of them we were flying over ocean, long dreaming patches of azure, dotted and patterned with islands green with jungle up to the summits, very different to the silvery Thibetan shamandoms.

The ship veered in low over the water, passing high-masted barques and solar-powered sailing vessels. I could see a bay ahead, rimmed with green. A great crimson-sailed ship was churning across it, the circles of laser cannon ports clearly visible.

'A war-junk,' the kappa said.

'One of yours?'

'Yes. Otherwise we'd be flying higher.'

We were coming in directly above the junk now and I looked down to see the multicoloured dots of people thronging the decks. Beyond, low buildings covered the steep sides of the bay. I could almost smell it: the lushness of alien plants. Beside me, Evishu straightened, as if paying respect. The ship left the bay behind and came in over a ridge. A small port lay there, sparsely populated with landing craft. I didn't know much, but these seemed old; their sides pockmarked and stained.

Then we were down, almost before I knew it. The copter

whined to a halt and the kappa stepped down through the hatch.
'Follow me.'

The road beyond was masked by trees, affairs like enormous
ferns. A sticky strand brushed my face. Evishu took my arm and
ushered me to a waiting vehicle. It was streamlined and spined
and the crowds gave it a wide berth. I thought I'd got used to it,
but different gravity made me stumble in the dust, despite
Evishu's anchoring arm. Blood rose hot in my face.

'What about the – the you-know?'

'Someone is dealing with it.'

I looked back and saw that a high van with blank sides had
pulled up beside the copter. Something was being loaded into it
on a gurney.

I ducked into the waiting car and the door slid shut behind
me, trapping me in cool air and an abrupt end to the stink of the
street. Malay was rank, sweat and spice and shit and a pungent
odour of decay. Many of the people I saw held handkerchiefs over
their faces, or wore masks in fanciful animal shapes. The heat had
made me dizzy. I leaned back on soft leather and closed my eyes
for a moment. When I opened them again, I found that we were
already moving: the car's motion an undetectable glide despite the
roughness of the road surface. We were moving along a broad
avenue, running parallel with a canal and sharing the road with
every manner of vehicle: small smoky cars, rikshaws, motorized
bicycles and the occasional air-car gliding down amongst the road
traffic before veering upwards once more. Compared with Mars,
everything seemed compressed into too small a space. Paradoxi-
cally, I felt that if I had been outside, I would have suffered from
a bad case of claustrophobia.

'Where's the Queen's palace?' I asked the kappa.

'In the city, not far. But we'll be going to her summer residence, high in the hills where it's cooler.'

That sounded better. I missed the cold. The avenue opened
out onto a broad sweep of bay and I realized that we were already

in sight of the war-junk. The sun was sinking, red in a roseate sky. I saw more kappa, squat toad-shapes holding their mistresses' parcels, and one over-tall flat-faced thing with mottled skin. The car passed a magnificent colonnaded building, stucco peeling from its façade. Behind it, and the jewel-fringe along the bay, lay a maze of back alleys. We drove past poverty similar to that of the outlying provinces of Mars; leprous children, shrivelled ancients, all watching the car go by without expression.

I said, 'This can't last. Can it?'

'It's lasted since the war,' Evishu said.

'Which war was that?'

A shrug. 'A gene war. Fought in the hills, over land. What else is there to fight for, these days?'

'We have too much land,' I said, but I thought of Mardian Hill, the excuse for the conflict with Caud.

'If you won't let us settle, what else can we do?' Evishu replied, unresentfully as far as I could tell. I thought of the dry basins of Mars, the empty plains. Did I really want them filled with the children of Earth? But we were all children of Earth, once upon a time. I was guiltily glad when the car pulled away on a wide white road out of town, leaving the slums behind. Now, the view was of tranquil rice paddies, a maze of irrigation ditches turned bloody by the fading sun. We started to climb, leaving the fields behind us and reaching the edges of the jungle.

'Not far now,' the kappa said, in quite a kindly tone, as though I was a child. Great hanging ropes of vines now fell across the roadway and the car slowed to shift itself over tall grass growing down the centre of the track. The ditches were thick with fallen leaves and undergrowth.

'How often do people come this way?' I asked.

'More often than you might think. The Queen doesn't encourage visitors. You're very honoured.' She spoke as though she meant it. I forbore from pointing out that the Queen, having been abducted, now had little enough say in the matter.

The road narrowed until we drove through a tunnel of green, the vegetation rustling along the sides of the car. Above, something gave a sudden shriek, making me jump in my seat. It could have been a bird, but it didn't sound like one. Evishu leaned forward and said something to the driver that I did not catch. Then we were out into a clearing, and a building glimmered ahead.

THIRTY-FOUR

Essegui – Winterstrike

Of all that nightmare time, I sometimes think now that the strangest and most dreamlike night of all was the night of the Matriarchy ball itself. I could scarcely believe that not more than a month before, I'd gone with Thea to a dress store on one of the smarter canals, a place the family had used for decades, and bought a gown. Standing in the bedroom at Calmaretto, with the city in its ominous curfew silence, under threat of invasion and filled with ghosts, I looked at myself in the mirror. The gown – dark red, high-necked, long-sleeved – made me look like a column of blood. I longed to take the armour of my great-coat, but the thing was too battered for formal wear, so I settled for packing my skating boots into a bag, just in case, and selected a velvet coat from the wardrobe instead, with a growing sense of unreality: we were at war, my sister had turned into a monster, and here was I worrying about my clothes. I took a last look at my swathed reflection and then, carrying the skates, went down-stairs to where my mothers and Canteley were waiting in the hall. It reminded me painfully of the night of Ombre itself: I almost turned to see if Leretui was following.

'The sledge is waiting,' Alleghetta informed me, resplendent in gold brocade that made her look like a pair of curtains. Thea, in bright blue, was similarly conspicuous.

'You both look lovely,' I said, insincerely. Canteley, in black and white, seized me by the hand. 'So do you!' Her eyes were brimming with excitement and I vowed to have a quiet word with Alleghetta as soon as possible, regarding the advisability of taking a child into a target zone. But looking at my little sister, I saw that she couldn't really be described as a child any longer, and was Calmaretto any safer? Maybe Canteley would be better off under my nose.

When we stepped out onto the garden path it was quiet and dark and cold. Winterstrike under curfew made me realize how well lit the city usually was, with lamplight gleaming from the gilt cornices, from the domes and weir-ward vanes. Now, it had become as much of a spectral city as the Noumenon, a realm of shadows. The only glitter came from the blacklight lamp on the prow of the sledge as it waited at the dock. Alleghetta went first, stepping over the side of the sledge and wrapping herself in furs. Her expression made it look as though she'd locked her face: determined that this night should still, despite it all, constitute her triumph. What must it be like, I wondered as I joined her in the sledge, to clutch and cling so tightly to a dream? My gaze went out to where I'd seen the demothea dancing, and I made myself glare straight ahead instead.

The sledge set off. The bare branches of the weedwood flickered by and then we were speeding down Canal-the-Less. We shot past the bridge where Leretui had met her disgrace and then the sledge made a quick turn into the Long Reach, the only really straight stretch of water in Winterstrike, which bisected the city across its widest points. Halfway down the Long Reach sat the island of Midis, where the canal split into two semicircles and then joined up again. The Matriarchy hall stood on Midis, separate from the Matriarchy itself and dating from a later and more frivolous period. Looking down the stretch of the Reach, the ghostly gold domes of the hall rose up from the ice, catching the faint trace of moonlight and spinning it back from its reflections. It looked as unreal as I felt. I watched as we shot down the canal towards it, Thea chattering nervously away until I thought Alleghetta might turn and slap her. Only Canteley, swaddled in her white and black furs, was genuinely looking forward to this: she was young enough to find it all exciting.

'What was that?' Alleghetta turned sharply in her seat as something dropped down into the canal – something solid, from the hole it left in the ice. But then the hole closed over, as swiftly as it had been made. I looked for writhing limbs under the ice but the sledge was speeding on and the ice was silent and dead.

Subconsciously, I think I'd been expecting us to be the only people stupid enough to venture out to a ball when the city was under such threat. I'd expected, at any moment, the sky to erupt around me, everything ending in a firework night, but when I looked up, all I could see were the stars, the reach of the Milky Way snaking overhead and the spangle of constellations over the city, interrupted by the bright sparks of the Chain. Usually, Winterstrike was too brightly lit for the stars to be seen; this was like being out on the Crater Plain, where the burn of them had reminded me of what Mars had once been like, before its atmosphere had been released.

As we came around the curve of Midis, the water-steps leading up to the hall were thronged with crowds and the canal beneath was a mass of sledges. It looked as though the whole Matriarchy had turned out for this. I glanced at Alleghetta and in the dim blacklight glow I thought her face was flushed, triumphant. They'd come in defiance of war, out of an innate and perverse conservativism that suggested one should not flinch merely *because* of conflict, but I didn't think Alleghetta would care. Half of Winterstrike was here and that was all she was interested in.

The sledge was slowing. We waited, impatient and chilly,

while the ushers engineered a parking place and we were guided out onto the steps, helped by staff in the Matriarchy colours. Thea took my arm as we moved out onto the terrace, and as she turned to me I caught a whiff of alcohol on her breath.

'Are you all right?' I hissed as I steadied her.

'Perfectly!' She stumbled. 'Whoops! Very icy!'

Oh dear, I thought. Meanwhile, Alleghetta was staring around with a sort of relentless, sweeping motion of the head, like a gun turret seeing who might have been coming into its sights. Canteley was hurrying ahead, presumably eager to see if any of her peers or scribe-mates were present.

'Good evening.' I turned to see Gennera Khine. She'd made some attempt to disguise her illicit profession: the bone necklace had been replaced by an iron lattice and iron drops hung from her ears, against a black formal bonnet of disquieting complexity.

'Why, it's you, Mistress Khine,' I said. Alleghetta greeted her with a murmur that I did not catch and then we were all going in together, one big happy party. At least it was a relief getting out of the cold: torches lined the steps and we were struck by a blast of warmth. Under my slippers, the ground was already dry and I could feel the underfloor heating seeping up through the soles. Inside, the hall was a hothouse, with great bunches of engineered orchids cascading over the window-frames and light beating down from immense chandeliers. It was so hot I took the velvet coat off and found myself still too warm. There were a lot of women in dresses that were no more than straps and scraps; out on the terrace, I'd have said they were mad, but in here, I envied them.

Canteley plucked at my sleeve. 'Essegui, there are cocktails! Can I have one?'

'Ask your mothers.'

'I can't find either of them. Can I?'

'Oh, go on then,' I said. Looking around I saw that she was right: there was no sign of Alleghetta or Thea. They'd disappeared in a remarkably brief time and that made me nervous. I couldn't see the majike either, but when I dispatched Canteley in the direction of the cocktails and headed for the hallway, I glimpsed Gennera marching down the corridor, threading through the crowds with eel-like skill. I seized her arm.

'Where's Alleghetta?'

'I'd like to know that myself,' the majike said sourly. 'I need to speak to her. Never mind. You'll do.'

'What's happened?' I asked, as foreboding filled me.

'I sent out a team to try to intercept your sister. She was seen by the Northern Gate; by the time they got there, she was gone.'

'She's left the city, then?' I was ashamed of how relieved I felt.

'Or wants us to think she has. What do you think, Essegui?'

I smiled. A passing staff member, a young woman in shadow-grey, thrust a platter of fluted glasses at me and I took one. The chilled wine gave me a moment of astonishing clarity, almost transcendental. Maybe this was the answer: simply drink more. 'Think? Why ask me, majike? Why don't you just look at that bit of stolen soul? She's not my sister any more, is she? She never was.'

'That's actually debatable,' Gennera said. She frowned at the drink in my hand as if she disapproved. 'She grew up as a human, knowing no different. The clone of Mantis, as I told you earlier, was the same, although Mantis was placed with people who knew what she was. In retrospect, a mistake.'

'Why would anyone take on an inhuman child?'

'The family were the Changed. I bargained, in return for citizenship favours. They were grateful, or appeared so. They filled Mantis's head with ideas.'

'About equality?' Impossible to blame them, it seemed to me.

Gennera snorted. 'Wasn't much equality in their opinions. More like domination.'

'Thank you for telling me,' I said. 'Frankly, I hope she's gone.'

'I don't,' Gennera answered. 'If Caud gets hold of her—'

'If Caud gets hold of her,' I said, 'it's likely that we'll already be past the point where it matters.'

We did not appear to have any more to say to one another. I went in search of Canteley. Dance while your city burns, I thought. The glass of wine had produced a welcome degree of insulation from reality, but I'd better not have any more. The orchestra had elected to perform a work that had last been popular in wartime some two hundred years before – not the most tactful choice. It now scraped and screeched its way through a mournful aria, while the members of Winterstrike's Matriarchy made their ponderous way around the floor. At last I caught sight of Alleghetta, her brocade billowing around her and clasping an elderly hatchet-faced woman whom I recognized as one of the council.

'Essegui?' I turned to find Canteley standing behind me. Her face was rosy with the warmth of the room and probably with cocktails, but she looked too worried to be properly drunk. 'Thea's – not very well.'

I should have expected that, but I'd only been out of the room for twenty minutes. How much had Thea drunk before we left Calmaretto? 'All right,' I said. 'We'd better go and find her.'

My mother was sitting slumped in a chair in a side parlour, with the crowd eddying around her. She'd evidently put the time since our arrival to good use, because she'd already reached the maudlin stage of inebriation.

'. . . always such a dear little girl,' she was saying to a concerned woman in mauve, and with horror I realized she was talking about Leretui. 'And now – now! – she's a—' Thea groped for a suitable adjective, '—nothing but a monster!'

'Mine were exactly the same,' the woman said, sympathetically. 'As soon as they start coming up to sixteen, what a nightmare! I thought the drugs they give them in schools these days were supposed to sort them out, not make them worse.'

'A monster!' Thea howled and wiped her eyes. I plucked her glass from her hand before she had the chance to take another swig and said to the woman, 'My mother. Slightly distressed, not feeling well. I'll look after her.'

'I know how it is with children,' the woman said. Against all the odds, she'd failed to recognize Thea: I supposed Alleghetta was the half of the marriage who was more in the public eye. Lucky for us. Together Canteley and I wrestled Thea out of her seat and hauled her out of the ballroom, up the stairs and into the winter garden, a world of red and gold, with fronds and skeins of crimson orchids billowing down from the struts of the ceiling, forming arches and arcades, while lilies erupted from the formal pools.

'It's ever so hot!' poor Thea complained.

'Here,' Canteley said. 'You can borrow my fan.' She fetched a glass of water from the dispenser by the windows and thrust it into Thea's hand. Thea glared at it.

'What is it?' she asked.

'Gin,' I said, before Canteley could reply. 'Sit there and drink it and don't move. We'll come back for you in a bit.'

'Where are you going?'

'Canteley needs to find the washrooms,' I said. 'We'll be back in a minute.' We left her perched on the side of a pool, staring suspiciously into the glass as hopeful golden carp rose up to the surface, cadging food. I hoped she wouldn't fall in.

Back in the main ballroom, a portion of the stage was already being lowered from the ceiling and most of the more senior members of the ruling council had abandoned the dancing and were now congregated in a huddle in the corner. Alleghetta stood by herself near the window, facing proudly inwards. I got the impression that she'd positioned herself to make maximum impact: the golden light sparkled and cascaded over her brocade gown and glinted on the pins that held up her mass of hair. Her face was as artificial as a mask. Somewhere, someone struck a small, tactful gong.

THIRTY-FIVE

Hestia — Malay

The palace of the Centipede Queen was old, white-plastered, cool. It stood on a slight rise, looking down towards Khul Pak, and behind the house were rows of fountains. Beyond lay the jungle. Now that we were down on the ground I was starting to realize how little of the islands was occupied, at least by humans. A rim of city lay around the shores, but the inner islands had been left to the jungle itself. When I stood at the window of the chamber allotted to me — plaster walls, a blue-tiled floor that was like walking on water, fretworked screens — and looked out, all I could see was an impenetrable emerald wall.

Not so impenetrable, perhaps. After dinner the kappa excused herself, murmuring something about an errand. Rubirosa took herself off to her room, saying that she was tired. I should have done the same. But I was on Earth, in a place of relative safety for the first time, and the meagre glimpses I'd had of the shaman-doms and Malay had intrigued and frustrated me.

Besides, I was a still a spy, even if I was working for myself now. Or for my mother? Best not to think about that. So instead of heading for my bed and my rest, I followed the kappa.

*

It was almost dusk when I slipped down the veranda steps in pursuit of Evishu. The sky had turned to a lambent green-gold in the west and Venus hung low over the treetops. A very faint breath stirred the leaves, but apart from that the heat of the day still hung in the air, making my skin clammy. I kept to the edges of the garden, just in case someone might be watching. The kappa took a path so narrow that it was almost invisible and I nearly missed it: one moment her stout figure was there and the next, she was gone into the trees. I waited for a second or two, then went after her.

The density of jungle growth was impressive. Enormous moths floated ahead of me down the path and something bit me hard on the neck. I had to stifle a yell and slapped it dead. Some spy you are, I thought. I was making enough noise for ten, but Evishu trundled on ahead, never glancing back. Very shortly, a bend in the path closed off the dim gleam from the palace lamps and the only light came from above, but the sky was quickly deepening to rose. It reminded me of the Crater Plains, or the winter sky over the city: all red and fire. Around me, the jungle was murmuring, coming to nocturnal life. A bird gave a loud startled cry, then subsided. I had no idea what lived in the forests of Malay and I couldn't help thinking of demotheas. How securely was our captive held? The kappa had already lost it once and they couldn't keep it under permanent sedation, unless the palace had more sophisticated equipment.

But the jungle was opening out. I found myself stepping into a clearing and moved hastily back in case I was spotted. The kappa was hurrying towards a round structure that rose from the centre of the clearing. It was squat, cylindrical, and surmounted by a huge plexiglass dome, a bulbous eye staring into the darkening heavens. An observatory.

Evishu opened a small door in the base and slipped inside. She closed the door behind her, but there wasn't any sign of a lock, and after a pause I cautiously opened the door and went in after her. A light high on the wall illuminated a spiralling staircase and the sound of the kappa's flat footsteps was retreating up it. When the footsteps stopped, I crept up the stairs, to where a landing led through a doorway. The kappa was beyond, in the observation turret itself, moving slowly about.

Something was hissing. It was a familiar sound: an antiscribe, experiencing heavy static. The kappa said something that I did not understand, but then the line cleared and Evishu said, in Martian: 'Do you read me?'

A voice, very faint and far away. 'Yes. But not well.'

'The women from Winterstrike are here. We have what you asked for.'

'Good.' And now I recognized the voice: I'd heard it often enough, over my own antiscribe, and in person. Gennera Khine. In spite of the heat, I went cold. Then the kappa said, 'And my Queen?'

'Still missing.' If I hadn't known her as well as I did, I might have missed it, but I didn't think I was wrong. There was a distinct note of satisfaction in Gennera's voice as she added, 'Everything's going to plan. At least on that score.'

'Make sure you keep it that way,' Evishu said, and I didn't think I'd imagined the note of warning, either. So the placid old kappa, unlikely research scientist and allegedly devoted servant of the Centipede Queen, was a little more than she seemed, too.

'Don't worry,' Gennera said. 'There's enough to occupy the Matriarchy at the moment without worrying about your lady. We'll get her out when we're good and ready.'

'Very well,' the kappa said. 'And the girl? The experiment?'

'Not going quite as well as it might. We'll need your captive, I think. Make sure you keep Hestia Mar in the dark about that. She's the daughter of someone who's become an enemy. And she's inquisitive.'

'She's what you made her,' the kappa said, back to placidity.

'Ah,' Gennera said, with a rattle of bones. 'They're all what I make them.'

The antiscribe started to power down. I went quickly back down the stairs and out, lurking behind the observatory until I heard the door close and the kappa's footsteps recede down the path. Then I followed, back through the black, whispering jungle, with Mars burning overhead like the spark of a spirit.

When I got back to my own room, I took the sphere from my pocket. 'Library,' I whispered, 'I want to talk to you.'

After a moment, the warrior appeared. I told her what I'd heard. 'You said you were sent to help me,' I said. 'Was it Gennera who hacked you, attached you to me? If there's a double game here, I need to know about it.'

'It was not Gennera Khine,' the Library said.

'Then who?'

'I told you. I cannot say.'

'Did I find you, Library? Or did you find me?' I knew the Library had her own agenda. 'Did *you* want that weapon to be used? And why did you want to see inside Mantis's tower?'

The Library's stringy mouth worked, but no words came out.

'Library?' I said in alarm.

'Find out who I was, Hestia. That holds the key to what I am now. Other than that, I cannot tell you more.' And she was gone.

That night, rather than sleeping, I went down the stairs to the office chamber of the palace and sat in front of the antiscribe. I dialled the secret code for Calmaretto, the one that Essegui and I had set up under the name of Aletheria Stole, and waited for my cousin to answer.

THIRTY-SIX

Essegui — Winterstrike

The gong gave another soft, sonorous note and the crowds still occupying the dance floor started to move back as the orchestra completed its tune with what I fancied was an unsettled speed. By the window, Alleghetta drew even straighter. She was scanning the room in a manner I'd seen a thousand times before at her own dinner parties and dances: looking to see who was there. She reminded me of a hunting bird, able to spot prey from the greatest of heights.

But now, the prey was hunting her, and she was well pleased. A staff member bustled up to her and spoke urgently in her ear. Alleghetta nodded, in a grand way, and allowed herself to be led across the hall, although 'led' is inaccurate: she swept the flunky in front of her like a ship in sail. As they passed Canteley and myself, she suddenly noticed we were there: I saw her mouth, 'Where's Thea?'

I frowned. 'What?' I said, pretending not to hear, and then, mercifully, she had gone past. She glanced back but I made sure to pretend that I hadn't seen, either.

'I hope Thea's all right,' Canteley said.

I nearly replied that we might never know. It had suddenly been given to me to wonder whether I shared something of

Hestia's pre-cognitive gifts after all. That sense of foreboding that had come over me in the sledge was very strong, almost as compelling as the geise had been, and all I could do was watch and wait.

Alleghetta was walking onto the stage with a measured stride. She must, I realized belatedly, have rehearsed all this many times and I felt a moment of supreme irritation, that during all the troubles with Leretui, Alleghetta had still had her gaze fixed on this purely political goal. Well, she'd achieved it now, for however long or brief a time, and I hoped it made her happy.

Canteley nudged me. 'They're coming forward.'

The members of the ruling council moved in a phalanx of red and black, their conical hats towering precariously above their heads. The city's principal costume had always seemed a bit ridiculous to me; I was glad to get away with the more practical and sombre garb of a simple ceremonialist. One of them bore a similar hat on a velvet cushion. I saw Alleghetta's face take on a familiar avarice.

'Well,' I heard myself say, although probably the only person to hear me was Canteley, 'she's got what she wanted.'

The council member handed the hat to Alleghetta. The gong struck once more, a ringing note that sounded throughout the hall and echoed in the sudden silence. I saw the orchestra readying itself to start up again and was profoundly grateful that we wouldn't have to sit through interminable speeches. Indeed, the council member's welcome was brief to the point of discourtesy, though Alleghetta bore herself proudly through it and accepted the hat with bowed head.

As soon as it was placed on her piled black hair, the violettas scraped up again and Alleghetta stepped back with obvious reluctance, at least to my jaded eye. But the music was drowned out by a high, unnatural whine. For a moment, I thought it was an insect next to my ear, then saw other people glance up and around and realized it was coming from outside.

'Canteley,' I said, 'get down!'

'What—?'

I grabbed her by the arm and dragged her under a nearby table. Seconds later, peering out from beneath the fringe of the tablecloth I saw a vivid flash of light, a weird red-green, and then the whole glass front of the hall imploded. Women were screaming, cut by flying glass, and a couple lay motionless.

'Stay there!' I ordered Canteley, without any real hope of being obeyed, and crawled out from the table. We were, I noted irrelevantly, surrounded by fragmented cake and I slipped on a lump of icing as I raced for the stage. Halfway there, I cannoned into Alleghetta, coming back. Her hair, and the new hat, were awry, but the blaze of rage in her eyes took away any comical aspect that she might have possessed.

'Essegui!' She made it sound as if it was my fault.

'Are you all right?'

'Of course not!' Never mind injury or death, the sudden explosion had robbed Alleghetta of her big moment and I doubted that anyone would be forgiven for it. Ever.

'What happened?' The Matriarchy members were running about like a hive on fire, with little result. 'Where are the excissieres? Don't you have any security?' The cursory scan we'd been given at the entrance had been barely adequate.

'I don't know!' But a moment later a team burst through from the corridor, weapons at the ready. I turned to face the shattered windows. Arctic air was blowing through, shrivelling the orchids and freezing my breath.

'They'll have a hard time fighting *that*,' I said. A vanguard of ghosts was pouring through the windows, some ignoring the gaps and coming through the few remaining panes. Spirits of the distant past: troops armed with spectral blast bows, and behind them, the Changed.

The weapons might be ghostly, but they were still operational. I saw a warrior kneel, take aim, and fire at the Matriarch who had handed Alleghetta her hat. There was no sign of injury but the woman went down and did not stir. Alleghetta and I, in unfamiliar accord, ran for the corridor, collecting Canteley on the way.

'Where's Thea?' Alleghetta hissed. 'Why isn't she with you?'

I was in no mood to be diplomatic. 'She was too drunk. We took her into the winter garden and left her there.'

Alleghetta turned on me as if about to strike. Another team of excissieres sprinted past, wounds glowing and shifting. Bit late, I thought. 'How could she get drunk at a time like this?'

'Because she's an alcoholic, Mother.' Alleghetta was taking it as a personal affront, which I supposed was fair.

'The winter garden's that way.' I pointed. 'I suggest you go and find her. We'll meet you outside if we can.'

Giving Alleghetta no time to argue, we made for the doors at the side of the building. I didn't want to meet Mantis again, and I couldn't help wondering who – or what – might be accompanying her.

I wasn't happy to be proved right. We just couldn't get to the doors: there was too great a crush. Shouts and the sound of weapons fire from behind made it impossible to head back the way we'd come. Then I remembered the stairs onto the gallery that led in the direction of the winter garden, on the opposite side of the building. Holding hands, we ran up the stairs. The corridor was deserted. We hastened along it until we found an open door. Inside, on the other side of the building from the ballroom, there was a long room. A series of small tables and some stuffy formal portraits suggested that this was one of the supper rooms used by the Matriarchy for visiting dignitaries. Another flight of windows looked out across Midis, sparkling with frost. Canteley and I ran to the windows and opened one that led out onto the balcony.

Outside, cushioned from the tumult within, the air was suddenly very quiet. It reminded me of Ombre itself, the still heart of winter. But I could hear distant shouts from the front of the building, and as I leaned over the balcony to see if there was a way down, movement attracted my attention. I heard Canteley gasp.

A demothea was standing on the parapet overlooking the Long Reach, poised like a dancer. I recognized her in spite of the changes. Her back was slightly arched and one foot was placed forward, the toe pointed. She'd got rid of her Calmaretto clothes and wore something tight and banded, with coils and drifts of loose material that reflected her limbs. Her sharp face was upraised to the balcony. Under the snaky mass of hair, her face was probably still more human than it should have been, though elongated and different about the jaw and the hollows of her eyes. Her cheekbones stood out like blades. An ice sculpture, I thought, almost translucent.

'Hello, Leretui,' I said. Her voice floated dreamlike up from the parapet, but there was a sharpness in it and a grating hiss which wasn't human at all.

'My name is Shorn.'

'All right,' I said. 'Be Shorn, then. What do you want?'

'Winterstrike.'

If you've never had any power, and then some of it is given to you, sometimes you become what you've most hated. I don't know how fine a line there is between envy and hate: not fine enough, if Shorn was anything to go by.

Canteley was gripping the balcony. 'Tui, I mean, Shorn – won't you just come home?' A child's plea that I couldn't have made. *Can't things just go back to normal?* But Canteley was old enough to know how impossible that was, even if there hadn't been the sounds of gunfire behind us. I'd like to say that Shorn's face softened, that some remnant of love for her little sister was enough to bring her back, just for a moment, but the white face staring up at us remained the same grinning mask. Then she flipped over and up in a blur, and was down onto the canal.

'Tui!' Canteley shouted. Moving almost as quickly, she fled

along the balcony to where a spiral stair stretched into the gardens. She ran across the snow to the parapet, with myself close behind, then went over the edge and vanished.

It was my turn to shout. I flung myself at the parapet and saw that it retreated down to the surface of the Long Stretch in a series of steep, elongated steps. Canteley was scrambling over the last one of these. I stopped to slip on my skates and that was the undoing of both of us.

It glided out from the shadows of the parapet, its robe swirling like a blizzard, just as it must have done all those months before. I glimpsed Shorn a short distance along the canal, watching and waiting, ready for flight. The vulpen seized Canteley around the waist and she screamed, but it was already skating fast down the Long Reach, with Canteley balanced on its hip like a captured doll.

I dropped straight to the ice and started skating, not stopping to think, just moving fast. I was damned if I'd lose another sister to the Changed, but it seemed to me as I skated that this was truly the end: the city would fall and Calmaretto with it, and if we did not die, then we would go to Earth and start again in another world, without my mothers, without Shorn. And what the hell had happened to Hestia? And the Centipede Queen?

The vulpen was skating faster than I could, faster than any human. As I followed, the cold air slammed into my lungs and made my feet feel leaden. In contrast, the vulpen skated with effortless grace, gliding along the length of the Reach with its robes whirling about it like snow. To think of it as merely an animal no longer made sense. I knew then that this must have been what Shorn had seen: perhaps half conscious of the change she was about to undergo, she'd recognized a dignity in the thing she had met, and this was why there had been so little remorse within her.

But there was no sign of Shorn now. She seemed to have been swallowed by ice and lamplight and shadows, and her disappearance brought my heart into my throat. I had no doubt that if she felt she needed to, she'd skate out of the night and take me down. We were nearing the end of the Reach now. I glanced back over my shoulder and saw a flickering brightness. The Winter Palace was on fire. A drift of smoke, fragile as a ghost along the Reach, filled my mouth with the choking bitterness of ire-palm. Despite everything, I hoped my mothers had got out alive.

'Canteley!' I shouted after the retreating figure of the vulpen, more to give myself a measure of courage than anything else. 'Hold on! I'm coming!'

Next moment, as if my cry had opened a door in the air, they were gone. I slid to a disbelieving stop, skates grinding on the ice, and looked frantically around.

We'd almost reached the end of the Reach, a T-junction where, in summer, a canal called Fountain Break ran parallel with one of the main lower promenades of the city. There were cafés along the length of Fountain Break and as its name suggested, a series of waterspouts provided coolness and ornamentation. Now, in winter, these central fountains were frozen tumbles of ice: they were left until spring, and there was a tradition of using the icicles in divination, examining the patterns they made and reading the results. All they spoke of to me now was failure. There was no sign of Canteley or her abductor.

I called her name and there was no reply. She hadn't made a sound since the vulpen seized her and that made me think that it had knocked her out, or drugged her. It wasn't like my little sister to bear things quietly. I bent down, fearing at any moment a bolt between my shoulder blades, and examined the surface of the ice. A thin, faint line told me that they might have taken the turn to the left, so I skated along it, weaving in and out of the masses of frozen water.

Then, a short distant along Fountain Break, something appeared which gave me hope. It was a culvert, leading under the bank to form a low, rough arch. It probably joined up with one of the other links of the canal network. I didn't like going into it unarmed, but I didn't think I had a choice. I skated into the culvert. It took my eyes a moment to adjust to the darkness and when they did so, I saw that I'd been wrong. The culvert was a dead end, terminating in a wall of ancient bricks. I was about to turn and skate out again when a very faint sound caught my attention. It was as though something had scraped against stone. Probably a rat, I thought, but it was worth investigating. Cautiously, I moved forward.

The scraping came again, then stopped. I waited for a moment, fearing a trap. Looking around the corner, I saw a line of barrels. At first I thought this must be the entrance to some kind of storage cellar: perhaps one of the waterfront bars kept its stocks down here. Then I realized that the barrels, which were made of some rubbery substance, had originally been floating and were now locked into the ice. This wasn't a storage place, but part of the canal barrage, used to regulate the water levels along with the complex systems of sluices and cisterns that lay beneath the city. At the end of spring, when the meltwater poured down from the heights, Winterstrike had in the last few hundred years been prone to floods. The barrages were emergency measures.

And someone lithe could easily have clambered around it. There was a narrow ledge running along the side of the arch, about two feet above the ice line, enough for a canal worker to sidle her way along in pursuit of her duties. Now, it wasn't necessary until one got to the barrels themselves, as one could skate over the ice, but the base of the barrels was wider than their upper parts – they looked as though they were half submerged – and I'd have to step up onto the ledge to get by.

That wasn't the hard part. The difficult bit was not knowing – or rather, suspecting – what might lie on the other side. I listened. The scraping had stopped, but I thought I knew what it had been – the sound of bladed feet on stone. Reaching the barrels, I hauled myself up onto the ledge and looked through. Balance was difficult with skates, but I didn't want to waste time putting them on again when I'd crossed over. I half expected to find myself staring straight down into the face of the vulpen, but there was nothing on the other side except more of the passage. Here, however, it was lit by lamps and I could see that the ice was scratched and scraped with a myriad twisting tracks. It wasn't just the vulpen and Canteley who had come through here. I dropped onto the floor and skated forward. I thought I knew what was up ahead: the same low arch and narrow expanse of tunnel, so I was startled to find that the space in which I was moving had suddenly opened out. And I wasn't alone.

Hastily, I hid behind one of the thick columns that reached down from the roof. The tunnel had become a hall: low-ceilinged but immense, and relatively brightly lit. After a moment I recognized what it was. The culvert led into one of the big cisterns that lay underneath the city and it was in one of these that I now found myself. Not to mention the crowd of the Changed that thronged its opposite end.

Luckily for me, they were facing away from the entrance, so no one had spotted me. I made sure to slide around the column, so that I would also be invisible to anyone coming into the chamber behind me. I saw aspiths decked primly in fluted black dresses, all ruffles and frills, sulpice in leather and brass. There were a handful of vulpen among them, but their robes were white and shadow-grey and if the one who had snatched Canteley stood there, I could not pick him out from his fellows. Canteley herself was nowhere to be seen and one of the vulpen's robes was spotted with bright splashes of what might be fresh blood. I swallowed hard and made myself keep watching. There was a palpable air of anticipation in the chamber, an electricity. A moment later, I discovered what they'd all been waiting for. There was a raised platform at the end of the room and Mantis stepped onto it, followed by Shorn. My sister's unhuman hand clasped Canteley's.

She followed Shorn meekly onto the platform with a bewildered air that seemed foreign to the girl I knew, even given the circumstances, and this lent weight to my suspicion that the vulpen had somehow drugged her.

'Look!' Shorn cried to the crowd in her new voice. She raised Canteley's hand high, swinging her arm up, and a murmur went through the crowd. 'This is what I used to look like!'

Mantis grasped Canteley by the shoulders and turned her this way and that so that the crowd could get a proper view of her face.

'I am a Harn of Calmaretto!' Shorn cried. 'I am demothea; I am of the Changed.'

Mantis said from the side, 'She is our pioneer.' A look of affection crossed her face. She reached out and touched Shorn's shoulder. 'She crosses boundaries, she has shown us the way.'

It all seemed very staged to me, choreographed. Then, 'She's a city aristocrat,' came an objecting voice from the crowd. I couldn't tell by the accent who, or what, had spoken. 'You told us Winterstrike would be ours. But this is a human.'

'I'm not human!' Shorn hissed.

'Human enough!' The crowd gave an uneasy shift of position and I thought I knew who it was who had spoken: a tall sulpice in a flowing robe of red and grey, a parody of Matriarchal garb which, in the city beyond, would have earned a fine or imprisonment under the Dress Code. 'Human until last week, and Changed because of what? An experiment begun in a Matriarchy laboratory!'

A note of alarm flashed over Mantis's features and I wondered what kind of story she'd been planning to concoct about Shorn. A religious transformation, perhaps? Some kind of miracle? But the truth seemed to have seeped out, as truth will.

'She—' Mantis began, but Shorn was obviously keen to test her new abilities. In the blink of an eye, a long black whip shot out over the flinching heads of the crowd and flickered across the head of the dissenter. There was a burst of what, in other circumstances, I would have described as blacklight. The tall sulpice fell as if poleaxed. Then the whip was gone and Shorn was smiling. The crowd fell silent. Very slowly, the sea of people around the fallen body of the sulpice melted away, until she lay unmoving in a huddle of red and grey. Only a vulpen remained, staring down at the corpse with its sad dark gaze. Canteley gasped audibly, as if she'd woken up, and I could see her trying to tug her hand away from her sister's grip. Shorn, however, did not let go.

The mood of the room was altering fast. I could feel fear building up from the crowd, washing over me in waves. Mantis evidently felt it as well, because as the crowd took a step forward, moving unanimously, her smile faltered. Shorn wasn't paying attention. The whip cracked again over the heads of the crowd and this time they surged towards the stage. I heard Canteley scream. Next moment, I was out from behind my hiding place, shoving and pushing through the mass of the Changed. I was, suddenly, pressed up behind the vulpen, my face against the musky robes. A hard, knobbly spine thudded against my cheek-bone. With a strength borne of rage I gave it a great push and the vulpen stumbled, then fell, carried down by my impetus and the weight of the crowd. I leaped over into the small gap left by its fall and found myself at the front of the stage. I was looking at Shorn's feet and she was looking over my head at the crowd. If I thought about that whip, I'd be lost, so I seized the front of the platform and hauled myself over it. Mantis whirled as she real-ized someone was coming onto the stage. I hit her full in the face and felt my knuckles crunch painfully on gristle. I knocked her off balance and as she went down I saw the crumpled imprint of my punch, as though I'd hit a sheet of plastic instead of a face. Then it rounded out, like someone popping out the dent on the door of a vehicle. I chopped down at Shorn's wrist and felt something snap. Canteley's hand finally broke free. Then the demothea was turning on me, whirling, and the instant between recognition and the whip flash was enough. I grasped Canteley by the wrist and dived for the back of the stage.

My main thought was of getting free of Mantis and Shorn.

My example seemed to have inspired the crowd and they were following me, a tide of the Changed breaking over the front of the platform and submerging Mantis and Shorn beneath them. Canteley and I made a run for the side of the stage and jumped down.

A passage snaked off into darkness. We bolted along it like rats. Halfway down it, past a bend, the lamps on the walls were once more lit: we were running over damp stone. We followed the passage upwards.

'The vulpen—' Canteley panted.

'It's all right,' I said. 'No one will know.'

'Tui knows!'

Suddenly I had an awful sense of history repeating itself.

'Canteley,' I said. 'You don't want to go back, do you?'

'Of course not!' We ran on and came to a flight of steps. There were cries from behind us, which reminded me of the scene at the Winter Palace. We seemed to be leaving disaster in our wake – but as long as it stayed in our wake, I didn't care.

The stairs were stone, and old. Something about them tugged at my memory, but I didn't understand why until I reached the top. Here, an ancient iron door stood ajar; the metal polished to a dull gleam that indicated that it had been cared for – this damp underworld was a haven for rust. I pulled it open and we stepped through into a vast, dim hall, with columns marching off into the distance. And then I knew where we were. I'd been here before, watching as an aspith spied upon me. We were in the Temple of the Changed, which explained why there had been so many of them in the cellars, and why those arches had been used. Had Shorn been told she'd rule here, Winterstrike's transformed queen? If so, her palace was empty now.

At least, as far as I could see. The hall looked empty and yet it felt filled with presences: as I stared, trying to see into the gloom, something flitted quickly into the shadows.

'What was that?'

'Canteley, I don't know.' But at least now I knew how to get out. Assuming we weren't stopped. Assuming we still had a home to go to. If Mantis and the vulpen had tried to snatch Canteley once already – as a hostage, or something even more sinister than that, a replacement if anything happened to Shorn – then they'd know where to find us if we went back home.

But there was another place that could be more easily defended. If we could reach it.

'Follow me,' I said to Canteley. We raced across the hall, footsteps echoing on marble that was slick with snow. At some point a window had been smashed, and the snow was already piling in, lying in drifts under the sill and scattering in tentative fingers across the floor. With Canteley behind, I made for the shattered window rather than the main doors, which might still be bolted.

We weren't quite fast enough. Just as I got to the window and boosted Canteley over the sill, taking care to avoid the sharp edges, someone cried out from the other side of the room.

'There they are!'

I didn't stop to see who it was, but scrambled after Canteley. A shard of glass caught on the sleeve of my coat. I tore it free and dropped down onto the terrace, landing in a drift. Canteley was already running in a panicking zigzag line across the terrace. I caught up with her and together we sped over the long courtyard. I glanced back once, to see the Temple of the Changed rising behind me through the snow; its immense façade like a skeleton in the night. Ahead lay the crater, and the bell tower.

Ire-palm does not shatter or break. It eats, melts, devours. I'd seen on the antiscribe newsfeed that there was still something left of the bridge that led over the crater to the bell tower, even though most of it had gone. It was fragile and I didn't know whether it would bear the weight of both of us, but I am not heavily built and Canteley was a girl. I hoped it would hold and I clung to that hope as I ran, with the snow starring cold on my face and my boots slipping and sliding on the black patches of ice that made the courtyard so treacherous.

It wasn't until we drew close to the lip of the crater and saw the ruined middle section of the bridge with struts peeling away into empty air and the long drop, that I fully realized how much damage had been done. I nearly turned back then. Nearly, but not quite. Canteley and I reached the edge of the crater and looked around.

The vulpen was skating across the snow, following the iced-over watercourse that led down the edge of the courtyard. His robe whipped out behind and his head swung from side to side, moving as a predator scents the air. He didn't need to smell us. We stood in plain view at the crater's lip. The vulpen slowed a little, perhaps reasoning that the last place we'd be heading was out across the bridge. The vulpen was wrong.

I looked at Canteley and saw her eyes become wide and frightened.

'Essegui?' she faltered.

'I don't think there's any other way,' I said.

She nodded, and swallowed. 'Then – all right, then.'

I didn't want to send her ahead of me, but nor did I want to risk the vulpen seizing her from behind. We stepped out onto the bridge. At this, its early stages, the bridge was as it had always been: filigreed black ironstone with rubberized treads against the danger of ice. We ran along it, ready at any moment for the bridge to teeter and collapse. I chanced a quick look behind and saw the vulpen pausing at the entrance to the bridge, its head on one side. Then it took a careful step forward, arching each foot so that the blades retracted into its feet, and started to run.

We were coming to the shattered part of the bridge.

'Hold my hand, Canteley,' I said, and edged onto the narrow rim. With one hand I grasped the fragments of the rail, and Canteley did the same, creeping along at an agonizingly slow pace while the vulpen followed. I could see other figures behind him, glimpsed in a shard of lamplight from the temple, and they looked like Mantis and Shorn.

I wanted to tell Canteley not to look down, but we had no choice if we weren't to fall. The vulpen was close behind now, a few yards away, and I thought he was having an even harder time than we were: his feet weren't designed for this kind of motion. And we were nearly at the end of the gap.

'Jump!' I ordered. We landed on the edge of the gap and Canteley's foot slipped on a piece of broken metal. She nearly went into the gap, but she grasped a strut as she slipped and I hauled her onto firmer ground. The whole bridge was starting to groan and shift as though it stood in a high wind and I was afraid that our movements might send it into destructive resonance. We couldn't turn back. We sprinted for the doors and behind me I heard a thud as the vulpen followed our lead and leaped. The bridge lurched, but did not fall. We reached the doors and I put my eye to the pad, hoping that the events that had befallen the bridge hadn't damaged the mechanism, or, once more, that what had been done to my soul hadn't damaged that, as well. The doors opened just as the vulpen lunged, and we were through and slamming the door shut behind us. I closed it on the vulpen's arm and heard something crack. The vulpen gave a whistling cry, whether of pain or surprise I neither knew nor cared. Then the door was shut and Canteley and I were alone.

My sister was shaking. 'Can it get in?'

'I hope not. We can get out through the base of the tower,' I said, thinking of that earlier flight into the crater. In a sense, though, we'd just be going round and round: back towards the arches from which we'd originally fled and full of vulpen. We'd have to go the other way.

But when we reached the entrance to the steps, we found that going down wasn't possible either: the spiral stairs had been blasted apart. I heard movement, elsewhere in the tower. It seemed our enemies had got here before us.

The only other option was up. I might be able to seal us off in the highest point, in the bell tower itself. We headed for the stairs. Memories of my usual duties were coming thick and fast. The hole in my soul felt as though something had taken it by the edges and pulled, dragging it further apart as we climbed. Then the door of the bell tower was up ahead and I was racing towards it, putting my eye to the scanner, feeling it read.

The door swung open and we fell through. I slammed it shut behind us, an echo of the main doors that, by now, the vulpen might have broached. I checked the security camera and saw that it had. Mantis stalked down the hall, her long coat swinging, catching the light and sending fractured reflections across the panelling. Beside her, the vulpen was no more than a prowling shadow. There was no sign of Shorn and yet, with some remnant of sisterly psychism, I felt she was there.

'What's happening?' Canteley asked.

'They've got into the building.' I didn't like the thought of Mantis trawling through those records, as if it was myself she would be violating, not merely a set of data. 'Let's make sure they don't get in here.'

As we were making our way across the remains of the bridge, a plan had been forming in my mind. I'd had no time to put it into action in the hallway, in case the vulpen had broken through immediately, but now we had a few minutes and I intended to make full use of them.

When we were children, and Hestia had taken Leretui's soul from her, I'd asked her how it was done. So she'd shown me, leaving herself open to having her own soul stolen, by myself.

I didn't share Hestia's eldritch gifts, however. I'd not been able to take her soul – which, frankly, had been a relief. But I'd been able to draw it out a little way and it had awoken in me an understanding of the patterns of the spirit, how they could be linked. In a way, it was more that Hestia had shown me the connection between us, how one soul might touch another, and this had been the interesting thing, rather than any real power it had given me.

I knelt down by the lock and looked into it, as if ready to be scanned.

'What are you doing?' Canteley's voice came from behind me.

'Wait. I need to concentrate.' I looked into the dark hollow of the lock and focused. It was as though the lock expanded outward, allowing me to glimpse the universe that it contained: spirals and whorls of stars and pinwheel suns, spinning galaxies and the traceries and networks between them. I wasn't looking at a universe, I realized. I was looking into my own soul and the links between it and the lock itself. Haunt-tech, where everything is animate, at least to some small unsentient degree. I drew the lock's spirit out into myself, sealing it in the hole in my soul. It felt strange, as though I'd put a large metal ball in my mouth and couldn't speak around it. But when I took my eye away from the lock and stepped back, I knew it had worked. Mantis wouldn't be able to open the door, unless she blasted it apart with ire-palm. I myself had become the lock: she'd have to reach me first if she wanted to open the door, and since I was behind it, that would not be possible.

Canteley was staring at me with curiosity.

'You look different,' my sister said. 'What did you do?'

Perceptive, and worryingly so. The thought that Canteley might be another of the majike's experiments came back to mind and I thrust it firmly away.

'Sealed us in,' I mumbled. Then I turned and looked out of the windows.

Our escape and its consequences had taken longer than I'd thought, although the ball had been timed for midnight, so it was hardly surprising to see a glow in the east. Dawn was rising over Winterstrike, banishing ghosts into the shadows, though not, I thought, for long. Through the crimson window the city was the colour of blood: red spires rising into the new day. Through the white window, the city was all snow and ice, as pale and ethe-real as a spirit city, and I remembered the Noumenon.

I turned back to the bell tower. 'We may as well be warm,' I said, and lit the brazier. It fired into life immediately, unaffected by the damage sustained by the tower, and we held out our hands to its heat in silence. Linking with the lock had given me a con-nection to the security system of the tower. It was very faint and I didn't think I could do anything concrete about it – no sealing of doors and locking my enemies behind them – but I could see things in a blurry, grainy, way. And what I could see was that Mantis had come up the stairs and was standing in front of the bell-tower door.

I gestured towards the door, motioning quiet. I could hear something scratching at the lock, a stealthy scraping. Outside, through the link and through the security camera itself, I saw Mantis bending in front of the lock with a thin tool. She was mur-muring. I watched. A few minutes later, she straightened up, frustration evident in the set of her shoulders. She turned to some-one beside her, whom I could not see, and spoke.

Canteley screamed. I whipped round and saw Shorn standing beside me. Up close, I was almost too intrigued to be afraid. The coiling tentacles, some as thin as worms and some thick as a finger, were piled on top of her head and gave Shorn the appear-ance of a grand lady of several hundred years before, as did the tight bodice and the drifting garment. She was holding out her hands as if beseeching me for help, but her face was mocking: still half human, despite the wicked pointed jaw and the huge hol-lowed eyes.

'Tui!' Canteley gasped.

'She isn't real,' I said, because I could still see that *nothingness* beside Mantis on the other side of the door, and I knew now what that was: Shorn herself, the young demothea using her illusions. Shorn, discovered, spat, but at that moment the door exploded inwards. Canteley dropped to the floor, her arms covering her head, and I was flung backwards against the wall. Mantis had decided to dispense with subtleties.

It wasn't ire-palm, but some other kind of melting explosive. Hot droplets spattered my skirt, missing my skin but eating into the leather. I rolled under the crimson window. Mantis strode across the room, reaching for me. I got to my feet and kicked out, sending the brazier flying towards her. She dodged, but the artificial coals had already spilled and one of them caught the hem of her coat and ignited. Her coat went up like a torch and then Shorn was there, dragging her out of the burning fabric and stamping it out. One side of Mantis's face looked like melted wax and I remembered how she had responded to my blow. Shorn's whip lashed out and I ducked. It struck the crimson window and shattered it into a thousand shards of bloody glass. I think it was this, even more than the abduction of Canteley, that made me act: that window had been in place for hundreds of years. I leaped over the remains of the brazier and sprang at Shorn. We went backwards through the door and down the stairs. Bruised and dizzy, I grabbed Shorn's head as soon as we hit the landing, and slammed her skull against the boards. We'd never fought as children, at least not physically, but we were fighting now. Shorn was trying to roll over and up and her strength was frightening: I could barely hold on to her. I shifted my grip to her throat to see if throttling worked, but Shorn's throat was hard and ridged. She hissed, the immense pupils dilating, and spat at me. I glimpsed her tongue, which also looked hard.

'Esse!' Canteley shouted from the top of the stairs. The brazier was rolling down towards us, bouncing and bounding, its metal sides clattering on the steps. I didn't know whether Mantis had thrown it or whether it had rolled, but I flung myself off Shorn, who tried to rise. As the brazier reached the bottom step I grabbed it by its handles, ignoring the sudden searing heat, and swung it at Shorn's head. The heavy metal canister hit home. The back of my sister's inhuman head caved in like a broken egg and Shorn collapsed.

I looked down in horror. Shorn lay in death, looking immediately smaller, more human. Her eyes were glazing. No time to say I was sorry, no time to say goodbye. She was simply gone, and I wondered whether she'd finally be free or whether her troubled spirit was already flying out to greet the ghost army of the Noumenon. I didn't have time to dwell on the issue. From above me, Mantis gave a thin, high wail. She came flying down the stairs, her burned face blackened now and her arms reaching wide. She cried something in a language I did not understand and I heard movement behind me, but Mantis was already there. She struck me in the face and knocked me to my knees. Up on the stairs, I was dimly aware of Canteley screaming. But Mantis had achieved what Shorn had not and I could feel consciousness slipping away from me. I fell forward but as I did so, I heard chanting.

I'd heard it before. It had ripped a piece of my soul from me, and now, with the later hole partially filled by the lock mechanism, I could see with my soul what my eyes could not. Someone was standing over me, someone familiar, and she was speaking. The majike had caught up with us and she was doing to Mantis what she had done to me. The chanting went on and on, horribly insidious, words keyed into soul-engrams, and of course the majike must have known what they were, since she was Mantis's creator. No wonder Mantis had sought the sanctuary of the Crater Plain, with such a weapon against her; she must have been very sure of the Noumenon army to return to Winterstrike.

It wasn't my soul but it hurt all the same. I didn't quite lose consciousness, however, and when my vision finally started to clear and I could sit up, Mantis was crouched in a huddle of skirts across the landing, her face as slack as an idiot child's. The majike was folding something into her reticule, primly, as if about to return home after a party.

'Essegui,' she said severely. 'Are you all right?'

'Leretui's dead,' I said, blinking up at her. It seemed as accurate as 'Shorn', now.

'Yes, I can see that. But we need to go.' She reached out a hand and after a hesitant moment, I took it and allowed her to pull me up.

'I know you don't trust me,' Gennera Khine said. 'But I'm on your side, you know.'

'And which side is that?' I didn't see how she could say such a thing, when I didn't know myself. 'Calmaretto's? The Matriarchy's?'

The majike regarded me calmly, as if I was a particularly slow pupil. 'No. Winterstrike's.'

We went quickly and cautiously down the stairs and out of the bell tower. There was no point in trying to secure the turret room any further – if someone wanted to try and make off with the festival bell, they'd have to go right ahead – but I released the lock, into the doorframe of the archive room. It might not stay secure for long but it was all I could do and I didn't want to go out of the tower with the lock still with me: it felt wrong. The majike watched as I worked, and said nothing.

When we finally stepped through the blasted doors to the remnants of the bridge, the sun was up and spilling brightly over the snow, sending sparks from the icicles. The majike pointed. 'Look,' she said. A figure was skating across the courtyard of the Temple, its robes a drift of cloud. The vulpen, leaving.

'They're still here,' I warned. 'They'll stay in the tunnels under the city.'

The majike gave me a reproving look. 'They've always been here. They come and go as they please, not as we do. I've sent squads of excissieres into the catacombs in the past and half of them didn't make it back. Where do you think Shorn's creature came from? All the way from the Crater Plain? Whenever a woman goes missing, or a child – chances are that's where they've gone.'

'What about the rest of the Changed?' I asked. 'Without Mantis, they might not be so keen to band together.' But we could not be sure. 'And what about the Noumenon?'

'The Noumenon will have to be fought,' the majike said. 'But I confess, I don't know how. We'll have to wait and see what happens with the Changed.'

'What about my soul, then,' I asked, but she only smiled.

We were on the bridge, and conversation languished until we were safely over the gap. The majike's vehicle was waiting by then, on the forecourt of the Temple which even now was melting into sunlight and snow. Canteley and I climbed into the vehicle in silence, and in silence, returned to Calmaretto.

THIRTY-SEVEN

Essegui — Winterstrike

I was surprised to find the mansion still standing, and appearing so normal. When we'd reached the Temple courtyard, I'd looked back to see the bell tower, the familiar crimson eye of the window no longer gazing out across Winterstrike. We'd mend it, I thought. Maybe. But it wouldn't be the same. The majike had told me that she'd send excissieres in to retrieve Shorn's body. I wondered if she'd be able to spare them. The morning city had a wary air, with no one about. I had no idea what might have happened in the course of the night. I saw neither citizens nor ghosts. Mantis had been led away, going meekly, by an excissiere waiting at the car.

When we reached Calmaretto, Canteley threw herself out of the car and up the steps, with myself close behind: it might not be wise to rush in. But the entrance hall was quiet, the black and white checkerboard of the floor and the tapestries that hung on the panelling were undisturbed. A moment later the parlour door was flung open and there stood my mother Alleghetta, her red and grey hat askew but still attached to her head. She'd probably take to sleeping in it, if we survived. She gave us all a glowering look and said, in the direction of the majike, 'Your crew fought off the ghosts. They've chased them out of the Winter Palace and put out the fire.' She looked grimly triumphant, although I couldn't see that she'd had anything to do with it.

'It won't be for long,' the majike said. 'The Noumenon have come too far. They might not be able to enlist the Changed next time, but they won't give up. This city is infested with ghosts now.'

'We'll see about that,' said Alleghetta.

Canteley clutched her arm. 'Where's Thea?'

'Sleeping it off,' Alleghetta said with a downward twist of the mouth, and for the first time it struck me that an actual Matriarch might not want to have a liability as a wife. Divorce might be frowned upon, but so was addiction. And something in Alleghetta's face as she looked at the majike, a sly, unexpected speculation, made me wonder whether Canteley and I might not be anticipating a new stepmother fairly soon.

'Leretui's dead,' I said, because the majike hadn't said anything about that and clearly it was falling to me. The result was more extreme than I'd expected: Alleghetta staggered back and clasped the banister for support.

'How?'

'I—'

'She tried to cross the bridge to the bell tower,' the majike interrupted. 'I'm afraid she fell.'

Alleghetta collected herself. 'Very well. Perhaps it's for the best.' And that was all she said about the matter, then, or for some weeks afterward, at least in my hearing. I suddenly felt exhausted. 'I'm going to bed,' I said. 'I don't care what happens now.'

Canteley yawned. 'I'm tired too.'

The majike nodded. I thought I caught a flicker of sympathy in her glance. Alleghetta clearly hadn't slept, but it didn't seem to make much difference. As I headed for the stairs, the majike caught my sleeve.

'I'll be in touch,' she said, in an undertone. 'We'll look after you, Essegui. I'll restore your soul to you, the missing parts.'

'All right,' I said. It had sounded more like a threat than a promise. I avoided looking at Shorn's door as I passed it, as if she'd left some eldritch trace of herself, her unhappy spirit still in there, drifting. I shut the door of my own chamber with relief, to see that the red message light on the antiscribe was winking at me. So I went over to see what was waiting.

Hestia's face floated onto the screen: tired, grainy, and deeply familiar. 'Essegui?' she said. 'I've got something to tell you . . .'